CW00607083

THE CAMEL TRAIL

THE CAMEL TRAIL
by Judy Jackson

Marsons London

First published in Great Britain in 2007 by Marsons
© Judy Jackson, 2007
Printed in Great Britain by Lightning Source

Typeset in Warnock Pro
Text design by Rachel Jackson
Cover design by DutchDesign2006@yahoo.com

A CIP catalogue record for this book is available from the British Library.
ISBN 978-0-9517220-2-2
www.marsonsbooks.com

for Michael

chapter 1

Things worth knowing and remembering:

Rubbing the temples with a slice of lemon can relieve a headache

A package or envelope sealed with white of egg cannot be steamed open

Tried Favourites Cookery Book with Household hints and other Useful Information, by Mrs. E.W. Kirk, 1926

LONDON 1944—ANNA

The envelope had no postage stamp. In the left hand corner were the words: *'To be opened after my death'*. Someone had searched the desk and emptied the walnut pigeonholes. Bills and correspondence were scattered in a heap. The letter had been opened. Anna turned it over and read the first few lines:

'My darling children,

As soon as I have passed away I beg you to ask the Doctor to sever one of my arteries.'

The request left Anna shaking. She wiped her eyes and put the letter back on the table. She was alone in the room. Her brother and sister were upstairs at their mother's bedside. Anna pulled at her knitted cardigan, stretching it to do up the buttons. She climbed the stairs and paused at the landing, catching her breath outside the door to the bedroom.

Dina lay on the bed breathing slowly. Her eyelids fluttered as if disturbed by the cracking sound when she inhaled. The air came out in a low whistle followed by a succession of laboured puffs. In the corner of the room Isaac sat reading. His older sister Boni blew a wisp of greying hair out of her eyes and leaned forward to stroke Dina's arm. There was room by the bed for two chairs but when Anna leaned over and kissed the soft skin of her mother's cheeks, Boni got up and without speaking she and Isaac left the room.

Anna moved her thumb over her mother's fingers, feeling the swollen joints and the buffed nails. She smoothed the bedjacket and leaned forward to whisper in her ear. What she said invited a reply but Dina was unable to talk. Would she have said anything if she could have spoken?

For three months Dina had been getting weaker. The doctor had been reassuring, claiming that his patients didn't die of old age:

> *"They always die of something. That 'something' can often be treated, even in an eighty-four year old."*

He prescribed medication for the heart and a glass of wine with meals. He advised her to continue walking up the stairs, even though the effort of climbing made her clutch the bannister every few steps.

None of them knew how long it took her to dress in the mornings. Dina adjusted the front buttons on the Liberty bodice and pulled on knickers and stockings. Then she'd have to sit down. Fastening the suspenders was slow and laborious and had to be done standing up. Before she could lift the petticoat over her head she would collapse into the chair again. Finally the black dress could be pulled down over her hips. Each stage took ten minutes with a fifteen minute rest in between. Dina refused to let Boni help. Her daughter would hear sighs and grunts from the next bedroom, but was only allowed to enter the room when the pearls were in place and the white hair smoothed into a bun at the back.

Anna stood up and walked to the window. A heavy fog hung over the back garden, blanketing the striped deckchairs piled up against the side wall. What had possessed her mother to move so far out to this double-fronted property in Finchley? It was the garden of course. Dina had always dreamed of a lawn, trimmed and rolled in neat lines, with dahlias and foxgloves in the borders. Anna could hardly remember her mother sitting in the garden. The pleasure had lasted only a few months. She had loved the summer sunlight, but when the sun disappeared and the clouds joined up to make a ceiling of grey, she would go indoors, no doubt regretting the move.

The flat in West Hampstead had been quite adequate. Anna had grown up there, in a mansion block called Kings' Gardens. There was nothing regal or green about it, apart from the leaves on the plane trees and a wide double entrance. Anna shared a bedroom with her mother so she was the one to hear the sobbing every night. Boni was eight years older; bossy, confident and forceful. It was Boni who decreed that there should be no onions in the

dn't care for the taste. Her mother gave in.
￼concerns and was preoccupied with Isaac's
￼ad poor eyesight, probably caused by a bout
of ￼za, but to outsiders all he needed was a pair of
glasses with thick lenses.

Dina was breathing more steadily so Anna smoothed the eiderdown and left the room. From the top of the stairs she could hear her brother and sister arguing. Isaac was shouting:

"You're not telling me she collapsed because of me."

Anna couldn't hear Boni's response. She knew they were talking about the money and when Isaac yelled the words 'you twisted her mind', she picked up her coat from the hall and pulled the front door closed behind her. The trolleybus drew up at the stop and Anna heaved herself into the nearest seat. By the time she'd changed buses and got off at Cricklewood Broadway to walk the rest of the way home, it was past lunchtime.

There was a placard outside the paper shop: 'Three killed by V2'. Anna was staring at the words and didn't notice that someone was holding the door open for her. She picked up a newspaper and read the first paragraph. Her eyes were blinking as she took in the news that five houses had been flattened and dozens of residents left homeless. It was what the paper didn't say that frightened her: the number of people left maimed and dying. There were no pictures of the victims. Her mind was whirling with images of families caught in a blast. In her head she could hear the wailing of someone who was searching for a husband, a daughter. She forced herself to calm down. She was forty-one for heaven's sake, not a child. By the time she'd reached the head of the queue her breathing had slowed to a normal rate and the full-blown newsreel pictures in her head were scaled down to a silent flicker.

When she reached the counter she asked the shop-keeper for a pack of Passing Cloud cigarettes. He mis-heard her mumbled request and ran his hand past the Players and picked out a pack of Woodbines. Anna looked round anxiously and repeated the words 'Passing Clouds please'. A man behind her sniffed and raised his nose as she slipped the pack into her bag.

The smell of fresh bread wafted out of the corner bakery but Anna hurried on to join the queue at the sweet shop. If she was buying cigarettes for Nathan she couldn't go home without the usual threepenny bag of toffees and tiger nuts for Nina. She handed in the Child's Green Ration book and added a few pear drops to make up the two-ounce allowance for the week.

Anna walked along Walm Lane hoping not to meet any of the neighbours. Who knows what conversations they might have had with Nathan? He had a habit of mixing up their names on purpose and pretending not to know who they were. With a glint in his eye he would make some outrageous comment—waiting for a reaction—but most people failed to appreciate his sense of humour and walked away, wondering whether he was quite normal. Anna quickened her step as she walked past number 169. The woman who lived there was ugly—there was no denying it. Her chin rested on folds in her neck and her mouth was wide and drooping. She never went out without her bulldog—a crinkled looking creature with leathery folds in his skin. Nathan told Anna that he firmly believed owners of dogs grew to look like their pets, so he named the woman 'Mrs. Dog'. Anna always feared that one day he would call her 'Mrs. Dog' to her face.

In the porch Anna took off her gloves and unwrapped the scarf. Nathan was in the back garden dealing with the chicken feed. He had a blade fixed to a long pole and was chumping a mixture of left-over porridge and potato peelings. He was wearing his usual crumpled clothes—an old sports jacket and baggy trousers. He'd never been one to care about what he looked like, so the restrictions on clothing didn't affect him at all. What did it matter that there were to be no pockets on pyjamas, no turnups on trousers? He was more concerned that there were no razor blades and he couldn't buy a new wireless to replace the old one.

He didn't hear her come in. She stood there watching as he mashed up the hot grey mess. When he had finished he put his hand under a pile of straw and pulled out a brown egg. He turned and smiled when he saw her:

"That makes five this week. You didn't think it would be worth the trouble, did you?"

Anna didn't answer.

"We might even have some left over to pickle."

Nathan looked up and saw that Anna wasn't listening. And then he noticed the tears on her face. He assumed she was crying because of Dina. He didn't know that his wife was terrified of the bombing. She couldn't admit her fears to anyone. She concealed them from Nathan, trying to stay calm as she waited for him to return from his fire-watching duties. When the air-raid warnings came, she hurried her daughter into the shelter, picking up her rag doll and blankets and settling down to wait for the all-clear. Throughout the long months of the blitz Anna had kept control of herself, turning her face away when she passed bombed buildings; refusing to join the huddles of whispering neighbours.

Her terror had begun at the start of the blitz, with the V1s, the first kind of rocket. Who would have thought that silence would be the cause of panic? It was that moment when the roar of the rocket stopped and the engine cut out—that was when the missile began to glide down, bringing its destruction to the houses and people waiting below. In those seconds of stillness Anna's heart beat faster and the perspiration dampened her forehead. When the blast came, yards or streets away, she closed her eyes and covered her ears with shaking hands.

After months of V1 raids there had been a short respite. And then came mysterious explosions of a new kind. At first no-one could explain why a street would be there one minute, and gone the next. The terror was finally given a name: the V2. This was a missile that made no sound. It took less than five minutes to cover its two hundred mile flight and reach the target. There was no warning and no defence. Yet Londoners endured it all. They never panicked; they stayed calm; they remained cheerful. Only Anna was overcome by fear. She struggled to conceal it, letting Nathan believe that her mother's impending death was the sole cause of her misery.

Nathan put his arm round her and stretched up to kiss her on the cheek. He handed her a large cotton handker-chief. Anna leaned forward and stroked his face and the wisps of white hair. She'd never known him with a full head of hair. He'd been bald when she met him but now, seven years later, he looked older than his age. Though he was only in his fifties he was used to people assuming that Nina was his grandchild and to be truthful he found it hard to summon up the energy to play with a five-year old. It was Anna who took care of the child; took care of him; bought the food; cooked it; cleaned the house; took down old curtains and made them into dressing gowns; mended their clothes and made sure the blackout material was in place when it grew dark outside.

The phone rang and Anna rushed in to answer it. Nathan wiped his hands and looked for a saucer for the egg. Anna put down the receiver and picked up her coat.

"It was Isaac. I have to go back."

chapter 2

LONDON 1944—ANNA

The fog had slowed the traffic till it was almost stationary. From the bus stop Anna kept to the nearside edge of the pavement and counted the houses until she reached her mother's gate. She blew her nose and felt the acrid taste of the thick air in her mouth. When Isaac opened the door he stepped aside and closed it after her to keep out the mist that was already settling in the hall.

He was about to say that she had taken her time to get there but his expression softened; Anna knew then she was too late. Boni was in the doorway wiping her eyes with an initialled handkerchief. Isaac began an account of Dina's last hours: how her chest began to heave and her breathing alternated from a gasp to a long, slow hiss. Boni joined in to say how her arms had suddenly become cool and mottled. Fifty minutes later—while Anna was halfway through her bus journey—their mother was finally still. The doctor had been called, had signed the death certificate and left.

Anna sat down, waiting for the tears to come. The thoughts whirling round her head brought a rush of misery. But it was too soon for the feelings of guilt and resentment to pour out; it was as if her brain had turned to ice, not yet able to melt.

Boni blew her nose and stuffed the handkerchief in her pocket.

"Anna, listen, Isaac's found this letter from Mother. Do you want to hear what it says?"

"I've seen it. It was open on the desk." Anna stared at Isaac.

Boni followed her glare. She narrowed her eyes as she looked at her brother.

"Have you been going through her things?" she asked.

"Since when is it a crime to look for your mother's will?" he answered.

"It is, if she's still alive," replied Anna. "I saw you had that letter on the table yesterday."

"Well I seem to be the only one who hasn't seen it," said Boni. "Typical. I'm always the last one to hear what's going on."

Isaac pulled up a chair and opened the letter. He exchanged a glance with Anna and then read the first sentence.

Boni gasped.

"What did she mean, asking a doctor to cut her arteries? It's too late, he's gone now."

Anna said nothing.

"Anna. What do you think?"

"Sorry, what did you say?"

"Well, it's obvious," said Isaac. "She had this fear of being buried alive. Bit odd really, because no-one thinks about that any more."

"She was old-fashioned" said Boni. "She had this Victorian idea that doctors often declared someone dead who was just unconscious."

"That's why they introduced the bells."

"What bells?" asked Anna, starting to listen to the conversation.

"Well, they used to attach a string to the finger of a corpse and then drill a hole in the coffin. The string was passed through the hole and attached to a bell by the grave. They had people whose job it was to listen for any tinkling. That's the origin of the phrase 'saved by the bell.'"

"Oh, shut up, Isaac," said Boni. "Mother's lying dead upstairs and all you can think about is stupid clichés. I want to hear the rest of this letter."

Isaac continued to read:

"and it is my wish that after the funeral, you have one night of prayers only and then carry on with your lives as usual. Do not grieve, my dears, I have loved you all so much and one day we shall meet. Meanwhile, love my memory and let it keep my dear ones straight and happy,

facing the trials and turmoil of life with courage and fortitude.

Since making my last will I have been blessed with a grandson and a granddaughter. Please give them £5 each from their Granny.

God bless you all my children and grant you happiness,

Your very loving

Mother."

"Trials and turmoil of life." Anna sighed. "She certainly had those. I can't remember her ever being happy."

"She was, before you were born," said Boni. "No, I didn't mean that. You know what I mean. When you were little. Before she lost father. It affected all our lives. Things might have been different if we'd never left Lisbon."

"All I remember is sharing a room with her," said Anna. "She cried every single night, for years. I learned to sleep with my hands over my ears so I wouldn't hear it."

Boni sniffed.

"You were lucky. You shared a room with her. I had that boxroom at the end of the corridor and no-one cared if I had nightmares or couldn't sleep."

Isaac was looking uneasy, clearly wanting to find the will that he knew must be somewhere in the desk. He'd already looked through the pigeonholes but the lower drawers were locked. He went to the cabinet and started to search. There were cut glass bowls, coffee cups and a silver sauce boat—all possible containers for the desk key. Eventually he found it, behind the candlesticks.

The drawers contained a stack of notebooks. There

was a recipe book of Dina's dated December 20th 1897. There were pages of handwritten notes and further on, printed extracts on cookery hints from the time of the first World War. The instructions for German Cabinet Pudding had the title crossed out and the words 'Victory Pudding' written in pencil above. Anna and Boni picked up other books: an account book in their grandfather's handwriting dated 1860, and a book of faded pages with the inscription 'Emily 1849' on the front cover. Who was Emily?

Isaac was still searching through a pile of papers. At the back of one of the drawers was a drawstring bag with something heavy inside it. He passed it to Boni as he carried on leafing through a folder of letters. Inside the bag was something wrapped in newspaper—a small silver teapot. It was a perfect sphere with a spout that was shaped like the head of a camel. The handle was made of ivory. Inside the lid was a note:

'Remember the sorrow; use the teapot with joy.'

"Hmph" said Boni. "all we ever heard was that it came from that place in Palestine. It certainly didn't bring Mother any joy."

Anna was fingering the silver camel's head.

"I can't believe our grandfather got this when he was fourteen; that it was all tied up with his 'tragedy'—the one he never talked about. It's far more likely that he got it years later when he'd gone up in the world."

"No, that's not true," said Boni. "If he'd bought it in England it would have a hallmark." She turned it upside down. "Look, there's nothing, it isn't English."

Anna was thinking that she knew so little about her

grandfather David; only what her mother had told them, that he lived in Gibraltar when he was a boy and that something terrible had happened.

"She never told us anything about his life."

"Why should she?" asked Boni. "She was too busy with her own problems."

"Exactly," said Anna. "Everything was hushed up. Maybe you knew more because you were older, but all I remember is Mother having secret conversations with the uncles. They used to stop whispering when I came in the room."

They were so absorbed by the camel teapot that they didn't notice Isaac. He was sitting in a chair, running his hands through his wiry black hair. A thick sheet of paper was on his knee. His face was white.

"She's left me nothing. Absolutely nothing."

"What did you expect?" asked Boni. "remember the money she gave you to start the button business, and the loan for all those cardboard boxes? She could hardly afford it and you frittered it all away."

Anna was looking at the will. It was short and uncomplicated. The house and contents were to go to Boni, the jewellery and funds in the bank account were to be divided equally between the two sisters.

At the butcher there was a queue of about twenty people. It moved slowly and as the customers neared the window, they looked at the sign announcing the government allowance for the week: 1s 4d. People started murmuring that you couldn't even get a scrag of lamb for that. By the time Anna reached the front of the queue the butcher was handing out a brown paper parcel to each customer. There was no point arguing. It wasn't as if there was a choice.

There was a rumour that there were onions at the greengrocer in Cricklewood Broadway but it proved to be wrong so Anna began the long journey to Petticoat Lane in the East End. She took the bus to Edgware Road and got the tube to Aldgate East. She couldn't remember the name of the greengrocer but joined a queue when she heard people talking about cabbages and sprouts. In front of her were two women with foreign accents. Everyone could hear them talking about buying food on the black market. She was ashamed to learn that they'd apparently paid someone £5 for a pineapple. When Anna got near the display of vegetables she was calculating how many potatoes she could carry and whether 3d a pound was reasonable for the onions.

With two heavy bags she moved on to a kosher delicatessen and waited her turn once again. When she reached the counter she asked if there were any pickled gherkins. The owner put his arm into a barrel with the greenish liquid coming up to his elbow.

"None left."

Without wiping his arm he put his hand into another barrel and pulled out a herring.

"Here, love. You can have this."

One last stop was a stall selling pieces of furnishing fabric. Anna picked through the remnants and found a bit of striped satin and a length of velvet. She was planning to make a toy for Nina. With a few inches of black-out fabric and an old cotton shirt she would have enough material. On the tube home she planned how to make the golliwog: a black face and body, legs in striped trousers and a velvet waistcoat. She fell asleep on the train and missed the station.

By the time Anna got home to Walm Lane it was six o'clock. Nina was in the back garden trying to catch one of the hens. It was her job to get them into the chicken house for the night. The bird flew out of her grasp and her shrieks made it even harder to catch it. Nathan was standing watching as Nina finally managed to creep up behind the hen and lift it into the coop. As she fastened the catch Anna called to her that supper was nearly ready.

A pile of bread and butter soldiers was on the table. Nathan couldn't understand why Anna wouldn't mix the butter ration with the margarine to make it go further, but she couldn't understand how he could consider mixing the precious butter with anything. She lifted the boiled egg out of the water and peeled off the top of the shell. Nina was just about to dip the bread into the yolk when the air raid siren began to wail. Anna hustled them all out of the back door and into the shelter, leaving the egg on the table. She settled Nina on the hard bunk bed and rushed back into the kitchen to grab the tin on the dresser. It would be bad enough if a bomb hit the house; far worse if the ration books went up in smoke as well.

24

chapter 3

Adafina—(Sabbath stew)

Set the onions and potatoes into a large
pot. Chop the meat fine and add to it spic-
es. Shape into balls. Add dried beans and
as much eggs as you can find, cover with
boiled water and a splash of olive oil. Cook
on the fire and keep warm overnight.

Gibraltarian recipe, 1840

1834—DAVID

There were never enough eggs. Hidden at the bottom
of the pot was a hen's egg, deep brown, soft and creamy.
It had a nutty flavour that came from cooking it with the
meat for twenty hours. But there was only the one—to be
shared between the six of us. When the Sabbath *adafina*
was ready to eat, we searched for the egg in the deep pot,
under the potatoes and the onions and the spicy meatballs that made the eggshell oily and dark. My mother
wanted to divide it up—I wanted the whole egg. I argued
endlessly that I'd rather have no egg for five weeks and
then on the sixth week, have the pleasure of cracking the

shell and biting off the top, sinking my teeth through the darkened white to the golden yolk inside. This never happened. I was only eleven. I had no say in the matter. When we sat down to eat we each got potatoes, a meatball and a morsel of the egg.

My father had no interest in the pleasures of food. His mind was on higher matters. We had lived in Gibraltar until I was ten and then for some uncertain reason we had left there to go to that place—that dreadful place. I remember the journey—the sea voyage and the sickness; those high waves and my stomach churning; the rolling ship and that taste that creeps into your mouth before the vile mess lurches out on to the deck. Was it days or weeks till we arrived in Acre? We watched as the massive anchor disappeared into the sea—no longer a murky grey, but as blue as the beach sky we had left in Gibraltar.

A man with horses and mules was there to meet us. We rode for days, first over flat paths lined with prickly pear trees and then through fields of thistles six feet high. The path turned into a rough and stony road. The mountain side was silver with olive trees. We set up our tents and began to fall asleep. I heard the voice of our guide whispering with my parents. Like all young boys, I was eager to listen to their conversation but the clicking of the crickets blurred the sound and I only heard muffled words: 'torrential downpour', 'houses damaged'. My eyelids were beginning to close but I forced them open as I overheard the man say to my father:

"Arab villagers attacked the Jews in the street. They stole their money and sent them off naked and barefoot."

That was the first of many times when I wondered why

we had gone there.

The next morning was cloudy and we continued, now walking over rocks and stones. We kept our eyes down, the adults stepping cautiously from one flat place to another, and the children kicking and throwing the pebbles. The path ahead was like a snake—a dusty zig zag, climbing to the top of the mountain. From there we looked down, catching our breath. The hills were covered with trees in blossom. My mother knew what they were. Fingering the leathery leaves she told us that the pink flowers were oleander and the white petals would turn into lemons. Through the branches we could see the roofs of the town. If only our life there had been like my first view from the mountain.

I tried to put these thoughts out of my mind when I returned alone to Gibraltar three years later. I was coming back to a town that I remembered well. Its heart consisted of three or four parallel streets, with lanes and passages leading downwards to the docks. The dark central thoroughfare, Main Street, was in shadow for most of the day. Steep flights of steps on the east side led to the caves and tunnels of the Upper Rock. It took fifteen minutes to go on foot from one end of town to the other.

Every day for the next few years I walked to school. The street was bustling with excitement. Donkey carts bearing barrels of water trundled over the wooden blocks and charcoal vendors called up to the three-storey buildings on either side. A Moroccan egg seller set down his wicker baskets at the corner of Tuckey's Lane, and chair menders worked in the shade of double-fronted doors. From the wrought-iron balconies women called to summon a tinsmith or a knife grinder. I never looked ahead as I walked, preferring to keep my eyes lowered. There was always a chance of finding something. I had seen a notice on a tree announcing that someone had lost a striped bag containing gold and silver dollars. Whoever found the bag would be rewarded with one-fourth of its contents. There was no sign of the bag as I dawdled along Irish Town, so I walked on towards home.

I lived with my guardian in a pink-washed house with a courtyard giving on to cool, shuttered rooms. At the end of the street there were forty-two steps, a sharp turn and then another twenty-seven steps. From the top you could look down over the curved roof tiles and wave at someone who was climbing up.

My guardian, Deborah Levy, was a spinster. She was in fact my aunt; a small, round woman, with pale skin. She was old—maybe fortyish—and apart from taking care of me, she seemed happy to spend her time cooking and visiting what she called 'connections'. Everyone who wasn't on the first level of cousins was a 'connection' so that included half the population of Gibraltar.

Every Friday afternoon I would take the *adafina* in its earthenware pot to cook overnight in the baker's oven. Before it got dark, the women would prepare the steaming pot of food for the Sabbath meal and someone would have to carry it down Baker's Passage. As the last of the loaves was taken out, the crocks were pushed into the oven to keep warm till the following day. The long slow cooking made the meat sticky and soft and the beans merged into the brown potatoes.

Ours was less than half full, because there were only two of us. Aunt Deborah would have liked more company. She brought up the subject of other boys in my school.

"Why don't we invite some of your friends for next week? she asked.

"I have no friends."

To take her mind off the question of company I asked:

"Do you remember when I went to the bakery to collect our crock and brought the wrong one back? We only found out because it had an unusual taste."

"It wasn't the taste. There was enough meat inside for a family of ten. But it's no more trouble to make a full pot. Don't you want to celebrate your birthday?"

"There's nothing to celebrate."

"When I was a young girl a birthday was a big event. We took a carriage to the beach at Catalan village and waited for the Spanish boys who came with baskets of *calentita.* Ah, the peppery taste of those hot slices. And the boys ... "

It was hard to imagine Aunt Deborah with flowing hair and a tight waist. She ignored my remark about having no friends and continued talking with the words spilling out of her mouth:

"It's not as if I have a dozen nephews. And besides, how else should I spend my time? I'd be pleased to have company."

How could I dissuade her? I was unable—or perhaps unwilling—to tell her what I was thinking. The 8th December was my seventeenth birthday. The memory of that other place was coming back. I tried to forget about those Sabbath meals—the *adafina* with the meatballs—*albondigas* I think they were called. I had blocked it out of my mind, with everything else. Each time the thoughts began I forced myself to concentrate on what was happening now, to forget why I was in Gibraltar, alone except for my aunt.

In a small community you might expect to find one synagogue and school. In this tiny British enclave there were four. I wanted to go to *Shaar Hashamayim* which was a hundred paces from our house. The words meant 'Gates of Heaven'. I wondered whether the orange tree in the patio was symbolic of our life on earth: beautiful, but sour? Inside there were carved mahogany benches lit by an array of lamps, of Dutch, Portuguese or English silver, hanging from the ceiling. My aunt preferred to walk five minutes to another synagogue on the corner of Bomb House Lane. The main gate was facing the sea. Birds flew across the sunlit courtyard under a trellis of vines and sometimes found their way inside. My school was in the next building.

The day started with prayers at 7 am—we called it *tefila*. Then Jewish studies for the next two hours, English after that, and finally, at the end of the morning some history. This always seemed to involve a battle; but I didn't care whether it was the Spanish or the English who won. Our teacher, Mr. Benzecry, had been telling us about the fourteen sieges and began to explain about a sortie in 1781.

"How big were the lead balls?" I asked. "How much powder did they contain? How did the fuse make the charge explode?"

Mr. Benzecry looked confused.

"David, if you want to know the details, go to the Garrison Library".

It wasn't hard to find. Library Street continued up a ramp and the building was set in a garden, with a racquet court at one end and the premises of the Gibraltar Chronicle at the other. Science was the only thing that stirred my mind and I knew that there would be books inside those reading rooms. But how could I get in? The entrance was guarded by an officer who asked if I was a subscriber. He told me that visitors should report to the Deputy Librarian, Lieutenant Frazer.

The lieutenant was seated at a vast table in the Upper Reading Room. He must have been surprised to see a boy in the doorway and putting back a heavy bound copy of the Times, he gestured to me to come outside. We stood at the top of the staircase and I used all the words I knew to persuade him to allow me to look at some of the books. He turned over the pages of the Rule Book and read:

"Every Subscriber shall have the liberty to introduce a Stranger to read in the Library Room which is open on Weekdays from 8 am in the summer till first Evening Gun-Fire."

"So may I be your Stranger?" I asked.

He smiled and whispered:

"If you obey the rules."

"Strict silence is to be observed in the inner rooms and the sand glass must be used to determine the length of time a reader may spend with the daily newspapers."

From that day I became a regular visitor, leaping up the

few steps to the doorway and searching for books in the glass-fronted shelves. School finished at noon. Everyone else went to the beach. I ran all the way home, eager to eat lunch and be back at the library in the afternoon.

I pushed open the big wooden door to our house, dropped my school bag and went into the dining room. Almost immediately the maid brought in the meal. Apart from her usual questions about my morning at school Aunt Deborah spoke little. We ate, in a pleasing silence. As the maid cleared the last of the plates, my aunt went upstairs to her bedroom for a siesta. I slipped out, ran along Cornwall Parade and pulled out my Visitor's Pass.

The library was a haven. In winter a log fire crackled in the fireplace at each end of the main reading room. Above each one was a mantelpiece with candelabra. It was always dark. The closed shutters protected the volumes from the sun that blazed down through the long, lethargic summer.

I carried books on physics and botany to the leather topped table upstairs and sat reading for hours. I never took them home or mentioned them to my teachers. At school we studied *Talmud* and worked in pairs. We were in the middle of a tractate—*Bava Metzia*—dealing with issues of ownership and business ethics. In the Rabbi's class we learned *mishna, gemara* and the mediaeval commentaries of Rashi. But my mind was buzzing with the excitement of chemistry. The patterns of behaviour of similar elements seemed like patterns of word-formation that grammarians tease out of our own language: mysterious and beautiful in their logic and terseness. Learning the equations and formulae was like learning a foreign language. Unlike physics, chemistry didn't involve a great deal of mathematics. It was about understanding; the distillation of much information into a neat, one or two-letter symbol.

I was in the library when a consignment of journals arrived from London. Lieutenant Frazer piled a dozen of them on to the table, next to the weekly delivery of the Times and The Morning Chronicle. I didn't recognize the title—The Lancet. At first I thought it was something military—lancers, or lances, but then I discovered that these were medical journals. I began to turn the pages, stopping at sections on *How to remove a stone in the windpipe* and *Poisonous snake bites*. I suddenly remembered the snakes in that other place, gliding around in the dust, not harming anyone.

I looked at the clock—four hours had passed. I'd been reading about the dangers of gases emanating from a dead body and a full description of an operation to remove a fist-sized tumour from a man's lower jaw. This was better than *Talmud*.

The summer passed and there was a shiver in the air. I pulled on my top coat as I walked. The sky was still as blue as the baby gowns displayed by the dressmaker. Why should I think of babies? The thought had not crossed my mind since I left that other place.

Each afternoon I spent hours poring over the journals. I became engrossed in amputations and head injuries; the club foot and female incontinence. I also found a series of Churchill's manuals. They cost 12s 6d each and I glanced at the ones on *Chemistry, Practical Surgery and Pathological Anatomy*.

The best one was '*What to Observe at the Bedside and After Death in Medical Cases*'. Part One explained the procedure. After examining the liver, spleen and stomach the doctor was to carry out a further inspection. He needed to check the lungs, colon and abdomen. I hoped our doctor had read this book. It was good to know that even the blood circulation was to be investigated before a body could be dispatched to the mortuary. Even more fascinating was Part Two. For those investigating death under suspicious circumstances was the advice: '*Look for burns, marks around the neck, and, if a weapon is discovered, compare it with the wound*'. In cases of suspected poisoning, '*one should search for arsenic and the contents of the stomach must be carefully examined*'.

I worked my way through almost a year's supply of journals. In a copy of the Lancet dating back to the previous September I read the opening article: '*Advice to Students on Commencing their Studies*'. The idea that had been stirring in my mind for months suddenly made sense—I wanted to enter the medical profession.

chapter 4

Salt biscuits

*Take half a pound of fine flour and a pinch
of salt. Put it in a bason. Warm an ounce
of butter and a sufficiency of milk to make
a stiff dough (about a gill). Knead the mass
and roll it out very thin. Prick over with a
fork, cut into biscuits and bake in a very
hot oven.*

From Deborah's notebook, 1840

GIBRALTAR 1840—DAVID

My father knew nothing of science but like me, he was
obsessed with learning. Did I ever see him without a
book in his hand? I remember him reading aloud to my
mother from a little book called 'Pat Lechem'—'A Morsel
of Bread'. I believe the author was related to our family
in some way. He was a great scholar but the aspect of
his work that fascinated my father concerned the tiniest
living things:

> *"Be especially careful, my child, with the veg-
> etables of our time which are full of worms, and*

are not clean. Pious women with good eyesight
should examine them carefully, and they should
do so three times."

"Is that why we can't eat mulberries?" I asked.

"Exactly," was the reply.

"But what about cauliflowers? Can't we just wash the worm out, if we see one?"

"But you can't always see them. That's why the vegetables must be examined."

To prevent any more questions he pushed a basket into my hand and said:

"David, I'm not disposed to talk about it. Please go to the market for your mother and bring back what she asks for."

In that place where he had brought us, there had been a thriving market every morning. The stalls were piled with wrinkled dates, oranges and mis-shapen peppers and the smell of fresh baked rounds of bread mingled with the scents of the spice pyramids, arranged on sacking under the awnings. My mother learned what vegetables she must avoid. My father immersed himself in Rabbinical texts—all to the same end, to pursue a pure life. He had a burning faith and was greatly admired. I found it hard to share their concerns at the possibility of consuming a minute worm or insect, and I let my thoughts wander as my father read out a different section each evening.

"We are accustomed not to eat lentils of the
current year, but we buy lentils of the previous
crop, which are at least twelve months old. Any
worms have disintegrated, and are regarded
simply as dust. Nevertheless we still examine

them, first in cold water, then in boiling water, and only then do we cook them. However beans and peas may be eaten in the same year, and the reason seems to be that they are large, and may be examined individually."

Aunt Deborah used to make pea soup when we had company for dinner. There were the uncles and Aunt Ledicia and what seemed to be dozens of cousins—Levys, Cubys and Parientes. They all took a great interest in our lives. One of them had seen me run up the steps to the library and reappear many hours later. If you know Gibraltar, you'll understand that even a visit to the library was worth reporting and could be a topic of discussion in the family.

The subject came up when Aunt Deborah was heaving a huge pan off the hob. The pieces of beef had been simmering for a whole day and the stock had to be strained into another pot full of green peas with some sprigs of mint. Aunt Deborah was pushing the mixture through a strainer. She began to talk:

"David, I don't know why ... ," she huffed, pressing the peas with the back of a wooden spoon "why you have to spend so much time surrounded by those dusty books."

"I like the library."

"But it would be better if you spent your afternoons on the sands."

"Better for who?" I asked, thinking about the sun smouldering on my back and the damp grains sticking to the pages of my book. To put her in a better mood I told her that I left the library in time to join my friends at about five o'clock.

I didn't tell her the real reason for my reluctance. Since I'd spent most of my boyhood away from the sea I couldn't swim well. When my friends dived off the rocks I felt my inside doing the somersault. I would have liked to walk past Windmill Hill Flats near Buffadero and throw stones over the bluff. As it was, I arrived at the beach long after the others, so I could hardly suggest we meet somewhere else.

The green puree was nearly ready. It seemed such an effort.

"Aunt Deborah, why do you spend so much time making pea soup? Why can't you make something simpler? The soup we had in that place was a broth made from vegetables and the bones of a chicken."

My aunt didn't like it when I referred to 'that place'. She usually started telling me how lucky I was. She put down the spoon, wiped her hands on her apron and went to put her arm around my shoulder.

"Don't touch me," I shouted and stamped out of the door. I shouldn't have pushed her away. In the beginning she had tried to help me with the memories, folding her plump arms around me and holding me tight to stop the tears. I should have understood: I was the centre of her world. Why didn't I explain how the books in the library had opened my mind to so many new things? I could have given her the satisfaction of knowing that I was in better spirits, passing my time happily. But the thought of the soup had brought back the memory of the table and the pile of spoons I used to put out. When the bad thoughts started coming I let myself remember the food, but for the rest, I pushed it away, out of my head, and imagined I was pressing hard against a heavy door which I had to keep shut.

Sardines. They weren't for eating. They were for buying and selling. The import export business seemed to support half the families in Gibraltar. In my last year of school Mr. Benzecry asked me about my plans.

"You could become an apprentice to one of the agents in Lisbon or London," he suggested. He knew that my mind wandered during the lessons and thought that I was dreaming of foreign travel.

"Do you remember when you sent me to the Garrison Library?" I began, thinking I might tell him about my interest in medicine.

"It seems you have become quite fond of the books there. We have books too. I don't know why you need to go there." He had long forgotten my original questions and had no conception of the world I had discovered in the scientific books and journals.

If I thought the subject was closed, it was reopened by my aunt a few days later. She also assumed that I was planning to enter the world of business. There was a package on the table.

"It's a gift, open it."

I began to unwrap the paper. Aunt Deborah was pulling at the loose strands of hair on her neck.

"It's a guide. Mogg's Strangers guide to London."

"Now you've spoilt it. You've told me what's in it."

She looked sad. I pulled out the book and turned to look at the *"List of the principal places"* on the first page.

"When you work in business you'll need to visit the big cities. I thought it would be suitable."

I was irritated with the way she spoke. She pronounced the words 'bissness' and 'vissit'. She spoke like many Gibraltarians with just a few words revealing that she was not quite English.

I didn't want to tell her that I'd already been studying an illustrated map of London with pale coloured pictures of the important sights. I could see in both plans a number of green places. I liked open spaces, like the Cork Woods near the Rock. They were a half hour walk from my house; an escape where the sun barely streaked through the trees and wild flowers and ferns grew by the stream at the bottom. In London there seemed to be four parks. One called Hyde had a lake, Serpentine, in the middle. Then there were smaller green areas—Lincoln's Inn Fields, Goodman's Fields and an Artillery Ground. The big river snaking across the map divided the south from the north.

My eyes wandered over street names—Cateaton, Great Bland, Queenhithe and Baalzephon Street. Where did a name like that come from? It was more like a street in that place. As my finger traced the roads it stopped at the title at the top of the map, showing the date it was printed: January 1st 1837. That was the day. The actual day. When it happened. I closed my eyes to stop the thoughts. Breathed. Pushed them away with the map.

Picked up the September issue of the Lancet. Kept my eyes on the words:

> *"It generally happens that a student has decided, previously to arriving in town, upon the school to which he shall enter. If he have not, the point of first importance is the hospital which he can best attend, and secondly the school nearest to that hospital where he may attain the greatest amount of useful information. Having decided upon his hospital, the student's next attention should be directed to the attainment of a lodging as near to the establishment of study as convenient."*

The chapter was full of information and the choice was confusing. Should I opt for an older hospital like St. Thomas's or Guy's in the south? Or apply to one of the newer ones like University College? For some reason the editor seemed opposed to King's and Charing Cross. In a state of indecision I considered where to attend courses. There were private schools like the Hunterian at Charlotte Street for the less affluent but I also pondered the advantages of going to lectures at one of the hospitals.

On the next page was a list of teachers and fees at The London Hospital. One session seemed to cost from three to six guineas but you could attend an unlimited number for as little as ten. The sessions began with medicine at 8 am. Midwifery with Dr. Ramsbotham was on Tuesdays, Thursdays and Saturdays at 10 am and on the alternate days there was Chemistry with Mr. Pereira. He also taught Materia Medica three days a week at half past three. But that wasn't all—the student still had to fit in Anatomy,

Physiology and Operations of Surgery by Messrs. Luke and Hamilton and a further session of Surgery by Messrs. Scott and Adams. The general fee for attendance at all of these lectures, qualifying for the examination at the College and Hall was £50.

It's strange how a page of details could make the black thoughts go away. I had to focus my mind on how to persuade Aunt Deborah to let me go to London, not as a visiting merchant selling sardines, but as an apprentice to a physician. Turning the page, I found the one fact that would convince her: The London Hospital employed a 'Hebrew cook' and had a kitchen supplying kosher food for the many Jewish patients there. There had to be Jews in London—at least that part of London.

I rehearsed what I was going to say. I walked into the kitchen to find Aunt Deborah baking salt biscuits. Her hands were covered in flour as she pulled and stretched the dough, rolling it out into thin strips till you could almost see through it. I was wondering how to begin:

"Aunt Deborah—I'm thinking of leaving Gibraltar."

No, that was too abrupt. She was pricking each strip with a fork and marking out the biscuits into two-inch lengths. When the trays were in the oven she began to talk about my leaving school and starting in commerce. I listened and said nothing.

"David, I shall miss you when you start to travel. But it won't be for long. You'll always be back here for *Shabbat*. We haven't done so badly, have we, since you came to live with me?"

Aunt Deborah went to take the biscuits out of the oven. I looked at the back of her head with her sleek hair parted in the centre. She used macassar oil to make it smooth and then pulled it back into a chignon and kept it in place with an ivory comb. I took one of the biscuits and pushed it into my mouth with a piece of salty cheese.

Since I hadn't replied she continued:

"and to think a spinster like me would end up raising such a fine boy."

I was far from 'a fine boy'. I must have been a disappointment. The boy Aunt Deborah had known as a child had returned with gangling legs and a face with broken skin and the beginnings of a stubbly beard. Did I remind her of my father, her only brother?

We existed side by side, in quite separate worlds. Her mind was occupied with cooking our food and visiting the cousins. As an afterthought she would pay attention to her appearance and choose a new bonnet for the spring. She was garrulous and inquisitive, sharing knowledge of the neighbours' lives in a tumble of English and Spanish words. I had little to say.

Our weekly visits to synagogue might have given me a chance to tell her my plans. But it was a short walk, often hurried as she wanted to be there in time to hear the weekly *Torah* reading from the scroll of the law. When we arrived she went up to the gallery and slipped behind the white ballustrade where the women sat. I picked up a fringed *talet*, threw it round my shoulders and joined in with the men, chanting the Hebrew words.

My father had taught me to read Hebrew. When I was very small he wrote out the *aleph bet* and I learned to put the letters together. But most of the prayers I knew by heart. We said them every day, from the moment we

43

woke up till we were curled up in bed at night. There was a prayer and a blessing for everything: on seeing the new moon, on eating a fruit for the first time in a season. As I got older my father left me to pray on my own, while he covered his head with his *talet* and rocked back and forth. He assumed I could follow and find my place in the book but the truth was that I would close my eyes and listen to the singing and not follow the words. I found that if I kept my eyelids half open I could make patterns with the light and see dancing cobwebs in front of my eyes.

chapter 5

JUMBLES

Unless you are provided with proper and convenient utensils and materials (butter paddle, hickory rods for beating eggs), the difficulty of making cakes will be great, and in most cases a failure, involving disappointment, waste of time and useless expense. Biscuits require only a mixing bowl and a baking tin.

Take equal quantities (a few ounces of each) of fine sugar, honey, butter and flour. Warm the sugar, honey and butter over a gentle heat. Stir in the flour, having first sifted it fine through a sieve with a pinch of ginger. Cook for a few minutes. Put drops on a well greased tin and flatten out. Allow room for spreading. Bake for about eight minutes. Lift off with a fish slice and press the biscuits round the handle of a wooden spoon.

From Deborah's notebook, 1840

Aunt Deborah was preoccupied with baking and bonnets. I passed my time in the library with Lieutenant Frazer, sharing items of interest from the Gibraltar Chronicle. The paper was full of information one might need at any time:

> *"Mr. de Vitry, Dentist to her Majesty the Empress Amelia, continues to fix without pain terro-metallic teeth. These teeth may be taken out and replaced at pleasure by the wearer. He also manufactures artificial Noses, Eyes and Palates. Apply Main Street, opposite the Exchange."*

I wondered about the eyes. Were these also done without pain? Why would anyone need an artificial nose? Would it work like a real one? I asked Lieutenant Frazer if he imagined Mr. de Vitry could replace the smell function.

He smiled and looked over my shoulder as I turned to the Shipping Section.

"Are you thinking of sailing somewhere?"

"As a matter of fact, I am."

"Look," he whispered. "the voyage to Southampton takes about five days. The Cunard Steamship Company offers *'superior accommodation at low rates.'*"

Someone at the end of the table said "Shhh". We carried on talking.

"I'm more interested in safety than comfort," I said. "Here's a report of a fire at sea. It says the crew were saved and taken to Dunkirk. I wonder what happened to the passengers?"

Lieutenant Frazer was pointing to a paragraph about an execution at Lisbon:

> *"To check the nightly recurrence of murders and robberies, the poor victim was hanged, after being paraded round the city for three hours."*

"I hope my Aunt Deborah hasn't read this." I said.

"Why?" he asked. "Are you going to Lisbon?"

"No, but I have other plans."

Before I could stop myself, I began talking about hospitals and schools of medicine.

Lieutenant Frazer reminded me of the 'strict silence' rule. We continued the conversation outside the reading room.

"Do you know enough physics and mathematics to study in London?"

"That's where you come in," I said. "Perhaps..maybe you could write a letter to say that I've been studying privately with you for some months?"

"I suppose you've taught yourself something poring over all those books, but a letter ... ."

I told him that I could write a few lines on what I had been studying and all he had to do was sign it, perhaps omitting his military title. I managed to convince him and then I broached another problem.

"I have to tell my aunt that I am leaving. And my teacher, Mr. Benzecry. He keeps asking me what I'm learning at the library."

"Haven't you told him that you spend nearly every afternoon here?"

"No, he thinks I go to the beach with the others."

"You're a funny lad, David. Give me the choice and I'd rather be sitting on the long sands looking out at that blue line on the horizon. And you.. you'd rather be sitting here reading the Chronicle."

"How am I to tell them? They'll never let me go to live in London."

"Why don't you invite this Mr. Benzecry to meet your aunt and you can tell them together?"

"I certainly can't tell him first. The news will reach Aunt Deborah before the end of the afternoon. Gossip travels fast in Gibraltar. Do you know that story about the young woman who was visiting from England?"

We began to walk down the stairs together.

"What does this have to do with your aunt?"

"It isn't related to her. It's about this place. The young woman I was talking about, she wanted to buy a gift for her mother. She went in and out of several stores, looking at different objects. In each one the shopkeeper took pains to bring forth a selection of goods. It was hard for her to decide: should it be the heart-shaped jewellery box or the porcelain doll? Maybe a hand-painted mirror would be more to her mother's taste? The young woman finally chose the doll."

"And?"

"Let me finish the story. By the time she returned to her lodgings the landlady already knew what she had bought. She even knew how much it had cost."

We agreed there should be no subterfuge. It transpired that my aunt was delighted at the thought of meeting Mr. Benzecry. The next day she sent me to school carrying a small envelope inviting him to come for tea the following Tuesday. I could already hear the conversation in my head:

> *"I'm planning to book a passage to England and find lodgings in London."*

Aunt Deborah would faint; Mr. Benzecry would help her up from the floor and my plans to study medicine would be finished. I needed a gentler introduction and imagined bringing the conversation round to a discussion of his family:

> *"Mr. Benzecry, don't you have a sister who lives in Secretary's Lane near the Cathedral? The one who was very sick last year? Wouldn't it be marvellous to learn how to cure people?"*

The reality was rather different. On the dot of three o'clock there was a tap on the brass knocker and standing at the front door was Mr. Benzecry, removing his leather gloves to extend a hand to my aunt. She was wearing one of the new fashionable crinolines and her skin was paler than ever with a dusting of pearl powder and some rouge tentatively applied to her cheeks. She led him into the parlour and invited him to sit in one of the high-backed chairs, smoothing down the starched linen of the antimacassar. The maid brought in a polished tray with a silver teapot and matching sugar basin and cream ewer. She set down a tiered stand with a cake made from Jordan almonds and a large plate of butter biscuits. On the top was a small plate of crisp, lacy jumbles.

A few hours earlier we'd had an argument about the jumbles. Aunt Deborah was spooning little mounds of the warm sugar and butter mixture on to trays when I came into the kitchen. She slid them into the oven where they bubbled and flattened and turned a dark brown. Immediately they were cooked she had to lift them off and roll them around the handle of a wooden spoon to make them curl. Of course some of them broke and I made myself useful by putting the broken pieces straight into my mouth.

Aunt Deborah slapped my hand:

"Stop it, David, there won't be any left."

The biscuits were tricky anyway, but the thought of the forthcoming tea made her nervous, so she wasn't working fast enough and many of the jumbles stuck to the tin or cracked as she peeled them off. She piled the few good ones on to a plate and put it on the top tier.

As she poured the tea I remembered the other silver teapot we never used. It was the only thing I brought with me from that place. It stayed in a cabinet in my bedroom, a precious possession, kept out of sight.

The conversation was in full flow with my aunt and my teacher discussing people they knew.

"David's a good student, you know" said Mr. Benzecry "but I think his mind is sometimes on other matters."

This was my opportunity.

"Aunt Deborah. What would you think if I were to go away, to live in London?"

"But there's no need. You can work as an agent and make the occasional visit to England."

"I'm not going to sell sardines. It's not what my father would have wanted."

"And what would he have wanted? He's not here. God rest his soul."

She was pulling at the sleeve of her dress, looking from

me to Mr. Benzecry. The tea was getting cold.

"I'm hoping to become a pupil to study medicine at a London hospital".

There was a long silence. Aunt Deborah was close to tears.

"Medicine? Mr. Benzecry, some more cake?"

He nodded and held out his plate. Flicking the crumbs off his trousers he said:

"That means years of study. How will you manage?"

Before I could say anything Aunt Deborah began a tirade:

"You'll be on your own in London. There'll be no-one to cook for you. There are dangers... ."

She was twisting her handkerchief into a knot. She turned away to refill the teapot.

Mr. Benzecry sat uncomfortably in his chair. He coughed and said:

"I know a man called Mendoza who can help David find lodgings. And there are kosher butchers and bakers in Whitechapel."

"Mendoza—Eliezer, isn't it? He's a connection" said my aunt. "So David will be acquainted with one Gibraltarian in a vast city."

"Perhaps we could telegraph and send word to his office that I will be arriving?" I suggested.

Aunt Deborah looked stricken. I wondered if I was right to stand by my decision to leave Gibraltar. Mr. Benzecry was finishing his cake. He set down his fork and then suddenly he was leaving and I was alone with my aunt. She turned away and brushed past the maid who had come in to clear away the plates. For the rest of the evening Aunt Deborah stayed in her room.

The next day I found her sitting at her desk looking through some correspondence. I asked what she was doing and for a full five minutes she said nothing. Eventually she sighed and said:

"David. I'm not sure this is wise."

"But my mind is made up. I've been considering it for weeks. It's not a decision I have made lightly. I've been finding out where to study and how much it will cost."

At the mention of money Aunt Deborah raised another objection.

"I'm not sure if there are enough funds to support you for five or six years."

"Funds? what do you mean?" I asked.

"Well, I told you some money was raised when you came back to Gibraltar."

I had a vague memory of that first week when I was taken to Aunt Deborah's house. The parlour was filled with people, neighbours who lived in the surrounding streets. They poured into the room and whispered in groups. They all knew my parents.

"Yes, but where did the money come from?"

"All the neighbours in Engineer Lane wanted to help," she began. "When the word went round even those who lived further on in Governor Street ... they all contributed to the fund. It's a considerable sum. I suppose now you are nearly eighteen, you are entitled to it."

Aunt Deborah sighed. "I have no notion of how much the lodgings and fees will cost." She had difficulty keeping her voice from trembling. "But be cautious, David, don't fritter it all away."

I wanted to thank her for everything she'd done for me; to say something to show how I appreciated her letting me go. Instead I put my arm round her shoulder and brushed my lips against her cheek, breathing in the faint perfume of powder. My face was damp. She dabbed at her eyes with the handkerchief.

The following week I bought a large trunk and began to fill it with newly acquired clothing. On top of the boots I packed trousers, some narrow cut with straps under the instep, others cantoon or 8s 6d tweed. I was arranging the waistcoats and ties when Aunt Deborah offered to fold my lounge jackets. She spread out sheets of tissue paper and then suddenly left the room. She returned a moment later with needles and thread.

"There'll be no-one to sew your buttons on," she said.

We finished packing in silence. She passed me porcelain cups and saucers, a tea caddy and cut glass tumblers. I looked round my bedroom and gathered together my hairbrushes and cuff links, hesitating over the writing case and pens—surely I'd be able to purchase some in London? I didn't think there would be room for the linen sheets and pillow cases, but it made sense to tuck them in around the heavier objects.

I picked up the velvet bag containing my *tefillin.* It was a long time since I'd used them at morning prayers. On the day of my *barmitzvah,* my father taught me how to place the black box on my forehead and showed me how to wind the straps around my arm. I'd done it every day since I was thirteen and even continued when I returned to Gibraltar and was given a new set. At the end of this school year I brought them home but I never prayed with them. They remained in the bag, untouched. I threw them on top of the linen, with my woollen fringed *talet* and last of all, the camel teapot. I closed the lid of the trunk, fastened the locks and moistened the luggage labels with my tongue, pressing them down, so they could be clearly seen by the porters.

At the quayside there was a large sign 'Peninsula and Oriental Steamship Company'. The whole of Gibraltar seemed to have turned out to see me off. Aunt Deborah wore a new, wide-skirted dress. Her bonnet was tied under her chin with a large bow. Small boys from the school in tunic suits with close fitting jackets jostled to get a better view of the ship. Their parents put out protective hands to ensure that the smart clothes stayed clean and unruffled. In the distance I heard the sounds of the Regimental Band in the Cathedral Square. I thought about Lieutenant Frazer. The letter he'd given me was safe in my pocket.

Mr. Benzecry came on board with me, found the steward and gave him half a sovereign. Aunt Deborah was pressing a handkerchief to her eyes. She pulled a shawl up to her throat and the fringes blew in the wind as she made her way down the gangplank. Alone in my cabin, I closed the door. I tried to recall some advice for frequent passengers that I had read in the Chronicle:

> *Never take a place opposite a newly married couple. It is tiresome, tantalising, disgusting.*
>
> *Never play at cards. Some people know too little for your temper and others too much for your pocket.*

If the berths are over each other, let the young
fellow climb and you take the lower one.

Biting my lip, I arranged my pyjamas on the top berth.
Presumably, being the 'young fellow' I had to be the one
to climb.

The ship was due to stop at Cadiz, Lisbon and Oporto
before finally arriving at Blackwall. My companion was
pleasant but untalkative and apart from assuming that
the middle aged couple waving to me from the shore were
my parents, he asked few questions and seemed keen to
acquaint himself with the various decks, shipboard activities and meal times.

Sea travel held no excitement for me. I studied the
daily weather forecasts as I was anxious about passing
through the Bay of Biscay and the infamous storms
and high seas often encountered there. But the passage
proved uneventful and I passed the days sitting on deck
reading.

The front page of The Morning Chronicle was a light
relief from the more serious literature I had brought with
me. A small announcement caught my eye:

'*Patent Aquatic Life Hat, guarantees total pre-*
vention from drowning, possesses such extraor-
dinary buoyant powers as to support four per-
sons from sinking.'

I was trying to imagine how four people could wear
the hat. Unfortunately it was not on sale on board ship
but was to be demonstrated every morning and evening
during the bathing hours on the Serpentine.

Disembarkation was slow and progress through the
customs house even slower. I was told I could leave my

trunk at the shipping office and collect it later. I made my way from the port to Smithy Street near Mile End Road. I was looking for Eliezer Mendoza, the 'connection' who had set up a business in the East End of London. He specialized in sardines, buying in Spain and selling, through agents, to Britain and Holland. His London offices were a couple of rooms at the top of a terraced house about half a mile from the river. When I arrived he was perched on a chair at a high desk, writing in a massive ledger. He asked me to wait while he entered the latest transaction, the name of the bank and the cash received. When he got down I was surprised to see how short he was. He enquired politely about my relatives in Gibraltar and handed me a list of addresses. Walking down the staircase with me to the front door, he barely came up to the height of my chest.

I took out one of my maps and set off along Sidney Street. The smell from the horses and the grime beneath my feet made me speed my pace, past Fieldgate and Stepney. I needed to get away from the bustle and chatter in the streets so I walked on to the castle, one of the monuments I had read about. It was less than a mile away and the round turrets were just visible above the slight fog. The Tower Ditch surrounded the castle on three sides. I looked at the vivid green lawn, so unlike the parched grass of Gibraltar or the sandy paths of that other place, and felt the cool grip of loneliness spreading up my chest.

chapter 6

BRAISED BEEF HEARTS

Wash the hearts; cut away the pipes and cut the dividing walls. Heat the dripping, brown the hearts all over and cook over a low light for about an hour. For the gravy, sprinkle some flour into the fat, add the water from the vegetables, bring to the boil.

From Anna's notebook, 1944

LONDON 1944—ANNA

The newspaper used to wrap the camel teapot was a copy of the Kent Herald, dated March 9th 1837. The matching jug and sugar bowl were in green baize bags. Boni had insisted that Anna should keep the tea set as she was clearly interested in her grandfather and how he came by it.

Nathan spread out the crumpled paper and leaned over to read the articles on the front page. A man called Nicholls had absconded from his home leaving five children. A reward of £10 was offered for information leading to his return. Another item reported that 900,000 people had been struck down by influenza in Paris.

"Nathan, move the paper, I want to chop the onions."

Anna was cooking the supper. The parcel from the butcher had contained a few bones and a couple of beef hearts. She was glad to have the onions as Isaac and his family were coming to supper and the thick gravy would eke out the small amount of meat. Would there be enough for four adults and two children? Anna peeled off the outer skins and cut the three onions into slices. She began to blink as they released their sting. In her mind onions were always linked with tears: not only the momentary discomfort in the kitchen but the tears that resulted from the constant rows she'd had with Boni as a child.

Outside the flat in Kings' Gardens was a long corridor. Anna used to slip out of the front door and push her doll's pram up and down. There was a sweet, roasting smell coming from one of the flats. The door opened and a woman appeared, holding an empty milk bottle. As she put it down Anna asked:

"What you cooking?"

"Liver and onions. Does your mummy know you're out here?"

At that moment Dina appeared and dragged her daughter inside.

"Why don't we ever have onions?" asked Anna.

"Because Boni doesn't like them," said Dina.

"But I don't like tapioca. Why do you make me eat that

disgusting mess and Boni can eat what she likes?"

"Anna, don't be rude."

The subject was closed. When Dina had lived in Lisbon she had learned to make every savoury dish beginning with a *sofrito* of chopped herbs and the essential onion and garlic. But when Boni started to stamp her foot and push her plate away the meals in the Levy household changed. Boni had got her own way.

Isaac was a gentle boy; brought up in a family with two sisters, he had none of the aggression of boys who had brothers. He had the train set to himself and was happy to include Anna in his games, chattering as he fixed the points and lined up the carriages. Boni took it upon herself to order him to clear up before supper and reported every quarrel to her parents. She was in charge. Eight years older than Anna, she saw the age difference as a licence to show her seniority. After all, she'd been there long before either of them were born. Her superior position in the family might have continued long after they'd left Lisbon but it changed overnight: her parents decided to hire an English governess.

Jo was about eighteen and came from a village in Dorset. She produced letters with impeccable credentials, speaking of her rapport with children and her knowledge of languages. When Dina read the references she had no hesitation and sent a wire in response. The new governess arrived in Lisbon and was met by the whole family who looked her up and down, taking in her pale complexion and wispy brown hair. In a short time Jo had assessed the situation: the oldest daughter was jealous of her younger siblings, the son was pampered, and the youngest child

59

was cherished, but not yet spoilt.

She was determined to bring a firm hand to the up-bringing of these children, but because of her irrepressible nature, even her rebukes were delivered with a twinkling eye. With the two older children at school, Jo spent hours playing with Anna. Dina watched from a distance. It was clear who it was that Anna adored.

When they settled in London Dina was grateful to Jo. She was pleased that she was keeping Anna amused with games and activities. But most of the time she didn't know what they were doing. One morning Jo brought in a toy stove and a bottle of blue liquid. Anna watched as she set light to the meths and put a pan of oil on to the stove. Then she sprinkled flour over some tiny fishes.

"What are they called?" asked Anna.

"Whitebait."

Jo tossed one of the hot fishes between her fingers.

"Taste it" she said.

"Why are they called whitebait if they're brown?" asked Anna.

Dina would have been horrified if she had been in the room. Frying in hot oil was far too dangerous. The pot could have tipped over. Anna could have been burned and scarred for life. Dina was always trying to protect her children from harm. Yet what she saw as caution, they regarded as an unreasonable restriction. Sometimes her attempts to shield them from danger were obvious. On other occasions it took months or even years before they noticed how obsessive she had become.

As children they probably didn't realize their mother was unusual. With no other mother to compare her with, life at home would have seemed normal. It was only later, when they looked back, that they pieced together certain incidents that at the time seemed unremarkable but from a more adult perspective, bordered on mania.

When Anna was nine she walked into Jo's room and found her packing a suitcase.

"I'm getting married, darling. I'm going far away ... to Jerusalem."

Anna sat on the suitcase, keeping the lid shut.

"You can't go. I love you and I want you here."

Jo was folding her clothes.

"But darling, I have to go. John is a doctor and he's going to work in an eye hospital out there."

"Then can I come too?" asked Anna.

"You can if you like snakes and scorpions."

Anna had jumped off the case and was climbing on to a shelf to get down a leather book.

"Where's Jerusalem?" she asked. "Is it the one in this bible?"

She had managed to lift down the huge volume of more than a thousand gold edged pages. On the back were her parents' names in gold with the date of their marriage. Inside, her father had written the Hebrew dates of the children's birthdays and their names. Anna's name was in a different handwriting, as if they hadn't known when she was born, what they were going to call her. Some of the pages were sewn up with cotton thread so they couldn't be opened.

"Why has Mother been sewing this book?" asked Anna. She was trying to rip the stitches with her teeth.

Jo replied that the pages might have been torn. But

Anna knew there was something strange and secret inside the book. The chapter that was sewn up stuck in her mind. It was Genesis Chapter 34.

It was not till some eight years later when Anna was sitting in synagogue that she had a flash of memory. The reader was chanting the Hebrew and she was following the English on the left hand page. Genesis Chapter 34. It was about Jacob's daughter Dinah. The conversation with Jo came back to her. The chapter told how Dinah was raped, and how the perpetrator and his whole family were murdered in a frenzied attack. What had her mother been thinking when she sewed up the pages of the family bible? She wanted to protect her children from every accident and uncertainty of life. Reading the story of her biblical namesake could only distress them.

The beef heart casserole was simmering on the stove. Isaac pushed past Anna and hardly managed a smile. He went to talk to Nathan in the sitting room, leaving his wife in the kitchen. Freda was showing Anna an eyebrow pencil she'd managed to find in the chemist. The two of them couldn't have been more different: Anna plump, with strands of dark hair waving in a curl at the side of her face; her sister-in-law with careful make-up, a slender, tailored skirt and trim ankles. The eyebrow pencil was not for her face. She had painted a solution of weak tea on to her legs to look like silk stockings and needed to draw a seam in a fine line up the back.

When Isaac had first introduced Freda to the family

at a dinner shortly before Anna's wedding, Nathan had said something mildly offensive. Freda had ignored him for the rest of the meal. Anna tried to compensate for the bad start to their relationship and made an effort to like her sister-in-law. But they had no common ground, since Anna had little interest in fashion and appearance and Freda had little interest in anything else.

Upstairs Nina was playing with her cousin Joel. The two children had been inseparable since they were born—a mere three weeks apart. While Freda kept to herself, resting in the afternoons and amusing herself with a growing collection of cheap novels, Isaac liked to spend time with his sister. As they drank tea and talked, their children were absorbed in imaginative games in the upstairs bedroom. Their parents were concerned at the lack of toys. Factories that manufactured non-essential items were given over to the production of munitions, so wartime children had no access to dolls or tin soldiers. Nina and Joel had no understanding of what they were missing. They had never seen a well-stocked toy shop.

What they were doing was far more exciting: at that moment Joel was tying Nina to a small wicker chair with a length of string. She had been captured by pirates and was awaiting her punishment. It was her turn to be strapped into the 'death chair'. The fastening was done with giggles and fake protests. Then the chair was heaved to the top of the half landing. This was the ship; the stairs below were a raging sea. Nina pleaded for her life. The chief pirate was bargaining with her; rocking the chair as he lifted the two front legs off the stair. On the count of three Joel released his prisoner into the depths, bumping her down the stairs, warning her of the sharks in the water. The string snapped and Nina rolled over, splaying out her arms to protect herself from the more real danger of the metal stair rods. The chair came to a stop before the turn that led to the long flight to the ground floor. Nina picked herself up and yelled 'my turn to be the pirate'.

Anna was mashing the potatoes and slicing up the beef hearts. Freda looked on, wondering how her sister-in-law had the patience to cook. She would have made do with a fish paste sandwich. Isaac came into the kitchen carrying the camel teapot. Anna kept on mashing, waiting for him to speak. He ran his fingers up the spout and over the mouth and said:

"So you're the one who got this."

"I told you to come and choose some things from Mother's house. You said you didn't want anything."

"I don't now. I might have done if she'd included me."

"Anyway, I didn't think you wanted this. You're not interested in our grandfather."

"I don't care about a crummy teapot. But I do care about my share of mother's estate."

"Isaac, don't start that again," said Anna. "You know full well that you've had your share already."

"How do you work that out? Just because she lent me a bit of money ... ."

"Remember the hundreds of pounds she put into the button business?"

"Don't bring that up again. When I took over that business it was flourishing. How was I to know that the holes for that huge consignment were drilled off-centre? And then there was the customer who wouldn't accept the covered buttons, claiming the dye was wrong. And then to cap it all, that garment manufacturer that went bust owing me a fortune ... ."

"It wasn't just the button business," said Anna. "What about the wine importing?"

"Mother was quite happy to help me get started again. Until you and Boni poisoned her mind."

"How dare you," yelled Anna. "Have you forgotten the help we gave you?"

"Help? Boni coming to the office for a few hours a week?"

"It's not as if she was twiddling her thumbs for the rest of the time. She was working for the uncles. Trouble with you, it was never enough. I was earning peanuts selling a few chocolates and I was happy to give you the odd hundred. But you always came back for more."

"Well, this time I'm not coming back at all. You can stuff the money. And your sanctimonious attitude. We can do without you. And Boni."

Isaac began to walk out of the kitchen. Anna wasn't taking in what he said. She was wondering about the beef hearts: a lower heat might have made them more tender; could there possibly be enough meat to go round? Isaac was standing by the front door, with his fingers on the handle.

"I've had enough of these conversations," he called. "You're always in the right. Well, you can talk to yourself from now on. I'm going."

There was a pause and Anna came into the hall, catching the last of his words:

"And don't think I'm coming back. I don't ever want to

see you again."

The front door slammed. Anna turned to see Freda and Joel standing at the bottom of the stairs. No-one said a word. Nina watched as Freda grabbed Joel's hand and pulled him out of the house.

Anna lifted the stew on to the table and removed the extra plates. She called Nathan and they ate in silence, broken only by Nina saying she hadn't finished her game with Joel. They spooned up the onion gravy and pushed the meat around their plates. They had no idea that Isaac had chosen his words with care and he would never speak to his sisters again.

When they'd gone home Nathan helped to clear the table. Anna straightened out the newspaper and was about to wrap the camel teapot when she noticed a paragraph on the back page. It was a short piece extracted from another newspaper, the Gibraltar Chronicle of January 1837. What it described was the tragedy experienced by her grandfather David.

chapter 7

Mutton broth

Take a scrag of mutton, put it in a sauce-pan, with a small piece of beef, and three quarts of water, some pepper, ginger, a little mace and salt. Let it come to a boil, and then skim it quite clean. Add a handful of barley. Put in some onions, a few turnips or carrots and let all boil together until tender.

From David's notebook, 1841

LONDON 1841—DAVID

My arrival in London might have seemed exciting but for me it was yet another move—the third in my eighteen years.

In Gibraltar we had always spoken English but I found the spelling hard. The rearrangement of a few letters led me to a decision that probably changed the course of my future. Remembering the advice in the Lancet to choose a hospital with a nearby school, I decided on the London Hospital and the Aldersgate school. The fees there were from three guineas per session and I judged that it was in the right location. What I failed to discover until the next day was that by confusing the name Aldgate East with Aldersgate I had given myself a considerable burden. The London Hospital, in Whitechapel, and the School, in Aldersgate, were almost two miles apart.

With Mr. Mendoza's list of addresses in my hand I set out to find lodgings. I walked back from Tower Hill into Mulberry Street. Number eight had a cracked wooden staircase and a room at the top with a window so small that at ten o'clock in the morning there was hardly enough light to read. I left and walked on into Aldgate East. I had imagined fine carriages and men wiping their lips with scented handkerchiefs. Instead there were strange sights: rows of handbarrows, carts with the horse gone and the tilt piled with old clothes, boots and damaged lamps. Green Dragon Yard was blocked with sellers of canaries and parrots. Further on a man standing in a dog-cart disposed of racing tips in sealed envelopes.There was a fish stall, the seller was shouting 'sevenpence', 'sixpence', 'fivepence'. Finally, shouting 'threepence ha'penny', he put the fish on a square of newspaper and bundled it up to give to the bystander. The room I'd come to see was on the first floor of a house in Old Montague Street, with barely enough space for the bed, cupboard and washstand but there was a large window. I agreed the weekly rent with the owner, a Mrs. Thomas, paid three months in advance and went to make arrangements for my trunk to be sent from the shipping office.

The London Hospital was a stone's throw from Aldgate East, though nowhere near The Aldersgate School. The walk between the hospital and the lecture rooms I had chosen took me nearly thirty minutes—a journey I was to make several times a day. Though I was accustomed to climbing the steps behind my house in Gibraltar, I found it irksome to trudge along the damp pavements, and perversely wished I could be back home kicking the stones along the path to the beach.

My first task was to buy books. I came home laden with volumes on anatomy and physiology. The professor of chemistry had remarked '*One fact learnt alone is worth a dozen pointed out by others*'. But no book prepared me for the dissecting room at the Aldersgate. It was small enough for the students to have a good view of the body under examination. The corpse was on a raised table and the lower part was covered with a piece of grey cloth. The surgeon began with a call for a strong, sharp scalpel. I heard a metallic scraping sound as he picked up the instrument. With a swift movement a central incision was made down the torso and the heart was removed. I was unable to concentrate on the explanation of its mechanical functions. Hanging over us was the heavy smell of putrefaction.

At the end of the class I was the first to reach the door. There was a welcome blast of cold air from the street. As I climbed the stairs to my room, I still felt sick from the foul reek of the corpse. Mrs. Thomas must have seen me looking pale as I passed and she called out from the scullery:

"Mr. David, I shouldn't say it, as I aint your mother, but you are going to do yourself an injury, rushing about like this."

"I'm late, Mrs. T. I have to be at Mr. Pereira's lecture in twenty minutes." I didn't tell her that on Mondays, Wednesdays and Fridays I was usually the last in the door at Dr. Ramsbotham's.

"Will you be going out again this evening?" asked Mrs. Thomas.

"Yes, I have to walk the wards with Mr. Adams." If I'd told her that he was one of the senior surgeons at the London Hospital. she would have understood better why my daily journeys were making me tired. Instead she sighed and shook her head.

Two years later, I found myself constantly exhausted, pushing through the fog and sleet and still unaccustomed to the chilling cold of the London streets. In my haste I hardly looked up, passing pawnbrokers and cabinet makers, assailed by the unfamiliar smells of cheesemongers and bacon dryers. I began to long for Gibraltar, for the sunbaked streets near the Library and a sweet *challa* from the kosher bakery in Irish Town.

Yet in one respect, little had changed. Because I attended classes in two places, I never had time to talk or smoke with the other students. They would meet in eating houses or spend the late evenings drinking, while I went back to my room to immerse myself in medical books.

The months passed. I hadn't even unpacked the porcelain cups or the camel tea pot. It stayed, wrapped in one of Aunt Deborah's fringed towels—unused, and out of mind. I found a laundress to wash and iron the linen sheets. They seemed preferable to the rough bedding supplied by Mrs. Thomas. One Friday I asked if I could use her kitchen.

"Will you be wanting to cook, Mr. David? Don't they give you meals in that hospital of yours?"

"I.. I'd like to make some soup," I answered "Like you make. What are you cooking that smells so good?"

"Mutton broth. I'll make you some," she replied.

"No, well, I'd like to do it myself. Will you show me how?"

She led me into the kitchen and lifted the lid off the heavy pot. She took a long fork and speared two chunks of meat, explaining to me that one was beef and the other a scrag end of mutton. She told me how to add the barley first and then showed me how to peel and cut an onion. I kept her instructions firmly in my mind and asked her a question:

"Would it inconvenience you if I left it on a low heat all night?"

"Don't know so much as inconvenience... p'raps it'll burn. Why do you want to leave it on? It don't take that long to cook soup."

How could I explain about not making a fire on the Sabbath? Or that I couldn't use the fat-encrusted pans of the house? I inched my way out of the kitchen, saying:

"You're a grand cook. But you'll be needing your heavy pan. I'll buy one of my own."

I hoped the flattery would take her mind off my strange request. Before I went out I stopped to write down the instructions in a small notebook. Was it a pinch of mace and a handful of barley or the other way round? I bought a solid pot with a lid, and went to the kosher butcher in Middlesex street for some saveloys and a few pieces of mutton. I left the meat to cook slowly with root vegetables, adding a spoonful of barley into the pot and then another one for good measure. On *Shabbat* I woke to the savoury smell of the stew. I slept most of the day, leaving my bed to walk to the stove and ladle the broth into a deep bowl. The thought of synagogue never entered my mind.

Prayer for me meant repeating the morning, afternoon and evening services and the purpose always seemed to be to conclude the repetition as speedily as possible. In Gibraltar the reader chanted the prayers in a sweet, trembling voice but there was no occasion for a dialogue with God, or for requests. It seemed to me—a subject never discussed with my father—that God required us to pray and in return he planned out our lives without consulting us.

The idea that prayers could be offered in song, soaring to the height of a magnificent building, had never occurred to me, until one day I walked into the Church of St. Botolph without Bishopsgate. Inside was a marble floor, wooden benches and large brass chandeliers with long white candles. Upstairs was a gallery. There were no ornaments and only when I turned round did I see the stained glass window and the altar with the cross. But it was the music that affected me—alto, tenor and soprano weaving repetitive phrases in a tapestry of sound that I could only compare to the joy of swallowing thick, dark chocolate.

For nearly three years I had kept no company with

Jews. There were no other students of my faith at either The Aldersgate or The London. Only the day before I'd had an unsettling experience. I walked into the lecture room and found some pupils huddled over a copy of the Lancet, reading an article by the editor, Mr. Wakley.

"He's at it again" one of them said. "Now I know why his journal is called The Lancet. He thinks the medical societies are an abscess on the body of the profession which has to be lanced."

I had come in at the end of their discussion. I did not anticipate their next comment:

"But then, what can you expect from him? He's the Honourable member who represents the Jew clothes-vendors of Finsbury."

I was stunned by their words. Did they know I was hoping to become a Jew doctor? I tried to consider how to respond, but in that moment, silence seemed the only possible choice.

Had I been in Edinburgh or Paris, I might have met fellow students who were Jews. There were none at Oxford or Cambridge, universities that excluded anyone who was not a member of the Church of England. I had hoped to find more liberal views in London, where University College was the first to offer an education to dissenters. Yet although I had embarked on a course of study, I hadn't considered the future. When the results of the examination boards were published, I began to have serious concerns. Among the successful candidates there was not a single Jewish name—no Cohen or Abraham MD.

On Friday 9th August 1844—I remember the date because the direction of my life changed on that day—I was walking from Aldersgate back to my lodgings in Old Montague Street at about six o'clock in the evening. Instead of my usual route from London Wall, along Houndsditch, I wandered down Camomile Street and on into a road called Bevis Marks. The painted signs above the doorways caught my eye: Jonas Levy—watchmaker, Julius Singer—jeweller. Even the house painter and the tailors had biblical names: Isaac Hyam and Emanuel Brothers.

In Gibraltar the community was prominent. On *Shabbat*, all the stores owned by Jews were closed—and that meant half the stores in the main street. Although I had exchanged glances with the poor Jews who were street traders in Whitechapel, and had been at the bedside of some Jewish patients in the London Hospital, I had little sense of the community that existed in this part of London. I did not even know that there was a synagogue here, in Bevis Marks. As I walked along, I noticed a stone archway leading off the footpath. Set in the stone was a wrought-iron gate leading to a paved courtyard. As I looked through the archway, a man in a long black cloak emerged into the courtyard and beckoned me in. He led me through an inner gate into the synagogue. He indicated one of the dark wooden benches, handed me a book and returned to his seat by the entrance. The building was tall, classic in design, and, like St. Botolph's, lit by hundreds of candles in brass chandeliers. For a moment I called to mind the cramped room where we had prayed in that other place, with a few seats and a reading desk for the scrolls of the law.

The cantor had a pure and clear voice and he chanted

the psalms in a melody I'd never heard. A group of young boys formed the choir and joined in the responses. The book I'd been given had a few sentences in Portuguese but the text was written in Hebrew on each right hand page and English on the left. For the first time in my life, I found myself reading the prayers in my spoken language:

> "Our Father, cause us to lie down in peace, and raise us up to a happy and peaceful life."

> "We give thanks for thy miracles, which are daily with us, and for thy wonders and thy benefits."

I read the words of the mourner's *Kaddish*, an unquestioning commitment to a magnificent God. I used to think it was sad, but seeing the meaning and listening to the tune, sung in harmony with the boys, it was almost joyful. The worshippers, many wearing top hats, joined in the final hymn, *Yigdal*, with the choir singing descant and bass and the cantor giving a concert performance in the final solo.

As the congregation filed down the aisles, he came over to me and introduced himself:

"I'm the *Hazan*, Reuven Zacharia." He looked at me with a faint air of suspicion.

"What brings you to the Spanish and Portuguese synagogue in Bevis Marks? Are you visiting?"

I told him my name and that I was studying in London. He asked me where I was living.

"About a thousand yards from here," I replied.

"But your family is not from here?"

I was about to tell him I had no family when he continued:

"I can always recognize a Gibraltarian accent. It's the way you say 'thoussand'. And how your voice goes up at the end of a sentence."

"You can tell the difference between a man from Portugal and one from Gibraltar?"

"I'm a cantor. If you sing you have to listen ... to language.. to sounds."

"And where do you come from?" I asked, conscious for the first time of the way I spoke.

"Tetuan, Morocco. We always spoke French at home, but now I speak in English and I sing in Hebrew."

The small congregation had by this time filed out, with a few ladies still descending the staircase from the gallery.

"So, Mr. Levy. Where do you eat on *Shabbat*?"

"I ... I have an arrangement for tomorrow," I replied.

"But what about this evening? We'd be honoured if you would join us for our meal. You'd be most welcome."

I accepted, perhaps too hastily, thinking about my usual solitary Friday dinner. I followed him out of the building into an adjoining house.

The Zacharias—the father and a daughter of about twenty—lived on the third floor, up a winding corkscrew stone staircase. In the dining room the table was laid with a damask tablecloth with two silver candlesticks in the centre. After he had recited the blessings Reuven Zacharia passed round small cups of wine, indicated a ewer for washing the hands, and came back to the table. He lifted the cloth covering the two plaited loaves and pulled off large pieces of the fresh *challa*, dipped them in salt and put the first piece in his mouth. He hesitated before offering the next piece to me. The third portion he threw to his daughter. I must have looked surprised because he immediately explained, laughing:

"We do it in order of descending age—I imagine you are older than Rachel."

chapter 8

SHORTBREAD (PETTICOAT TAILS)

*Work into a paste two pounds of flour,
one pound of warmed butter, a quarter
pound of powdered loaf sugar, two ounces of blanched almonds and the same of
candied orange and lemon peels. Form it
with the hand into a round, about an inch
thick, cut it into quarters and pinch each
at the edge. Prick the top with a fork, bake
upon paper on a tin.*

The Family Handbook—Choice Receipts and Valuable Hints,
1838

LONDON 1844—DAVID

In a fairy story, I would have decided then and there to
marry the beautiful Rachel, but at that time my thoughts
were far from the prospect of marriage. Also, since this
is a true account, I have to admit that although her complexion was fair, she was not strikingly handsome.

In the months after my first visit, I returned often to
Bevis Marks, and was frequently invited to the Zacharias'

table. I learned that Reuven Zacharia was a widower so Rachel always prepared the food. She would set down a platter of chicken and *pimientos* on the dresser and return from the kitchen carrying a dish piled with rice, while her father spooned some olives from a pot. Like most people in London he would have had little conception of what olives were really like.

My mother used to choose from the great barrows in the market and bring home purple skinned olives the size of a plum. My favourites were the crinkled, black ones, with the oily juices dripping out of the bag on to the floor. Father preferred the chillies, crunching them whole while he waited for his food to be put in front of him. One day my sister picked up a fiery red pepper, took a bite and rushed, screaming from the table. "Don't drink water" said father. "Eat some bread to get rid of the heat."

Rachel was looking at me. "You look sad," she said.

I shook my head, conscious that I had once again transported myself back to that place. I could not stop scraping away at the memories, like a fingernail digging into a scab. Rachel's few words were the first she had aimed directly at me. Usually she spoke little, with her head bowed, replying politely to her father's questions, with the occasional phrase in French. Over the next weeks we settled into a less strained relationship, even what an observer might have called a courtship.

Yet during the week I had no thoughts of romantic trysts; my studies were arduous. In addition to the lectures on general medicine and paediatrics, there were classes in midwifery and gynaecology. I walked the wards of the London Hospital every day with Mr. Adams but although I stood with him at the bedside I was still not entitled to be a 'dresser'. Every Friday the students went to the operating theatre and watched from above. One evening at dinner I described it to Rachel:

"We look down on the operations and watch as the patient suffers eight or ten minutes' agony."

"How do they stand it?" she asked, turning pale.

"Their veins are constricted with a tight band. That and the alcohol help them to sink into unconsciousness."

"How can you bear to watch?"

"I sometimes feel faint but we each carry a snuff box in our jacket pocket." I was thinking of the infernal heat, the constriction of the stand-up collar and neck tie.

As I walked back to my rooms I reflected on the possibility of marriage, though I had grave concerns about the financial implications of such a step. My board and lodging—at 30s a week—was costing more than half of what I could hope to earn as a physician.

One Friday evening, Rachel was clearing the dishes from the table. She seemed preoccupied and had a sad look in her eyes. She clearly resented the task of looking after her father. He had tactfully taken his leave and left the room to prepare his *Torah* reading for the following day. We began to speak.

"Tell me about your life before you came to London," said Rachel.

"There's little to tell," I replied. "I lived with an aunt. My parents were killed in an accident."

"How?" persisted Rachel.

"I prefer not to talk about it," I said, hoping to end the conversation there.

"I'm also an only child" she began again, assuming from my brief comments that I had no other family. I stayed silent. I could see that she wanted to tell me more, so I listened while she continued:

"My mother died five years ago. I was sixteen. She had been weak and sick for two or three years. When she finally died ... " She broke off and looked down at her long, thin fingers.

"... it was as if a burden had been lifted. Is that a dreadful thing to say?"

I couldn't imagine nursing a sick parent; my only experience was of a mother caring for her children, not the reverse.

Rachel explained: "There was endless changing of linen and bringing bedpans ... afterwards there was only my father to look after." She lowered her voice and ran her thumb over the fingernails of the other hand.

"Of course he would like me to be married."

"Has he anyone in mind?"

"About a year ago he suggested a man of about fifty. He was stout, partly bald but he had good teeth and was in perfect health." She laughed.

"There must be some handsome young men in the synagogue?" I enquired.

"There are, but what would Papa say if I chose someone who had been brought up in the orphanage next door? On the other hand I'm not exactly a match for the more affluent members of the synagogue. The *Hazan*'s daughter would hardly be accepted by the Montefiores or Mocattas."

It would be untrue to say that I had given the question

of marriage no thought. I was twenty two years old, living a lonely life with an uncertain future. We could both benefit from a new start, sharing a home and acquiring furniture and plate.

I kept my head down, trying not to look directly at her. She was brushing aside a few wisps of brown hair and smoothing the poplin of her slate coloured dress. A voice came from my throat and before I could catch the words escaping from my lips, I heard myself whispering:

"Would you consider marrying me?"

Rachel looked up and gave me a shy smile. "I would, if you want to."

Taking a deep breath I replied:

"I like you very well and together, we could better our lives."

"But do you want to?"

"I do, yes I do."

Mr. Zacharia was overjoyed. He had become fond of me and welcomed me to his family, as he had done all those months ago, when he invited me to that first meal in his home. The wedding was planned for the summer—the end of my academic year and a quiet time in the synagogue since most of the congregants left the city for the seaside.

With months to go, there seemed no urgency in the preparations. That winter I was still struggling with my anatomy studies. Falling asleep in the class I was woken by the booming voice of our Professor:

"*Know your bones and dream about them.*"

More frequently I found myself dreaming about figures. One evening, I was sitting at a table, enjoying a fish dinner in Billingsgate for a shilling, calculating how much I would need to support a wife. I knew that a physician's wages would bring me no luxuries so I decided to sink all my capital into a speculative venture—buying railway shares. I began to study the newly formed companies and bought shares in two of them: Great Western and York & North Midland. Sixteen new corporations had been registered in January and capital was being raised for thousands of miles of new track. Shares were at a discount as the cost of construction had risen by 50% over the estimates. Without discussing the matter, I made the decision and in January entered the market when the shares of Great Western stood at £100 each and York at £50.

Rachel and I were to be married in the Spanish and Portuguese Bevis Marks synagogue on the third Sunday in June. By May the price of the shares had risen to £207 and £108. By the time the invitation cards were posted the shares were still rising. Replies came back from Aunt Deborah and Mr. Benzecry. Mr. Zacharia encouraged me to invite Mrs. Thomas, Mr. Mendoza and some other 'connections' I had mentioned. In the mornings I picked up the post, put it aside and turned to the stock market page of the newspaper.

Reuven Zacharia had no knowledge of the fortune that was soon to come my way. He was exploring other financial possibilities, in particular the authorisation of a dowry for members of the synagogue. He told me about his conversations with the Secretary, Simon Almosnino. The running of Bevis Marks was entrusted to the gentlemen of the Mahamad. Simon kept the minutes of their monthly meetings and being somewhat indiscreet, he shared matters of interest with his friend, the *hazan*. Reuven told me that funds were available for brides who had no father, but was unsure of the position for Rachel who had lost her mother. He promised to talk to Simon the next day. When he came into the room the secretary was dipping his pen into the ink and writing in a careful hand:

"Purchase of sacks of flour for Passover matzot agreed
Whitewash for the school room - four guineas"

Simon turned the page of his rough notes and pointed to a paragraph headed *Permission for Marriage.*

"Is this about David and Rachel? Have they granted permission?" asked Reuven.

"It's no simple matter" replied Simon. "What do you know about David?"

"He comes from Gibraltar."

"But he'll have to prove it."

Reuven reported this conversation to me because he was aghast at the idea that his daughter might not be allowed to marry in Bevis Marks synagogue. There was a strict rule that only Sephardim (from Spain and Portugal) could be members. I would need to produce a copy of my parents' marriage certificate to prove my authentic Sephardi descent. The alternative was for the marriage to be solemnized at the Great German Synagogue nearby, where the members were Ashkenazim from Northern Europe.

As I had no such certificate, and did not wish to explain why, I embarked on a lengthy correspondence with Rabbi Abecasis of Gibraltar. He knew of my predicament and eventually found the details I needed in the community records of the town.

Simon was dealing with a pile of correspondence when Reuven walked into his office.

"You'd think the Mahamad had better things to do. I have to send letters to the parents of boys who have behaved badly" he began.

"Simon, about the dowry ... "

"and then they spent half the meeting discussing whether they could afford £8 to help a young man find a place in a lunatic asylum. Half an hour earlier they'd agreed to send £500 to help the persecuted Jews in the Middle East. And then they quibble over a paltry sum like £8."

"Ahem ... " Reuven coughed. He wanted to return to the matter of his daughter's dowry:

"What's the position for a widower like me?"

"Strictly speaking Rachel doesn't qualify but the Mahamad have discussed the matter and are prepared to grant a dowry."

Reuven never recounted the details of the conversation but it was clear that the congregation would make a generous allowance towards the cost of the wedding. The ladies treated Rachel as if she were a daughter and consequently began to help in the bridal preparations. Together they summoned a dressmaker, selected a design and fabric and then put their minds to the choice of a floral bouquet. The wedding was to take place in the afternoon to be followed by a small reception in a nearby hall. As well as the sweetmeats, there were to be rice fruit tarts and cocoanut cakes.

Rachel couldn't wait to tell me about the menu:

"There'll be marrons glacés, jaune and blanc mange and petits gâteaux taillés."

I was confused by the French terms, but she went on:

"You know what they are—petits gâteaux taillés—petti-coat-tails, they're called in English.

I still didn't understand.

"Those biscuits—shortbread—they're cut from a circle and they look like... " she lowered her eyes "a petticoat."

To cover her embarrassment she continued:

"And we must have Maids of Honour." I thought she was referring to bridesmaids but she explained:

"No, they are those lemon cheese cakes they make at Richmond in honour of Queen Charlotte."

I must have missed a few more details of the reception because I heard Rachel asking:

"David, which do you prefer with the pine apples, lemon or raspberry water ices?"

My conversations with Rachel were centred on fabric and flowers, gâteaux and guests. Her shyness with me diminished. As the months passed we were becoming closer and found ourselves happy in each other's company. Her pale complexion began to take on some colour and her grey eyes, which had seemed dull, now began to look at me with a loving warmth. For my part, I was struggling to show affection—an emotion I had kept hidden for nine years, since my life was shattered on that January day in 1837.

The 19th June 1846 was a Sunday of intense heat. The day dawned with a haze in the cloudless sky. Every candle in the synagogue was kindled. I remember standing under the canopy with the choir singing the welcoming words of *Baruch Haba* as Rachel walked in on her father's arm to join me. Aunt Deborah and Mr. Benzecry came forward to stand by my side, in the place of my parents. Looking from one to the other, I half-closed my eyes, trying to remember the touch of Mama's hand or my father's arm round my shoulder. I bit my lip as I realized their features were fading in my mind. I forced my eyes to remain dry but had no control over the steady drip of perspiration pouring down my sleeves to the end of my fingertips and from there on to the floor.

chapter 9

2½ oz flour, 1 oz butter, 1 gill water, 1 egg, pinch salt, vanilla essence

Coffee icing, cream or custard

Put water, butter and salt in saucepan and bring to boiling point. Add flour. Cook for a few minutes until mixture comes away from side of pan. Add essence and egg. Force into sausage shapes on to greased tin. Bake in fairly hot oven, Regulo 6. When cooked split down side and remove any soft inside. Fill with stiffly-whipped sweetened cream or custard and coat with coffee icing.

From Dina's notebook, 1916

LONDON 1944—ANNA

In his methodical way, David kept notes of his income and expenditure. The account books had entries for household expenses, starting with modest acquisitions for his home in Gravel Lane, a stone's throw from Bevis Marks and a few streets west of his lodgings with Mrs.

Thomas in Old Montague Street. On one page he wrote a scribbled note about how to make mutton broth. Anna read the instructions, wondering why her grandfather had written this among the details of his purchases of railway shares. She moved her grandfather's notebooks aside, and turned to one in her mother's handwriting. The recipe for coffee éclairs brought back a vivid memory of her brother and how he used to lick off the icing.

Anna was thirteen and she was on the tennis court with Isaac. She was winning the game. She had given him the usual two point lead to compensate for his poor eyesight but when she got to 40-30, he slammed his racquet into the net and refused to continue playing. It was only when they got home, settled in the kitchen with a cup of tea and an iced pastry, that he apologised for his bout of temper.

He'd been angry at the prospect of losing to his younger sister; cross at the thought that he could hardly see the ball as it came over the net. Was it any wonder that many of her shots sailed past him? But his frustration was mixed with embarrassment: that he was carrying on a normal life, spending time playing tennis while other eighteen-year olds were lining up to enlist for the war.

The atmosphere in the house was tense. In 1916 Boni was twenty one. She should have been planning a celebration dance. Instead she was poring over a list. She had a small book marked 'Dances etc.' and she had written down the names of forty seven girls and forty nine men. A heavy black line had been scored through at least fifteen of these: Costa, de Pass, Benzimra ... . There was no note about where they had died; whether it was Ypres or Verdun. One of these men was more than just an acquaintance, but no-one in the family had any suspicions. Boni kept her feelings to herself and didn't want them to know that she'd lost the man she'd hoped to marry. She worked in her uncles' office every day and dealt with correspondence about olive oil and sardines. Her mind was full of the death announcements in the newspaper. When she came home in the evenings, Isaac was sulking and all her sister could talk about was her backhand. To make matters worse, Anna was pretty, with long black curls and a smile for everyone. The corners of her dark eyes would wrinkle as she giggled over something no-one else would think funny—the only one in the house who found anything to smile about.

Five years later, when Anna was eighteen, the laughter faded as she and her mother embarked on a row that lasted for weeks. It began with an invitation. Jo was living in Palestine and had sent a letter asking if Anna would like to visit her:

8th July 1921

Dearest Anna,

John and I would like you to come and stay with us in Jerusalem. There is so much I'd like to show you. Don't be worried about the heat; the evenings are pleasantly cool. You can live with us for a few months and then decide whether or not you are going to do a maths degree at university. We shall be back in London next week and you can return with us.

Much love, as ever

Jo

Dina had a habit of making a pencil-written draft of any letters she sent. It may not have been an accident that Anna came across the copy:

22nd July 1921

My dear Jo

I write to explain the unfortunate scene last Thursday. Anna's tears and protestations were not unexpected. Her outburst at my refusal to allow her to go to the Holy Land with you and John was highly unreasonable. The anger and accusations of selfishness were, I admit, hard to bear. The words 'ruined my life' were particularly cruel. In all these years I have only had the interests of my dear children at heart.

I gather that you are planning to return to the Ophthalmic Hospital in Jerusalem next month. The journey itself would cause little concern. After all, you were so calm and organised at the time of our last dreadful sea voyage from Lisbon. That was a long time ago and the circumstances of our hasty return to London are in my thoughts every day.

As I say, the sea voyage is not my worry. What makes me fearful is the danger of living in a place so far removed from European customs and values. Anna is ill prepared for life in a hot, sandy city. She has no idea how to bargain with the Arab traders who have been known to pursue young white women through the alleys of the souk. She has no clothes for the relentless heat of the day. She might easily catch cold in the cool evenings. She would have to deal with insects, dust, winds and burning sun. Is it any wonder that I prefer her to prepare herself for university by giving mathematics coaching in Hampstead? She will have other opportunities to visit Jerusalem.

My reasons for forbidding the trip are, I admit, not solely caused by concerns for Anna. The losses I have suffered have convinced me of the importance that a family should remain united. Boni and Isaac have expressed no wish to leave us. Anna is argumentative and persistent, as you know well, but I believe her character will be strengthened by my refusal to give in to her.

I shall be grateful if you would now let the matter drop. Please do not renew your invitation to Anna to travel with you.

Yours truly

Dina Levy

Anna was angry and resentful but it never occurred to her to go against her mother's wishes. There was to be no further discussion on the subject of going abroad. She had no choice in the planning of her future. She would go to London University, to Bedford College, and continue to live at home; the question of going away to Oxford or Cambridge was never raised. Throughout the long summer she fumed at her mother's control over her. She could hardly look at her but she said little and the fury stayed buttoned inside, only to be released on the tennis court. She joined a club and threw herself into physical activity. Working on her service and backhand pushed out the thoughts of how her mother had controlled her since she was a child.

It was surprising that Anna was such a good tennis player: she had always been overweight. Though she blamed much of her childhood sadness on Dina, the weight had never been a source of friction between them. It wasn't Dina who made Anna feel ungainly. When they sat down to a tea of home made cakes and sweets there was no mention of Anna's figure. In Dina's eyes her daughter was just 'well built'. Anna saw it differently. As a child she was dressed in frills of white broderie anglaise with long puffed sleeves; 'like a meringue' she would say later. When she came to buy her own frocks, she would always choose clothes that disguised her bulges; collars that concealed a less than swanlike neck. If she looked in a mirror, she preferred to turn sideways, lifting up one shoulder to make herself look slimmer. She would never appear in a photograph alone, but always behind a group where only her face could be seen.

In the autumn of that year Anna was enrolled at Bedford College to do a maths degree. There must have been happy memories of her three years there; but it was typical of Anna that instead of recalling the excitement of mathematics and the opening of a new circle of friends, all she could recall were the bad moments in her life. It was the conflicts that were foremost in her memory: the rows, the confrontations.

After she finished her degree her mother persuaded her to take some cookery classes. The suggestion was not made with any criticism, though it was pointed out that Anna had no skills in the kitchen. On the first day of the four-week course she arrived with as much enthusiasm as a housemaid faced with cleaning up the grate before setting up the coal fire.

Her first impression was one of shock. The teacher was preparing meat and told the students never to wash it but simply to wipe it with a cloth. She used the same, blood-flecked dish rag to blot joints of lamb and chicken, and then, in a display of apparent cleanliness, swept it over the board before proceeding with the next dish.

The students were handed leaflets on the ideals of the school, epitomising its attitude to the importance of appearance in food:

> *Colour in cookery is almost as smart as in dress and the garniture of dishes a serious subject in the kitchen.*

> *A joint of meat looks best without ornamentation. But if it is a leg of mutton, wrap a pretty paper ruff round the bone.*

> *The one great art in decorating dishes is symmetry. Every dish to be a success should have a tiny speck of green somewhere. A garland of parsley or watercress is suitable for everything from the fish until the salad is reached.*

During the demonstrations the students watched. Then they were encouraged to follow the recipe to the letter. When Anna was given the ingredients for beef tea and devilled turkey legs no-one noticed that she never put a spoon in the consommé or took a bite of the meat. She'd decided it was too hard to explain that she only ate *kosher* meat and on the day the class was making a collared pig's head Anna simply stayed at home.

When she returned the next day she took her place in the chocolate making class. It was worse than being in school. Her absence had been noticed and the Principal turned to her and said:

"Ah. Miss Levy. We are glad you are honouring us with your presence."

The first part of the lesson involved melting the chocolate. It wasn't a simple matter and required a precise approach. That suited Anna. She had a mathematical mind and appreciated what the teacher was saying:

"The temperature in the room should be between $60°$ and $65°F$. The couverture has to be heated over simmering water. On no account must you let this water boil. If a drop of water gets into the chocolate it will be ruined. You must stir it constantly ... "

The students were getting impatient. They'd already been standing watching the chocolate for half an hour. Anna was entranced. The others wanted to start making fondant and marzipan but Anna realized that making sweets was a science. The correct temperature for the sugar was essential for these fillings. Nougat and caramel would require even more skill than chocolate couverture.

The warm smell of the melting chocolate seeped into Anna's clothes. When she got home that evening she could still feel the smoothness of the mahogany mixture and remember the rhythmic stirring of the cocoa butter. She couldn't wait to go back the next day. Once the chocolate was tempered the dipping and piping could begin. By the end of the class she was turning out coffee creams and chocolate almonds, pralines and truffles.

Anna had graduated from London University with a good degree. After the course she took a job as a teacher in a local school. It was hard to go back to elementary equations when her mind had been filled with university mathematics, with projective geometry and complex numbers and the integral calculus, and with the need for rigour in reasoning—how you can be confident that a result is true. Instead of working on analysis of functions and the study of conic sections she was now spending time in front of a class of restless ten-year olds who couldn't wait for the bell to ring.

At home she relaxed by practising the skills she'd learned at the cookery school. She was making caramel when Isaac came in and almost tripped up on the sheets of newspaper covering the floor.

"What on earth are you doing?" he asked.

Anna was holding a wooden stick in one hand and waving a spoon covered in boiled sugar backwards and forwards, till it fell in long threads.

"I'm making spun sugar."

"Careful" he said "it looks dangerous."

The transparent strands were ready and Anna was arranging them on top of a pile of round choux buns. Isaac watched as she explained the difference between a Gâteau Saint Honoré and the long iced buns which were éclairs. Isaac picked one up and started to lick off the top.

"Sis," he began, with his mouth full of creamy custard,

"will you lend me some money?"

"Come on, that's the third time you've asked. I've already lent you more than I can afford. Just because you don't want to work with the uncles in the sardine business......"

"I'm fed up with sardines. It's not as if I ever get to travel. I've got an idea for a quicker way to make money. All I need is a few hundred to get started."

"I can't, Isaac. I'm not a millionaire on a teacher's salary. Anyway, I'm going to need money to start my own business."

"What business?"

"I'm going to sell hand-made chocolates."

At that moment Dinah walked in and heard the tail end of the conversation. "But I thought you enjoyed the maths teaching..." she said.

"I don't know which are worse—the lessons or the break times."

Anna had never told her mother how much she missed the university maths course. She elaborated on her other complaint: "The staff room - it's like a hotbed of gossip. They never stop... Every time I come in the door I wonder what they've been saying about me."

"What about this business then?" said Isaac. "We could be in it together. I could do the selling and deal with the invoices."

"I'll be lucky if I have ten customers a week so I hardly need sales staff and an accounts department."

"You're not going to resign from the school, are you?" asked Dina.

"Yes, I am, but I'll do some private coaching, just in

case it doesn't work out."

"Well then," said Isaac, "you could still lend me some money."

Anna had been calculating how much she would need for her business. There would be small premises to rent, boxes and equipment to purchase. With no experience of book-keeping or marketing, she woke up each morning dreaming about how to produce the perfect truffle. The lessons at the cookery school had been worth while. She had only a patchy knowledge of sauces and fish, but she had mastered the techniques of tempering the chocolate and whisking up a faultless cream filling. She knew how to decorate the tops with traditional swirls. Within a week she was producing boxes of exquisite sweets. In the evenings she carried on with the maths coaching, often turning up at a pupil's house with chocolate under her fingernails and a smear across her forehead.

As for the money, she wrote Isaac a cheque, but she knew from the way he shoved it in his pocket that it was for less than he wanted.

Isaac never stopped asking for money. His requests came at infrequent intervals: a few months after Anna's marriage to Nathan, then none for a few years. In 1942, when Nina was about three and the talk on everyone's lips was of food rationing, Isaac nagged his sisters again for loans. He persisted for another two years, and only stopped when Dina died and the bitter quarrel erupted. Since then, seven weeks had gone by with no word from

Isaac.

"You don't think he means it, do you?" Anna asked Boni.

"What, never speaking to us again? It's possible, knowing him."

"Maybe he'll write a postcard. Or maybe Freda will let Joel come and play."

"Anna you're not being realistic. He hasn't replied to our phone calls or letters. Didn't you send him something last week?"

"Well, that was just newspaper cuttings, cartoons from Punch. I thought if I didn't mention the quarrel he'd come round."

Boni shook her head:

"I doubt it. I'm beginning to think it's final. He's not going to get in touch."

At first Anna did not believe that she would never hear from her brother again. For weeks she pretended that everything would be all right. She wanted to make up the quarrel and couldn't imagine that he didn't. Nathan reassured her as well as he could. She heard Isaac's voice all the time, in her mind. She thought about Isaac calling out to her in Lisbon:

'Hey, wait for me. You know I'm out of breath. I can't catch you.'

She thought about what he'd said when Mother wouldn't let her go abroad:

'I'll take you one day. I'm going to go travelling.'

Anna's letters were returned; there were no telephone conversations and months went by with no communication. Then came the realization that he wanted no further contact with her. Finally she came to accept that the rift was permanent; it was as if he were dead, gone from her life forever. There were no more shared memories, family meals, ordinary conversations. She never heard his voice again.

chapter 10

CHOCOLATE CARAMELS

*1lb loaf sugar, ¼ lb butter, ¼ lb unsweet-
ened chocolate, ¼ lb syrup, 1 gill thin
cream, vanilla essence*

*Grate or shred the chocolate, and put it
into a saucepan with all the other ingredients. Melt slowly over the fire, and then
boil to the "crack" or to 300°F, stirring almost constantly. When ready, pour out,
and, when set, mark in squares.*

Cookery for Every Household, by Florence B Jack, 1931

LONDON 1945—ANNA

The house in Cricklewood had an air-raid shelter in the
back garden. Nathan was out on fire watch duty. Anna
was sitting on the lower bunk trying not to lean back
against the damp concrete wall. It was cold and the musty
smell made her long for her warm bed inside the house.
But for Nina it was an excitement, running between the
house and the shelter, poking her head out of the door,
watching for the searchlights. Anna jumped up, almost

banging her head on the top bunk, as she leaned out to pull her daughter inside.

"Come and cuddle up and I'll tell you a story."

"Will you tell me again about the sweets?"

Nina picked up her golliwog and put him on the pillow, stroking her finger along his striped trousers and round the buttons of his scarlet waistcoat. Then she lay on top of him with her cheek pressed to the round black face. She'd heard the story before, but she wanted Anna to tell her again about how she used to make the fillings and dip the chocolates in the smooth dark covering.

"There were whole brazil nuts, strawberry fondants and cocoa dusted truffles. But the best were the caramels. They were a mixture of cream and butter and chocolate and when the mixture set, I cut it into squares and wrapped them in cellophane. Then I used to tie up the boxes with satin ribbons."

Nina had never seen a box of chocolates. Production had stopped soon after the beginning of the war and the only sweets available were on ration. She was allowed to go to the end of the road and queue at the sweet shop with her coupons, hoping that there might be a little extra from the broken sweets at the bottom of the jar. A boy in front of her told her a story about how he'd heard there was chocolate at a chemist:

"Brought it back, I did. Ex-lax, it was called. How did I know what it was? Made me ill for days, it did. Me Mum said it was a laxative, whatever that is."

The shelter was dark and Anna turned off the torch. Nina's eyes were beginning to close. It was late and Nathan was still out. Anna began to worry that he wasn't home yet. The day before they'd had an argument: he was always talking about 'ganufs' and brigands. 'Ganufs' were people who tried to cheat you. Brigands were profession-als who succceeded. He'd gone into a shop and accused the owner of overcharging for a waistcoat made of a poor cloth. He'd ended up calling him a 'ganuf' and stormed out, leaving Anna to face the angry looks of the other cus-tomers. When she got home, there was Nathan, large as life, writing something secret in his spidery handwriting. It was a poem for her birthday—twenty verses declaring how much he loved her. Why wasn't he back? She hated it when he was on duty checking for fires while she and Nina were in the air-raid shelter, waiting for the sound of the all-clear.

To take her mind off thoughts of Nathan trapped in a burning building, Anna began to think of how they'd met nearly ten years ago, and how it was all because of the chocolate business and the maths lessons.

Dina could see that her daughter was exhausted. She suggested they should take a holiday together. They booked into a kosher boarding house in Eastbourne and Anna carried the leather suitcases up the stairs. The room was adequate, with chintz curtains and two high single beds. There was a washstand with an ornate jug and bowl. She arranged their few lonely frocks alongside an empty row of hangers in the vast wardrobe.

Dinner was at 6.30pm. They sat down at one of the three tables in the dining-room, keeping their elbows off the starched white cloths and fingering the EPNS cruets while they waited for the food to arrive. The meal began with chopped fish patties topped with a circle of carrot. A livid beetroot sauce formed a pool on the side.

"What is it?" whispered Dina, pushing a forkful around her plate.

"It's gefilte fish—all Ashkenazi Jews eat it."

"But it's sweet" she hissed. "What have they put in it?"

"Chopped onion and sugar" said Anna "and then they boil it for hours and spoon the stock over the top when it's cold."

The next course was chicken soup—a golden broth with vermicelli noodles—followed by roast chicken. The breast meat was as dry as sawdust and Anna leaned over to her mother and whispered:

"They boil the bird to make the soup, then when it's completely dead, they roast it till it's dried out. It's lucky we've only booked in for a week!"

After dinner they went into the drawing-room where the other guests were settled in deep armchairs, reading the newspaper. At a card table in the corner was a couple playing piquet. The woman was dressed in purple shantung and had a silver and amethyst ring on her right hand. She wore no wedding ring. The man was thin and his bony wrists protruded from the sleeves of a crumpled jacket. From the back he looked about sixty, with balding hair and a slight stoop, but when Anna looked closer, she could see he was much younger—probably in his forties.

At breakfast the next morning the man was sitting alone at a table by the window. He smiled at Anna—a broad, direct smile. She looked down at her poached egg and tried not to look at him. He poured a cup of tea and unfolded an Ordnance Survey map.

Anna spent the day on the beach with her mother. She fetched two deckchairs and turned them to face the sea. They sat watching the tide come in. A weak sunlight trickled through the clouds and they pulled woollen shawls up around their necks when the wind came up. Back at the boarding house, there was a smell of simmering vegetables. Dinner was stewed meat and boiled cabbage. As Anna pushed away her half-eaten plate, the man looked at her and smiled again.

After three days the man plucked up the courage to speak to her:

"I'm Nathan Grunthal. I'm here from London. Where are you from?"

It crossed her mind to tell him that she was born in Portugal, but instead she gave him the short answer:

"Hampstead."

They exchanged some information and Anna discovered that the woman he was playing cards with was his cousin.

"Is he a writer?"asked Dina, when Anna walked back to join her in the drawing-room.

"No, he's a patent agent. He seems very clever, he was telling me that he specialises in chemical engineering." Anna tried to sound nonchalant.

"He asked if I want to go for a walk tomorrow."

She arranged to meet Nathan at the bandstand near the Grand Parade. As she approached she could see him, wearing a tweed overcoat with the buttons done up wrong. Slung across his chest was a camera on a leather strap. They took a bus up to Beachy Head and then walked along the coastal footpath.

"This is the highest chalk sea cliff in Britain," said Nathan. "If you look to the east past the town and the pier, you can see Pevensey Bay and Hastings. I think we should walk the other way, towards Brighton."

"It sounds as if you've been here before," said Anna. "I've never been to Eastbourne. Nor to many other places, either."

She stopped and thought before adding: "I had the chance of going to Palestine and I desperately wanted to, but Mother wouldn't let me go."

She began to tell him about the pleading and the arguments but as soon as she'd finished the story she regretted it. She didn't want him to think her mother was a monster so she chattered on, telling him about Boni and the onions, explaining why Dina was so protective.

"Do you know, I have never spent a single night on my own, and to this day I still hear my mother crying in her sleep. She won't let me go away because she has a fear that something will happen to me."

Nathan listened and said very little. He didn't respond by telling her about his family. They just walked and for much of the time there was a peaceful silence. They climbed along a steeply winding road and looked down at the beach. It was low tide and there were a few children playing in the shingle.

When they got back to the boarding house he told her he was leaving the next day and promised to look her up in London. She didn't hear from him for a couple of weeks. And then he phoned to invite her for tea at Lyons

Corner House in Coventry Street. When she arrived he was already seated at a table. He got up and grasped her hand.They ordered a pot of tea and Nathan began to tell her about his new secretary. Anna was imagining a slim, blonde woman.

"She's a dragon—about fifty eight, I think. She's going to rule my life."

"I can't imagine you being ruled by anyone. You seem so ... certain about how you want things done."

"Set in my ways, you mean."

"Perhaps I should try to get you un-set?" Anna looked directly at his grey blue eyes.

Nathan squeezed her arm and then, quite unexpectedly, put his hand on her cheek. She was the first to look away and grasped the clutch bag in her lap.

The next time they met, Anna suggested a change of venue, but he preferred the Corner House. The waitress put down a pot of tea and Nathan ordered a slice of Battenberg cake. Anna wasn't hungry but must have been looking intently at the marzipan covered slice.

"Is something wrong? Are you sure you don't want anything to eat?" he asked.

"No, I'm sorry, I'm just intrigued by the way it's put together—the pink and white chequerboard pattern."

She started to tell him about the cookery course and must have talked about cakes and chocolate for a good ten minutes before she noticed that he had lost interest in what she was saying. Anna changed the subject and they talked about university—her time in London and his years in Cambridge.

When they got up to leave Nathan looked nervous.

"I don't want to go back to the office. This secretary, she's very impatient and looks at me angrily while I'm dictating letters to her."

Anna could imagine the scene because Nathan spoke slowly, weighing up every word.

"I keep forgetting her name. Each morning I call her something different—Miss Packet, Miss Peacock—I don't think she likes it."

"I'm not surprised. Would you like it, Norris, or is it Norbert? No I forgot, It's Nathan."

They both laughed. He squeezed her hand, sliding his fingers up the sleeve of her cardigan. Anna imagined what it would be like to take him home. She could see the scene, with her mother and sister eyeing him critically and quizzing her when he'd gone.

They continued to meet every few weeks. Sometimes a month or more would go by and then he would telephone and invite her to a production of Gilbert and Sullivan. Boni teased her about her 'young man', knowing full well that Nathan was fourteen years older than Anna.

A year later Anna still knew little about Nathan's family. He lived with his parents in a house in Clapton and was planning to move to Cricklewood. His father was 'something in the City' and spent his time watching a pile of dwindling shares. His mother was from Sunderland and was never happier than when she was talking about her only son, explaining to people what a patent agent did.

Nathan became a frequent visitor at Kings' Gardens, though for both of them the meals were an ordeal. Anna was aware that his clothes, his conversation, everything was under scrutiny. He was simply trying to deal with unfamiliar foods, separating recognizable pieces of meat from the sauce or scooping the cream out of pastries. Anna watched him with a growing affection, silently preparing responses to the questions which would come later.

Another month passed. Anna realized how the weeks dragged when she wasn't with him. She had no idea that he was preparing a speech that would change their lives. They were in Maison Lyons at Marble Arch. The orchestra was playing an Ivor Novello melody. The waitress was standing waiting for Nathan to give his order. Anna was looking at the Nippy's white apron, her trim waist and the tiny buttons down the front of her dress. Nathan had started a conversation about Boni and broke off to ask for two portions of baked beans on toast.

"What does she think about her younger sister having a 'beau'?" he asked.

"Is that what you are, my beau?" asked Anna tentatively.

He answered without hesitation:

"I'd like to be."

She took this reply to be a serious suggestion, as Nathan rarely said anything that wasn't carefully considered. The waitress came back with a tray of food. Anna didn't remember the exact words of Nathan's proposal but her response was carefully considered:

"I have to ask you a serious question before I agree," she began.

"What is it?" asked Nathan, looking worried.

"Well, if we're to be married, we need to know if we

like the same things and ... "

Before she could finish, he broke in:

"Well of course we do, we both like reading and ... "

"Yes but there are more important things, I have to know. Do you like onions?"

chapter 11

Tea Cakes (Excellent)
> *four ounces butter, four ounces sifted sugar, 4 eggs, four ounces flour, ¼ teaspoon baking powder.*
>
> *Beat the butter to a cream, add sugar, keep on stirring and add the eggs, separately. Finally sift in very gradually the flour and baking powder. Put a little less than one tablespoonful into each baking cup or tin and bake in a very hot oven. They only take about 5 minutes to bake. Make a thin syrup, pass the cakes through it whilst it is still hot and dust them over with cinnamon and sugar.*

From Dina's notebook, 1937

LONDON 1937—ANNA

The invitations for the wedding were spread out on the table. Anna looked up from writing addresses and confided in Dina:

"I'm worried about Nathan's Ma. She's a cold fish, isn't she?"

"It's hard to tell. When we first met her I thought she disapproved of the match. But now, poor woman, who knows what she's thinking?"

A month after the engagement was announced Nathan's mother Estelle had suffered a stroke. Her left side was paralysed and she spent her days on a chaise longue, gripping a knitted shawl to her chin with the fingers of her good hand. It was clear that she had once been good looking. A photograph on the piano showed a woman with eyes as dark as blackberries and hair plaited on top of her head.

When they went to visit her Anna hovered in the background while Nathan tried to speak to his mother. She replied in a whisper and was unable to take any interest in their wedding plans. Anna dreaded going to the house. Everything about it was dark: the walls, furniture and heavy drapes were in tones of brown. A lace tablecloth covered the oval dining table—the only splash of white in the room. Nathan's father Julius was more welcoming. Immaculately dressed, with white hair and a trimmed beard, he spent his days in the City. Even when he was losing money, which was much of the time, he had a smile for Anna and engaged her in conversation about the accounting side of her business.

To take her mind off the problem with Nathan's mother, Dina began to tell Anna about the plans for the wedding reception.

"I've found this house in Chesterfield Street. The rooms are magnificent—high ceilings and marble fireplaces."

"Mother, I want to ask you something."

"What dear? Where was I? Fireplaces. They promised

to light the fires. Oh, and I've agreed a price with the caterer. He comes highly recommended. It'll be elegant. I think everything is under control."

"Mother, about Nathan … Are you happy about me marrying him?"

Dina still seemed preoccupied.

"Mother, did you hear what I said?"

"It's not for me to say. You've made your choice."

"But you like him, don't you?"

"As much as I'd like anyone who was taking you away."

"Please, don't be like that. He's not taking me very far."

"It's got nothing to do with the distance. It's just … that I'm not prepared."

Dina would never have been prepared—even though she'd had thirty four years to imagine the day when her daughter left home. She turned the conversation to a concern that they all understood:

"Who'd have thought you'd be the first one to get married? Poor Boni."

In the silence that followed they both thought about the effect of Anna's engagement on her older sister. Boni herself was managing to hide any feelings of jealousy. She showed no reaction to the arrival of gifts in the post and shared the family's enthusiasm for cut glass bowls and silver sauce boats. She didn't mind hearing about wallpaper and carpets and even went with Anna to choose a stove for the new kitchen.

But when it came to cooking she needed to prove that Anna wasn't the only one with skills. Boni had learned from Dina how to bake. She could produce elaborate desserts. She would show them. She decided to make something spectacular the next time Nathan came to dinner. The photograph in the book showed a *dobostorte*, a Hungarian gâteau usually attempted only by professionals. The cake had six layers of sponge, sandwiched together with the smoothest filling—a chocolate buttercream. It took all afternoon to make. The top was glazed with golden caramel, marked into segments before it set and the sides were finished with toasted hazelnuts. When it was carried into the dining room everyone was impressed—except for Nathan. He looked uncomfortable as portions were lifted on to glass plates. He didn't like the look of it. It was too rich and wasn't anything like the cakes his mother made. He'd never had such an elaborate concoction and saw no reason to try one now. Anna glanced at his bone-thin fingers, knowing that he would have preferred a piece of seed cake or a madeleine to dip in his tea.

He and Anna made an odd couple. She was taller and certainly wider than he was. She had shiny black hair, parted on the left and waved at the sides. Her wardrobe was full of home-made skirts and jumpers of 2-ply wool, knitted on No. 13 needles. He wore the same suit every day, the trousers bagging at the knee, the turn-ups slightly frayed. In his waistcoat was a pocket watch on a chain and a cigarette case full of Wills' Passing Clouds.

Anna knew that her mother disapproved of Nathan's appearance, but was slightly in awe of his intellect. She herself could see beyond the shabby clothes and found, for the first time in her life, that she was unaware of her own flawed figure, and felt calm and relaxed when they were together. She must have had romantic dreams of love but the men she had known—many of them good looking—had made her feel inadequate. Nathan's quiet adoration brought a certainty that was more valuable than moonlight and roses.

Was he concerned about the over-possessive mother-in-law? If so, he never showed it. A younger man might have been fearful for the future. Nathan had reached the age of forty-eight with an understanding of parents' attachment to their unmarried children. He had never lacked company on the sands of Scarborough or Broadstairs but the young women he had admired could never pursue a real conversation or appreciate his passion for reading. Any discussion of emotion was concealed in a facade of jokes that only he found amusing; the outpouring of love for Anna expressed only in poems and written notes.

The marriage ceremony was to be held in an Ashkenazi synagogue. The first Anna knew of this arrangement was when Nathan told her he'd been called before the Mahamad, the governing body of the Spanish and Portuguese synagogue at Lauderdale Road. They suggested it might be better if the couple were to marry in the bridegroom's synagogue.

"What do they mean, better? I've been going to Lauderdale Road since I was a child."

"They won't allow it. I'm not Sephardi so we don't have a choice."

"I can't believe they're so old fashioned. They're behaving as if I was marrying someone who isn't even Jewish."

"Anna, forget it," said Nathan. "They don't want people who've just come off the onion boat. Think how they would lower the tone of the membership."

Anna was embarrassed at the snobbery in her synagogue and was wondering how to respond when Nathan asked:

"You will still marry me?"

"I will if you behave yourself," she replied.

She had already had a taste of Nathan's jokes and was nervous that he might come out with an impudent remark to one of the guests.

A week before the wedding Isaac was planning a dinner party for his sister. He was arranging a celebration at the Trocadero. When they arrived the table was set for eight. Anna couldn't work it out: there were four of her family, then her two uncles, and Nathan, but who was the eighth? The guest turned out to be Freda. Isaac had chosen this moment to announce their engagement.

"Look at her ankles," Anna whispered. Nathan seemed unaware that slim ankles were something to be envied. He was too busy studying the menu card. In the left-hand corner were the initials of the restaurant, set in red sealing wax. Underneath were the words *J. Lyons & Co. Ltd. Proprietors.*

"I'm glad to see we're being entertained in a Lyons Corner House," he whispered.

"Look," she said, "the main course is pheasant. They've found a kosher caterer who can get game birds."

"There's nothing unkosher about birds," said Nathan.

"I know. It's catching them that's the problem. They're not kosher if you shoot them."

Nathan didn't reply. Anna continued. "Anyway, shooting them can't be a good idea—you get all those bits of shot stuck in the flesh."

There was no response. Anna knew what he was thinking. He was probably imagining how you would catch and kill a bird. A slow moving chicken or turkey would be easy; one on the wing would be a different matter. For once she had guessed wrong; he was just wishing he was eating a plate of baked beans.

Nathan had been warned to be on his best behaviour. He engaged Freda in conversation about music hall stars but couldn't resist a joke: suggesting she was a contemporary of Marie Lloyd. She made a quick calculation and realized that would have made her sixty seven. Freda looked back at him, not sure whether he was being stupid or plain rude. She ignored him for the rest of the meal.

At the other end of the table Anna was laughing with Isaac and they were both happy to see that for once, their mother was smiling. The uncles, enjoying the generous quantities of wine, were in good form. When the party broke up Anna hugged her brother and thanked him for a wonderful dinner. When the bill came, Isaac picked it up. It was only later that Anna realized who had paid for it all: it came out of the money she had lent him. Not a penny had been repaid.

The day of the wedding arrived. On February 4th 1937 Anna walked up the aisle of Brondesbury Synagogue. An operatic choir boomed out from behind a screen above the ladies' gallery. Anna wished there'd been Sephardi tunes, with young boys singing in harmony. But more than that, she wished she'd been holding her father's arm, instead of walking with Uncle Solomon. When she reached the wedding canopy Nathan seemed overcome with emotion as he gripped her hand.

Immediately after the service they left in a car, but while the guests went straight to Mayfair, they had another call to make. Nathan's Ma was confined to the house so they'd arranged to go and see her before going on to the reception. The visit must have taken over an hour and it was five o'clock when Anna and Nathan finally arrived at Chesterfield Gardens. The guests had been there for some time. The bridal couple walked through the door, past the pillars with stone carvings and up the staircase into the drawing room. There were high bay windows with a balcony at the front. In each of the reception rooms was a roaring coal fire.

To Anna the rooms seemed over warm. Everyone was mingling and talking happily. A few of Nathan's friends called out to greet them as they walked in the door. Anna recognized groups of people she knew. She overheard snippets of conversation:

"Can you believe it? ... I don't expect it's her fault ... "

On the tables were teacups and saucers. Why was no-one sitting down? Dina was whispering with Boni, trying to catch the eye of one of the waiters. And then Anna realized what was missing. There was no sign of any food. On the tables were empty dishes: the remains of a plate of sandwiches, a few sprigs of cress, and the paper cases from what might have been fairy cakes. In the hour since the guests had first arrived the carefully calculated number of vol-au-vents and fondant iced cakes had rapidly disappeared. By the time the bride and groom arrived nothing was left from the promised elegant tea. Dina tried to collar a waiter to find out if there was anything in reserve.

A message came from the kitchen that everything had been put out—and most of it eaten—in the first half hour. Nathan joked that there were no madeleines, and tried to reassure Anna. She said she wasn't hungry and that it didn't matter. The rest of the reception passed in a haze: there must have been speeches, cutting of the cake, portioning out inch-sized pieces to put in boxes to take home. But for Anna it was a disaster, what she always referred to as the 'fiasco of my wedding day.'

The tears were welling up in her eyes. It wasn't that she wanted a few finger sandwiches or a cream cake. She was thinking of her mother. All her life Dina had never served a cup of tea without something sweet and delicious to go with it. The guests were beginning to leave. The family were all going back to Dina's flat where Anna would change into her going-away outfit. On their way out they overheard a couple talking in the entrance hall:

"Remember climbing all those stairs in Kings Gardens and those tiered cake stands?

"Shame. We could have done with some of her éclairs today."

They sat around awkwardly. Anna took off her shoes and removed the corsage of freesias from her frock. Nobody mentioned the wedding reception. Dina went into the kitchen and brought out a plate of tea cakes: little buns that had been dipped in syrup and dusted with cinnamon sugar. She picked up the camel teapot and poured tea into fine porcelain cups. Nathan refused the cakes. Anna spilt some of the dark sugar over her wedding dress. She brushed it off and went into the bedroom to change.

✵

chapter 12

SWEET CROQUETTES OF RICE

*Take about six ounces of rice, which soak
in lukewarm water, and then cook it in
milk and water (half of each) with two
ounces of butter, half of a rind of a lemon
well grated, two or three ounces of sugar,
four yolks of eggs beaten with a little lukewarm water and a little salt. Stir now and
then, and add milk and water, in case it
should become too thick. Turn on a flat
dish when cooked, and let cool. Make
balls with the rice, and dip them in the
four whites of eggs well whisked then roll
them in fine breadcrumbs, dip again and
roll again in the same, throw them in hot
grease, drain them when fried, dust with
sugar and serve.*

What to Eat and How to Cook It, by Pierre Blot

The teapot. I dropped it. I hoped it wasn't dented. It slipped out of my hand when I went to make the tea for Papa. Mercy, what would David say? He gave it to me on our marriage day. It was like a silver ball with an ivory handle. The water came out through a spout that looked like a camel's head and neck. I liked to run my fingers over the mouth and the eyes and the fine silver work around the lid.

It was the first beautiful object I had owned. But, if truth be told, I'd owned nothing of value before. When I lived in my father's house, I had a garnet ring of my mother's, and frocks and bonnets and lace petticoats. It was when I became mistress of my own home in Gravel Lane—what a joy—that we started to acquire all manner of fine objects. David left before seven o'clock in the morning and often returned as late as nine in the evening, so the furnishing of the rooms was my task. At first I spent the days idly comparing linens and asking the prices of carpets, but then I ventured into clockmakers' shops. Did we need a tall-case clock or a bracket clock? How could I tell the difference between mahogany and oak, and whether the inlays were made of boxwood? I began to search the newspapers for announcements of where bargains were to be had.

We had settled into a contented life, though for me it was more lonely than I'd imagined. What did I know of marriage? My father was alone so I had no expectation of a married couple spending time together, but maybe … maybe I hoped it might be different. There was an imbalance in our energies: he was often tired from the long hours of his medical studies; I had the whole day to myself and spent much of it dreaming of his tousled hair on the pillow, his lips parted in sleep.

Strangely—because I had never taken much interest in it before—I took pleasure from planning and preparing dinner. David appreciated my efforts and welcomed additions to the menu. My father would never contemplate anything new and looking back, I believe he must have been nervous when he came to dine with us. He was visiting one day when I started to turn the pages of a book on the art of cooking. He looked over my shoulder and read:

"Written by Pierre Blot. He must be a Frenchman. Where does he get receipts for bear and buffalo?"

"It's published in America. Here's a section on how to prepare meadowlarks and fig-peckers."

"I wouldn't bother with the birds," he said in all seriousness.

"You do see the odd blackbird or thrush outside" I smiled "but he doesn't tell you what to do with those."

"I trust you won't be giving me spinage and salsify, whatever that is. And what's this in the meat section: sweetbreads? "

"Listen to this Papa: It's about puddings. Monsieur Blot says:

> *"The English think the stomach requires to be filled with something heavy due to the perpetual fog."*

I copied out Sweet Croquettes of Rice. I didn't wait for fog but made them on the next rainy day. First there was the boiling of the rice, then the tedious beating of the eggs. When I'd finished the frying there was a pile of creamy rice balls all dusted with sugar. In truth, it was more than enough for just the two of us.

In the evenings after dinner David retired to his study. He was working for his medical examinations. He'd passed the botany and chemistry with good marks. He was also expecting to do well on the pharmacy and physiology as the questions had been easy. It was the anatomy that concerned him. Every day he rushed to see what was in the post. When the familiar envelope arrived, I put it on the top of the pile of correspondence. He took out the letter and a look of dejection came over his face. I knew he had failed.

"I'm not sure whether I should attempt the final examination," he said.

"But you've done so well on all the other papers."

"That's not my main concern. Even if I obtain a medical degree, how do I know if patients in London will welcome a foreign Jewish doctor?"

"How do you know they won't, if you never try?" I went to kiss him but he turned his face. I put my hand on his, trying to encourage him.

I understood his fears. I had come across something recently, quite unconnected with medicine. It was in a book about furnishing:

> "On the subject of auctions, take care if you have set your mind upon something for which there is lively competition, that you are not 'run up' by the Jew brokers who swarm at all sales."

Perhaps David was right to be concerned. It was some

months after this discussion that I discovered he had almost decided to give up the medical profession. I was alarmed when he began to have business discussions with two men. The first one was called Eliezer Mendoza.

"Who is he?" I asked.

"You remember? He was the man who helped me when I first arrived in London. No, you wouldn't remember. That was before I knew you. He was a connection from Gibraltar. He has a business selling sardines."

"He's a merchant," I said. "If you work with him you'll have wasted all those years learning about blood and muscles and bones. Is that what you want?"

He didn't reply but I could see that he was troubled. Then a few days later he had a visit from a man called Moses Costello from an Estate and House agent called Mullins and Co. I left the room but overheard snatches of their conversation.

"3% on the first hundred pounds ... drawing up agreements 10s. 6d"

I imagined that David was intending to invest some of his trust funds in the purchase of a dwelling. I only discovered later that he had already put all his capital into a highly speculative venture and was planning a grander move.

David was a mild-tempered man. He never scolded me but he sometimes treated me like a child. He didn't know that I spent many hours reading. He believed I should be content sitting in a rocking chair, stitching or painting flowers. I would have liked to go with him to the Chiswick Gardens or to Kew.

What I wanted more than anything was to have a baby.

No, that is not the truth. I wanted to have four or five. I dreamed of a large family. I dreamed of David in those long hours when he was out; I could barely wait for him to return. When I raised the subject of children, he said:

"Maybe one, but not more."

"Why?" I asked. I put my arms round his neck and was about to pull him towards me. He lifted my hands from his collar and replied:

"Large families do not bring happiness."

"How do you know?" I continued "you never had one." He turned away and left the room, the conversation clearly concluded.

I became pregnant in the autumn of 1847. David's eyes clouded over with tears when I told him the news. I kissed him on the mouth but he drew away, as if there were someone else in the room. He didn't speak. Did I ever wonder what had made him so withdrawn? What stopped him from showing affection, from stretching out a hand to touch my face or pulling me close when I needed comfort? Perhaps I should have asked, but he had a maddening way of ending a discussion in the middle, so to speak. I simply accepted that I had married a man whose emotions were locked inside, like a cabinet without a key.

In company, however, he was always good-tempered. Eliezer Mendoza became a frequent visitor to our home.

"I don't trust that man. His legs are too short," I said when David returned from calling a Hansom cab for his guest.

"Rachel, you do say the strangest things. He's been here but a minute … "

128

"And that's a minute too long. He's going to persuade you to give up the medical profession," I interrupted.

"He is looking for a partner in his business. He's made a proposal to me."

"But all you ever wanted was to be a physician," I protested.

David thought for a moment and then said:

"I was obsessed with the idea. It was something I read... what was it now?"

He began to mutter something about 'man being created as a beautifully constructed mechanism'. I silently agreed that he certainly was. He went on to talk about 'an everlasting monument to the Almighty's architectural skill.'

I don't know what came over me. I burst out:

"The Almighty gave you a skill—to cure people—and you want to give it all up to work with a man who buys and sells tinned fish?"

He agreed that I was right, that it would be a waste of all those years of study. Then he began to talk about the brain and the nervous system; the arteries which carry the body's fluids. He stopped and a sad expression came into his eyes.

"I've had a fearful weight on my mind. I'm not at all sure I am suited to it."

"You may be right. It's too hard to distinguish the metatarsals from the metacarpals," I said. He showed no sign of appreciating my foolish jest. I understood his feeling of disillusion but what I failed to comprehend was his growing desire to acquire property and possessions. Our child was to be born in the house in Gravel Lane. I would have been content with a small home but David wanted fine furniture and paintings, fitting to a man of substance.

"I want to dine with intelligent, influential people. I want cooks in the scullery, a footman to hand the soup, a servant to bring in the entrée ... "

"David Levy," I said "Where do you get such notions?"

He often said I interrupted his thoughts. This was one of those moments. He continued as if he hadn't heard me:

"We are living a life of mediocrity. We have no time to see beautiful things, to grasp them, to own them. I want to take us beyond all this, and that's why I'm going to join Eliezer Mendoza. Sales of olive oil and sardines are rising and I'd have the prospect of foreign travel. It would be a relief from the strain of studying."

What could I say? I believe I muttered: "I hope it's the right decision."

David had no idea about my concerns. He just went on talking:

"You may be content to live as your father has, remaining in the same occupation for twenty years, with no chance of bettering himself."

"How can you say that? What is 'bettering yourself'?"

It was another one-sided conversation. He carried on:

" ... and as for my parents, they went from a comfortable life to one of hardship. They chose it—and what was the result of their piety? A miserable death and one son who has no place in English society and even less in the alleyways of Safed."

Where was Safed? That was the first time he had named

the town where they had lived. I so much wanted to talk to him. When I asked David to tell me about his parents he simply replied:

"It's in the past," closing the door on yet another conversation.

To make up for his silences he began to buy me small presents. They were not for a specific occasion because he had no understanding of birthdays. The gifts would arrive in the post, addressed to Mrs. David Levy. He would push them across the table and then pick up his own letters, saying little as I unwrapped a book or a needle case. Perhaps it said something about the difference between us: I would have liked to feel the crinkle of fine paper and a satin ribbon. He was more interested in what was inside. I remember one box in particular; it contained 'Blackwell's Inimitable Curling Comb'.

"How does it work?" I asked. David looked at the instructions.

"You insert it in hot water, press the spring so the comb disappears, withdraw it and the curl is complete!"

If I laughed at the curling comb and his growing collection of snuff boxes and cigars, I was apprehensive about his plans. He presented me with a small book called "The Art of Conversation (and Miscellaneous Thoughts and Reflections on General Conduct)". It consisted of advice for those who wanted to improve their station:

"Is this meant to apply to me?" I asked, pointing to a passage about how to behave in company:

> 'Do not sit dumb. That looks either like pride or stupidity. Give your opinion modestly.'

I continued reading:

'Listen attentively to your superiors. Talk entertainingly.'

"What if I don't think little men like Mr. Mendoza are my superiors?"

"Rachel," said David wearily, "it's not about you alone."

"It certainly isn't. Here's what an accomplished man requires: *'good natural parts'*—what does that mean?"

'A good temper; good and general education, begun early; choice, not immense reading.'

Enjoying the haughty tone, I continued:

'He also requires conversation with men of letters; and knowledge of the world, gained by business and travel.'

He wasn't amused. From the outset I should have resisted David's attempts to improve our social standing. Instead I remained silent and let the campaign continue. He purchased a copy of Robson's Housekeeper's Account Book.

"Look, there's a column for each tradesman—baker, grocer, oilman, corn chandler, cheesemonger etc. Then there's a list of items of expenditure—poultry, fish, tin, turnery, washing and mangling, coals and wood etc."

"But all this about wages and taxes," I interrupted. "It doesn't exactly apply to us. We don't have a grand house or servants."

"We will one day," replied David. His positive tone turned to one of dejection as he added "I thought you'd be interested."

I found it hard to respond. I was feeling heavy and ungainly. All I could think was that for the time being

I was mercifully exempt from fulfilling these duties. I turned the pages and saw that there were some notes at the beginning of the book. They gave the times of the seven daily collections of letters in town and hints on the management of duck keeping. I copied into my note book *'bread burnt over charcoal and pounded in a mortar produces a cheap but good tooth powder'.*

David picked up the housekeeping book and turned to some information at the back: lists of bankers and judges, tables of weights and measures and new stamp duties.

"There's nothing here about the management of children and babies" he said, brightening up. "Perhaps it isn't much use after all."

He must have seen that I was upset at his transparent attempts to improve us and insisted once more that the book was not meant as a criticism of me.

The positive effect of his changing profession was that he was able to spend more time at home, leaving later in the mornings and arriving early for dinner. Towards the end of my pregnancy David was gentle and considerate. The weather was getting warmer and he brought me cool drinks. One day he walked in with a Japanese fan, hand-painted in a riot of colour. That evening the contractions began.

Our son was born on 12th June 1848. The labour lasted two days and like all mothers, I find it hard now to describe, or even recall, the pain and the stretching. David said it was lucky there were no complications, since he hadn't completed his midwifery course! We called the baby Solomon, after his paternal grandfather. I remember nothing of the circumcision party held eight days after his birth. A Mr. Albert Moses, a pastrycook in Norton Folgate, provided confectionery and fancy biscuits.

chapter 13

GRIDDLED MACKEREL WITH A COMPÔTE OF GOOSEBERRIES

Ingredients: one large mackerel, a little salad-oil or butter, salt and pepper.

Method: Do not wash the fish, but wipe it clean and dry. Split it down the back, sprinkle it well with seasoning, and brush lightly over with warm butter. The fire must be clear, and the fish should be turned frequently. Allow 15–20 minutes for a mackerel of medium size, and a few minutes longer when broiled in paper.

Gooseberry sauce

Gather gooseberries before they are ripe, pick and scald them till they are quite tender, but not mashed. Strain them from the water, and put them while hot in to the basin or tureen. Lay upon them some boiled parsley chopped, fine Lisbon sugar upon that, and then pour rich melted butter over the top. This sauce is proper for Green Goose, Mackerel and boiled Leg of Lamb.

From Emily's notebook, 1850

I had set my mind on a career in medicine. I wanted a wife and one child. Only one of those wishes became a reality.

As a student my head was filled with idealistic notions. Then came the difficult years when I was rushing hot foot between Aldersgate and the London Hospital. After one of my morning lectures, I spoke with Dr. Ramsbotham about my chances of success. He was frank and open, with regard to my abilities and my religion. The decision to abandon my medical studies brought with it considerable regret. The exhilaration of working with the human body was a sensation I never again experienced in any business venture.

Shortly after our marriage, in June 1846, the railway shares rose again. Great Western now stood at £224. I decided to sell at the end of September. By October there was some apprehension in the share market. The newspapers reported that 'a storm was at hand' and there was anxiety, but not, as yet, panic. If I had waited another two months I would have faced financial ruin. Investors who had been persuaded by the offer of a 6% dividend soon realized that their railway shares were overpriced. The enormous depreciation in value had begun. But by that time I had already become a rich man. I never told Rachel about my original investment—probably out of a fear that being more cautious, she would have disapproved. The moment to tell her about my prosperity came later when I decided that we should move from Gravel Lane.

We found a large house in Finsbury Square. Number

40 was the fifth in a row of thirteen terraced houses along the north side of the square. There were three or four hotels at the corners and in the centre was an ornamental garden—a parterre, I believe, with a drinking fountain. Like many fine neighbourhoods in London it had livery stables and a hospital nearby, but within a stone's throw, near the New Artillery Ground, were the saw mills and a timberyard. On windy days smells wafted in from the pickle manufactory and distillery in nearby Ropemaker Street. The house itself had four floors and imposing reception rooms—large enough to hold a ball.

I had gambled everything I possessed and the venture had paid off. Having put the proceeds into the purchase of number forty, I needed to turn my mind to business. I worked for a year with Eliezer Mendoza importing olive oil. There was much to learn. Although I knew Spanish, I had to acquire enough words in Portuguese to deal with the trade in sardines.

A year later I established my own company, Levy and Co., taking advantage of the demand for highly priced sugar. I acquired warehouse space to store sacks of cinnamon and coffee beans, chestnuts and rice. I imported chalk, seeds and candles and employed agents to sell the dried fruits, as well as phosphorus and petroleum. It was clear there was a market for cheap goods like soap, as well as fine pepper and tea. I saw no need to disturb Rachel with details of my dealings. We barely spoke half-a-dozen words about the business. There is a wide difference between men and women and I doubt if Rachel would have shared my enthusiasm for searching out new products. Yet one thing she would have understood. There were times when I found myself remembering the patients in the London Hospital and wondering what had become of them.

At home my life was also changing. Although I had no desire for a large family Rachel's mind was fixed on having more children. When Solomon was two our second child Jonah was born. We chose a biblical name which had a great personal significance. Jonah was a survivor, being cast up, still alive, from the bowels of a whale. I imagined his sense of isolation as the whale slid away and left him gasping on the shore.

The children brought me great joy, though it seemed to Rachel that I spent little time with them. Solomon was a good child, placid and unadventurous. He was wiry and agile and when he was learning to walk, he pulled himself up to look at the fine ornaments on the small tables in the drawing room. I never remember him breaking a single one. Jonah was different—a heavy, restless boy who screamed for the first few months of his life. Rachel passed many nights rocking him in a carved wooden chair that was one of the many pieces of furniture I had bought at auction.

We engaged a houseparlourmaid called Betsy and then employed a girl called Emily who had replied to the announcement we placed in the newspaper for a Good Plain Cook. Rachel and I had many conversations about furnishing the dining-room and she even came with me to purchase the Chippendale chairs with the lion's paw legs. When it came to planning a soirée we seemed to have totally opposing views. My wife would have liked to cook a small dinner herself; but we were now in a position to employ staff, so the kind of evening I envisaged was different. I bought a book which I thought would solve the problem. "The Lady's Guide to the Ordering of Her Household and the Economy of the Dinner Table" was exactly what was needed. I used to read aloud from it in the evenings:

'Ladies must take a greater degree of interest in every part of household work, in order to reform their dinners. The poorer classes, in England, do not, unfortunately possess a natural aptitude for cooking. They enter service early, pass a few years in sculleries doing dirty work, pick up some scanty knowledge and call themselves "plain cooks".

The book contained examples of a carte for dinner for up to sixteen people, written in French (and English for the kitchen staff). Each one had two soups and for the fish course, elaborate sauces. The entrées which followed required considerable skill—quenelles or croquettes. The main courses were more in the English tradition—a saddle of mutton and some roasted birds with a variety of vegetables. The desserts would have presented no problem for Rachel as she had a growing repertoire of creams, jellies, cakes and puddings. At the side of each carte was a helpful list of items to be purchased. For the soup alone the order included 12 lbs of gravy beef, 6 lbs of knuckle of veal and a set of calves' feet.

To my surprise Rachel showed no interest in achieving such a dinner. I had given her a small notebook and she used it for receipts for one or two dishes that took her fancy. I must confess to meticulous notekeeping myself but I believe she wrote out the instructions for the cooking and passed the book on to Emily. I recall a particular discussion about fish. Rachel had copied out '*Griddled mackerel with a compôte of gooseberries*'.

"That's a strange combination" I suggested "I'd prefer sole with wine sauce. It's more refined."

She replied that the sauce contained lobster. Rachel had been brought up to follow the strict dietary laws of *kashrut,* as I had, but my father's dominant views on the suitability of every mouthful had left me sceptical. I would not have minded the addition of a crustacean, but since my wife was concerned about what foods were permitted, I decided to leave all such questions to her. Returning to the idea of the mackerel she continued:

"I don't think the French eat fish with green berries. It's strange that they call gooseberries '*groseilles à maquereau*' and never eat the two together. They don't know how good it is."

We never did eat the mackerel with gooseberries. It may have been the wrong season for the berries. All I remember was an exchange about the cutlery:

"Rachel," I said "you've forgotten to put out the fish knives."

She replied with surprising force:

"Why do you always pick on me? Tell Emily to put out the precious fish knives."

I took them out myself. They had ivory handles and a design of a fish engraved in the silver. Rachel didn't appreciate the things I bought. She seemed content to pass her days in the kitchen with Emily or in the nursery with Solomon and Jonah. Although she blossomed with motherhood she still lacked confidence in the company of our growing number of acquaintants. There were the stockbrokers and bankers from the neighbouring houses and merchants from Bevis Marks synagogue. I wanted to use the fine rooms in our house to entertain people of breeding. Rachel had no such wish. Some of my efforts to help her were rebuffed. One evening when we were dining alone I pointed to the silver sauceboat on the table:

"Where is the stand for the sauceboat?" I asked. "You can't set a silver piece on a china plate."

She didn't seem to understand my concern that the table setting should be correct. Instead she began to talk about the anchovy sauce she had made:

"It's not made with the essence. I scalded the fish, took out their spines and mashed them. ... but all that concerns you is the silver stand."

We were spending too many evenings at home. I discovered some places of amusement and we began to go to the Hanover Music Rooms or the Diorama in Regent's Park. Occasionally I purchased tickets for the theatre.

On one occasion we were preparing to go to the Pantheon, when I called out that we were going to be late. Rachel was reading to the boys and was engrossed in a book called "Easy Chat for Little People". Solomon loved to hear about boys who walked on frozen ponds or played with loaded guns. Each tale had a simple warning and an accompanying drawing. That evening Rachel was reading of a girl who fell into a river because she leaned over the side of a boat. By the time she'd closed the book and smoothed out her frock, we were already late. We arrived at the theatre in the middle of the first act. Instead of enjoying the play, we stood outside. I can't remember the words of our quarrel but we left the theatre and returned home.

I pulled off my gloves and said:

"You've ruined our evening."

"And you ... you consider no-one but yourself," she started. "You don't read with the children, but you resent it when I do."

I opened my mouth to reply, attempting to arrange my thoughts into words. Rather than confront the truth I argued:

"You don't understand ... "

"No, I never understand. Because you never tell me. You never explain. You ... " Rachel's voice trailed away as she wiped away tears. I took her hand, pulled her towards me and began to stroke her wet cheeks.

I sat her down on the chaise longue next to me and linked my fingers with hers.

"For half my life, since I was fourteen, I have been trying to keep control of my emotions," I began.

"But if you tell me why, I can help you," cried Rachel.

"No-one can help. The problem ... the reason I can't be close to you—or the children—is nothing to do with you. It's because ... I lost everyone I loved and the only way I could continue my life was to try never to feel deeply for anyone again."

The words were like a needle I had thrust into Rachel's flesh, an unintentional wound that I couldn't repair. In an attempt to limit the pain I had caused I decided to tell her some version of what had happened. I began with the easy parts, about my childhood. The story began in

1834 and even as I was speaking, I was wondering how to describe the event that occurred three years after that.

"When I was eleven my parents left Gibraltar with me, my two sisters and my brother."

"But I thought you were an only child" she interrupted.

"That's what you assumed. I didn't tell you that."

I fell silent for some minutes and then continued.

"Abraham was thirteen, Miriam nine and little Rebecca was only three. We travelled by sea to Acre in the Holy Land. From the port we journeyed by land past Rama, through a country of wild gorges and huge precipices. We reached a village called Jauna, overlooking the Jordan valley, with magnificent views of two lakes: Tiberias on one side and the Lake of Huleh, on the other. We rode on mules, climbing over rocky paths till finally we reached Safed. The town is perched on the summit of a mountain nearly 3,000 feet high."

Rachel said nothing, but moved closer to me as I carried on speaking:

"Solomon, my father, had brought us to this place to follow a Rabbi—Haim Josef Tzarfati—and to live in his community. We found a shell of a house—typical of the dwellings in the town—and with help we made it habitable. The walls were made of stones, very thick, held together with a slurry of mud and straw. We plastered them white inside. For the floors we laid flat stones on top of the ground. Then we covered them with straw mats and rugs. Young men came to put timbers on the flat roof and to cover the cracks with layers of beaten earth. On top of this they sprinkled sea sand, which they wetted and compacted with a kind of roller made from a heavy cylinder. The houses were built on the slope in a step-like fashion, so that the roofs formed a sort of street. Abraham and I would run along the roofs, jumping down to the next level, till we came to the market.

When I was small I didn't know my mother's name. To me she was Mama, to my father 'my dove'. She was actually called Paloma, but in the observant community we had joined, there was no-one with a non-biblical name. My father would disappear for hours but Mama was always at home. I never saw my father kiss my mother. There was no display of affection between men and their wives in public or in front of the children. Perhaps that's why she showered us with tenderness. She would never pass without brushing a cheek, squeezing an arm or at the end of the day, folding us in her arms. She was large and had long, unruly hair which fell in strands around her face. Most of her time was spent providing food for us."

I told Rachel about the markets and the rare occasions when a cow or goat was slaughtered; of the way the animals were brought to the house and milked by the doorpost. I described the games I played with Miriam and the hiding places I found with Abraham in caves on the hillside outside the town.

Rachel's eyelids began to close. I had been speaking for two hours. I promised to continue the next day.

chapter 14

C<small>AULIFLOWERS</small>

Be very careful in your examination and washing before you put these in the sauce-pan for their stalks and branches afford peculiar facilities for 'squatting' to many insect settlers.

The Dinner Question or How to Dine Well and Economically, by Tabitha Tickletooth.

<small>LONDON 1851—DAVID</small>

In the afternoon there was a storm, though at one stage bright sunshine flooded into the room before the rain began again. I was waiting to continue the story but remained in my chair for hours without speaking. Rachel said that our quarrel had unleashed a stream of words, like a broken pot that first released a trickle, then a gushing flood of water. She told me I had revealed more in those few hours than in all the time we had been married.

I was about to continue my account of what happened when Jonah began to cry. He was waking up with colic every few hours. Rachel took him out of the crib and put him on her shoulder, stroking his back. I thought it was wrong to keep picking the child up but I could see we would get no peace until he was calm and I was unsettled by his tear-stained face and constant sobbing. Rachel rocked him to sleep and Emily served our meal. Afterwards we took a tray with the camel teapot and poured out two cups of tea. We sat in silence for some time before I could bring myself to speak again:

"My father ... it's hard for me to talk about him. He was so preoccupied with study and keeping the laws that I fear he couldn't see things that were under his eyes. For him the sight of an insect in the food was of more concern than a major event in the town. Not that anything of consequence ever happened in Safed. That is, until ... I am at a loss where to begin. Perhaps I should tell you about my sisters?"

"Rebecca was a golden child—blessed with curls the colour of sand and a sunny nature which made everyone smile. She would laugh and giggle and invent stories. She never stopped talking. Because she was the youngest, she was told not to interrupt, so she waited her turn and then chattered incessantly, until we had quite lost the trail. She loved to dress up in Mama's clothes, clattering along the stone floors in shoes that were too big and tripping up in skirts far too long for her. Everywhere she went, she took her small woollen bear and when she was tired she put a paw in her mouth and sucked the end till she fell asleep.

Miriam was quite the opposite—dark haired with long

ringlets and always lost in her own thoughts. At meals Mama would ask her to pass a dish of rice and she would continue eating, as if she hadn't heard. So much so, that at one time my parents suspected that she might be deaf and consulted a healing man in the town. He pronounced that her hearing was perfect, so we all became accustomed to Miriam's periods of silence and behaved as if she were not there. We discovered later that though she spoke little, she spent her time observing everything around her. The first time I discovered that she could draw was when I found a few sheets of paper on her bed. She saved the paper from notices fixed to trees and I suspect, tore out the blank end papers from books she found in the house. She had a few sticks of charcoal and drew pictures of the streets and the vendors in the market. My father wanted us all to learn Hebrew very well and gave us passages to copy every day. Miriam would decorate her page with flying birds, turning the letters into legs or wings.

Abraham went with my father to the synagogue every morning and again in the late afternoon and evening. He had learnt to pray with great fervour, swaying with his feet close together and his eyes shut. I did everything I could to avoid going to *tefila* and tried to persuade my father that I could pray just as well outside under an olive tree. He dismissed my complaints, yet sometimes failed to notice that I wasn't by his side, as he was often in a trance-like state. One day, Miriam revealed a secret I had been keeping for weeks: I no longer said my night prayers at home and kept a small book of stories inside the covers of my prayer book in synagogue. Mama, of course, knew. She smiled at my excuses and I suspect, had a sympathy for my lack of interest. My father was furious. He never shouted and although there was no ear-rending outburst, I felt the full force of his pained anger.

For a week I planned my revenge on Miriam. I knew she was putting together a collection of line drawings—pictures of the family and the Rabbis. They were remarkably life-like; the charcoal strokes capturing a fleeting expression or a look of concentration in the eyes. In a moment of glee, I took the drawings and hid them under the covers of my bed.

The next day was Sunday, 1st January 1837. I woke to a clear, bright day. It was cold outside so I put on warm clothes. In the afternoon my mother came to the room I shared and sat on the bed.

"I know you don't want to go with your father."

Before I could answer, she continued:

"Try, just try ... to find a prayer that speaks to you, bring it into your mind and send it to God. He likes to receive messages."

I had never thought of the hurried words as part of a conversation. I promised to go to the synagogue in the evening, but my mother was happy for me to remain in the house. Maybe there were some tasks to be done ... . A few minutes later Mama left and went with the girls to a neighbour's house. My father put his arm round Abraham and they walked down the street to the synagogue of the Ari. I'm not sure why it was called the Ari—I knew it as the place where the great Rabbi Isaac had prayed. I would have gone with father but I stayed behind to look for my shoes, which Miriam had hidden in retaliation for my trick with her drawings. Mama complained that my feet seemed to grow every few months. But I remember those shoes: they were brown, with punched holes and laces made from thin strips of leather."

I stopped talking for a moment and looked at Rachel. She took hold of my hands to stop them shaking. Through the mist in my eyes I could see that she was perplexed.

"Why did you never tell me about your brother and sisters?"

I took out a linen handkerchief and passed it over my eyes.

"Because if I didn't talk about them, it was as if they had never existed. And that was less painful."

She squeezed my hand and urged me to continue.

"It was still light and I couldn't find the shoes. The table in my room began to tremble with a gentle motion—yet there was no wind outside. The walls began to rock. There was a faint rumbling noise outside and from deep down a roaring sound, muffled at first, and then bursting, cracking, shattering, heaving ... I looked out of the window. Everywhere stones were falling, roofs collapsing. The house opposite split in two and then crumbled, dust falling everywhere. People started running into the street, their faces smeared with white powdery grit. Shouting filled the air; screams; cries; and the clatter of feet—everyone running, stumbling away from the lower level of houses which was about to be crushed by the cascade of stone and roofing.

The ground had cracked and the dirt road was gaping open. I stood glued to the window, not knowing whether to stay or run. Even if I had known that this was an earthquake, I would still have been unable to move, terrified that the house would fall on me or the path out-side would open up again. Across the road a vast stone fell from a tottering wall on top of a woman carrying a baby. She was crushed to pieces with her child. The walls of the upper houses were giving way under the weight of the timber roofs and the compacted sand and earth was flying in the air—a thick black dust whirling down and covering everyone who had rushed out for safety. I pulled the blankets from my bed and crawled underneath the table, shaking and sobbing. A moment later the walls began to heave again and another deep rumble retched up from the floor beneath. Then everything was falling, the wardrobe, the ceiling, the sky itself seemed to be fold-ing in and spewing out on top of the bed and the table. There was the sound of creaking wood and pieces of the roof started to fall; then a grumbling shower of earth and water dripping from a broken jug. And after that silence … nothing … nothing except … the whimpering of a baby. The shouting outside had stopped.

I stayed under the table with the blanket pulled up to my chin. All around me was broken plaster, shattered furniture and an eerie quiet. Then I must have fallen asleep. When I woke up—who knows how much later—I was stiff and could hardly move; I blinked and saw there was nowhere to move. Above the table were layers of broken timber and plaster. Outside were voices, calling, pleading. I tried to shout but my voice seemed so small in the depths of the shattered room. I heaved at a piece of wood, hoping to lift it off the table, but it was embedded in the remains of the wall at the other side of the room. I realized then that the plank had taken the weight of more debris which would have demolished the table. I kept calling, for Mama, for my father, for anyone who would come to help me. My voice was getting hoarse so I put out my tongue and licked the slick of water which had poured from the jug. It tasted dirty. I must have been under the table for the whole of that day and night because when I woke again, I could see shafts of light coming through the cracks in the pieces of wood. A light rain was falling.

Suddenly there were voices outside and I started to call out again. 'Mama', 'Mama'. There were sounds of a spade thudding above me and a heaving of stones and wood; and an arm reaching out to me and pushing the table and lifting me out.

The next thing I remember was waking up with the sound of moaning and sobbing all around me. I was lying on the grass at the bottom of the little hill leading up to our house. The rain was drumming on the ground. People were sitting with water dripping down their backs.

"I have to go back," I cried out. A man with blood on his face looked at me and shook his head: "You can't, there's nothing left."

I started to run back up the hill. My feet were scratched from the rubble on the ground. People were poking through the debris of where their houses once stood. Groups of men were digging and humping stones and planks, trying to find anyone who had survived. I slowed down, looking for the neighbour's house where my mother had gone. There was nothing there—it had been completely crushed by the weight of the house above it, fallen like the sole of a shoe on an autumn leaf.

I turned the corner and ran to the Ari. A few men were

sitting outside with their heads in their hands, intoning psalms. The synagogue too was a pile of rubble. I started running, searching for anyone I knew, looking at the faces streaming with tears and grime. I went through the alleyway back down past one of the other synagogues, all the time calling out 'Mama'. Someone took my hand and led me back down the hill. Everywhere there were ruins; the streets cracked and full of rubble; the air thick like fog. We clambered over bodies and hands and I turned my head to watch people leaning over and tugging at a sleeve, a leg. A man walked past with a woman slumped over his shoulder, a blanket draped over her body."

Rachel stopped me and whispered:

"How did you get news of your parents? Why did I think that they had been lost at sea? When you told me there was an accident, I had no idea ... "

"I kept hoping that I would look up and see my mother and my sisters running towards me; that my father had somehow survived the collapse of the whole building he was in. But in the next few days, more and more bodies were pulled from the rubble and laid out in one of the synagogues that had survived the earthquake. There was an urgency to get them buried. People walked slowly past identifying a friend or relative with a nod of the head. The body was removed. A list of names was posted on a board. That was when I learned that the whole of my family had died: my father, Mama, Abraham, Miriam and Rebecca. I was fourteen with no more than a gash on my leg and a head brimming full of tears."

The tea was cold. Rachel took my hand and led me to bed.

✳

chapter 15

*"Immediately after a death, close relatives
are obliged to perform Keri'a, the rending
of a garment. For a parent, this is done
on the left side of the garment, a tear to
the extent of a hand's breadth being made
near the top of the garment. For a son,
daughter, brother, sister, husband or wife,
the garment is rent on the right side."*

From Sephardi Home Ceremonies, by Dayan P Toledano

LONDON 1851—DAVID

The days after the earthquake were smudged in my
mind, like the encrusted dirt on my face. There was no
water to wash. People came with tents to protect us from
the driving rain and the cold of the night. We huddled
together—pressed against bodies that sobbed in the
darkness, murmuring names—children calling for their
parents, parents looking at a child through eyes wet with
pity and anger. The digging continued. Those who had
no spade used their hands, passing the stones from one
to another, hurling rubble aside in the feverish search. I
saw two boys squeezed out, one gasping and choking,

the other with part of his leg crushed and the rest still embedded under the stones. What had once been a road was now an impassable mound of rocks. Some buildings had their sides sheared off, others were left intact as if a giant had pointed his finger at the houses and then brought down a mighty foot on those he chose to destroy. Money changed hands for an axe or a piece of wood and gravediggers were paid a thousand grush to pull out a body, lifting a boulder that revealed a hand or just a finger. They worked in silence. Walking up and down, picking their way over the debris, were a few Rabbis, followed by groups of students. Some were mouthing prayers, others were holding up their hands to the sky, a pointed accusation against the God who had done this act.

The terrible shudder had thrown one row of houses on top of another, till they all came crashing down the slope. The ones on the lower levels were buried under the weight of floors and roofs, pressed together with a filling of crushed possessions. The survivors—Muslims, Jews and Christians—speculated on the number killed. Some guessed it was thousands, but the number was changing every day as many who were not killed immediately died days afterwards, breathless beneath the fragments of wood and stone, dust and gravel. I learned later that fourteen synagogues were destroyed that afternoon. Any belief I might have had that God was good, was buried there, among the *Torah* scrolls and the holy books. But of course those thoughts came later. My immediate concern was the daily search for a scrap to eat or a sip of water. The thirst was unremitting, a sour, dusty taste in the mouth and a feeling that the inside of my body was withering like a crinkled fig leaf.

A few days after the earthquake I went back to the wreckage of our house. My feet were bleeding, the skin broken from walking over rubble without shoes. I was looking for something to bind up my toes. The rooms were strewn with clothing and broken pots. Under the table where I had hidden, was the blanket and bed cover. Nearby were several sheets of paper, scattered on the floor, with a doll of Rebecca's and Mama's shoe. The crockery lay around, all broken. I stood in the doorway, looking at my feet and the jagged pieces. The first object I could reach was the silken cloth used on Shabbat to cover the *challa*. I picked it up, ripped it with my teeth and tore it into two strips. As I was binding up my feet my eye was drawn to an object, shining in the dirt. It was the silver teapot. I wrapped it in a piece of cloth and took it back to the tent.

I am not sure of the moment—whether it was one, two or three days after the quake, that I realized I was completely alone. My whole family had been wiped off the earth. I remembered how, a few days earlier, Abraham and I had been watching a line of ants. We played at pushing them with our finger and suddenly one of us swept them all off the table. We stamped a few to death and watched the others making another laborious climb up the table leg.

In the remains of Safed there was no point in shedding tears. In every tent, someone had survived with only a memory of a soft cheek or a gentle touch. Few people could bring themselves to move. Only the older children like me had spurts of energy to go and search for something that would ensure that we woke up the following day.

I never told Rachel about the camel teapot. For her it was simply a wedding gift and one that she treasured. For me it was like a stone around my neck; a source of guilt that I had saved that object and nothing else.

The telling of the disaster was in some way a relief—as if I had let out a long breath, held for too long in bursting lungs. I imagine Rachel was grateful for the flood of words I had released, but it didn't change the tight control I kept on what she called my 'feelings'. I was unable to be angry or passionate. It was as if the part of the brain that controlled my emotions had been severed on that day in January 1837.

Rachel, by contrast, seemed to be more contented. As our sons grew and started school, she had more time on her hands. She was taking trouble with her hair and I noticed that she had chosen a new style—with a centre parting and the sides slightly puffed out and a chignon at the back. I believe she waved it with the heated iron tongs I had purchased for her.

I tried to interest her in collecting antiques. After the move from Whitechapel I gravitated more and more towards West London. Visiting my tailor in Jermyn Street, I noticed a particular window display of fine carpets, between the hatter and the bootmaker. When I returned I suggested to Rachel that she might like to look at them.

"It's next to Harvie and Hudson" I explained. She wasn't

paying attention.

"Rachel, did you hear what I said about the carpets? On your way back, you might go into the cheesemonger and pick up some Buxton Blue or Cheshire."

"Yes. I'm all ears." She seemed distracted, picked up her latch key and went out.

She returned a few hours later with two packages.

"I thought we'd try some Parmesan for a change. That apricot-coloured cheese looked so dry."

"What's in the other parcel?"

"Open it up and see."

I unwrapped the paper and took out a box. It contained a silver sugar basin and cream ewer to match the teapot I had given her.

" ... How in the world?" I began.

"I was looking for someone to make the copies," she said. "I found a notice in the Chronicle about a silversmith in Cornhill, opposite the Bank of England."

"But ... " I began.

"I knew he could make the Cottage and King's pattern but I asked if he took commissions for other styles. I took in the teapot and he's reproduced the rest of the set with the same ivory handles. Do you like the design? He's done it well, don't you think?"

What could I think? I didn't have the heart to tell her that the original teapot was never part of a set. The piece had come from Tangier. When we lived in Gibraltar—that was before we went to Safed—my parents once took the short passage across the sea to Morocco. I was about ten and Abraham was a couple of years older. We wandered off on our own and found that we were lost in the alleyways. I thought it was exciting but Abraham was frightened. We started running, past the piles of terracotta pots, in between the spice vendors. I told him our parents wouldn't go back to Gibraltar without us. We turned a corner and there was Mama. She was standing by a display of beaten copper pots, bargaining about the price of a silver teapot. My father didn't wish to join in the negotiations and walked off carrying a huge sack of oranges. We all got on the ferry; Mama happy at her purchase and Abraham complaining all the way home about the smells and the noise of the market. I think it was the crowds that made him unsettled. We ate some of the oranges; the taste was wonderful and the juice dripped down our sleeves. My brother just kept moaning till we got back to the Rock.

It was pure chance that the teapot made the return journey from Safed to Gibraltar and from there to London—one object retrieved from a mass of misery.

chapter 16

1856

Glazed secretaire bookcase—mahogany
Vienna wall clock—walnut and beechcase
Chenille Axminster carpet
Mahogany chest (rosewood crossbanded top)
Gilt wall mirror
French polishing, 17s.0d
Broadwood piano, 100 guineas

From David Levy's account book

LONDON 1856—RACHEL

I remember once at the seashore at Ramsgate, sitting by a rock pool and stirring the sand with a stick. The water turned thick and muddy and then it ebbed away and a wave brought fresh, clear water into the pool. David's emotions were like that—stirred up by his account of the earthquake which explained everything but resolved nothing. The two people he loved best, Mama and Rebecca, had gone. He felt a bubbling anger towards his father, for taking them to Safed in the first place, and immersing himself in a mystical world that did not include children. But what about his feelings for Abraham and Miriam? His brother was a pressed-out copy of his devout father, yet he was still his best friend and playmate. And Miriam—I don't know how he felt about her—the sister who taunted him one minute, and then disappeared to work like an angel on her drawings.

His answer was to suppress it all—not to talk about anything: the flashes of joy or the simmering arguments. When he told me about Aunt Deborah, at first I didn't understand—his detachment, his secrecy about the library. But now I could see how a frightened boy would be unable to accept a substitute mother. It was all making sense: why he kept a distance from his school friends; how he never went drinking with the medical students. As for me, he didn't know how to accept that I loved him as he was, from the shock of unruly hair and dark olive skin to the way he spoke, measuring his words, revealing little of what he was thinking. I sometimes wonder what kind of man David Levy MD would have been; certainly different from the detached, elegant businessman who wanted a wife and household in keeping with his position.

Perhaps I am being harsh. He had no more control over his feelings than a sick man has to control a fever. He used to purchase flowers for the house—stiff purple irises that Emily would arrange in an ornate vase. Yet he never put a bunch of flowers into my hand. I would have liked the scent of freesias or sweet peas, or even a dozen daffodils. They are such complex flowers. They grow almost wild but the cultivated ones have intriguing names: Angel's Whisper, Cornish Cream ... but the beauty is in the way the petals unfurl from a tight bud, revealing a cup of palest peach or bright orange. Where was I? Ah yes, David and the flowers. But it wasn't just that. He ordered toys for his sons but never knew if they played with them. He decided to purchase a bagatelle board, and spent some time choosing whether it should be faced with ash or oak. It had a hand-turned cue and brass nails around the target areas. The boys used it only once. Solomon accused Jonah of losing one of the ten balls, so they went outside to play French cricket instead.

David had become an English gentleman. His clothes came from Jermyn Street and he encouraged me to buy the best bonnets and frocks. He spent a hundred guineas on a Broadwood piano—finely veneered and handsomely decorated. We spent some time together choosing between a piccolo or a semi-grand and finally settled on a 'cottage' which the shopman assured us was an '*instrument for the noble and wealthy*'. David wanted me to play and suggested that he should find a tutor. We pored over copies of The Musical World and there, amid announcements for the latest dance music, was a notice:

"Monsieur Laurent du Col has the honour to announce that he has returned to London and will be happy to receive Pupils for the Harmonium and Pianoforte".

The following Thursday at two o'clock Monsieur du Col came to our house and began the weekly lessons. He was much younger than I expected—I judged him to be about twenty-eight years old. He was about five feet seven in height, with firm muscles and a narrow waist and hips. I noticed this because he wore close fitting trousers and a brightly coloured waistcoat. His eyes were dark brown and he had wavy black hair but no beard. His face had the appearance of a young boy who hadn't yet taken a razor to his skin. David stood next to him, several inches taller, waiting to discuss the lessons. I looked from one to the other, suddenly embarrassed.

"I don't want to work through dull studies suitable for a child," I began.

"Madame Levy" said Monsieur du Col "you may be assured that my pupils do not find my lessons dull."

David turned to leave the room. Fingering the tutor's card he looked up and smiled at me:

"I'll expect an invitation to your first concert performance."

Monsieur du Col sat down at the piano and moved his fingers up and down the keyboard.

"These are arpeggios. You need to learn scales, but that is like preparing a canvas for a painting. But ... ," he added "to play well, you also need to listen."

He began to play and told me that these were the first bars of a Schubert piano sonata. The lessons progressed. I was impatient to get on with finger-demanding pieces.

"Teaching you is like ... " his voice trailed off, then he began again:

"It's like teaching the works of Molière and Balzac to a child who can't read."

His comment disconcerted me. I was embarrassed that he thought of me as an uneducated child. Would I ever be able to play like him? He must have seen that I was downcast because he said in a softer voice:

"I've been listening to music all my life. This is all new for you. You can't suddenly acquire an instrument and

162

play it to perfection the next week."

What he said had an unsettling effect on me. One moment he would make me feel inadequate; the next he was full of encouragement. After about a month, he made a suggestion:

"I should take you to some concerts ... .We could go to hear Thalbert, Clementi."

"But what would people say?"

"We wouldn't be doing anything out of the way. I've taken many of my pupils to concerts."

"But for me to be seen, alone, with my piano tutor—that would be shocking," I said.

He simply ignored my comment and replied:

"We shall go in the afternoon. Instead of having the lesson here, we shall be in a hall."

The following week, he called to collect me and handed his gloves to the maid, who ushered him into the drawing room.

"Madame Levy—may I invite you to lesson one, of the Laurent du Col Concert Series?" I laughed and when we were alone, I told him:

"Betsy can't pronounce your name and told me that Monsieur Duke was here."

"That's because she has never learned French. But you have, I know."

"How do you know?" I asked.

"Because when I come in you say "Ah, Monsieur Laurrrent du Col."

I blushed and walked to the hallway, waiting for him to follow. The first outing was to a piano recital. The programme consisted of a Prelude and an Etude by Chopin, and Liszt's new Sonata in B minor. I asked Monsieur du Col how many years it took to achieve such a performance. We talked about the hours of practise and I understood why he was amused by my impatience.

I began to look forward to Thursdays and practised for hours before the lesson. Solomon and Jonah were at school and Emily had some time to herself in the afternoons. The house was quiet. David noticed that my playing had improved and he must also have seen how contented I was. What he didn't know was that as two o'clock approached I began to feel nervous and excited.

As Monsieur du Col sat beside me at the piano, I kept looking at the softness of his face. It was so different from David's heavy growth. He spoke with a pronounced accent and often broke into phrases in French, the words tumbling out of his mouth in his urgency to explain a phrase to me, or to describe a piece of music he had heard.

"Madame Levy" he would say, if I played too loud. "You are not in the English music hall, you are, *comment dit-on*, in a French salon, with me."

That made me laugh, because our carpets were French and some of the furniture was French but it was the Frenchman himself who made me smile. Every Thursday he arrived, sometimes before two o'clock, and we would sit side by side playing and talking. We spoke about the mazurka—the triple time and the dotted rhythms—about French composers and eventually, about him. It was then that he invited me to call him by his Christian name. It took me a moment to understand his meaning. We must have talked long past the allotted hour of my lesson. I discovered that he was four years younger than me; his parents lived in Carcassonne in the Languedoc and he had been to a Catholic school. Although he taught keyboard instruments, he had a passion for strings. He couldn't believe that I had never heard Vivaldi or Bach and promised the next week to take me to hear one of the Brandenburgs.

Just before the performance began he explained to me the three movement form of Bach's violin concertos. I looked round the hall nervously. He must have known what I was thinking but pretended there was no cause for concern. As we were leaving he said in a voice loud enough for anyone to hear:

"Next week I shall take you to hear Mozart. Your education will begin with the Divertimento No. 3 in F major."

As promised, he reserved seats at the Exeter Hall and on the journey there, began to explain about criss-crossing parts, wide melodic leaps and the vibrant sound of the Allegro movement. I wonder now if most people who hear Mozart for the first time feel what I did then? The second half of the concert was Symphony No. 40 in G minor and by the time the orchestra was playing the andante I felt that the soaring music was carrying me away. It was as if I was floating and looking down, from above, on the correctness of my life in Finsbury Square. But of course, it was not just the sound of the strings. The force of Laurent's presence made me feel stimulated and alive. On the way home the happiness changed to unease.

I said nothing to David about our excursions. He was so taken up with his new business ventures that he was sometimes away from the house for days or at meetings that continued late into the evenings. Laurent began to ask me about my marriage and the children and I told him only that David was quiet and reserved, but very generous. Seated at my piano, it would have seemed disloyal to reveal my concerns and the isolation I felt.

I was playing a scherzo when Laurent put his hand over mine. I thought he was about to correct my fingering, but instead he said:

"Why don't you come to my house at Kensington and we can go from there to St. James' Hall?"

I should have refused. Instead I agreed that it made sense, pretending I didn't know that Kensington was about four miles to the west of Regent Street and not at all on the way to the Quadrant. What was I thinking? After he had gone I went over the words he had used. But it wasn't the words—it was the way he looked at me with eyes that smiled. But perhaps I was mistaken.

I left the carriage at the Palace and started to walk. It was late March and the pavements were dotted with the first fallen blossoms.The trees were like pink candy and the painted facades of the houses were draped with woody branches of wisteria. I meandered for nearly an hour, round Edwarde's Square and through a covered walkway past a small church, St. Mary Abbot's. Across the main street, I came to Duchess of Bedford's Walk, passed through Holland Street and finally found myself in Pitt Street. The house had three storeys and no basement. Laurent opened the door before I knocked, as if he'd been standing there, waiting.

He led me upstairs to his room at the top of the house,

laughing:

"Now you can see where 'the Duke' lives."

He closed the door and we stood there, not speaking and then both expressing the same thought:

"I thought you wouldn't come."

"I wasn't going to come."

He was wearing a waistcoat in a plain cloth edged in braid. I remember it because I couldn't take my eyes off the lapels and the buttons as I was trying so hard not to look at his face. My frock had a close fitting bodice, long waisted and pointed in the front. It was fastened by hooks and eyes at the back.

chapter 17

How to make coffee:

The Turk roasts and pounds the berry at the moment he requires it, stews it with a very small quantity of water, and drinks it boiling hot, with the grounds, without either milk or sugar.

French coffee is very seldom either fresh or pure, the liquor from the boiled-up grounds of the preceeding day being very generally used.

English coffee: begin by procuring good berries (the Mocha are the best), roast them at home. Next grind the quantity you deem sufficient, put it into a broad-bottomed block tin or iron coffee pot, pour on boiling water, then put the pot on the fire and boil quickly, stirring all the while. As soon as the bubbles begin to rise, take the pot from the fire, pour out a cupful, hold it a couple of feet above the pot, and pour it back again; repeat this three or four times; give the pot a smart knock, to cause the grounds to settle, keep it warm but do not simmer. Strain through fine muslin. Fining with isinglass, salt, egg-shells or sole-skin always destroys the flavour and is quite unnecessary.

From How to Dine Well and Economically, by Tabitha Tickletooth

LONDON 1856—RACHEL

The first mistake was to go to the concerts. I should have stopped the lessons. But by then, it would still have been too late. When I was not with Laurent I tried to pretend that it was an infatuation, that I was bored with my life and excited by the prospect of an adventure. Nothing was further from the truth. I was in love with him and could think of only two things: an immense joy and a fear that what we were doing was wrong. Yet David had no knowledge of the outings. No suspicion. Not an inkling. Of that I am sure.

In April school was closed for two weeks at Easter. For the first days I was preoccupied with preparations for Passover and encouraged Solomon and Jonah to help. Of course they took no part in the cleaning; the scrubbing, the carpet beating, the boiling of silverware. They were charged with searching the rooms for leaven; crumbs from the seed cake that Emily made at this time of the year. Surprisingly, given his views on the details of *kashrut,* David took a great interest in the observance of the laws of Passover and insisted that every corner should be swept and pronounced free of the minutest speck of bread or flour. A mouse would have had a hungry search in those days before the Festival—the cupboards were bleached and spotless in readiness for the stocks of *matzah* and sweet almond cakes.

In the afternoons the boys went to spend time with my father. Since Reuven was their sole grandparent, he was more than happy with the regular arrangement. He had a collection of playthings waiting for them. Their favourites were the Game of Beasts and a Chinese puzzle. He also gave each of them a set of magic cards. When the Festival was over and the special plates were put away, the pattern of our lives returned to the rhythm of days when each of us pursued our own business. I left Betsy and Emily to run the house and as soon as I knew David was going to be away for a day I sent a note to Pitt Street and went to meet Laurent.

I walked up the steps, closing my silk parasol. I had told David I was going to buy finger bowls for dessert and arrived with the package in my hands. Laurent came towards me and put his arms round me. I looked over his shoulder at the calico curtains swaying in the breeze, at the clock on the narrow mantelpiece ticking loudly.

"Are those the finger bowls you had to buy?"

"Yes."

"Are they for one of your dinners?"

"Laurent. Please don't talk about that."

"Why, can't I talk about your life?"

"Not that part of my life."

I was pulling at my tight white gloves. He turned away and picked up a bottle of curaçao. He filled two small glasses and handed one to me.

"When is he back?"

"Tomorrow morning. But I have to be home before dark. My father is bringing back the boys ... "

"Rachel, we ... we can't go on like this. Stealing an hour or two ... "

And then he was stroking my hair, covering my face with kisses. I closed my eyes and all my intentions evaporated. There was sobbing, sweet kissing, a great explosion of love.

As I prepared to leave he leaned against the inside of the door and pleaded:

"Stay. Stay and eat with me."

"No, I can't. You know it's not possible."

By the side of the cherrywood bedstead was a small table. On it was a plate with a chunk of bread, some ham and a piece of cheese.

"I'll make you something hot to drink before you go. You like coffee, don't you?"

"Yes, but ... well, just one cup."

He went down the stairs and came back a few minutes later with a jug, a small cup and a larger one. He poured coffee into the *demitasse* for me and for himself he added some steaming milk.

"I know you like it strong. Will you have some bread? I wish I could buy a *baguette* but this English bread is all I can find."

"No, I'm not hungry."

"I'm sorry. I forgot. You don't eat ham, do you? I can't offer you any cake; not like the ones you give me in Finsbury Square."

"Laurent. Please stop. Don't keep talking about my

house."

We sat in silence while we drank the coffee. I began to walk to the door but I turned and threw my arms round him. I couldn't find the words to paint the anxiety of my mind. I was filled with a confused exhilaration. What started with a touching of hands and a kiss, so often ended with an argument and tears. Of course he wanted me to be with him for the whole night but I resisted all his invitations to stay.

Several months elapsed. My sleep was troubled. I often awoke before it was light. At least in the early hours I could dream of him undisturbed. Whether I was at home with David or in Pitt Street with Laurent there was an intangible uneasiness. Sometimes I would notice David glancing at me but his gaze never penetrated my thoughts. I could imagine him thinking:

> *My wife seems a little upset. Women can be bothered by trifles.*

We met less frequently during the summer. The boys were home from school and it was impossible for me to leave the house unnoticed. I needed to spend more time with them, filling the long days with activities and outings. I bought them a chess set and the new Game of the Lamplighter. I took them to the Egyptian Hall to see the magic of Maskelyne and Cook. We watched the dexterity of the plate spinning and then gasped as Mr. Maskelyne removed Mr. Cooke's head.

"Why don't you take them to hear Jullien?" asked Laurent. "They will love him—Louis Antoine is a showman. I could even come with you."

It is strange how foolish a woman can be when her

heart is breaking with love, for I almost agreed. In an effort to sound tranquil I said:

"No, that would be unwise."

I enquired about tickets. Covent Garden was full but there were a few left at Her Majesty's Theatre. Laurent was right. Solomon and Jonah loved the histrionic display and it kept them amused and attentive for several hours.

When they went back to school I slipped out in the middle of the day and my visits to Laurent began again. As we climbed the stairs, I started to say what I had been rehearsing in my mind on the journey:

"I shouldn't be here," I whispered.

"Don't talk," he said. We were standing by the small settee in his room.

"Sit there opposite so that I can look at you. I suppose what we have been doing is improper, but it is not in the least wicked."

He closed the shutters. He was holding something in his hands behind his back.

"I bought you some flowers, you said you like roses." He handed me a dozen blooms, just beginning to open, pink tipped with a sweet fragrance. He took one out, broke it off and slipped it into the bodice of my frock.

"You've pricked your finger," I said. "It's bleeding." I took out a handkerchief.

I began to pull the petals from one of the roses.

"These last weeks ... I have been close to despair ... I wanted so much to be with you."

"And me?" He picked up the petals that lay in a heap on the table. "How could I bear to stand behind the piano stool, waiting for you to turn and look at me, expecting at any moment that the maid would come in ... "

He took hold of my hand and ran his fingers over my nails. He used to tell me they looked so white, like almonds.

"Laurent, I must talk with you." I bit my lip, trying to take a tight grip on my heart.

"When we went to the concerts, everywhere there were prying eyes, folks who would stare. But what would people think ... if they knew?"

"No-one knows. Those people ... they have nothing. They move through life without touching it."

"And what about us? What about me? What am I doing to David? I have to stop seeing you."

Laurent was silent for what seemed like five minutes.

"But how can you stay with him, when your heart feels like this for me?"

He pressed his cheek close to mine and I felt the smoothness of his skin.

My judgment evaporated and in the next weeks we continued to meet. My days were spent in anticipation; dreaming of climbing the stairs to his room, closing the curtains on the world outside. Yet when I was there, I was tormented by guilt. I could hear David's voice, feel his hands, imagine the pain in his eyes if he knew.

Barely a month after I had resumed my visits to Pitt Street, I arrived one day in a state of anxiety. In the carriage I had been preparing my speech. When Laurent closed the door behind me and drew me inside he was holding a bunch of cornflowers—a vivid blue with a profusion of petals. I broke one off and slipped it into his buttonhole. It was then that he saw the tears in my eyes.

He pulled me towards him, squashing the flower as he pressed me against his chest. I lifted my face and whispered:

"It would have been better if he'd bought me a violin."

"Why?"

"Then you'd have had no reason to sit beside me on a piano stool."

"But I would have made sure you were holding the bow correctly."

I was thinking about that first touch of his fingers and began the speech I had been preparing:

"We have to end it."

"Why now, Rachel? I've managed the whole summer, sharing you with your children, but now we will have time again."

"It isn't right. I should never have let it start. I have to stop coming." I turned towards the door.

He touched my hand but he didn't speak.

"Please, let me go."

He was holding both my hands but his face was turned away.

I pulled one hand away and said:

"I wish it had never happened."

"Is that the truth?"

"Yes, it's the truth."

I didn't know I was capable of inflicting such hurt. I turned and left, looking back to see him standing at the door, as he had done those months before, but this time with a look of torment in his eyes. I felt a pain in my stomach. It reminded me of the time when Jonah had sliced the top of his finger with a knife and I looked at the open wound and the blood and felt the cut in my own hand.

chapter 18

1946—October 19th. Under a Treasury Order, travellers leaving Britan can now carry £20 sterling.

1948—March 16th. Restrictions on foreign travel are being withdrawn. Sir Stafford Cripps, the Chancellor of the Exchequer, announced in the House of Commons that tourist travel will be permitted to Austria, Denmark, France, Italy, the Netherlands, Norway, Portugal and Switzerland

From UK Government directives

LONDON 1948—ANNA

There was no notepaper with a black border. When someone you love walks away without a word there is no funeral, no closing chapter. For Anna the loss of her brother was as real as if he had died a sudden death; a chasm in her life, as deep as if it had been caused by a heart attack or cancer. Overnight there was no more contact. Now that the Government had lifted restrictions on travel he might have gone abroad. Who knows whether he was in London or Australia: the distance was immaterial. Two years had passed since the day when he walked out. On her birthday Anna would open her cards slowly. There would always be a poem from Nathan, a sweet verse declaring how much he loved her. There was never anything from Isaac.

There were constant reminders. She would turn to look at a man wearing thick glasses and realize it wasn't Isaac. Every time the phone rang she hoped, for a brief moment, that the voice would be his. She continued to hear his words going round her head: the way he called her 'Sis', the good-humoured requests for yet another loan: *'come on Sis, it's only fifty, I'll pay it back.'*

She missed Joel too, with his serious brown eyes and the way he would never finish a sentence. She even missed his bitten fingernails and the way he lost his temper playing games with Nina. They had played together three or four times a week for six years and then one day he wasn't there. Nina couldn't understand why Joel had disappeared. In the first few days she kept asking for him. Anna's reluctance to confront the truth and the natural hesitation of parents to reveal any flaws in their family led to a virtual silence on the subject. Nina pretended that nothing was wrong. Yet though she rarely mentioned her cousin, she wandered around the house, unable to play on her own. Joel had been like a brother; one minute they would be giggling over a new game and the next, she would be shrieking at him, saying he had cheated and it wasn't fair.

Anna remembered an afternoon when they were both three. The children were getting ready to go to a birthday party. Nina was wearing a smocked dress with short puffed sleeves. She wriggled as her mother fixed a ribbon in her hair. Nathan had been putting a picture on the wall, knocking in a nail with a hammer, and he left the hammer on a low table. Joel began to tease Nina, pulling at the ribbon. Most small children might resort to a pinch or a shove to resolve a quarrel. Nina picked up the hammer and hit her cousin on the head. A line of blood trickled from his forehead. He took a long breath and then started to cry, his screams reaching the neighbours' garden, making them look up from watering their potato plants. Inside, Nina was still holding the hammer, yelling at Joel that it was all his fault.

The ribbon was on the floor; it was entwined with a few strands of her hair. Joel kept sobbing as he fingered his bruise. Nina wouldn't stop crying. Of course neither of them went to the party. Anna stayed in the house to find witch hazel and plasters, and Nathan put Nina in the push chair and began to wheel her out of the house, along Walm Lane and up the hill towards the railway. When they got to Lydford Road they stopped on the bridge to look down at the railway line. Nathan said very little. Nina watched as several trains passed and stopped at the station. When she got tired of waiting for the next one she agreed that they were ready to go back. By the time they got to the house Isaac had already taken Joel home. Anna was ironing a pile of linen. Nina rushed into her arms and it was then that she began to understand what she had done. As Anna explained that a head wasn't like a ball, but more like a fragile bubble, there was a smell of burning. The iron had singed a dark yellow mark on the pillow case. Nathan lifted it off, took Nina's hand and went to read her a story.

Nina claimed that she didn't like boys. She preferred to play with the cat, a crossbreed that seemed to have no owner. When it first squeezed its way into the house she offered it a few drops of milk in a saucer; by the end of the week Anna was boiling up bits of stale fish that she'd bought from MacFisheries just before closing time. It was agreed that the cat could stay.

When Joel heard that the cat had remarkable eyes—one green and one blue—he brought a friend, Richard, to see if it was true. The boys agreed that the eyes were in fact different and gleefully told Nina that the cat was probably blind. They played with it for a few minutes, but at the first scratch they lost interest and disappeared into Nina's bedroom while she stayed downstairs, chasing the cat under the table, trying to lift it on to her knee. Joel and Richard were acting out a scene involving gangsters and the police. They needed an extra character. Nina's gollowog, Oggy, seemed to be the best candidate. Joel didn't quite see how he would fit the role of troublemaker or policeman, but he liked the golliwog's face and clothes. He was trying to take off his striped trousers and waistcoat when Richard, wanting to get on with the game, started to pull one of the legs. Joel held on tight to the other leg and both boys yanked and heaved until one of them fell over. The sound of ripping fabric made them drop the golliwog on the floor. At that moment Nina appeared in the doorway. When she saw Oggy, ripped up the middle, stuffing oozing out in lumps, she began to shake and shout. She was crying big, wet bubbles of tears. She picked up the golliwog and tried to push the bits of his inside back.

Hearing the cries and shouting Anna rushed upstairs to see what was going on.

Nina was gasping and holding her breath. Her beloved gollywog was lying on the floor, the trousers torn and the buttons hanging off the velvet waistcoat. While her daughter sobbed '*They've spoiled him*' Anna started to look for Oggy's mouth: the yellow smile had come unstuck and was lying on the carpet with a pile of kapok stuffing. Anna took the golliwog and sat with Nina on the stairs, promising she would take Oggy to hospital. His treatment would be painless and quick. Three days later he reappeared with slightly thinner legs and neat stitches up the inside of his trousers.

Richard never came to play again. But Joel was forgiven and their games continued; pirates and gangsters, 'operations' on each other done with imaginary scalpels and bandages. On a cold January day they decided to warm up the cat which had come in with snow on its fur. Joel heaved open the oven door and Nina lifted up the cat. She tried to push it in, but there was a large casserole in the way. The cat scampered away but was caught and dunked in a hot bath instead.

On Sunday mornings Nathan settled himself in the kitchen for the weekly shoe cleaning ritual. He would spread newspapers over the lino floor and begin the task of polishing five pairs of shoes. It was an odd sight. He'd come in, take off his battered hat and the old jacket and roll up the sleeves of his shirt. He might remember to lift the trouser legs so they wouldn't crease at the knees before beginning the process of smearing black or brown polish on each shoe. Then he would take a brush and pass it rhythmically across the leather until each pair shone. A final buff with a duster and the shoes were in a row, gleaming. The job took about an hour. As he worked Nathan would make the odd comment:

"Where's the *shtik* put my spare laces?" Anna ignored his reference to Beatrice, who never touched his things while she was cleaning or ironing.

"You can't get decent boot polish any more—it's not like the good old days."

Everything, in Nathan's view, was better before the war—preferably before the first war.

"Did you know that Prince Charles was christened in the Gold Music Room at Buckingham Palace? I doubt if his parents can play a note."

None of these pronouncements required a response but Anna couldn't resist a remark about his obsessive shoe polishing:

"Why do you take so much trouble with your shoes when you look so ... so ... "

"Don't start about my clothes," he interrupted.

"I don't understand. You don't mind going out in a battered old hat but your shoes have to be shining."

"Clothes don't matter. Shoes are what people look at. Educated people don't have dirty shoes."

Nathan had such fixed ideas. Certain things had to be done properly. There was no discussion. It must have been hard for him to become a father at the age of fifty. He had no experience of babies or small children but he knew how to tell stories. He used to tell Nina about his travels and show her photographs he'd taken with his box brownie. He brought out sets of Players cigarette cards and let her sort them by colour or uniform. He had an album with postcards of his favourite music hall stars. But when Nina wanted to know what was written on the reverse, he quickly turned them over so all she could see was a picture of Vesta Tilley or Zena Dare.

Anna had thought she could have some influence on him; change some of his habits, but although she would have liked more company he wanted to be left in peace. *'Leave me be'* he'd say if she suggested going out or inviting friends for a meal. He had no need of company and disliked social occasions. He pretended to forget the names of their friends and embarrassed Anna by asking them outrageous questions. At fifty-eight all he wanted was time to read the biographies he brought back from the library. He immersed himself in stories about F.E. Smith the famous criminal barrister, repeating them endlessly to the family. But while F.E. Smith could get away with offensive comments to judges, Nathan's outspoken remarks were less well received. Anna found herself giving in to his desire to stay at home, rather than risk an awkward social encounter.

His professional work was beginning to pick up again. After the war years when there was hardly any call for patent agents, Nathan was happy to be back in the office. He had a meticulous way of filing and dictated letters so slowly that his secretary had no need to use shorthand, but could write every word in the neatest handwriting. At home he enjoyed sitting by the coal fire, wearing a pair of worn slippers.

It was through the synagogue that they were introduced to a couple called Jaffé. Janine and Jacques had recently arrived in England after spending the war years in occupied France. They had a son called Raoul, a boy of nine, with straight brown hair, a serious expression, and glasses that he pushed on to his nose every few minutes. It was decided that he should go to the same school as Nina though as she was a year younger, he wouldn't be in her class.

Anna told Janine that it was perfectly all right for the children to travel the few stops together on the bus, without an adult. The Jaffés were horrified. Had they gone through the terrors of Nazi occupation for their only son to be abducted by a stranger or killed while he was crossing the road? Nathan understood why they were fearful but he also knew why his wife was so keen for Nina to be independent. It was all connected with Anna's childhood. Dina had made such efforts to protect her children that she refused to give them any freedom. They were hardly allowed out of her sight when they were young and the first time Anna went away, to visit a cousin, she received a letter from Dina with every post, sometimes twice a day. Because Anna had never slept alone and had always shared a bedroom with her mother, she had been determined not to interfere when Nina closed the door to her room and put up a notice saying "Keep Out." As a result she knew little of what was going on in her daughter's life.

When Nina was nine she left the primary school and was enrolled at a private girls' school. For her parents this was a step up in the world; an entrance to a better education with girls from good families. For Nina it turned out to be a daily torment.

On the first day the girls lined up for the form photograph. They were all wearing the regulation uniform—a navy skirt with a striped blouse. Seated in the front row, in a hand-sewn cotton dress with a sash was a small girl with wavy brown hair. That was Nina. If the photo had been in colour her face would have been red with shame. Her uniform hadn't arrived in time so she had to wear one of the dresses her mother had made.

Clothes were a big embarrassment for Nina. While the other girls talked about buying skirts and blouses from chain stores she had dresses made from Liberty prints. While Anna pinned up the hem, Nina would squirm and ask:

"Why can't I have a bought dress like anyone else? They get theirs from C & A."

"Exactly," said Anna. "You know what that stands for: Cheap and Awful."

Anna wanted her daughter to look pretty. And that included having pretty hair. There was nothing wrong with the way Nina looked. She had a sweet face, framed with shiny dark hair. But Anna thought it should be curly, so every night she sat her daughter on a stool and divided her hair into strands. Strips of white cotton, cut from an old sheet, were wrapped round each strand of hair and tied into a knot. Nina had to get used to the rags pressing into her head as she lay down on the pillow. The next morning when she took them out, her hair was a cascade of curls. It didn't make her feel pretty. It made her resolve to grow her hair into long thick plaits which wouldn't need to be curled.

Nina tried to explain to her mother why she desperately wanted to have long hair. There had been endless discussions about it. Anna thought it was easier to manage short hair. Nina wanted to have plaits. She decided that if she couldn't have real ones she would have the next best thing. She found some pieces of brown wool, divided them into three piles and formed them into pigtails. Then in the secrecy of her bedroom she fixed them to either side of her head with hairclips and swung her head from side to side, feeling the long 'hair' on her shoulders. When it was time to go to sleep she took off the clips and hid the plaits under the pillow.

At school Nina had problems that were more significant. She came home one day and told Anna she was in trouble.

"What do you mean, trouble?"

"I can't tell you. It's too awful."

"It can't be that bad, darling. Tell me what it is."

"No. It's nothing."

Because Anna didn't want to interfere she let the matter drop. A few days later she was summoned to the school for a meeting with Nina's form mistress.

"We're worried about your daughter. Nina can't sew."

Anna smiled with relief.

"Have you brought me all the way from Cricklewood to tell me that? It's taken me an hour to get here." Then, regretting her sharp reaction, she changed her tone:

"I'm sorry that she can't do cross stitch. Is there a problem with her maths and spelling too?"

It was not long before the real cause of the trouble emerged. Nina had been stealing from the girls in her class. At first it was small things like a hair slide or a fancy pencil case. A week later she walked into the cloakroom to see a pair of shiny patent shoes on the floor next to her coat. She picked one up and slipped the strap over the button. She looked at her own brown sandals and then she lifted down her shoebag, pushed in the black pumps and hung it back on her peg. Days passed and the class were asked to search for the lost shoes. Nina kept quiet. She added more items to the bag with her name on it: a leather purse with punched holes, a small box of Caran d'Ache crayons.

Anna was summoned to the school. If only she had picked up the message that her daughter was in trouble she might have avoided the scene that followed. Nina was waiting in the headmistress' study and the shoe bag was on the desk. She was simply asked to tip the contents out on to the floor.

chapter 19

STUFFED BREAST OF LAMB *(SERVES 4)*

3 breasts of lamb, 4 large onions, 2 oz beef fat, 1–2 fl oz water, 4 oz fresh bread-crumbs, small bunch fresh parsley, 6 large potatoes

Ask the butcher to bone the lamb breasts. Trim off the fat and flatten them with a rolling pin. Chop one of the onions and leave the rest whole. Fry the chopped on-ion in a little beef fat. Make the stuffing with the fried onion, parsley, breadcrumbs and a little water. Spread the mixture over the breasts of lamb and roll them up. Tie with string.

Put the rest of the beef fat in a tin. Roast the stuffed lamb, the potatoes and the onions in a hot oven Gas Mark 7 for quarter of an hour. Turn the heat down to Gas Mark 5 and cook for another hour till everything is brown and tender.

From Anna's notebook, 1949

A heavy smell hung over the school dining room. The serving tins were heaved on to the table: potatoes roasted hours earlier sitting in a pool of fat and globules of congealed mincemeat submerged in a mud-coloured liquid. Nina pushed some overboiled cabbage round her plate. She was the only Jewish girl in her class. No-one knew about the laws of *kashrut* or why she couldn't eat ham or pork. The teachers had invited the girls to talk about their people, meaning their families, but it didn't take long before Nina realized that her 'people' were different from everyone else's. Penelope and Arabella were blonde and had never met anyone who lived north of the river. Serena and Heather belonged to a tennis club. None of them rushed home to Hebrew classes twice a week or celebrated New Year in September.

When Anna found out that Nina wasn't eating anything at lunchtime she offered to send her with sandwiches. The suggestion was refused. There were only two possibilities: eat the lunch at school or go home. Since Cricklewood was too far to go in the middle of the day Anna came up with another solution. Nina was to have lunch with the local Rabbi and his wife. Rabbi Senitt lived a hundred yards from the school. His wife seemed happy to have a small girl join them for half an hour while they ate their kosher meal. For Nina it was a disastrous plan. She came to dread the short walk to the house; sitting with the elderly couple, trying to think of something to say as they brought out soup, *gedempte* meat balls and mounds of mashed potato. It was bad enough having to eat food that wasn't the same as her mother's. She knew that something was expected of her—a polite finishing of everything on the plate and answers to questions about her class and the school lessons. As the weeks progressed she became silent, asking for smaller portions, eager to leave the table and get back to school.

Because she went out for lunch Nina had few friends. She'd sit down at her desk to find cliques of girls talking behind her back. She was never in the club. The leader, the one in charge, was Rhona, with perfect skin and curly eyelashes. But it wasn't her looks that set her aside from the others. She was the one who 'knew'. What was it she knew? Well, that was a secret. If you were in her crowd, she would tell you. She would tell how it was done. She might even give details of how her parents did it. Nina heard the whispering and walked away.

For her tenth birthday she planned a party. She wrote invitations and sent them to a dozen girls in her class. The replies came back, one after the other, saying that Cricklewood was too far away, or they were busy. Only two girls accepted. Anna suggested she should invite Raoul, but that would have meant Janine and Jacques coming too. They went everywhere together and, apart from sending their son to school, they wouldn't let him out of their sight. Nina protested that it would be too embarrassing. It was bad enough that her father was bald and looked like her grandfather. Inviting a French-speaking family who spoke too loud would be an even greater humiliation.

To make up for the lack of school friends, Nina decided to invite two boys she'd met walking down Walm

Lane. On Tuesdays and Thursdays she went straight from school to Hebrew classes at Cricklewood synagogue. Derek and his brother lived in the next street. They went to the local school and had scuffed shoes and black hair that was smoothed down with brilliantine. Nina could hardly believe her mother's reaction: 'Make an excuse and tell them the party has been cancelled'. Anna hadn't even met them; she'd certainly never heard the language they used when they joked together. Nina argued that her mother was a snob. Anna had heard enough from Nina's garrulous accounts of her brief acquaintance with the boys to know that it was a bad idea to invite these boys with the girls from school. She tried to explain that it was possible to move in different worlds, but trying to create a social mix of people from contrasting backgrounds needed more skill than her daughter had at the age of ten.

The party was a disaster. Nina told the boys they weren't invited after all, and was left with just the two girls who had accepted. They played games and for tea Anna brought out sandwiches, cut into fancy shapes. The girls put one or two on their plates and then asked what was in them. Each sandwich was an unpleasant surprise: cod's roe, cream cheese with olive, or egg and anchovy. Their plates went back untouched.

Nina was the only one eating. Anna cleared the table and brought out the cake. She'd been saving the sugar ration for two weeks and had produced a sponge filled with strawberries and a custardy cream. Nina was wishing she'd had a bought cake and a plate of Penguin biscuits.

To make up for the party, Anna asked Nina if she'd like

to invite Derek for supper. A few days later she brought him home after their Hebrew lesson. They were both starving. The only thing they'd had to eat since lunch was a snack at the class where they were each given a sticky poppyseed bun. They spent the next hour picking at their teeth, trying to remove the gritty seeds with their nails, unable to concentrate on the *aleph bet* and the stories of brave pioneers in the deserts of Israel.

When they walked into the house in Walm Lane there was a smell of roasting meat. Nathan pulled up a chair for Derek and they all sat down at the kitchen table. Anna brought on a tureen of soup. The bone stock had been bubbling away with vegetables all afternoon. The soup was to fill them up before the main course. There was a small amount of meat—no chops or shoulders of lamb, but a boned-out roast made from the breast. It was filled with a stuffing of fried onions, breadcrumbs and herbs. The potatoes were roasted around the edge of the tin, crispy and brown.

Derek handed back the empty soup bowl and licked his spoon. He and Nina began to laugh about the poppy seed buns and the teacher.

"'E rolls up this newspaper an' 'e flicks it at our ears, like this," he said, demonstrating with a napkin.

As soon as the main course was put in front of him Derek started to eat. He didn't wait for the others. He spoke with his mouth full:

"I don't half like this meat, Mrs. G" he said.

The summer term came to an end and Nina was to transfer to the senior school. To help her forget the humiliations of the stealing incident and the party, Anna planned a holiday with the Jaffés. Nathan would have preferred to stay at home, but because Janine and Jacques had become close friends, he was prepared to consider it.

The French couple were complete opposites: Jacques was tall and well groomed, with a well fitting sports jacket. A faint scent of cologne followed him into the room. Janine was under five foot tall and wore high heels and tight skirts to the knee. A slash of scarlet lipstick was slicked over her lips, as if she never used a mirror. She was finding it hard to settle in England, missing the sound of the French language and the familiar way of life they'd been used to before the war. Whereas she talked about cafés and *haute couture* he concerned himself with Raoul's schooling and his future. Neither of them said a word about what they had gone through during the occupation.

Janine walked into the kitchen and pinched Nathan's cheek:

"Natan, you 'ave to come with us. You are offul. You don't take Anna anywhere. And your clothes ... why you look so offul?"

He looked up: "I'm cleaning my shoes, look at them."

"But the rest, the trousers are so—how you say, like a bag."

"Baggy", said Jacques. "Leave him alone. He's promised to come. Now tell me about Weymouth. Is it like Nice or Juan?"

196

"Not exactly, there are no casinos," smiled Anna.

It was settled. Jacques, Janine and Raoul were to join them in the house they'd rented on the south coast. They spent the days on the beach, with Anna providing tomato sandwiches, wrapped in greaseproof paper. Nina complained about the swimming costume that Anna had knitted for her. It wasn't the colour; it was the shape. When she came out of the sea the waterloggged garment sagged to her knees, giving off the sour smell of wet wool. Nathan didn't hear her complaints as he sat in a deckchair reading. After supper the children went to their room, Nina smarting from the reddened patches of sunburn on her back and Raoul scratching at the mosquito bites that covered his legs and arms.

When the children were in bed the French couple began to talk. For the first time they spoke about the mistake they had made in 1941.

"We should have left before the ban on emigration."

Jacques could tell that Anna and Nathan were too embarrassed to ask, but clearly wanted to know what had happened.

"But after that we couldn't get out."

He described how they walked all the way to the Swiss border. They each took a small suitcase with some clothes, but on the way they tipped half of them out.

Janine explained:

"We had to carry Raoul and our feet were sore from the shoes." She stopped for a moment and then went on:

"And then we got there and the frontier police sent us back. It was, how you say? the French Militia. I remember how we pleaded ... but we were so terrified of them.

Everyone was."

Janine dropped her head and looked down. Anna didn't know how to respond. She waited a few minutes for Jacques to continue:

"We made our way to a small place near Lake Geneva, Saint-Gingolph, I think it was called. We were trying to find a room to stay. Suddenly we saw a woman falling from the fourth floor of a hotel. She had thrown herself out. That noise when she hit the *terre* ... the ground. Ay."

They were all silent till Janine took up the story again:

"We found a truck ... someone who would take us. Of course we had to pay. I had two rings and notes that we had sewn into the bottom of our coats. We wanted to go to Lyon but he left us at a village in the hills, Sainte-Claire-à-Caluire. It turned out to be for the best—it was harder for them to round up Jews in a mountainous area."

Over the next week the Jaffés described their life, hiding in a barn, sometimes waiting days for the farmer to bring them food. Nathan was imagining the danger for all of them; how the farmer must have been terrified at the risk he was taking. None of them wanted to mention the other fear: of being taken to Drancy, the 'collection centre'. Jacques was remembering the packed trains leaving from Lyon; the priests on the platform arrested for sheltering people. He described the day when the Nazis sent two vans to an orphanage in a village called Izieu where they rounded up forty-four children and sent them to join 15,000 other Jews waiting in the Winter Velodrome in Drancy.

"I don't know how they knew, but the children had a name for Auschwitz. They called in Pitchipoi."

They were all silent, aware of the gulf between them. Anna and Nathan had thought that food rationing was a problem. How could they imagine what their friends had endured for four years?

Jacques was the first to speak:

"When did you know in England? When did it become known what had happened in the camps?"

"We heard it in '45. That radio broadcast from Belsen when the camp was liberated."

Anna didn't say a word. She was thinking of how she'd been so frightened of the bombing in London. She wondered what it must have been like to live in fear of marching boots, a thumping on the door.

For the next few years Anna and Nathan shared summer holidays with the Jaffés. They took the train to Broadstairs and Torquay and once ventured north to Scarborough. Nina wanted to go somewhere else. She'd grown into a teenager with strong opinions, wearing tight waisted skirts and fine knitted boleros. Anna persuaded her out of the backless sundress in white cotton piqué, saying it was not suitable for a fifteen year old. The velvet shoes with stiletto heels were under discussion. Also at issue was which seaside town to visit next. One of Nina's school friends had stayed in a kosher hotel in Bournemouth.

"I don't want to go to Bournemouth," said Nathan.

"Why not?" asked Nina. "It's got a putting green and a lift from the top of the cliffs down to the sands."

"I don't want to go," said Nathan.

"Leave it," said Anna. "Your father doesn't want to go there."

"But why?" persisted Nina.

"Just leave it. He doesn't want to talk about it."

Nina wondered why her father was so adamant but she knew better than to carry on the argument. That year, 1954, they went to the Irish lakes. If they'd gone to Bournemouth they could have eaten kosher meat. But in Killarney there was plenty of fish. The Jaffés were happy with whatever they were offered. One evening there was soup on the menu.

"Not for me, thanks," said Anna.

"Why not?" asked Janine. "It's vegetable."

"But it's made with meat stock, probably ham bones."

"How do you know?" asked Janine.

"It's like the peas, they put little bits of ham in them— they put it in everything." Anna turned up her nose.

"I don't understand" said Jacques. "We would have been happy to have a little piece of sausage; when you are starving, you don't think about things like that."

Anna felt embarrassed. Nina was pushing a piece of fish with her fork.

"It's 'things like that' that have kept the Jews going, not a piece of sausage," said Nina.

Everyone at the table stopped talking. The sudden outburst was a surprise. Nina, usually silent at meal-times, launched into a defence of her belief in God. Raoul stared at her without saying a word. Janine argued that she couldn't believe in a God who allowed evil to prevail. Nina answered in a quiet voice:

"Of course you know there's a God. Just because he hides sometimes, it doesn't mean He's not there."

Raoul gazed at her with a look of admiration that would have been appropriate if he'd been listening to Albert Einstein explaining his Theory of Relativity.

The next day Nina and Raoul went off to explore the town and walk round the lake. Several four-wheel carriages were lined up and the drivers were standing by their ponies, looking for business. One of them was a young man of about eighteen. He called out and asked if they wanted to go for a drive.

"No thanks, we're walking," said Raoul.

The driver looked at Nina and winked. She looked back at him and smiled.

"I'll do it for half price," he said.

"No, really. We'd rather walk."

Raoul started to walk faster and Nina had to run to catch up with him. They walked round the lake for an hour but the weather was changing. The sun had gone in and there were dark clouds overhead. A few drops of rain began to fall and Raoul started to run.

"I can't keep up with you," called Nina.

"Come on, we're going to get wet."

"Well, I can't run in these shoes." Nina was wearing pointed toed shoes with a heel.

"Take them off then."

"Don't be daft. I can't do that."

At that moment the pony and trap appeared in the

distance. The young driver was heading straight in their direction. He stopped beside Nina.

"I'll take the young lady for nothing. But I've no room for the both of you."

Nina climbed up and the other three passengers made a space for her. She looked at Raoul and then looked back at the driver who was winking at her again.

The pony and trap arrived back in minutes. Raoul was left walking round the lake for another hour. When he got back he was completely soaked.

chapter 20

SCONES—(MAKES 12—14)

8 oz self raising flour, 1 level tsp baking powder, ½ oz sugar, 1 oz butter, 5 fl oz fresh or soured milk

Shake the flour and baking powder through a sieve to get rid of any lumps. Rub in the butter and stir in the sugar. (It should be crumbly.) Add the milk and stir till the mixture comes together into a ball. Sprinkle flour on a board and knead the dough quickly till smooth. Level the top with a rolling pin—it should be about ¾" thick. Cut into rounds and arrange them on a greased baking tray. Brush the tops with a little milk and bake in a hot oven (450°F gas 8) for about 10 minutes. When they are cooled, pull them gently in half. Have ready a bowl of thick cream and some strawberry jam.

From Anna's notebook, 1956

The letter from Freda was dated March 9th and had a second class stamp. The news came as a shock—Isaac had died of a heart attack. The burial had already taken place. Anna had always believed that they would make up their quarrel, but it had lasted for eleven years: eleven years of silence from his side. The first year was the hardest. Anna simply couldn't believe that her brother was no longer a part of her life; that Joel wouldn't grow up with Nina. Each year, as she prepared for the Passover *Seder,* she hesitated as she set the table, wondering whether to add three extra place settings. After all, they always left a wine cup for the prophet Elijah in the hope that he would come. There was a similar chance that her brother's family might ring the doorbell at the last minute.

Anna couldn't bring herself to tell her friends that she had no contact with Isaac—apart from Janine and Jacques, who knew the whole story and, having little family of their own, understood how Anna was feeling about the rift with her brother. When people asked after him she told them that Isaac was fine and that he'd moved away. Boni was more practical and tried to reach him through Joel; she'd sent a letter to the last known address and had received a reply:

> *"Thanks for your note, Aunt Boni. We're all well but Dad would prefer you not to write to me."*

And now he was dead. Any hopes of rebuilding the relationship were shattered. Anna prepared to sit *shiva.* She took a pair of scissors and made a cut in her blouse. Should it be on the right or the left? Did it matter? The custom came from the time when mourners would rend their clothes in anguish. Would they have stopped to consider where to make the first tear? In the sitting room the fire was going out. Anna took the tongs and put more coals on to the grate, waiting for the flames to bring some heat into the room. She found a book of psalms that had belonged to her mother. She sat reading, wishing for visitors to come and comfort her. But no one knew. Not even the Jaffés. They were making plans for Raoul to go to university in France and she didn't want to disturb them with a piece of bad news that would remind them of their own losses during the war. So she told no-one and didn't even contact the Rabbi. There was no evening service and no memorial prayer. Only the flickering of a *jahrzeit* candle that burned for seven days.

A few weeks later Nathan made a gesture to help her get over the loss:

"Anna, dear. Why don't I take you abroad on holiday?"

She thought she'd misheard. Maybe he'd said he could afford a holiday. For once Anna had no enthusiasm for going away. Nathan suggested they should wait till the beginning of June for warmer weather, which made Anna think he was already changing his mind. But the planning was already in progress. It was decided that they should start in Rome and travel from there to Venice and Pisa. Nathan brought guide books from the library and they discussed whether to fly or to go by boat and train. There was one factor that made them uneasy. They would be away on Nina's seventeenth birthday. The problem was not that they were leaving her alone—she could go and stay with Boni for a fortnight. The dilemma was more complicated: for some months their daughter had been in a situation that caused them concern.

It had nothing to do with school. Nina's life seemed to be running smoothly. She couldn't wait to leave in the mornings for a game of tennis before the first lesson. In the afternoons she was in the team on the lacrosse field. She did well in exams, picking up Latin with ease and choosing to specialize in three modern languages for her A-level year. Her social life was centred on her two closest friends, Eva and Rosemary. She sat next to them in class and saved a place for each of them at the lunch table. In science they worked on the same bench, comparing experiments and sharing test tubes. In the art class they would chatter and giggle over their attempts at life drawing. At the end of the day, they'd walk to the station together, squashing their regulation school hats into their bags. When Nina got home she would pick up the phone and have a half hour conversation with each of them.

And then the phone calls stopped. In the holidays Nina had been to a dance one evening, and that had changed everything. She told her parents with excitement:

"I've met someone wonderful. He's Moroccan. We spent the whole evening speaking French."

The man was called Samir. He had sultry eyes and dark eyebrows. His face reminded her of one of her film idols, Mario Lanza, a star with a huge voice and equally large frame. For a couple of years, since she was fifteen, she had been taking herself to the local cinema, sitting in the vast auditorium of the State Kilburn. She'd buy a choc ice and listen to the Wurlitzer organ as she waited in the interval between the B film and the main feature. When the lights went down Nina could no longer tell whether it was Caruso himself or Mario Lanza on the screen, but she was convinced that he was singing to her alone. Samir had the same effect on her, but he was considerably thinner.

What Anna saw was different. There was something about him she didn't like. Nathan thought it was because he was older—about thirty—but with the age gap between him and Anna, there was little he could say on that score. Nina was obsessed with Samir and talked about him at every meal:

"He thinks I should do my hair like this, what do you think?"

"Samir says I shouldn't wear big petticoats. They're not elegant."

"Samir is the most brilliant dancer. Samir ... "

Anna hoped the infatuation would pass. Nathan wanted Nina to go to university.

"I suppose the Moroccan is coming round again," he said one evening.

"Could you be a bit nicer to him if he does?" asked Nina.

"I will if he stops talking about settling down and having ten children."

Anna and Nathan left for Rome on the 4th June. It was the first time they'd been away alone since their honeymoon and when they weren't talking about their daughter they were writing her letters. They wrote home almost every day, telling Nina and Boni the details of their trip.

Anna joked that Nathan was expecting to be confronted by brigands at every turn. If you went abroad, you were bound to be the victim of a gang of thieves. Nathan knew you couldn't trust foreigners. In Rome he was proved right—they were jostled by a crowd of young men at the railway station and when they got on the train Nathan saw that his wallet was missing. He consoled himself with the thought that the brigands hadn't found the pocket with the travellers' cheques. Anna was not sorry to leave Rome; her feet were sore and she was tired of looking at ruins.

They were concerned about managing their money. Cigarettes were cheap at 3s. 4d for twenty but a boiled egg for breakfast cost them 2s. Anna wrote proudly:

"What a swindle. We soon put a stop to that by not having any more."

Nathan was in good form, talking to the Italians, making jokes and getting in little digs that most of them didn't understand. They went to buy fruit at a small shop and while Anna was choosing peaches, Nathan looked at the owner—a very large woman—and opened his dictionary. In perfect Italian he asked:"how are you, my little one?" Anna thought the woman was going to hit him.

At the hotel Nathan made remarks to the staff in the dining room. Anna asked the waiter if he'd met many English people. He replied:

"Like the Signore? No. But in our training we took lessons in psychology to help us with such people."

While they were away Nina saw Samir every day. Since he had no car they went by bus to the cinema and on picnics. In the evenings they went dancing. Samir held her close as the saxophone played. He whirled her round and whispered in her ear. On the fourth night they were in a crowded hall, dancing to the slow beat of *"Blueberry Hill"*. Nina felt her insides were melting. Her handsome partner moved her gently away from his cheek and started to swing. The sound of *"Wake up Little Susie"* filled the dance hall and she knew he was going to ask her to marry him that night.

Anna kept the letters coming:

> *"Please don't get too involved whilst we are away so that we have an awkward situation to handle when we come back. I don't think Daddy and I do that kind of thing very well! By the way I've bought a pair of sandals that Janine would say look 'offul'.*
>
> *fond love*
>
> *Mummy"*
>
> *PS I've been very good but this afternoon I ate a huge strawberry sundae (which cost 5s). Your Dad had a cup of tea."*

Nina replied:

> *"How do I wash my can-can petticoat? Someone said I should do it in the bath so all the layers don't get creased. By the way, Aunt Boni is teaching me to make a dress from a pattern. What does 'cut two on fold' mean?"*

Samir had proposed and Nina had accepted. She planned to tell her parents when they arrived home. She was unsettled. Samir had talked about where they would live and what she should wear but had never said the words 'I love you'.

Nathan's next letter was about the Leaning Tower of Pisa. The guide spoke good English and explained the history to the group.

"When he'd finished I took him to one side and introduced myself as the head of an important English firm of constructional engineers. I told him that if they would entrust me with the work, I was sure that in four to five years my firm could bring the Tower back to the vertical position."

Anna added:

"The guide took him quite seriously. He was horrified."

At the end of the letter she put in a PS:

"You know, darling, you never really know a man till you live with him, and as it isn't the done thing to do that before marriage, the future is always a bit of a gamble."

Although Nina had told them nothing about Samir's proposal, Nathan must have suspected what was going on because he wrote in more detail:

"In matters like this most people would agree that age and the accompanying experience of life count for something, and after all I am about on the last lap whilst you are only just out of your childhood. What I find is that in a vital matter that would affect your whole future you should not make up your mind too hastily. At seventeen you still have practically everything to learn of the world in general, manners and men (generically and individually!) and you should have

the opportunity of making a more extended acquaintance with young people like yourself on the threshold of adult life. So go steady my dear and above all cherish your freedom whilst you are still in the formative years."

When they returned Nina was at London airport to meet them. It was then that she told them she was engaged to Samir.

Nathan's reaction was calm.

"Ask him to come and see us, darling. I'd like to talk to him."

"What are you going to say?" whispered Anna, while Nina was helping to find their suitcases. "You're hardly going to tell the Moroccan that you think he is shifty and we don't want him to marry our daughter."

"Leave it to me."

Samir turned up the following day and they all sat in the drawing room. Anna brought in a tray with the camel teapot and four cups and saucers. On the trolley was a plate of scones. There was a shuffling of feet and uncomfortable glances before Nathan began:

"So, you and Nina are engaged?"

Samir looked uncomfortable. It was clear he didn't know what to do with his scone. He watched as Nina spooned on some cream and topped it with a dollop of jam.

Nathan continued:

"She's very young. We just want to be sure you're doing the right thing. I'd like to make a suggestion."

Samir waited for him to go on:

"Don't announce the engagement now. Wait six

211

months. Then if you still feel the same, go ahead."

There was a long silence. Samir ran his fingers through his hair and without looking at Nina replied:

"I don't think so."

What did he mean? A look of shock crossed Nina's face.

Samir looked at her parents and said:

"I want to get married. I don't want to wait."

They understood what he was saying. Nina opened her mouth to speak and then stopped and left the room. Samir left without finishing his tea.

For three days Nina didn't speak to her parents. She was furious and blamed them for wrecking her engagement. On the fourth day she came down to breakfast and announced:

"When I leave school I'm going to get a job. I've decided not to go to university. It's lucky really, I could have been married."

The days of silence had made her realize what a fool she had been. Samir never loved her. He was always comparing the way she dressed to more sophisticated girls. He showed no interest in what she was studying. He wanted a wife and thought he could fit her into the mould. She had been captivated by his black eyes and the way he danced.

If it hadn't been for her father, Nina would have become Mrs. Samir Shamani. Nathan was clever. He had a double first in chemical engineering from Cambridge and had read all the novels of Trollope. He'd never studied psychology. Yet when Samir came to announce their engagement, Nathan knew instinctively what to do. Far from the

212

expected outburst, he'd asked a reasonable question. If he had forbidden Nina to see 'the Moroccan', she might have rushed into marriage at eighteen. She would have spent the next ten years struggling to be elegant, bearing numerous children.

A few weeks after their break-up, Samir went abroad and within three months he was married. Nina put him out of her mind but a year later she had cause to think of him again. She'd been invited to a May ball in Cambridge. Nathan wondered whether going to the college ball would make her regret her decision not to try for university. Anna was otherwise preoccupied; she was making Nina a dress of yellow tulle, with a bodice dotted with irridescent sequins.

Nina seemed to think the dress was too luxurious. Anna took her into her bedroom and opened the cupboard. Inside was another gown, wrapped in a white sheet, pinned tight to protect it from dust. The gown was also yellow, a golden satin with ribbons.

"I've never shown you this, have I? It belonged to my grandmother, Rachel. I always wanted to wear it. But then there was the war, and your father never wanted to go out ... Anyway, what does it matter? I don't have the figure for a dress like this."

Nina ran her fingers over the ribbons.

"How do you come to have it? It must be a hundred years old."

"It is, almost exactly. It must have been for a ball. I found it at the back of Mother's wardrobe after she died."

Nina picked up her own dress and slipped it on. The layers of net petticoats made it stand out. It also made it hard to sit down. She looked in the mirror and turned around. For a moment the thought of Samir came back to her and she said wistfully;

"It's a wonderful colour, but is it really elegant?"

chapter 21

*With good management and patient drill-
ing, everything for a small party can be
cooked and served by two female servants.
Do not crowd your guests, for nothing is
more annoying to them than to have to use
their knives and forks with their elbows
pinioned to their sides; it is also incon-
venient for the servants in changing plates
and offering dishes.*

*Let every lady who would make sure of her
dinner going off without mishaps, person-
ally superintend every detail connected
with the arrangement of her table, her dining-room, and her kitchen. Let her draw
out a plan of the table, and mark on it the
spot where every dish is to be placed.*

How to Dine Well and Economically, by Tabitha Tickletooth

LONDON 1857—RACHEL

I walked out of Pitt Street for the last time on Tuesday,
8th September, with no arrangement for a piano lesson
on the coming Thursday. I passed through the streets of

Kensington with my head down. My feet were scrunching through the leaves, the path in front of me blurred through the tears in my eyelashes. I tripped on a stone and looked up to see that the wisteria had flowered for a second time—silver blue cascades around the windows of the houses in Holland Street.

The days that followed were the most wretched of my life. At times I felt ashamed at my dismal mood; at others I was enveloped by the fearfulness of my loss. I walked around the house taking in the aroma of fine linens, preparing for dinner at seven. At night I turned back the embroidered sheets and laid out David's cotton night cap. I bought him a blue silk cigar case. One day he surprised me with a bunch of lilies. I found a cut-glass vase and turned away from him as I arranged them in the water.

To avoid suspicion I knew I would have to continue playing the pianoforte. I told David that Monsieur du Col had gone back to see his family in France. But whenever I pulled out the stool I was overwhelmed by the empty space beside me, behind me. Soon I stopped playing altogether. I wanted to try to forget the immense joy and the depth of sadness that the music had brought me. I spent more and more time alone, sleeping away the afternoons, trying to hide from the cloud of gloom that was enveloping my days.

It didn't occur to David to find the cause of my unhappiness—he must have observed something, though not the full extent of my misery. In his view all I needed was to be occupied. He continued to buy me books on household management, hoping I would show interest in his small dinners.

I must confess that for a full month I had no knowledge of anything regarding my husband or the running of the house. I was so absorbed in my own thoughts that I had no notion of what David was planning for the coming winter. If I'd been myself I'd have been amused; he was making preparations for a grand ball in our house in Finsbury Square. He wanted me to be involved in the organisation. Having established that the rooms were large enough, he was arranging to bring in a dance band.

"We'll need double woodwind and percussion, a few strings, but no viola ... .

A polonaise is a good way to start the evening. Then we could have a cotillon, a waltz and go on to the quadrille."

He rushed from one thought to another:

"We shall have fine Havana cigars, floral arrangements and ... "

"And who is to be invited to this grand ball?" I interrupted.

"People of breeding; financiers, the man who's moved into number 80, he's an underwriter at Lloyds, I believe."

"I think we'd be more comfortable with the traders we know from Bevis Marks."

"We can invite them too, but I want to expand our social circle."

For the first time David made it clear what was behind the books of management and manners. I could only think of the occasions when we had been rebuffed.

"Like Lord Petersham and his wife," I said. "They refused our dinner invitations three times."

"Rachel, people like that have busy lives. They'll come if we have a large ball."

I left the room and went upstairs, dragging my legs in fatigue. I thought that sadness was a condition of the mind, not the feet. I closed the door, eager to welcome the sleep that for a while would mask the melancholia. Every waking hour I thought of Laurent. Over and over I played in my mind the scenes of our first concert outing, the times we spent in his room at Kensington. I repeated to myself every word he had spoken to me and tried to feel again the touch of his fingers and his kisses on my face.

David was concerned at my apparent ill-health. He called in a physician and obtained patent medicines for me. He wanted me to join in the planning of his ball. But he must have been aware that I was unable to make decisions. In order to spare me the trouble of searching for a suitable ball gown, he procured some silk satin fabric and arranged for a seamstress to come to the house. I have a recollection of her arriving one day with patterns of ribbons. She needed to take my measurements. Some short time later—it may have been a week, or two—Betsy our parlourmaid took delivery of a large box. She could hardly contain her excitement. Inside was a yellow gown with five tiers of ribbon embroidery round the skirt. It had wide floating sleeves. I had never worn anything like it. My gowns were usually maroon or olive green taffeta with a tight collar and cuffs with tiny buttons and loops. This one was golden satin with a low cut bodice.

The invitations arrived in the next post: embossed cards printed in fine black lettering. David wrote the names and addresses and I put the stamps on the envelopes. We sat together in his study as he went through the guest list and decided on the food to be served.

"Emily can't cope with this" I began.

David drew some cards from a leather case and handed them to me:

Mrs. Hammond, Professional cook,
17 Balcombe Street, Dorset Square;

William Willes, Waiter,
34 Cambridge Street, Edgware Road,

"Yes, and here's the piano tuner:"

Mr. Charles Taylor, Lupus Street.

The thought of all these cooks, waiters and musicians passed through my brain and all I wanted was an escape. I imagined walking out of the house and taking the carriage to Pitt Street. I came to my senses and heard my husband talking again:

"We need candles—at least twelve pounds, and we should order the groceries from the Civil Service. They can deliver wafers, petit fours, caraques ... "

I looked up at him. His eyes were sparkling and he was so clearly happy at the thought of this grand event that I felt an immense rush of pity and guilt sweeping over me. I remembered what he had said when he asked me to marry him: "We'll have a better life together". The elegant house, the clothes, the dinners—they were all for me too. Even the piano tutor who had brought such turmoil to my life, had been a gift to me.

After a few minutes I saw that David was waiting for my response. He continued to talk about the desserts:

"What about those chestnut sweets you like, the marrons glacés?" he asked.

My mind was so confused that I misunderstood his meaning. I thought he intended me to make them but I discovered later that he had always intended to order them from Paris. I searched through my receipts and found the page headed 'preserved and glazed chestnuts'. I sent Emily to purchase the raw nuts and when she returned I was reading the instructions. They began with a warning:

> "This is a long and extremely intricate process and is therefore seldom undertaken in the home."

> Materials required for experiment:

> A block tin or a very clean iron saucepan, a pound of sugar (best), a jug of water, 2 lbs of fine sound chestnuts, a basin containing brown sugar, a few thin wooden skewers about 8 inches long and a good fresh lemon.

Emily continued to read while I began the cooking.

> Make an incision in the outer skin only of the chestnuts and boil them till they are tender but not soft. At this early stage it is very easy to make a mistake. We want to keep the chestnuts whole and if we boil them even a little bit too much they break into small pieces. Afterwards peel away both the inner and the outer skin.

> The chestnuts being ready our next point is the sugar. We put a pound of sugar and half a pint of water in the saucepan and set it on the fire. Until it is dissolved we may stir it but after it has boiled we must on no account stir it and we must move it about as little as possible. When

220

it has boiled ten minutes we dip a fork into it.
In a minute or two, when we hold it in the air,
there will be seen a long silvery hair. Now we say
that the candy begins to 'hair' and this is a les-
son that is to be borne in mind. We now squeeze
into it the juice of a lemon or add about 2 table-
spoonfuls of vinegar, watch it still more closely
and let it boil rapidly for a minute or two. We
have ready a cup of cold water and keep drop-
ping therein a morsel of the syrup. When it
sets in the water like toffee, so that it leaves the
finger clean and so that a morsel tried by the
teeth feels brittle it has arrived at the degree of
boiling known as the 'crack' or the 'snap' and is
ready for our purpose.

Up till this point there was no cause for alarm. But when I started to dip the chestnuts into the hot syrup, they stuck together and began to break, so instead of fine whole candied chestnuts I had a sticky mess of nuts and sugar. Emily just sat watching, occasionally reading out further instructions:

The varnish is to be very thin and there is to be
no portion of the nut left untouched.

She didn't notice me brushing away the tears as her eyes were on the book:

If we can so arrange matters that we can give
the chestnuts a second coating they will look
handsomer.

I had no wish to continue with the cooking. I had no enthusiasm for any part of David's ball. When I returned to the drawing-room he was writing in his notebook. He looked up and paused, with his pen in the air:

"We'll need at least three waiters, and we shall serve champagne, sherry, claret and brandy. We shall also need maraschino and curaçao."

That was the liqueur that Laurent had offered me in Pitt Street. Why was it that everything in my life was either insignificant or brought back memories that caused me pain?

The day before the ball a package arrived from Paris. It contained five boxes of the finest marrons glacés. I folded the wrapping paper and was winding the ribbon round my finger when David came into the room. I hadn't told him about my farcical attempt to make the sweets but the thought of that miserable afternoon made the tears spring to my eyes. A look of tenderness crossed his face and he squeezed me very tight, pressing me against his jacket. He smelled of the soap I'd bought in Jermyn Street; sharper and more musky than the lily of the valley at my side of the washstand. We spoke a little about my state of mind, which he interpreted as nerves.

I agreed with him that the culmination of weeks of planning was making me agitated. The house was full of people bustling from one room to another, clearing furniture, spreading a linen drugget over the carpet. The doors had been taken off their hinges. Muslin hangings were suspended at the sides of the doorways. Four iron stands stood empty in the hall. David assured me that plants would be delivered within the hour.

The night arrived: Wednesday 25th February 1857. A linkman led the guests from their carriages to our door. The drawing room was ablaze with candlelight as the dancing began. I looked at the young musicians. Did they count as 'people of breeding'? Was a violinist or a pianist of equal standing to a wine merchant? David's eyes were flitting round the room, making a mental calculation of the number of invitations sent out and the assembled guests. A part of me wanted to run up the staircase, close the door of the bedroom and bury my face in the pillow. I thought for a moment that we should have invited Laurent and imagined myself dancing with him, our eyes and fingertips meeting in the sea of guests. Then I came to my senses and took a deep breath and moved closer to my husband. We stood watching as the men selected their partners and marked their cards. I caught a glimpse of Jonah and Solomon peering through the bannisters. We didn't think it appropriate for boys of seven and nine to be at the ball, though I would have been proud to show them off in such a large gathering.

David held out his hand and we lined up for a quadrille. It was already half past eleven. I began to notice a slight frisson in the room. The men's eyes were darting around and they seemed to be manoevring into position to be in proximity to a particular partner. David explained that they were taking significant care over their choice for the last dance before supper, wishing to escort a particular lady to the dining room. The meal was served at midnight. There was hardly an inch on the tables that wasn't covered by an exquisite platter of food; each one highly decorated with the aspic glaze shining in the candlelight. David and I took our places at a table next to the stockbroker who lived at the north end of Finsbury Square. His wife complimented me on my golden satin gown. I had thought of the colour as 'honey' but her description matched the impression that David wanted to create. In the corner of my eye I could see my father hesitating over where to sit, looking for a familiar face from Bevis Marks.

I had no appetite and to my surprise David was also toying with the food in front of him. He was relieved to see that our guests had eaten the meal with relish and when the waiters cleared the plates, ours were the only ones where the food was scarcely touched. Some hours later they brought on candied fruits and cassata. The first few couples began to leave at about three o'clock.

When the last guest had gone and the servants had cleared the platters, David and I sat on the chaise longue together, eating the sugary marrons glacés. I started to lick the syrup off my fingers but he passed me a linen handkerchief to wipe my hands.

"I wonder how many of them will return the invitation?" he asked, "whether any of them want to socialize with an olive oil merchant?"

My heart jumped at the sadness in his voice. I put my hands on his face and kissed his mouth. When we drew apart I squeezed his hand and said:

"I don't think a Jewish doctor would have done any better."

chapter 22

To wash a Turkish Handkerchief

*Put the handkerchief in a basin of fresh wa-
ter, make a quantity of soap suds in which
let it soak for ten minutes, rub it carefully,
and put it afterwards into another basin
of fresh water for five minutes, squeeze it
well and let it half dry in the wind then put
it between two linen rags and pass an iron
over it not very hot.*

From Emily's notebook, 1856

LONDON 1856—DAVID

Before the ball I was apprehensive; concerned that some
of the guests would have a prior engagement. Would they
want to come to the home of a Jewish businessman—even
in a substantial house in Finsbury Square? Every detail
had to be perfect, yet I had little knowledge of what was
to be served or how best to plan the evening. I was particularly anxious about the musical ensemble: perhaps
we should have had a harpist, but that would have taken
up space needed for the dancing. In the end we found a

talented cornet player.

During the daytime I was preoccupied with the enlargement of my business. I had acquired premises in Fenchurch Street and employed several clerks to assist with the paperwork. Dealing with bills of lading and letters of credit was tedious and I preferred to devote my energy to matters in Spain and Portugal. My agents were selling to grocers and wholesalers in the provinces, leaving me free to travel in search of new sources of oil and sardines.

It was on these journeys that my mind turned back to my childhood. The memories continued to haunt me. I had nightmares of running through the rutted streets of Safed, searching through the splinters of the house. Even in the daytime I would find myself going back to that room, looking for something hidden underneath the table. The thoughts were always accompanied by cries and the whimpering of a baby.

At about this time I noticed that Rachel was listless and withdrawn. At first I thought she was anaemic and suggested she might need a tonic. The patent medicines seemed to make her more contented for a while. But the gloom returned and we lived under a cloud for several months, when even at midday she would retire to the bedroom and take a nap.

By contrast, I was finding it hard to sleep at all, lying awake for hours listening to the long case clock chiming midnight, then one, then two. Counting the strokes, I subtracted them from the time I was to wake up, worrying that it would be impossible to concentrate on the business the following day.

To calm my mind I tried to relax my body, concentrating on every muscle. First I would tense my neck and shoulders and then breathe out slowly, relaxing the muscles, keeping my eyelids closed and my jaw still. Then I would breathe in again, clenching my fists and tensing my ribs and pelvis until I was stiff all the way down to my toes. When I breathed out I would recite to myself the list of bones I remembered from my anatomy class: phalanges, tarsals, fibula, tibia, patella, femur, sacrum, clavicle, vertebrae, mandible. The purpose was to make every part of my body limp. I even believed I could uncurl my eyelashes. Eventually I fell asleep. According to Rachel, I mumbled and talked, speaking more in my night-time conversation that I did during the day.

Though I have no memory of it, we must have discussed the possibility of having more children. I was more than content with our two sons, but Rachel assures me that we talked about it one evening when we were planning the guest list for a ball.

The balls had become an annual event, with furniture movers and musicians transforming our home into a society venue. Although I planned most of the first one myself, Rachel began to enjoy devising dishes for the supper and choosing unusual sweetmeats. But it was the organisation of the servants that took much of her time. In the days before the ball, there were frequent deliveries and the boys had to be paid after the goods were checked. Envelopes with the correct money were left for the cook and the removal men. There had to be beer for the waiters and linkman. It was left to me to write a note to the piano tuner and arrange the hire of plants for the entrance hall.

Rachel took charge of the final purchases: dance cards with pencils from Swan and Edgar and paper ribbons and white ties from Peter Robinson.

When we were planning the guest list for the third ball I suggested we should invite the piano tutor called Du Col. We hadn't seen him for some while. He was the Frenchman who used to give Rachel lessons. For many weeks she had seemed animated and looked forward to the weekly session. Her playing improved and I would often come into the house and hear her practising a Chopin nocturne, memorizing the notes till the technique was right. And then, for some reason, she stopped the lessons, so I no longer left money for the tutor. I believe she told me that she needed to practise more, rather than continue with the weekly tuition. Or maybe he had gone back to Paris or wherever it was that he came from. I was waiting for her to reply to my suggestion and she became quiet.

"I don't think so," she said. "He went back to France. He's probably still there."

I have no detailed memory of this conversation nor of the discussion about having another child. Perhaps I was hoping that we might have a daughter. When Solomon was thirteen and Jonah eleven, Rachel became pregnant again. For the first three months she felt constant nausea and, for the only time I remember, took no interest in cooking and the food we ate. The strangest things made her feel sick. She claimed that cooked apples had an unspeakable smell but an infusion of jasmine leaves helped to calm her stomach. She never went into the kitchen and Emily provided the meals with almost no supervi-

228

sion. Without Rachel to guide her, she had reverted to the plain English cooking she was brought up with and on one occasion produced a monochrome meal that began with potato soup and stewed white fish.

"This dinner is infernal," said Solomon.

"Where did you learn to say things like that?" I asked.

"He's an oaf" said Jonah "it's no good jawing, just eat it."

"Why can't we have mamma's lamb chops with asparagus sauce?" asked Solomon, as Emily came in to clear the plates. The poor girl couldn't resist a reply:

"Because, as I couldn't find the receipt. There's nothing in the book, 'cept instructions for washin' a Turkish handkerchief."

She left in a huff and returned with lemon custard and stone cream. Jonah, who was getting quite plump, ate both puddings while Solomon pushed the bowls of white food away. Their mother, of course, ate none of it.

In the September of 1862 Rachel was eight months pregnant. I was happy to see that once again she seemed to take pleasure in planning small dinners, sitting with Emily every morning to decide on the entrées. One day I overheard them discussing the desserts:

"I think we should call this baby 'Marron," I said, joking.

"How about Bathsheba, after my mother?" said Rachel. "or if it's a boy Ebenezer."

I was imagining how a boy with a name like that would be teased in school.

"There are plenty of biblical names," I said "ones that are shorter, easy for a child to write."

Rachel asked me to make a suggestion. I asked if she knew the story of Jacob's children.

"Well, I know Joseph, of course—and that's a good name for a boy, but there weren't any girls, were there?"

"Yes there was one, Dinah. She was out in the fields one day and met a young man. He..he ... um ... dishonoured her."

"What do you mean?" asked Rachel.

"Well, he loved her and wanted to marry her, but he took her by force. When Dinah's brothers found out what had happened they were furious and told their father. But by then Dinah seemed intent on marriage and Jacob finally agreed. But there was a condition: the young man and all the men in the city would have to agree to become like them, in other words, to be circumcised."

"And was that the end of the story?" she asked.

"No—two or three days after the circumcisions when all the men were in pain and presumably resting and unprepared, two of Jacob's sons came with swords and killed Dinah's husband and every male in the city. They took her out of the house and brought her home."

"And Jacob? How did he feel when he discovered his sons were murderers?"

"He was frightened. When he heard the news his first thought was "what will the neighbouring tribes think of us?"

All I could think was that Dinah was a survivor, like me. Rachel seemed overcome by the story I had told her. When I came to the part where Dinah's lover was killed her eyes misted over.

She said the name aloud:

"'Deenah'—it sounds the same in Hebrew and English. I like it. But I think we should drop the 'h'. Otherwise it sounds like 'Dynah' and that's too harsh."

Our daughter was born three weeks later. She weighed six pounds three ounces. It was a hard confinement and both mother and baby needed great care for the first month. Rachel was finding the boys difficult as they were constantly bickering and she took little interest in their boisterous games. I hoped that she would form a closer bond with Dina, but the baby found it hard to suck and became tearful and angry. Rachel too seemed to be suffering some discomfort.

I was overjoyed to have a daughter. She had Rachel's grey eyes but fair hair like my sister Rebecca. I ordered frocks from Paris and bonnets with silk ribbons. It was a while since we'd had a small child in the house and with some guilt, I found it a pleasure to play with her. I would have done anything for her. Yet in my subconscious mind I had a fear of losing her and imagined her, a pretty six year old, walking away, holding her mother's hand—never to return.

chapter 23

THE FABRICATION OF ICES

As at present ice is so easily obtained, and at a price so very moderate, we should render ourselves quite remarkable for meanness did we not indulge our guests with such an inexpensive refinement. You can avail yourself of one of the newly-invented freezing machines so liberally offered to your patronage, otherwise you can operate quite as satisfactorily with the old-fashioned pail and ice pot.

The Lady's Dessert Book, 1863

LONDON 1867—DINA

My first memory is of green ice cream. Mamma told me it was pistachio and I remember tasting it at one of the dinners. Betsy used to bring me treats once the company had arrived. The ribbons on her cap went flying each time she ran to open the front door. I crept down to see the guests. When they were sitting at the table eating the dinner Betsy poked some tidbits through the bannisters.

After a long time the ladies left and the gentlemen stayed to drink the port.

"Why aren't the ladies allowed the wine?" I asked. She was busy clearing away the coffee cups.

"Do you think Mamma likes the dinners?" Betsy slipped a creamy meringue on to a plate for me and answered:

"To be sure she does."

But we could both see her face when the cards on the silver trays were brought in. Her lips were tight shut and she'd put her fingers through her ringlets and pick up the fan, flicking it open. It was Papa's idea to have the dinners. He sent notes to important people and sometimes they didn't reply. He did all the planning—'military style organisation' Mamma called it. I didn't understand that and asked Betsy once what millinary-style meant.

"Your father likes to write lists. He makes notes in his account book."

"Is that the one with his best handwriting?"

"Dina, that's enough questions. Yes, he writes down everything: *Ribbons for poultry 1s. 8d, Bay leaf 3d.* But mostly it's for Emily. She needs to send word to the butcher. Like for the grand ball next week: *1 turkey, 14 quails, 12 fowls for boiling, 2 ducklings*"

My brothers didn't like the balls. It was the dancing they disliked. We all stood watching as the gentlemen and ladies lined up for the polonaise. Jonah was looking at the bustles on the frocks; Solomon had his eye on what the men were wearing:

"I wouldn't mind a top hat like that," he said.

"Papa would never allow it, you're only eighteen."

Jonah was smiling:

"At least they can't pinch my cheeks while they're dancing."

Papa was standing in the doorway watching too. The room was filled with candles lighting up everyone's faces.

Mamma was telling me the names of the dances:

"'*Cotillon*', say it again: 'cotiyon'."

Papa whispered something to her. I think he said: "So they came after all."

"Who's they?" I asked, but I don't think he heard me. The band was playing a polka called the '*Can't Stop Galop*'.

There were two violinists, a drummer and a man who played the clarinet. During supper they left—someone said they had disappeared, but I saw them come back again later. Before the supper started there were drinks. The waiters wore white ties and they passed round glasses of champagne. The food was on long tables. First there were steaming hot cups of chicken broth and then there were slices of meats—roasted veal, a kind of smoky beef and can you imagine, tongue? That was bad, but even worse were the platters of small birds—pigeons or quails, I think they were—with their little wings and legs all tucked in. Then there were bigger animals—carved turkeys and capons, which Mamma said were grown-up chickens. These had been sliced and put together again and covered with a kind of jelly to make them shiny. I thought it was called aspect but I didn't like the taste. Glass bowls were filled with new potatoes and a cucumber salad with a herby smell. They said it was chervil, but that sounded like one of those small pets. When I came to choose, I took some asparagus sticks and Papa made me try a crispy red ball which turned out to be a radish. I hated it. I couldn't wait for the desserts. There were grapes and fruits with a sugar coating, rounds of yellow pine apple and oranges in dark caramel. Mamma's favourite was marrons glacés—a kind of syrupy nut which got stuck in my teeth.

In between the balls our life was ordinary. Solomon and Jonah didn't play with me because they didn't like dolls or dressing up. Papa bought me clothes which came in parcels in the post. One of the frocks he ordered was too big for me and Mamma cut a piece off the bottom. She asked me to bring her my favourite doll and when she'd finished sewing I saw that she'd made a tiny copy of my own frock.

Papa didn't have any interest in photographs. There are no pictures of me with my brothers or with him. But one day when I was about five I went with Mamma to a photographer. I remember standing on a chair while he put a black cloth over his head. I was wearing a frock that came from Paris with fashionable puffed sleeves. The bodice had an inverted triangle of pink smocking, with matching lines of pink embroidery on the skirt. I still have the picture today.

It took many years before I understood why my brothers didn't want to play with me. It had nothing to do with the fact that I was a girl; it was simply the age difference. I was a child and they were almost young men.

When Solomon left school he joined Papa in the business. At the time I was bored with the conversations at dinner. Employing new agents? Dealing in phosphorus and petroleum? It was only when I was older that Solomon and I began to talk.

"It's the negotiation that's exciting" he said. "Knowing that another half hour of discussion can result in a far higher price for the product."

"He's being modest" said Papa. "He has a natural flair for commerce."

Jonah looked much like his brother, with our father's brown hair and dark eyes, but they had a different build. People used to say the boys looked like two peas in a pod because they resembled each other, but as far as I was concerned one looked like a broad bean and the other like a shrivelled green pea. Their characters were different too. Papa had acquired a new office in Fenchurch Street but Jonah took every opportunity to disappear during the day, leaving his father and brother to manage the business. Whenever there was a question of one of them travelling to Gibraltar Jonah would go, extending his few days with a weekend in Deauville or Paris. He'd return to a shivery silence, often followed by an explosive quarrel. When I walked in the room they'd usually be talking about money and Papa used a term I didn't understand at the time—'settling your gambling debts.'

The atmosphere in the house was like being on a carousel. At times we were up, with Jonah playing practical jokes and Papa attempting as usual to 'improve' us all. We refused to take seriously his comments on etiquette and his desire to cultivate acquaintances of good breeding, so mealtimes were filled with laughter and wisecracks—

mostly at Papa's expense. But there were weeks when he hardly talked and I sensed there were financial problems that he wanted to keep from me.

Maybe he discussed them with Mamma, but perhaps he didn't. We all felt we needed to treat her like a bird's egg that we'd found in a nest—delicate and easily broken. There were periods of gloom and misery when she disappeared into her room for hours, emerging tear-stained or silent. Yet at times she was easy to talk to, eagerly joining in our conversations. Then some minutes later, we'd be in the middle of telling her something and we'd catch a faraway look on her face, with her grey eyes focused in the distance.

"Mamma, you're not listening. You haven't heard a word of what we've been saying."

"I'm sorry, my darling," she admitted "tell me again."

In the winter of 1877 when I was fifteen Mamma seemed preoccupied. They were planning one of the big balls and she went out to place an order for cassata and strawberry ices. When she returned she appeared agitated:

"I've forgotten the beer for the servants. Then I went to speak to Mrs. Hammond and she wasn't there."

"Who is Mrs. Hammond?" I interrupted.

"The cook who lives in Balcombe Street. She was thinking of going to live in the country with her daughter. She might have gone. What are we to do, David?"

"Rachel, it's not important. We'll find another cook. I don't want you worrying about the ball."

Papa noticed that Mamma was shivering and suggested that she should go to bed. The next day she woke up and complained of a sore throat and pain in her chest and muscles. Papa took her temperature and immediately summoned the doctor. By the time he arrived she was perspiring so much that her night clothes were soaking wet. Her temperature was 102. I could hear Papa talking with the doctor:

"If she gets breathless, it could be bronchial."

"Does that mean it would affect patches of tissue in both lungs?"

"Maybe" said the doctor.

"So what's the prognosis?" asked Papa.

I knew nothing about medicine but I understood what my father was asking. The doctor waited a moment, then replied:

"In a debilitated patient it may result in respiratory failure. You were a medical man, Mr. Levy, so you know something about acute bronchial diseases. We have to hope that the inflammation can be contained."

"And if it can't?"

The doctor didn't reply immediately, as if he was turning over in his mind what was to be done. Eventually he said:

"There was a paper published recently suggesting the use of oxygen in cases of pneumonia."

When I heard him mention the word 'pneumonia' I was alarmed. He went on talking:

"I remember seeing something about it in a journal. Now I remember. A man named George Barth, calls himself an 'inventor and patentee'. He is selling an Oxygenator for about six guineas. Somewhere in Bloomsbury, I believe."

Papa left the house immediately to find out where Mr. Barth was located. I was sure that he would be able to find a cure for Mamma. Knowing that he'd been a student of medicine made me even more convinced.

I stayed with Mamma, turning over the dreaded word 'pneumonia' in my mind. For some hours her condition remained stable but then her temperature rose to 104. The oxygen machine was brought in but by then her breathing had become rapid and laboured. We sat by her bedside telling her not to talk. I looked from father to Solomon and then to Jonah—all of us were silent and shocked. I wonder what Mamma was thinking as she looked at our stricken faces?

It was two days later, on December 31st, that Mamma died. Papa was alone with her in the room. When he came out his eyes were red. He was twisting a handkerchief in his hands. I was not allowed to go in to see her. I waited outside, thinking it would be wrong if I cried, so I kept blinking and looked away. I'd never noticed the mouldings on the ceiling before, but now I kept me eyes up away from the door. When I went downstairs I was expecting to cry but I found that the tears were blocked. Jonah took my hand and sat me down next to him. We didn't speak for a long time. I wanted to tell him how much I had loved her. Instead I asked:

"Do you think I was a trouble to Mamma?"

"What do you mean 'a trouble'?" he asked.

"Well, when I was born you were both old enough to look after yourselves. It must have been hard for her, having another baby."

"She always had time for you. Think of how she made

240

frocks for your dolls." He lowered his eyes and added "I think she just loved small children."

"More than older ones?" I asked.

"She used to read to us when we were young, but then later ... we spent a lot of time with Grandpa Reuven."

"But remember how she took us to the circus?" said Solomon "and to hear that band leader Jullien, or Julliard, what was his name?"

"But why do you think she was sad? Why did she go up to her room to be alone?" The three of us had never talked about this before.

"I asked Grandpa Reuven once," said Solomon. "He said she was always quiet."

The men went to the funeral and I stayed at home. The ladies never went to the graveside. Emily began to prepare a meal and the next thing I remember was someone urging me to eat a hard boiled egg. I cracked the shell and began to peel it off and then I began to cry. And the tears filled up my eyes so I couldn't see anyone around me. People were eating in silence. I left the table and rushed out into the hall. The mirrors in the house were all covered with white sheets. I couldn't see my face.

For the next week the drawing room was filled with people who came to visit. When I came down in the mornings there were women sitting in groups. In the afternoons Papa's friends came to console him and every evening the Rabbi from Bevis Marks synagogue led the prayers. Jonah and Solomon joined Papa in reciting *kaddish* and I stood numb and dry eyed.

For a year Papa went twice a day to the service at the synagogue. When he came home he was silent. He refused to allow anyone to enter Mamma's dressing room. The cupboards and drawers stayed untouched.

On a cold day in March I found him sitting at her writing table, looking through a pile of papers. She had kept everything—receipts for new dishes she wanted Emily to try out, every single bill for the dinners and balls, programmes from concerts. I was standing by the door, holding the cut-glass handle, when Papa suddenly rushed past me and left the house. I ran down the stairs and called after him but he had gone. I went back upstairs, pulled open the curtains and saw him walking down the street, without a coat or hat. I went to the desk and began to pile up the papers when I saw some sheet music tied up with a red ribbon.

It was a piano work by Schubert. There was a handwritten note pinned to the corner.

> *"Rachel—I thought you would like this piece for four hands. Did you know that the composer worked as a piano teacher for Count Esterhazy in Hungary? An unusual feature of the music is that the hands of the players often cross. It was Schubert's way of making physical contact with the young Countess Karolin, with whom he was in love. Think about it on Thursday—Duke".*

When my father came back I asked him: "who is the Duke?"

"I don't know. There was a young piano tutor called Du Col," he replied. "Maybe it was him." His voice was controlled but his hands were shaking.

"What did he mean by 'on Thursday'? I persisted.

"Your mother had piano lessons on Thursdays."

"But why would he send her notes?" I asked.

His eyes filled with tears and he whispered "why, indeed?"

chapter 24

SUCCESSFUL 'AT HOMES'

Simply opening a suite of well-furnished, well lighted and gaily decorated rooms will not answer the purpose. Desirable people should be made acquainted with each other. In the absence of popular musicians, famous travellers, well-known speakers or missionaries, the hostess should possess a large amount of tact to put strangers on an easy footing.

Cassell's Household Guide, 1869

LONDON 1883—DINA

I first saw him at a ball. The 13th February began with a heavy snowfall. The carriage arrived at the mansion in Piccadilly. Flakes the size of a thumbnail swirled round my bonnet and I complained about my shoes slipping on the pavement. Papa was glowing at the prospect of what he called 'a significant occasion'. Our hosts, Marie and Leopold de Rothschild, had recently returned from a year-long honeymoon voyage.

I handed in my velvet cloak and was given a pencil and a dance card. Before I could write my name at the top a tall young man appeared in front of me:

"Miss Levy, may I have the first dance?"

"How do you know my name?"

"Because I've heard about you. My name is Joseph Levy."

"Are you being serious?"

"Yes, of course I am. Let me explain. I'm from Gibraltar and we are cousins."

"... and I should dance with you because we are related?"

I didn't mean the words to sound rude but I was taken aback by his directness. He looked crestfallen so I held out my card and invited him to fill in the first line. When he handed it back I noticed that the name 'Joseph L' appeared on six other lines. I laughed as he led me on to the dance floor, putting one arm around my waist and holding out his left hand as the waltz began.

"How do you know the Rothschilds?" I asked.

"You ask a lot of questions Miss Levy. I met them when they spent a month in Gibraltar last year. The whole community wanted to entertain them. Leopold asked me to take him round the Rock. I helped him to miss afternoon tea in at least five elegant salons!" he laughed.

His eyes were a deep blue and he had a way of smiling straight into my eyes as we talked. He was taller than me and well built, with a bronzed skin that was offset by the whiteness of his dress shirt. During the third waltz he suddenly pulled me towards him and his lips brushed my hair.

"I beg your pardon," he whispered.

I looked up at him and wondered if his apology required a response.

We walked back and sat down at a small table. He asked me for the dance card, took out a pencil and started writing on it. When he handed it back he had written the names of each of the dances: 'Cherry Pie', 'My Queen' etc.

"These aren't really the names are they? 'Yours Sincerely', 'Snowdrift'?

"Do you think I would make them up?" Before I could answer he walked away and whispered something to the bandleader. They were playing a quadrille.

"I've asked them to play my favourite, 'Star of the Night', specially for you." He smiled again, crinkling his eyes.

"How do you know so much about dance music?" I asked.

"Because I love dancing ..."

"And what else do you like?"

"The sun on my skin and diving off the rocks into the sea. And when I'm away from Gibraltar—fine meals and ... young ladies with fair hair." His voice trailed off as he looked straight at me again.

Embarrassed, I turned the conversation to his work:

"and what brings you to London?" I asked.

"The dreary business of olive oil and sardines," he replied.

"That's the same as my father's business—at least it was, until he started selling anything that came in a barrel or a sack," I joked.

"Of course it is, all the Levys are in the same business.

But enough of that. I want to talk about you. Start at the beginning on 3rd October 1862."

"But that's my birthday" I gasped "how did you know?"

"I already know a lot about my beautiful cousin Dina Levy," he smiled.

We danced and talked for the whole evening. I discovered that he was the same age as me, his parents were called Samuel and Regina and he had one brother, Dan.

"He thinks he is clever, but he can't put two consecutive thoughts together."

"Don't you get on with him?" I asked.

"Yes, when I'm travelling and he is in Gibraltar. But don't let's talk about him. I've come to London for a month and I'm staying with a cousin at Billiter Street. It's near your father's office."

"And I suppose you know where that is," I said.

"Of course. It's at Fenchurch Street. It could happen that we might both be there at the same time."

And we were. Every day for the next fortnight. I had made a habit of going to the office sometimes after Mamma died so it was not unusual for me to be in the vicinity of Fenchurch Street. When I turned the corner Joseph was coming towards me, as we had planned. He took my hand and slipped it under his arm. We walked through the streets, down towards the river, near the Tower.

I don't recall the moment when we fell in love. We were captivated with each other from the beginning. It was as if a letter had slipped into a matching envelope. All it needed was for the top to be folded over and sealed. He must have proposed some time in those two weeks but I only remember the day he came to the house to ask Papa's permission. They went into his study and I believe there was some talk of a dowry. Everything happened so quickly. It was taken for granted that we should be married before he returned to Gibraltar. That left two weeks to plan the wedding. Joseph was impulsive and forceful, accustomed to making decisions. After the shortest discussion between us it was agreed that we would go to live in Portugal.

"Why must you live abroad?" asked Papa.

Joseph replied:

"The business is based in Gibraltar but I want to open an office in Lisbon."

I knew Papa was wondering why the office couldn't be in London and before he had a chance to ask, I said:

"We're going away because Joseph couldn't live with the fog and snow."

I was secretly looking forward to a new life with just the two of us, with no-one to tell us what to do. Perhaps we both misunderstood or were too selfish to understand that Papa was trying to tell me how much he would miss me.

He raised a new objection:

"Anyway I can't think about a wedding at such short notice. I have matters to settle."

He didn't want to talk about it in front of Joseph but a month earlier he had lost a large amount of money. He'd bought a quantity of olive oil and the price had suddenly dropped, leaving him to sell at a loss. Whether it was a miscalculation on his part, or sheer bad fortune, I don't know. This had never happened with the sardine sales;

249

the price seemed to be more stable. Papa must have had financial problems before but the result of the olive oil catastrophe was serious: he was contemplating the sale of our house.

I tried to reassure him, telling him that we had no intention of arranging a large wedding. Joseph added that his parents were planning a celebration in Gibraltar, as they couldn't make the journey to London at two weeks' notice.

"But ... " began Papa.

He still looked concerned. In an attempt to cheer him up, I said:

"You're the man who has organized balls for a hundred and eighty people. What we have in mind would be as easy as one of your elegant dinners."

He didn't reply.

"We could even have sole in white wine sauce," I added, planting a kiss on his cheek.

The marriage date was fixed for Tuesday 13th March 1883. On the Monday evening Papa was sitting at his desk. We began to talk as we had rarely done before. It was as if we had both discovered that words were needed for a conversation. Speaking with him had never been easy. When I was small he tried to play with me but when I wanted to talk he seemed unemotional and withdrawn. After Mamma's death we developed a closeness, though a strange and sometimes silent one.

I asked him if he was disappointed that he had given up his medical studies and he began an animated account of his years in medical school. He talked about his life as a boy in Gibraltar and told me about the library and

Aunt Deborah. The one subject that he avoided was any mention of his parents.

"What were my grandparents like?" I asked. "I don't mean grandpa Reuven. He died when I was little, didn't he?"

Papa ignored the first part of my question.

"Yes, you were about three. For a whole year your mother didn't go out or invite company for dinner."

"Solomon says he spoiled me."

"He did," said Papa. "He adored you. We couldn't stop him bringing presents. Every time he walked in the door he brought you dolls and toys."

"Did he spoil the boys like that too?"

"Maybe, when they were young. But he was more interested in teaching them to sing. Jonah didn't want to go to synagogue, so he never learned the tunes. Solomon went—but then he didn't have a voice."

"What were your parents like?" I asked again.

We were interrupted by Solomon who burst in to give Papa some news which clearly shocked him. I was so mesmerized by the breathless excitement of my love for Joseph and the plans for our marriage that I had forgotten Papa's business concerns. Putting the house up for auction must have been a hard decision and Solomon's news that night added to his worries: Jonah's gambling debts exceeded all his fears and the house sale was now urgent.

Papa put his hand on mine:

"It's just as well you are leaving to go to Lisbon, otherwise you might be homeless." He managed a smile. And then quite unexpectedly, he added: "Like I was once."

I didn't ask what he meant. Mamma had told me the story and made me promise never to mention it to Papa.

He walked over to a cabinet, took out the silver teapot with the camel head spout and handed it to me.

"I want you to have this, Dina. It came from my family's home in Safed and it was the only thing that came out of the earthquake with me."

I hesitated and then said:

"I didn't know that's where it came from. Why do you say it was 'the only thing'?"

"When I went back to the house I found the teapot. There were other things I didn't take. I should have done," he whispered.

"You've never told me about the earthquake. What was it like?"

"You don't want to know about the buildings collapsing ... I've tried to push it all out of my head."

"But afterwards, where did you sleep? I know so little about it. Tell me," I said.

"They brought tents. The rain was drumming on the canvas and I was shivering inside."

"I had no idea. I thought the climate in Safed was hot."

"But this was winter. The next day it began to snow and the white flakes turned to slush. When I put my head out of the tent I could hardly see. There was a dust like ash which had been spewed up from the cracks in the ground."

"At least the earthquake was over," I said.

"That's not true. There was an aftershock. It started again ... the rumbling, the shaking and more stones flying and falling."

I couldn't imagine it. He went on to tell me what it was like inside the tent, listening to the screams and the clawing of hands and the hurling of rocks.

When he stopped talking I waited a moment and then I asked:

"How long did you keep looking before you found out everyone had died?"

"I ... I ... knew. There were the lists. The names. Of course there were bodies that couldn't be identified, but we all knew who was missing ... "

The words tailed off. Papa broke the silence and said:

"The Japanese believe it's a fish."

"What do you mean?" I asked.

"They think that earthquakes are caused by a giant catfish called a 'namazu' that lives in the mud beneath the earth."

"And is that what you think?" I suggested.

"Of course not. It's an act of God. When I was a child I believed that God was good and omnipotent. But now I'm not so sure. The two don't go together. Well, that's to say 'good' in the sense we mean it. He may have a plan for us that is eventually for our own good, even if we can't see it at the time. We may never know, but on the other hand, in the next life we may ... "

In all those years of brief exchanges we had never spoken of anything significant. Now my father was talking about belief in God and a life after death. To be truthful I had never thought about such things. I turned the conversation back to the days after the earthquake. I wanted to know how he felt when he was sent to Gibraltar, alone, to stay with his aunt, with no parents, no brother and sisters.

"I don't remember the journey back. I must have gone with somebody. Those weeks are blurred in my mind. I was taken to my Aunt's house. It seemed very quiet. There were no other children. The nightmares lasted for months then I found ways of blocking out the memories and decided not to think about them."

"Is that why Mamma told us not to mention it to you?"

"Is that what she said?" he sighed. "People thought I was cold, unfeeling. I couldn't make friends and even when I married Mamma I couldn't share my thoughts with her. And now it's too late … "

He breathed in and let out a deep moan. And then he picked up my hand and brightening up, said:

"How about this wedding tomorrow? He's not exactly a 'man of breeding' is he? He's a Levy, after all." We laughed—at Papa's pretensions and his honesty.

The wedding reception was at No. 22 Clifton Gardens. The house had four storeys and was set back in a private roadway. The service was conducted on the ground floor, in a drawing room with large bay windows. Why do I remember nothing about my gown, the guests or the ceremony? I have no photographs and it all passed so quickly. I do have the menu from the dinner—a small folded green card printed in silver. There were many courses and I suspect there was no discussion with the bride or groom about the choice of food. It included a 'refined' fillet of sole and to my amusement, looking back, beef tongue and aspic! It was written in French. Mamma would have liked that.

✳

chapter 25

CARAMELLED DATES

*Remove the stones from the dried dates. Fill
with almond marzapan. Cook a quantity
of loaf sugar with a dash of water over a
low fire until the sugar is melted. Stir with
a wooden spoon but after it boils, on no
account stir it again. The sugar will start
to bubble and by degrees turn to a dark
colour. Immediately dip each date into the
caramel and leave to set on an oiled tin.*

From Dina Levy's notebook, 1883

GIBRALTAR 1883—DINA

It took four days to make the sweets for the family celebration in Gibraltar. Joseph's mother bought a mountain
of ground almonds and sugar and worked with aunts and
cousins to turn them into tiny *queijinhos.* The almond
paste was rolled into barrel shapes to look like little
cheeses. Each one had a lid to hold in the sticky golden
filling which they called *yemma.* Then they were rolled in
more sugar. Meanwhile Joseph and I were having our own

sweet time, sailing from Southampton on the Peninsula and Oriental Line.

It was my first sea voyage. Although Papa was used to travelling, the furthest I'd ever been was to Brighton. We left our baggage in the cabin and went up on deck. It was too cold to sit out for long. The cabin was so small that we had to climb over each other to get anything out of the trunk. We hardly bothered to dress at all and the days and nights in bed merged into a haze of ecstasy.

When we arrived in Gibraltar Joseph pretended to be my personal guide:

"We are about to enter the most remarkable possession of the English Crown. There are but few features of interest in the town, most of the buildings being sadly wanting in the picturesque element."

"Where are we going?" I asked.

Joseph handed 1s 6d to the driver of the one-horse carriage:

"On a tour. That'll be enough for an hour."

"Do you want a guidebook Sir?" asked the driver.

"No thank you" said Joseph, smiling "I have been here before."

He squeezed my hand and said "You are now entering the narrow and gloomy thoroughfare called 'The Main Street'. There are two principal hotels—the Club House and the King's Arms. And from here we shall go to Beef Steak."

I thought he was referring to the hotel dinner but it turned out that this was the name of one of the sea caves on the eastern face of the rock. As the carriage rumbled through the streets Joseph put his arm around my shoulder:

"What are those round things you have on frocks?"

"Buttons."

"No, the shiny things."

"Diamond brooches."

"No. Those sparkly things—sequins—that's it. Your eyes remind me of sequins."

"I've never been in such sunlight. It would be grey and drizzling at home. Here it's so bright."

By the time we arrived at his family's house my face was flushed with excitement. I was about to ask why the street was called Engineer's Lane, but Joseph's parents came to the door and scooped me up in their arms. They took me inside, whisking me round the room, introducing me to uncles, brothers, cousins. At the 'small family celebration' I met a hundred more members of the Levy family. Great Aunt Deborah, now in her eighties, patted my hand and asked after my father. Joseph's brother Dan drew me aside and spoke in a low, measured tone:

"I understand you live in a fine house in London. He'll never be able to keep you in such style" he continued with a sneer "in the manner to which you have become accustomed."

I didn't know if he was being serious, but he added:

"Joseph doesn't believe in hard work. He … " I had heard enough and interrupted:

"Dan, I don't know anything about business. Women in our family have better things to do. You'll see. Joseph will manage perfectly well. Why don't you come and visit us when we're settled in Lisbon?"

A waiter was passing with a tray of caramelled dates. I

took one and lifted it out of the paper case. On an impulse I held it out and popped it straight into Dan's mouth. It was too big to swallow and he went to take it out but the caramel had stuck to his teeth. I moved away, leaving him struggling to retrieve pieces of the glassy sugar coating. Joseph was at the other side of the room. I never told him about our aborted conversation but I sometimes thought about it. Years later it came back to me, when the subject of money was the focus of a fraught exchange between my brothers and me.

The next day at breakfast Joseph picked up a knife and began to carve a block of butter into the shape of a rock.

"This is Gibralter. Here … ," he said, flattening the top of the butter at one end, "are Windmill Hill Flats, and at the tip is Europa Point."

"Can we walk up there?"

"It's uphill and it'll take three quarters of an hour."

"Well if I can manage all those flights of steps, I think I can do it."

We walked up an undulating road with the sea on our right. As we looked back at the town Joseph said:

"Did your father tell you much about the Rock?"

"About the town, yes. But nothing about his life. I imagine the places haven't changed that much, like the library with the log fires in the reading room. But there don't seem to be as many street sellers as he described."

"I wouldn't know about the library."

Our hands were linked and I looked down at his dark fingers and my pale ones. We'd arrived at Europa Point.

"We can't go anywhere from here," I said. "Let's go back."

Joseph resumed his role as my guide: "a few adventur-ous spirits have risked their necks in scrambling round the eastern side of the rock."

"Well, I don't feel that adventurous. I'd like us to be married for a bit more than a week."

"We can do it" he said. "I've ... " the rest of his words were lost in the wind. He was already finding a path, so I lifted my skirt and followed him. My last memory of Gibraltar was sitting on Dead Man's Beach with Joseph, my clothes covered in sand, catching my breath and gaz-ing out into the calm blueness.

When we arrived in Lisbon we had to give up our pass-ports at the police office in the custom house, waiting for authorization to reside in the city. We stayed at the Hotel Braganza and had a room with a balcony overlooking the wide river.

"We can just afford the 7s.6d a day" said Joseph. "But I think we do need a guide book here."

He purchased The Stranger's Guide and immediately started reading from a section on the Public Baths.

"There are floating objects, unpleasant to contemplate, which have been deposited nearby."

Joseph shook with laughter.

"You have a puerile sense of humour," I said.

"It's better than my brother Dan. He thinks it's amus-ing to criticize people."

"Yes, he does" I said, remembering our brief conversa-tion at his parents' party. And then, to conceal that I'd had first-hand experience of his insinuations, I added:

"I mean, there's no reason why two brothers should be alike."

"We're like cork and cheese," said Joseph.

"Chalk, you mean, I don't know about Portuguese, you're going to have to learn English," I smiled.

We stayed only a few days at the expensive Hotel Braganza and moved to a small boarding house in Baixa. It was a short street but I had a problem remembering the name 'Rua da Porta do Carro do Hospital Real de S. Jose'. We began to look for an apartment to rent. It seemed that houses were let by *semestre* or half year. Towards the end of May and December, tenants posted squares of white paper in their windows, informing passers-by that they intended to leave. For a few days around those dates we, like everyone else, kept our eyes turned towards the upper floors, wanting to know who was moving.

We walked and walked. The streets were paved with small hard stones—not rounded like cobbles but flat. At the sight of the first blister under my foot I bought a pair of thick-soled shoes. Joseph bought tobacco, a silk hat and kid gloves from Seville.

Now that I had the stout shoes, Joseph walked me the length of the new Avenida. Lined on both sides with trees and statues, it had small gardens and ponds, with cascading fountains. At the north end was a park with hot house plants. Joseph started to teach me some words of Portuguese, reading from a book by the poet Luis de Camoes.

"Are you going to read the whole poem?" I asked, closing my eyes.

"Since you don't appreciate it, I won't," he answered.

"It's not that I don't appreciate it, I can't understand it."

"It's a fiery love poem," he said.

"Well then, do read it."

"I don't think I will. There are more than eight thousand verses."

I thought of the poet a week later when we found an apartment on the second floor of a house near Praça de Camoes. It was in a *travessa*—a cross street called Rua Garret. Our building was covered in the blue and white azulejo tiles and when the summer came I found out that they kept the walls cool by reflecting the rays of the sun.

I was getting used to living in Lisbon. I loved the markets. There was the one with large white umbrellas where they rang a bell at 2pm to announce that all the stallholders had to clear the fruit and vegetables from the square. At the Ribeira Nova—the fish market—I joked to Joseph that the local people were always calling 'fish', but it was just their way of calling one's attention with that strange sound 'pish-sh'. We bought herring and sole because they were familiar but I soon learned to bargain for tunny and anchovies, as I'd learned the words *'atun'* and *'enchovas'*. One day Joseph came home with a live lobster.

"You know we can't eat lobsters."

"So Jews can't eat lobsters. But lobsters can eat Jews. I'm sure they're not fussy when they bite people," he replied.

"What a ridiculous argument," I said.

I gave the whole writhing, clicking bag to my neighbour and asked Joseph never to bring such a thing into our house again.

"You don't have a spirit of adventure," he complained.

"The last time we talked about that we nearly killed ourselves climbing over those rocks."

"All I'm saying is that we should try new things."

"If you want to do something adventurous, why don't we go to a bull fight?"

The following Sunday we took the tram to the Praça de Touros, buying two tickets for 100 reis, and for another 500 each (about 2s) we bought seats on the shade side of the galleria. We had read in our book that Portuguese bull fights had none of the '*barbarous cruelty and disgusting brutality*' of the ones in Spain.

"How do they fix those wooden balls to the tips of their horns?" I asked Joseph as the bulls were paraded round the ring. His answer was lost in a roar from the crowd as the cavalleiros in high boots appeared on their horses. I couldn't take my eyes off the men walking behind in their embroidered jackets and velvet breeches.

"Look at their thin shoes and white stockings" I said, trying not to watch as they fixed iron-barbed darts into either side of the bull's neck, just behind the horns. The noise from the crowd swelled again as the men jumped over the barrier to escape the bewildered and maddened animal.

"I don't know about bull fights in Spain, but this is brutal enough for me," muttered Joseph. I had stopped watching and was shielding my eyes.

"What's happening?" I asked.

A group of negro men had thrown themselves at the bull. It tossed one of them into the air and injured several others. A few stopped to pick up the coins that had been thrown from the stands. Six muscular men seized the bull by the tail and dragged it away. By this time I couldn't take my eyes off the drops of blood running down the animal's back. The whole performance was repeated with two more bulls. One had a glossy coat and bright black eyes. The other, which had fought before, had scars on its neck from the wooden darts. By the end of the evening I realized with horror that what had shocked me the first time no longer made me turn away with revulsion. The following week we went to the Opera.

Joseph found some rooms in a crumbling building at the corner of a square called Praça do Municipio. He carried on his business, exporting olive oil and sardines, but unlike my father who found commerce stimulating, he had no enthusiasm for finding new outlets or products.

"As long as I make enough for us to live, I am happy," he said. "I don't want to spend my time in a dusty office."

"I know. The sun is shining outside and you want to enjoy life." I'd taken the words out of his mouth, so he had to say something persuasive:

"Anyway, I can't be with you if I'm poring over a ledger."

He spent the minimum time in the office and for the rest we were hardly ever separated. On Saturdays we went to the synagogue and I had to climb up to the second level balcony where the women sat. On Sundays we were together again, walking through the orange groves of Belem, overlooking the river Tagus.

I loved Belem. I'd learned how to pronounce it properly—'Beleing'—and every Sunday we went to Black

Horse Square and waited for the tram. The journey took about thirty five minutes and wasn't particularly scenic, with the docks and the railway line on the left and old houses on the right. The tram went along Avenida da India in line with the river and passed the municipal library which used to be a 17th century palace. I always looked out for it because there were railings with thick stems of wisteria winding in and out of the metal and white flowers tumbling down till they brushed the ground. I could almost smell the scent from the tram. Wisteria was Mamma's favourite flower.

We explored the palaces and monuments and then walked the back streets where the houses had knockers in the shape of hands. Joseph wanted to buy one to replace the heavy brass knocker of our apartment and while he was looking for an ironmongery I watched the vegetable carts trundling along in the middle of the narrow streets. They were stacked high with leeks and broad beans, garlic, carrots and the most huge green cabbages.

We always ended up at the famous pastry shop—Pasteis de Belem—with tables inside. They only make one kind of pastry, called *pasteis de nata*. It has a crisp base and the creamiest custard—just set, so it doesn't ooze out when you bite into it. At the counter there are sugar sifters filled with cinnamon to shake over the tarts. They are the most delicious things I have ever eaten. Three or four aren't quite enough but five are just too much.

chapter 26

DINNER FOR 14 PEOPLE

games	*9s.9d*
crackers as name cards	*£1.17s.0d*
records	*14s.3d*
soup meat	*4s.9d*
poultry	*£1.14s.6d*
fish	*6s.9d*
laundress	*2s.0d*

From Dina Levy's account book, January 3rd 1924

LONDON 1960—ANNA

If the Levy family had kept diaries it would have helped Anna in her search for the truth. All she had was a collection of notebooks, filled with comments about the food they bought and ate. David's began with the mutton broth he'd copied from Mrs. Thomas and ended with pages about the annual balls, with meticulous detail of every penny he spent. The dinners and balls were the key to the door of upper class society; the success that would never have been his, had he remained a doctor.

Yet for Rachel the love of cooking was an escape; her kitchen was a haven of warmth and comfort where she could withdraw from society and spend time with Emily, creating unpretentious meals.

But it was often the gaps in the notes that were as revealing as the details. Dina kept two books: one listed the expenses for small dinner parties, the other contained recipe notes that were almost entirely sweet. They must have started when she was trying to recreate pastries she'd had in Gibraltar and Lisbon. And then for nineteen years there was no record of any entertaining in Dina's home. Anna, of course, knew why. After they left Lisbon their life changed. It was only in 1924, when Anna was twenty-one, that her mother resumed the entries in her book. The page was strangely worded, with the date at the top, the number of guests—fourteen—and a list of items including balloons and cigarettes. Yet there was no mention of the occasion, not a word that it was her daughter's coming of age.

Nina's twenty-first was another matter. Anna was planning a party. It was an opportunity for her to try out some of the recipes she'd cut out from magazines. Since Nathan never wanted to try anything new it would be a chance for her to pore over pictures in her French cookery books and experiment with galantines of poultry and nougatine baskets. Nina herself had never learned to cook. She saw no need: her mother was an expert patissière and chocolate maker, who turned out soups and roasts that defied the constraints of rationing.

Some weeks after the Samir episode they had gone to the seaside for the day. Nina had offered to help prepare the picnic. The sun disappeared behind black clouds and they sat in a beach hut facing the sands at Frinton. Anna unpacked fish patties and cucumber sandwiches but Nathan was waiting for a hard boiled egg. Nina cracked the first one, rolled it on the biscuit tin to break the shell and then peeled it carefully before handing it to her father. She did the same with the second egg—but when it hit the hard surface out came the slithering white and a ball of uncooked yolk. A sickly smear was sliding down her skirt, but as she scooped the mess out of her sandals she had to explain that anyone could make a mistake and pick up the wrong egg—it had nothing to do with being able to cook.

Nathan tried to distract her by asking whether she was planning to go away in the summer. Then somehow the discussion turned back to Samir and Nina's decision not to go to university. It made no sense to Nathan that his daughter was planning to leave school and start work immediately. How could anyone not want to go to Cambridge or Oxford? How could she prefer to work in an office, rather than pass the days punting on the river or walking through cloisters with manicured gardens? Nathan had won the battle to convince his daughter that she was too young to be married but he hadn't put enough effort into the next skirmish: persuading her to take up a place at university.

She had turned it down after the briefest investigation of the modern languages course. Because medieval French was an integral part of it, she rejected the whole idea of going away to learn about the literature that formed modern day European language and culture. For a while she toyed with the idea of going to the Interpreters' School in Geneva. Nathan had dismissed it in a couple of sentences:

"You have to spend all your time listening. I'm not sure you'd like that. You've always got plenty to say."

Nina hadn't bothered to reply. She was thinking of the rigorous training and wondered if she'd be good enough. Perhaps it was the self doubt that led her to make her own decision, without asking for further advice. She was keen to begin work; to start earning money and be independent. To her father's dismay she enrolled on a short secretarial course. He saw it as a waste of her education. She saw it as a way to acquire the skills needed for a job as a bilingual secretary.

After the first week she could hardly admit that the course was dreary. Typing was taught to the sounds of march music; fifty girls tapping away rhythmically, learning to place their fingers in the correct position on the *querty* keyboard. Bookkeeping was even more tedious. But after a month a chink of light broke through the boredom: half of each day was spent in learning a new skill that fascinated Nina. Shorthand proved to be the translation of language into a system of cleverly linked written strokes. She learned how to break down words into syllables that on the page turned into a series of lines, curves and circles. Transcribing the spoken word into code was exciting and the urge to reach greater speed was a challenge. But she had underestimated the difficulty of reading back her work, turning these marks into intelligible prose.

A bi-lingual secretary could hope to earn £9.50 a week.

Nina's first job was translating letters for a French drug company, with an office in London. On her first day she followed her boss into his office, smoothed down her skirt and took out her shorthand pad. She filled pages and pages as he dictated at speed and as she was so busy concentrating on the French words and the unfamiliar names of the drugs, she failed to have any understanding of the meaning of the correspondence. When she sat down at her typewriter she attempted to make sense of the hurriedly written lines and dots. She began to type, leaving gaps where she couldn't recognise what was on the page. She started again with a clean sheet of paper and decided to fill in the spaces with words that seemed to fit. The finished letters were delivered at the end of the day, ready for signature. The boss took one look at the nonsense she had produced and burst out laughing. The next day Nina was looking for a new job.

Tallino was a company that manufactured Italian knitwear. The work here involved liaison with the factory in Milan, explaining that a garment had two left sleeves or not enough buttons. The manager told Nina she could buy anything she wanted at cost price. The first time she went down to the packing department the staff were cold and pretended there was nothing to fit her. Each time she returned there was nothing in a size 12. After the third attempt it was obvious; the packing staff were furious that someone younger was on a higher salary, just because she could write letters in Italian. The atmosphere in the office became increasingly uncomfortable. Nina ate sandwiches for lunch while the other typists went to the local pub. In the afternoons, no one would show her

269

where to find a new typewriter ribbon and the post boy somehow forgot to pick up her mail at the end of the day. After a few weeks she decided to leave.

The next job was in the sales department of an engineering firm. The work was technical and challenging. Nina somehow made sense of the correspondence that came from Europe, translating into English with some skill. But when it came to putting sentences into a foreign language, this was vastly different. They gave her a brochure to translate into German. It was about spherical ball valves. *Kugelrundtanzgesellschaftklappe* was the word she came up with, but something told her that wasn't quite right. She handed the work in to her boss and immediately began to worry. She'd found all the words in a dictionary, but doubted whether a German engineer would make sense of her clumsy sentences. She pictured the finished brochure, with glossy pictures and prose that would make the reader cringe. It was too late to get it back; the manuscript had already gone to the printer. There was only one option now—to leave before publication day.

Nathan was concerned at the frequent job changes. He was still disappointed in his daughter's choice. While Anna was poring over pictures in cookbooks, deciding what to serve at Nina's party, he raised the subject again:

"My three years in Cambridge were the happiest times of my life."

"Thank you," said Anna, sensing that this was not one

of his jokes.

"No, what I mean is, we were carefree. We sat up late at night talking. There was always stimulating conversation. Not like the places we go to now where there's nothing but small talk. No one wants to discuss politics or books."

"But you were lucky. You had the choice to go away," said Anna.

"I know what you're going to say. You didn't," said Nathan.

"No, I didn't. I had to live at home so it had to be London university."

Nathan thought it better not to dwell on Anna's disappointments.

"It wasn't so easy for me either. After what happened in Bournemouth, Ma didn't want me to go away either."

Nina overheard the end of this conversation.

"Dad, don't you think it's about time you told me? About Bournemouth, and why you never wanted to go there?"

Anna interrupted:

"Look, it's a painful subject. Leave your father alone now. We'll tell you later. I want to talk about your 21st. I need to know about numbers and ..."

"I don't know why people make such a fuss about their 21st birthday. Was it always like that? Did you have a big party?"

Anna looked pensive.

"Actually it was the one time I remember my mother being happy. For all those years she'd cried and dressed in black. What I remember most was the white lace collar she put on for the evening. We had a dinner. I think she hired a cook for the evening."

"I thought she had no money. How could she afford that?"

"In those days you didn't need to be well off to have staff. Look in the notebook. The cook cost 16s and the whole of the dinner cost £21. Remember there were no machines then, so it made sense to spend two shillings on a laundress."

Nina turned to her father to ask him if he'd had a party for his twenty-first. He replied abruptly:

"No."

"Why not?"

Nathan sighed.

"Well, I suppose you have to know sometime, so I'll tell you. But promise me two things: you won't interrupt and when I've finished, you won't ask me to keep talking about it."

He began by describing Queen's College in Cambridge, punting on the river with his friends and the structure of the Wooden Bridge. Nina wondered what this had to do with a seaside town. Nathan was following a train of thought that would lead him to explain why he never wanted to go to Bournemouth.

chapter 27

NEW PICTURE PALACE

*The proposed theatre will be luxuriously
furnished, and will embody the acme of
ease and comfort. There will be a Tea-
house where afternoon tea may be taken
by Patrons of the Theatre. The exterior will
be attractive and the lofty facade when
electrically lit will be seen for some considerable distance.*

The Bournemouth Echo, 1910

LONDON 1960—NATHAN

"It was the end of my second year at Cambridge. Looking back, I wonder now that I was ever able to go back for
Part II of the Tripos."

He took a deep breath before he continued:

"I'd been working exceedingly hard. Pa suggested I
should go on holiday with Emma, my sister."

Nina waited for him to explain. Who was this sister
he'd never mentioned before?

"Emma was eighteen. She was very pretty. She looked

like Ma when she was young—black hair, coiled up at the back. And those long dresses, nipped in at the waist. And a parasol. She always carried one of those."

Nathan took a cigarette out of his case and tapped it on the lid.

"Where was I?"

"You were telling me about Emma. What she looked like. Was she like you?"

"Not at all. She wasn't serious like me. I was always reading, but she loved to paint."

"Where did she learn?"

"I don't think she ever had lessons, but she had a natural skill. She could look at a scene; fields or a cottage, and bring it to life with a few brushstrokes. She adored Monet and she practised his style of layering the paint. He did it in a seemingly careless fashion. I think she copied some of his themes—the rippling water and faded sunlight."

"Anyway, we went to stay at a boarding house in Bournemouth. It was in Bath Road, near the East Cliff. It wasn't far from the railway station. I seem to remember there was a cricket ground too."

"Did you go swimming with one of those horse-drawn bathing machines?"

Nathan didn't seem to hear Nina's question.

"In the evenings we went to the Theatre Royal in Albert Road. During the day we went to the Pleasure Gardens. Bournemouth was very genteel, it wasn't trippery."

"What does that mean?"

"You know, day trippers. They went to places like Margate and they'd spend the day on the sands. There were stalls where you could borrow a novel and take it to read in a deck chair."

"Did you go swimming?" Nina had seen old postcards of people strolling along the sands in their best clothes and wondered how the bathing machines worked.

"Not much. We did some wading in the sea at low tide. I rolled up the legs of my trousers and Emma hitched up her skirts. There was an ice cream stall on the beach and we queued up for wafers and cornets."

Nathan stopped for a moment as if he was remembering the taste of the vanilla ice cream.

"On the Thursday morning Emma said she was going for a walk. I arranged to meet her at a tea room at three o'clock. I got there early and she wasn't there. I waited for half an hour. I wondered if she'd forgotten. So I went out to look for her. She was nowhere to be seen."

"And?"

"I went back to the boarding house. They said she'd left hours before."

Nathan got up and poked the fire again. When he sat down it was as if a switch had been turned: he wanted to finish the conversation.

"She never came back. She just disappeared."

"How can anyone just disappear?" asked Nina.

"She went out perfectly happy. I never saw her again."

"But what happened? Did she have an accident?"

"I really don't want to talk about it any more," said Nathan.

"But you haven't finished. You can't just stop there."

Anna put her arm round Nathan's shoulder and gave him a hug. After a few minutes he got up and left the room. Nina waited for her mother to continue the story:

"By the evening Nathan was frantic. He'd looked everywhere so he went to alert the coast guards. He thought Emma might have gone to take a walk along the sands, and got swept out to sea. He sent a telegram to his parents and his father came down on the next train."

"For five days the two of them walked the streets of Bournemouth. They waited till the evenings to go down to the sands, as there were fewer people around then. They walked along the beach searching the sea shore for a sighting of something; an item of clothing, who knows what? All they could see were footprints of dogs and rubber soled shoes criss-crossing in patterns across the sand. Nathan and Pa trudged as far as Boscombe pier and then all the way back along the West Promenade."

"They called in the police and after a few days they decided to hire a private detective. There had been no news: no evidence that Emma might have been kidnapped, or murdered. The coast guards told them it could take days for a body to be washed up on the shore. Nathan waited and his father went back to London. His mother was inconsolable. She must have known then that something terrible had happened; that she'd never see her daughter again."

"Nathan didn't give up. He went back to Bournemouth four times in the next few weeks. He pestered the police. He put notices on trees and posted advertisements in the local paper. The detective was searching for clues. Was Emma unhappy? Had she been ill? Was it likely that she'd gone to meet someone? They came up with negative responses for every avenue they tried."

"Nathan returned to London. His mother was in

mourning. He and his father said *kaddish* and went to synagogue every day. His mother had a small prayer book that she read at home. In the back was a list of short blessings—one for each occasion: seeing a rainbow, smelling a sweet-scented fruit, moving into a new house, returning safely from a journey. She just sat reading psalms. In the back of the book was The Burial Service. It ended with the words *'The Lord God will wipe away tears from off all faces.'* There were no prayers for when someone had disappeared. There was no grave. Only a gaping void in their lives."

Anna looked drained. Nina came over and said:

"Why didn't you tell me before? All those times I kept asking Dad why he didn't want to go to Bournemouth."

"And now you know why he never wanted to go on holiday. Why he buries himself in his books; why he doesn't bother about trivial things like clothes."

In a low voice Anna continued:

"It took me a long time to understood about his Ma. It wasn't that she disliked me. She simply couldn't bear the thought of anyone replacing her daughter."

chapter 28

WANTED

Smart boy for office work and errands. Must be quick and willing. Apply: Edward Johnson, Private Detective, Old Christchurch Road.

The Bournemouth Echo, 1910

LONDON 1965—ANNA

It was only after his marriage that Nathan had felt able to talk to Anna about his sister's disappearance. It was twenty-seven years after the event. He relived that morning in 1910 when Emma had gone out and never returned. And then he didn't speak of it again, until the day when Nina asked him why there were no celebrations for his twenty-first birthday.

By keeping silent he had tried to heal the wound, but for years he kept picking away at the scab, opening up the sore. He paid the private detective for six months and all the time he was doing his own investigations. He would turn his face in a crowd and follow a young woman with the same hair as Emma. He kept in contact with the police and long after they had lost interest he continued to search for clues, following up any possibility. He visited asylums, checking on lists of inmates; he read books on amnesia and melancholia. He was never prepared to close the door.

Eventually he started to go out again—to theatres or the music hall. But when the lights were turned low, he would scan the faces of the artistes, wondering if perhaps, somehow Emma had walked out of her own free will and chosen to join a troupe of actors. Nathan couldn't bear to go to picture galleries: even if the exhibition featured Cezanne or Pisarro, he was nervous that there might be a Monet and the sight of the short and feathery brushstrokes would bring back memories of Emma's paintings.

Worst of all was the feeling of guilt—that he should have prevented the disaster from happening; that he was somehow to blame. His parents never gave him cause to feel responsible. They had a strong faith and believed that Emma's disappearance was '*beshert*'; that it was predestined, a question of fate.

In the first few years their friends learned not to mention that Emma was missing. Yet Nathan heard the whispers, the speculation about what might have happened. During that period he received strange phone calls. He would pick up the receiver and wait for the caller to speak. Then there'd be a click and silence. On one occasion a voice spoke: telling him that Emma had been spotted, working as a governess in a house in South London. Nathan took down the address, went to the area and found that no such street existed.

By the time he married, Nathan had relegated the tragic

event to the past—just as long as no-one talked about it. Anna was different; she could never let go of the things that worried her, bringing them up over and over again. Her resentment at her mother's control over her early life simmered away, even after Dina's death. Then there was a bitterness about money. Her mother had few funds, due entirely to an act of deceit in 1905, two years after Anna was born. Neither of them ever forgot the dishonesty or the perpetrator.

It wasn't that Anna talked about the events incessantly; it was as if she was always looking through a pair of glasses that were cloudy, never able to see a clear picture. Anna's mind was filled with thoughts of what might have been and the constant reminders of other people's prosperity. A wealthy cousin acquired a sports car and asked her if she wanted to go for a ride. He drove up to the house and took out a handkerchief to wipe a speck of dust from the highly polished wax. Anna stepped on to the running board, marvelled at the dashboard and squeezed herself into the passenger seat. The driver revved round the streets and when Anna got home Boni couldn't wait to hear what the car was like.

"Squashed," replied Anna. "There's no room to swing a cat in those seats."

When Anna went shopping she tried to make small economies. Yet her appreciation of fine leather gloves or tailored costumes was at odds with the price, so instead of buying new, she would make her clothes last another season. With Nina she solved the problem by sewing; she would never set foot in the dress department of Debenham and Freebody, though her daughter would have been delighted with a bought dress—perhaps even more thrilled with one from a cheaper store. When it came to presents it was a different matter. Anna would spend hours searching for the perfect gift, trying to outdo Boni in the size of the box or the ribbon on the wrapping. When Nina was twelve Anna bought her a Slazenger tennis racquet. It had to be the best. She herself had only ever had second-hand racquets. She brought it home, wrapped the box in crêpe paper and tied the parcel in an extravagant flourish of velvet ribbon. The morning of the birthday arrived. Nina went to answer the doorbell. A van driver was delivering a bicycle; a bottle green Raleigh with three-speed gears and shiny wheels. The card said: *With love from Aunt Boni.* Anna signed the delivery slip, pulled the bicycle inside, and slammed the door.

Nina had little understanding of her mother's oscillating behaviour: one moment she would be trying to save a shilling; the next she would be buying Nathan a fine fountain pen that cost her a week's housekeeping money. Anna's attempts to avoid interfering were a mystery to her daughter. While other parents kept their teenage children on a tight rein, Anna encouraged Nina to go on holiday with Rosemary. They'd been together all through their school days, so what was wrong with them spending two weeks in Italy in the summer? Rosemary's parents had doubts about letting two seventeen-year olds travel alone. Anna dismissed the dangers and convinced them that it was perfectly safe. They exchanged phone calls every day the girls were away, yet neither set of parents had any idea of what their daughters were doing. When Nina returned from Sorrento she said nothing about rid-ing on a scooter with an Italian waiter and going on a date with a man she'd met on the ferry to Capri. Anna tried, as she had with Samir, not to be inquisitive. She looked at the letters postmarked 'Positano' and passed them on without a word. Nina was grateful for the tactful silence but she must have sensed her mother's underlying feelings of regret and missed opportunities.

Nina seemed unable to hold down a job—or a boyfriend. Her parents watched as she moved from one office to another. They lay in bed awake as their daughter brought back a series of young men, serving them coffee till the early hours of the morning. What was she doing? Nathan didn't want to go downstairs in his pyjamas; Anna lay awake, unable to fall asleep, thinking she was doing the right thing by giving her daughter the freedom she never had.

By the age of twenty-six Nina was feeling stifled. She wanted to leave home but could offer no explicit reason. Her parents allowed her to stay out late and asked no questions. Most of her women friends were married, settled in homes in the outer suburbs, bringing up children with the help of a Swiss au pair. Nina felt the need for change, for another job, perhaps in a new place.

She decided to apply for work in America. She signed up with an agency in New York, claiming she could speak three languages, though her German was far from fluent. Anna outwardly approved of her plans but listened with more than a tinge of jealousy as Nina talked about the relative advantages of living on the East or West side of Manhattan. Why did she have to go so far away? She could have rented a perfectly respectable flat in London, somewhere off the Edgware Road, perhaps, near to the tube and within walking distance of Marble Arch.

The date was fixed. Nina was to leave on the 5th May. For two weeks Anna prepared for a party to mark her going. They hadn't entertained on this scale for five years, since Nina's twenty-first. Nathan had persuaded Anna that they were happy as they were, rarely going out and hardly ever inviting guests. When Nina left, who would be there to try the Stuffed Tomatoes Egyptienne or Chocolate Profiteroles that Anna had added to her repertoire?

The cooking was done in stages: tongues were left to pickle in brine, egg yolks were whisked into mayonnaise for the Salade de Boeuf, pastry was rolled and cut into tartlets and boats. Days before the party the house was filled with the smell of chicken stock simmering on the hob and apples stewing for the sauce for the duck. Anna's fingernails were breaking as she lifted pots and peeled vegetables. Boni came to help with the sweets, pressing out almond paste to form the *queijinhos* and stirring the golden *yemma* sauce for the filling. While it was cooling she called to Anna that she was going out to buy a present for Nina.

Anna was too busy to take much notice. She checked the menu and wondered, not for the first time, whether it made sense to offer duck, chicken and beef. She wrote out the order for the greengrocer and piped chestnut purée into the pastry boats.

On the eve of the party, two days before Nina was due to leave for New York, Boni arrived with her present. She got out of a taxi, asking the driver to help her bring in the heavy packages. Both the parcels were wrapped in crisp paper and tied with fine satin ribbon. Nina ripped open the first one and stood there, amazed. It was a suitcase made of cream-coloured leather with a scarlet silk lining. The other parcel contained a matching case, this one in two parts, with hangers for dresses on one side and red silk pockets for clothing on the other. Anna was speechless. She hadn't bought her daughter a going away present. She'd been stuck in the kitchen, preparing the food for fifty people. Nina was too excited to notice her mother's tight lips.

At the party Nina took Rosemary into her bedroom to see what Aunt Boni had bought her. Anna stayed downstairs. As she cleared away the plates she thought about the cream leather. What a ridiculous colour for luggage. Anyone could see that the cases would get scuffed and you'd never be able to get the marks off.

Anna and Nathan drove to Southampton with Nina to see her off. They went on board the liner and when they had found her cabin they explored the decks and the 700-seater dining room. The moment came when visitors were asked to leave so they walked down the gangplank and waved goodbye. Anna couldn't remember where they had left the car. Nathan, who never drove, had made a note of the street name on the back of a cigarette packet. On the journey home Anna took her hand off the gear lever, wiped her eyes and passed the handkerchief to Nathan.

When Nina arrived in New York she knew no-one. The agency suggested she could find a furnished apartment between Lexington and Third Avenues. The buildings all seemed to have doormen so she assumed the rent would be too high. She took the cross town bus to the West side and started walking the side streets between Riverside and West End Avenue. She eventually found a building on 86th Street. The kitchen was dark with a small window facing the fire escapes at the back. The view from the bedroom was more promising: a bustling cross street with grocery stores and neon lights. Nina moved in and set up a desk with her typewriter, a stack of red/black ribbons and carbon paper. She arranged her dictionaries on the bookshelf along with the Penguin paperbacks. She unpacked her records and arranged clothes in the wardrobe to the sounds of The Seekers.

Now all she needed was the work. She'd spent too long arranging and re-arranging her possessions and was happy to begin work on a set of training manuals that arrived in the post. The agency followed these with divorce documents and adoption certificates. Nina returned the translations within days. She dealt with a fifty-page medical brochure, but didn't return the double-spaced sheets until she had checked and double-checked for errors. And then she heard nothing from the agency for a few weeks. She went into the office and scanned the noticeboard. There was a request for a Spanish speaker to *traduccir poemas.* There was no work for French or Italian.

After the fiasco at the engineering company Nina was reluctant to offer German as one of her languages. Her vocabulary was poor and by the time she'd looked up the nouns in a dictionary and worked out the complex word formation with the verb at the end, she'd forgotten the meaning of the first words in the sentence.

She phoned home to take her mind off concerns about how she was going to pay the rent. Anna answered the phone and told her some surprising news: she'd persuaded Nathan to start going out more. She chattered on about a play by Harold Pinter and how Nathan was even prepared to go to a cinema to see Dr. Zhivago. Nina wanted to tell her mother about the work problems, but instead she listened as Anna said:

"He calls it a picture palace. He's so old fashioned."

"Mum ... " said Nina.

"We went to a Gilbert and Sullivan last week. I've even got him to agree to go to a new restaurant—the one at the top of the Post Office Tower."

Nina sighed. It was ironic that her departure had forced Nathan to be more sociable. Her parents were evidently happier than they'd been in years. She didn't want to spoil their pleasure by telling them that life in New York was not quite as good as she'd hoped.

The restaurant that Anna had chosen was in a revolving glass area 540 feet above central London. They ordered a bottle of wine with their meal. The menu offered little choice if you didn't eat meat or shellfish. Anna of course refused the *vichyssoise* soup—it was bound to be made with stock from a non-kosher chicken. They opted for *sole véronique* which came with a floury white sauce and two or three grapes. When the bill came Nathan looked glum. Anna reminded him that people only came to the

Post Office Tower for the view.

On the way home Nathan complained that he was feeling tired. At the front door he fumbled in his pocket for the key. He walked through the hall into the sitting room and had a strange sensation that he was about to lose his balance. He lowered himself into a chair and closed his eyes. He couldn't wait to go bed but he had to walk slowly as the walls seemed to be closing in on him. He shouldn't have agreed to go out to the restaurant. He'd only had one glass of wine so it must have been the rich food that was making him feel unsteady.

chapter 29

IN FRANCE, TEA IS USUALLY MADE BADLY. HERE IS
THE BEST WAY:

> *A glazed crockery teapot is preferable, but
> one of porcelain, metal, or enamel may be
> used. Pour one cup of boiling water into
> the pot. Put on the lid. Shake to wet and
> heat all the interior. After a minute, pour
> out the water. Put in one small teaspoon of
> tea for each person, fill the pot, cover and
> let steep for three minutes. Serve at once,
> otherwise bitterness will spoil the aroma.
> Water that has been boiled several times
> or too long will not make as good tea as
> freshly boiled water.*

The Art of French Cooking, 1965

LONDON 1965—ANNA

Nathan woke up the next day, dressed and went down
for breakfast. Anna passed him some toast and a cup of
tea. He moved his hand forward but his fingers wouldn't
close around the handle. The cup tipped over, pouring

the steaming liquid over the table. Anna began to mop it up and when Nathan leaned forward to help he felt a rush of dizziness in his head. He wanted to go and sit in the armchair but couldn't stand up. His right foot was fixed to the floor. He sat back again and started to talk:

"I want sssssshhhhh I want to ... "

The words wouldn't come out. They were floating round his brain and he couldn't get them lined up. He shook his head to shut out the confusion. When he opened his eyes a man was taking his pulse and shining a light into his pupils. He heard the words 'doctor' and 'ambulance' and let himself sink into unconsciousness.

At the hospital a junior doctor confirmed the GP's initial diagnosis: Nathan had suffered a severe stroke. Tests done in the next few hours revealed that the blood supply to part of his brain had been blocked and within minutes the brain cells had died. The right side of his body was paralysed and he was unable to move his arm and leg.

Anna sat by the bedside, stroking the fingers of a hand that had no feeling. She wondered if anything could have been done to prevent the stroke. He wasn't overweight; he ate and drank in moderation. The doctor had confirmed what she knew: the cause was more likely to be hereditary.

When he woke up Nathan asked what was happening. He spoke slowly as if his mouth was full of bubbles, but the words made sense. It was clear that the link between the lips and the brain had not been seriously affected. Anna didn't tell him about her conversation with the consultant. When she'd asked about the prognosis the answer had been direct:

"One third of patients recover well; one third have mild to severe disabilities and a third die. In your husband's case, it looks as if he will be in the second category."

The tests had shown that Nathan was unlikely to make a full recovery. The doctors prescribed drugs for the next forty eight hours to get him past the imminent danger of a further stroke. The crisis passed and a physiotherapist was called to discuss rehabilitation. Anna was realistic: was it likely that a man of seventy-six could learn to walk again?

When he was ready to leave, a hired wheelchair was brought into the ward. Two nurses helped to lift Nathan out of bed into the chair and wheeled him out to where Anna was waiting with the car. Skilled hands lifted him from behind, moved the paralysed leg and pulled him on to the seat. They closed the door and Nathan sat staring ahead. Back at the house Anna struggled to unfold the wheelchair and find the brake. She positioned it alongside the car and strained to lift Nathan out. What had seemed easy with two nurses now seemed impossible. Nathan could move his left leg but didn't have the strength to stand. How could she heave his body out of the passenger seat on to the wheelchair? Each time she tried Nathan slumped back, convinced he was going to fall. It began to rain and with a final effort Anna moved him to the edge of the seat, sliding and pulling till she finally manoevred him on to the chair and clicked down the foot supports. She lifted both his feet off the pavement and turned the chair round to negotiate the two steps up to the house. When they were inside she left Nathan sitting in the wheelchair, with one arm hanging down, both of them too exhausted to perform the whole process in reverse and get him comfortable in an armchair.

Anna went into the kitchen and filled the kettle. She had to solve the problem of how to move him from one seat to another. A cup of tea would help. She brought the tray into the living room and they drank the tea in silence. Anna looked at the wheelchair and the armchair, trying to work out the best way to deal with the lifting. Nathan had to learn to stand on his good leg. She lifted him up, put her arm firmly round his waist and held him for several minutes.

"I can't do it," he said, sinking back into the wheel-chair.

"Yes you can. Try again. Let's get you up and have you facing the right direction. Lean on me while you take one step."

It took several attempts but eventually she got Nathan settled and left him with the newspaper on his knee while she folded the wheelchair and put it away in the hall. When she came back half the paper was on the floor and the rest lay crumpled in his hand. His fingers were cold. Anna brought a rug but as soon as she turned her back it slipped off, leaving him trying to lean over and pick it up with his left hand.

Nathan looked up and said:

"Well, that's me done for, isn't it?"

Anna was close to tears when she replied:

"We'll manage. It may get better in a few weeks."

The doctor had said that if one area of the brain had been damaged, it was possible for another part to take over. She knew this was unlikely.

Anna had arranged for the beds to be brought downstairs. The large front room had been hastily converted into a bedroom and the walnut side tables were piled with books, table lamps that needed plugging in, slippers, pyjamas and her own handcreams and reading glasses. She looked at the mess, wondering where to start. She turned and went into the kitchen.

In the next few days the full implications of Nathan's stroke began to sink in. He had to accept that he had become totally dependent on someone else. He needed his wife to lift him on to the toilet, wash him all over and struggle to get his legs and arms into his clothes. Thank God he still had the use of one hand so he could wipe his own bottom.

For Anna the realization came gradually. She accepted at once that it wasn't like caring for a patient with 'flu who was expected to get better the following week. She could see the days stretching ahead, filled with tasks she would be required to do. She'd have to take the top off his boiled egg, butter the bread and find the simplest way of making sure she would hear when he called. That was obvious. a small brass bell would solve the problem. In that first week she was happy if she'd worked out how to prop up a book, how long it took Nathan to read a page of the newspaper before she was needed to take it from him and turn it over. If she'd known then that matters would only get worse, that paralysis brought with it inevitable complications, she might have been more gloomy.

Nina offered to come straight back from New York.

"Wait a few weeks, darling. There's no immediate danger and your Dad may feel a bit better in a while."

As soon as Anna had said the words she regretted telling Nina not to come. Nathan couldn't be left alone for ten minutes, so she was trapped in the house, unable to go beyond the post box without making arrangements for someone else to be there. Boni phoned to ask if she needed help:

"Help?" Where could she begin? There was no bread in the house. The milk in the fridge had gone sour. Perhaps she could use it to make scones? But there was little point in that if there was no tea to go with them.

"Well, yes, Boni, you could do some shopping for me."

"Sure, as long as it's not too heavy. My back's playing up."

"Don't bother then. The district nurse is coming this afternoon. I can pop out while she's here."

Anna had worked out that it took half an hour for the nurse to give Nathan a bath. She came twice a week. That would allow seven minutes to walk to the corner shop, five minutes to pay the paper bill, eight minutes in the queue at the greengrocer and another ten minutes to walk back. But when the nurse came Anna slumped into a chair to read the newspaper and fell asleep. She was woken by a cheery voice calling "Bye now" and the sound of the front door closing. There was still no milk for a cup of tea.

Nathan was settled in his chair wearing clean pyjamas. The nurse never bothered to dress him; it was so much easier to pull on two loose garments than struggle with vest and pants, socks, shirt and a tie. Anna didn't like to see him in pyjamas during the day. If anyone were to come to the house, it would look as if she hadn't bothered.

But lifting Nathan out of the chair and pulling his clothes on or off took forty five minutes—nearly an hour twice a day, of heaving, stretching and struggling with sleeves and bending down to tie shoe laces. By ten o'clock she was exhausted; it was too late for the television news and she was too tired to read a book. She sat at her desk to pay the bills, trying to ignore the pain running down the back of her calves, and finally went to the bathroom and brushed her teeth. Nathan rarely woke during the night and Anna lay in the high single bed, listening to his slow breathing. When she finally fell asleep she dreamt she was in a deserted street with newspaper pages floating down from the sky and someone telling her she had to pick them all up.

The next morning Anna phoned her neighbour to ask if she could borrow some milk. The woman came round with a small cup and stood in the doorway, waiting to be invited in. Nathan was calling. The woman was asking if she thought he'd be out and about in a few weeks.

"I expect so," said Anna.

She closed the door. Nathan called out to tell her that the physiotherapist was late for her weekly visit. With little to occupy him, his eyes were fixed on the clock, watching the minutes pass.

"I don't want to exercise the fingers of my paralysed hand," he protested.

"But you have to," said Anna gently.

"And there's no point in her pummelling the limbs I can use."

He was supposed to keep moving every day, but apart from the walk to the bathroom, he'd persuaded Anna

295

that the caliper fixed to his bad leg was painful and it was best to 'leave him be'. They both dreaded the woman's visit. It made Anna feel like a child who hadn't done her homework. She was reminded of her Latin lessons, when she'd failed to learn the passive tense. Now at the age of sixty-two she felt she'd finally mastered it; in the space of a few weeks, her life with Nathan had changed from the active to the passive, with little chance of the process being reversed.

chapter 30

PLUM CAKE

*6 oz butter, 6 oz sugar, 6 oz plain flour, 3
eggs (separated), grated rind of half a lemon, 1 lb red plums or greengages*

Preheat the oven to 375°F, Gas 5.

*Cream together the butter, sugar, egg yolks
and flour. Add the lemon rind. Whisk the
whites and fold them into the mixture,
which should be fairly stiff. Spoon it into
a buttered and floured oblong cake tin.
Halve the plums and take out the stones
and arrange them on top of the cake, pressing them down lightly. Bake for 40—50
minutes.*

From Anna's notebook, 1965

LONDON 1965—ANNA

Nina was in the middle of an important assignment.
The agency had put her in touch with a man who was
writing a biography and had a hundred letters to translate from Italian into English. At first she'd agreed to her

mother's suggestion that she should wait a few weeks before going to London, but almost immediately she changed her mind: there was no reason why she couldn't take the work with her. She booked a flight and arrived the next day.

When she walked into the house she took a deep breath when she saw her father. He was slumped in a chair, sleeping, with one arm hanging down. He was wearing a new jacket but it looked as if her mother had chosen the wrong size. The sleeves were the right length but there was a space between the buttons and the bones of his ribs.

Her parents seemed to be in a routine. It was clear to Nina that Nathan couldn't be left on his own. He couldn't move from one position to another; couldn't do any of the things that needed two hands: cutting up food, shaving, or opening toothpaste. He was unable to write, to open an envelope, to pick up a towel from the floor. She was planning to stay for two weeks but how could she go back and leave her mother with such a burden?

The air ticket wasn't changeable. But it was paid for and she could buy another one in a few weeks, perhaps a month or so. Maybe she could pick up some more work in London? Or she could stay indefinitely and give up her life in America.

Nina listened to her father talking about cleaning his shoes:

"I can't even do that any more. You need two hands—one to hold the shoe and another to put on the polish and hold the brush."

Nina didn't reply. She was thinking about the lease on

her New York apartment.

"But I suppose it doesn't matter. I don't get out much nowadays."

"I know." Nina thought it best not to remind him of their last conversation when he'd told her he'd been gallivanting all over London.

As if he'd read her mind he said:

"It's funny, your mother got me going to the theatre and the cinema. That was probably what brought all this on."

Nathan gave a weak smile and lifted a glass of water to his lips. Anna brought the bottles of pills, took off the caps and watched while he lined up the tablets and swallowed each one separately. The three of them sat in silence.

Anna had lived her life under a cloud of resentment; always thinking of what might have been. If it hadn't been for Dina she would have travelled more; if it hadn't been for the war she would have had a successful business; if she hadn't quarrelled with Isaac she would have had a normal relationship with her brother. All of this seemed insignificant compared with what was facing her now. Overnight Nathan had become disabled and she had become a full time carer. There would be no outings and no holidays. There were two windows in the week when she could pop out to buy food. The days of wandering around in the West End, looking at dress materials, buying ribbons, they were gone. Yet for some reason even she couldn't understand, Anna no longer felt resentful. It was hardly Nathan's fault that he couldn't move. She watched as he sat all day in the same chair with little to say, even wishing that he would come out with one of his outrageous remarks. He was like a child at a birthday party, on best behaviour, waiting for his mummy to collect him so he could complain about the colour of the balloon or the way he'd nearly won at 'pass the parcel'.

When Nina had unpacked she offered to stay with her father so that Anna could go out. The offer was refused. Nina gave her five good reasons why she should accept so Anna changed her mind and finally agreed to leave Nathan at home for a few hours the next day. Nina was asleep while Nathan's pyjamas were removed, pants and vest tugged into place and shirt and trousers buttoned and zipped. She took a long bath and came out of the steamy room to find her mother preparing breakfast and lunch. By nine thirty Nathan was ready to face the day; a book propped up on his table, the radio within reach of his left hand and the pills counted out and lined up on a tray.

By force of habit Anna walked quickly to the bus stop. By the time she reached Oxford Street a quarter of her free time had evaporated. The stores were almost empty and she rode up the escalators, unable to decide whether to stop at the fashion floors or the home furnishings. She wandered through the blouse department and watched a young woman flicking through a rail of skirts. Anna felt fat and depressed. She pictured herself trying on a tight-waisted tweed costume, struggling to do up the zip in a cramped changing room. She took the lift to the ground floor and breathed in the heavy scent of the perfumery department. A young man approached, brandishing a spray of the latest fragrance. In the haberdashery department silks and knitting wools were stacked up in rainbow lines. Anna kept looking at her watch. Three hours had passed. She needed to get home. With nothing to show for her outing, she crossed the road and waited for a bus.

Nina was surprised to see her mother arrive home empty-handed, Nathan had been no trouble—in fact he'd been asleep most of the time. She was beginning to think it wasn't so hard after all. She'd spent an hour working on her translation and then she'd woken him up for lunch and heated the meal that Anna had left. They'd listened to the one o'clock news and Nathan closed his eyes again while Nina took the tray into the kitchen and left it on the worktop. There wouldn't be any need to change her air ticket. The situation wasn't as bad as she'd thought. After all, there was nothing she could do for her father and her mother seemed quite cheerful.

Nina was in the bedroom putting on mascara when Anna returned home. As soon as he heard the key in the door Nathan rang the bell. It was clear that he was agitated and needed to go to the bathroom. Anna hoisted him out of the chair, put his arm round her shoulder and walked with him along the corridor, repositioning the paralysed leg after each step. It would have been quicker in the wheelchair, but that involved taking it out, fixing the foot supports and more lifting. If he didn't make it in time, there was no one to blame but herself. She couldn't be angry with him; he'd waited for hours for her to come back. He wouldn't have wanted to ask Nina to help him.

A few months after the onset of the paralysis, Nathan had a particularly bad day. He was having difficulty swallowing and asked to have his food mashed up. He had stopped reading; the library books piled up unread as he was unable to concentrate for more than ten minutes at a time. The television flickered in front of him but he had no interest in the afternoon stories for children and was dozing in front of the black and white screen by the time the comedy shows gripped the nation in the evenings. The last thing he wanted was company. He would have been content never to see anyone else but Anna.

In fact, hardly anyone came to the house apart from the Jaffés. They came every week and never arrived empty handed. For Anna there would be a French loaf and some cheese that Janine would take straight into the kitchen. But first she would pull out a small bag of pear drops and put them on the table in reach of Nathan's good arm. Jacques was the only friend who could engage him in conversation. Instead of assuming that his mind was half paralysed like his body, he talked about the news. While Nathan found it hard to concentrate on reading the papers, he was keen to discuss the conflict in Vietnam. Jacques defended President Johnson who had recently committed a further 50,000 troops to the region:

"What a dreadful burden for a leader, sending what he calls 'the flower of our youth, our finest young men' into battle."

"Reminds me of the first World War" said Nathan. "I have more sympathy with the men that their commanders. You should read Wilfred Owen. We've got his poems somewhere."

When the visitors had left Anna tried to keep Nathan talking. She told him that Raoul was living in France and was going out with a girl his parents disapproved of. According to Janine she was ugly but it was clear that any prospective daughter-in-law would have been an unwelcome addition to their tight knit family. Nathan had stopped listening and began to sink back into his shrunken world, saying he was tired. It was the silence that led to Anna's suggestion that she should start a new activity:

"You know they keep telling you to exercise your limbs? I think I need to exercise my brain. What would you say if I started to learn bridge?"

"I don't want you to go out. You'll leave me with one of those agency nurses, like the one who came on Tuesday."

Anna had indeed hired a nurse, at Boni's suggestion. They had booked a table for lunch at a restaurant with pink tablecloths and the menu propped up against a vase with a single rose. Anna was jumpy with the waiter and seemed unrelaxed as they waited for the food. Boni told her that she just needed to get out more often, and they planned to make it a regular arrangement.

Anna reassured Nathan:

"I'll only go out once a week. And the bridge games, they could be here. But you've got to promise not to say anything rude to my friends."

Nathan replied:

"I don't have many pleasures. Why do you want to take that away?"

It was the first time they'd laughed for months. Anna had a friend, Elena Marouk, who was a bridge teacher.

It was arranged that she'd invite two other friends and they'd have a lesson once a week. Somehow it was decided that Anna would give them all supper instead of paying for the lessons. The game was fixed for Monday evening.

With Nathan asleep in his chair Anna began to do the cooking. She'd planned to make a leek soup, followed by sole in mushroom sauce. Elena was particularly fond of Anna's plum cake, so she started by weighing out the butter and sugar. She was about to line the cake tin with greased paper when Nathan rang the bell to ask for a glass of water. She came back to the kitchen, ready to whisk the egg whites, when he called out, saying that the newspaper was in a tangle. Anna went in crossly and replaced the paper with a book, opening it at the page with the bookmark. Just as she started to spoon the cake mixture into the tin, he called her again to say that his shoe was hurting and he needed to take it off.

Anna cut the plums and laid them on to the batter. She slid the cake into the oven and went to deal with the shoes. It was six thirty. In half an hour they'd be here, ready to eat. She hadn't peeled the potatoes or made the mushroom sauce. When the doorbell rang Anna was far from ready; the cake was nearly cooked but the sauce for the fish hadn't thickened and the new potatoes still had the skins on.

The bridge lesson went well. Elena explained the rules of bidding and walked round the card table, arranging the hands and pointing to the best card to lead. By eight-thirty they were all hungry so the table was cleared and covered with a starched tablecloth. Anna carried in the soup. Nathan was asleep in his chair. She served the rest of the meal, watching to see if he was waking up, needing to be helped with his food. When she brought in the cake, she cut it into squares. It was crumbly and buttery with halved plums oozing red juice. To her surprise her guests took a couple of mouthfuls and then pushed away their plates. Anna cleared away and took the cake into the kitchen. As she ran water into the sink she could hear them dealing the next hand. She turned off the tap and saw by the side of the weighing machine a bowl of sugar. She'd forgotten to put it into the mixture. No wonder the dessert was inedible. Anna picked up the remains of the plum cake and tripped as she went to open the bin. The red juices dripped down the tiles and the cake landed on the floor. She picked up a cloth, wiped the wall and went back into the living room. Nathan was snoring; the other three were waiting for her to continue the game. Anna noticed a red stain on her skirt. She picked up her hand, looked at the dreadful cards she'd been dealt and burst into tears.

chapter 31

Yemma (can be used as a spread on buttered matzah or sandwiched between layers of sponge cake)

Take a whole vanilla pod and cut it through. Boil ½ lb sugar with ½ glass water and to this add the seeds scraped from the pod and the pod itself. Once the sugar has melted it is advisable not to stir the syrup. Cook until the syrup becomes fairly thick. It should reach what is called the 'thread' stage, that is, it should form a thread when tested between the thumb and first finger. However, take care: sugar syrup is very hot so if your fingers are unused to great heat, pour a little on to a plate and lift it with a spoon.

Then pour the syrup gradually on to 12 yolks of eggs, beating all the while off the fire. Put the pan back over hot water and stir the yemma on a slow fire until it thickens. On no account leave to attend to tradesmen or other matters, but beat constantly for 10—15 minutes. Pour it into a clean jar and let it cool.

From Dina's notebook, 1892

Life in Lisbon was sweet. On the corner of our street was a pastry shop. What I remember most about that shop was the *yemma*—the golden filling for cakes and almond biscuits. I'd first tasted it in Gibraltar, at the time of our wedding, and here it was again—a smooth thick mixture, flecked with black dots from the inside of a vanilla pod. One day when I was in the shop, the owner invited me to go into the back and watch them making it. Fifty egg yolks were being stirred over simmering water and a sugar syrup was poured in and mixed until it thickened, like jam. Perhaps he shouldn't have shown me the process because after that I made it myself and I put it in everything—dates, sponge cakes—and at Passover we spread it on buttered *matzah.*

For the first five years we lived in a two-roomed apartment. It was large enough—given that we had no children—and unlike my father, I had no interest in searching out antique furniture or possessions. I was happy with what we had, though I couldn't resist fine linen. I found a woman who did exquisite embroidery and she sewed our initials on to sheets and pillowcases, even on to a set of fringed towels. It was only later, when I had no help, that I realized these were washed and starched after every single use. We had tablecloths and tray covers; drawn-thread napkins, appliquéed place mats. Joseph claimed there was no room for his clothes in the chests of drawers.

As our linen collection increased, Joseph insisted that we should move, hoping that, apart from added wardrobes, we would soon have a need for an extra room. We were drinking tea and spooning *yemma* on to slices of cake when the black-edged envelope arrived. As I fingered it, an extraordinary thought came into my mind. How fortunate it was that we lived in Rua Garret and had moved from Rua da Porta do Carro do Hospital Real de S. Jose. A telegram to that address would have been an expensive nine words longer. I opened the folded sheet and read the message:

> *London 5th October father died today come back. Solomon*

How do you measure sadness? Not in the number of words. If I added up, over the years, the terse sentences on telegrams and the grim pronouncements from doctors, they would amount to less than a paragraph. Yet each event made it harder to live and breathe—as if the blood flow to my heart had been interrupted.

I arrived back in London after the funeral but in time to join Solomon and Jonah on the low mourning chairs in our father's house. Jonah found it hard as his legs were long and the stools were uncomfortable. Solomon's unshaven face looked pale and I could see that he was beginning to lose his hair. The week of *shiva* was nearly at an end and in between the stream of visitors I made my brothers repeat the events of the previous days. Solomon began:

"It started on Sunday. Father had a fearsome headache. The pain seemed to be pressing on the back of his neck."

Jonah joined in: "The next day it got worse. It was your birthday, 3rd October. We were talking about you."

"Don't say it."

309

"Say what?"

"You can't believe I'm thirty. It makes you feel like middle-aged men."

"Which we are. Do you want to know about what happened or not?"

"Yes of course I do. Go on."

"Well, we were talking, father was quiet. We persuaded him to see the doctor and he prescribed some medication. The pain was excruciating. He called it a 'thunderclap headache'. No-one could do anything."

I waited for Jonah to continue, wishing I'd been there.

"He started vomiting, on the Tuesday, was it? The next day he was dead."

I must have said something about missing the funeral. Solomon tried to explain:

"We had no idea. He only lost consciousness just before the end. We telegraphed you straight away. Then there was the business of the post mortem. The doctor said the cause of death was 'unknown' so he insisted on calling in the coroner. We did everything we could to arrange it quickly. The verdict was 'A subarachnoid haemhorrage—a small aneurism on the cerebral artery'."

"Papa would have known what that meant," I said.

I stayed indoors for the rest of the week, as visitors came and went. There seemed to be a constant stream of people, lining up to pass on their condolences. I don't remember a single word that anyone said. The room was full of people sitting in groups, talking about the new omnibuses and the illuminated signs in Piccadilly. I felt strangely detached and was relieved when it was time for me to go. I packed my suitcase and was just about to close it when Jonah came in and handed me a large envelope.

"Papa wanted you to have this."

Inside was a newspaper dated 1837. Folded round the paper was a sheet of notepaper. The letter was in my father's handwriting:

40 Finsbury Square, London.

12th March 1890

My dearest Dina,

I have already given you the silver camel tea-pot and I want you to know that your brothers are happy with that decision. It has come to you with love and memories.

I brought it from the ruins of Safed. When I left that place I had no parents, no brothers or sisters and thought I could never be happy again. With God's help my life has been good: I have had a family of my own and enjoyed some degree of success which enabled us to live in an elegant home.

My one regret is that I have passed on so little from my parents. It was difficult for me to tell the story and it took many years before I was able to recount the events and emotions that have formed my life.

You may have wondered why there are no pictures of your parents' wedding day or why no photographer was hired for your own. The truth is that I feel a tremendous guilt that I had no images of my family and therefore take no pleasure in looking at photographs.

On that day when I went back to the rubble that had been our house, I found some papers. Under the bed, where I'd hidden it, was a sheaf of my sister's drawings. Miriam had done charcoal outlines of the Rabbis and the streets of Safed; completed portraits of Mama, my father and Abraham and sketches of little -------- Rebecca. There was an unfinished picture of me and a few attempts at a self-portrait. I picked up the teapot and left the drawings.

It is a matter of considerable sadness that on that fateful day I made the wrong decisions. I have lived with a feeling of guilt for all these years.

Your mother loved the teapot. Forget the sorrow and use it with joy.

The letter was signed:

'Your loving father—David'.

On the journey home I read the letter again and noticed he'd written a word before 'Rebecca' and crossed it out in a heavy pen. I thought about my father and the talk we had on the eve of my wedding. Maybe he was trying to tell me something? Why else would he now refer to 'wrong decisions'? Surely he had no choices when he was struggling to survive. Was it such a mistake to bring the teapot and leave the drawings?

Joseph was at the quayside to meet me when I returned to Lisbon. He took me home and with the afternoon sun streaming in through the windows, he laid me on our bed and kissed the dampness on my face. I knew immediately what was in his mind.

We had been married and childless for nine years. For the first few years I can truly say that we never thought about children. We were so engrossed in each other, so enraptured —it sounds unbelievable, but it was so. To some extent we had each been overshadowed by our siblings and the escape from doting parents to a life of total freedom was a joy we had no wish to complicate with the arrival of a child. Yet at some stage this changed and certainly Joseph began to talk of babies. We'd pass a woman in the street, pushing a perambulator, and he'd look at the child and squeeze my hand. There was a boy who lived in the apartment upstairs. If he came to borrow a bag of sugar, Joseph would put his hand behind the boy's ear and produce a coin with a flick of the wrist. Was there a tinge of jealousy when I saw the two of them laughing? I watched as he tickled the boy, knowing instinctively when to stop, before the giggling turned to tears. From that moment I was aware of each passing month when I failed to conceive.

For a full five years—sixty months—I dreaded the arrival of those first drops of blood. until a day in December 1892 when I realized there was nothing. It was exactly three months after papa's death. When I visited the doctor he confirmed what I already knew: I was finally pregnant.

My first thought was one of apprehension but when I told Joseph he was ecstatic. He picked me up and danced round the room, his eyes sparkling like that first time, when we met at the ball.

In the early days I felt tired walking up the hills of Lisbon and I was pleased to close the heavy wooden door of our apartment and fall on to the bed. The middle months passed in a contented haze. My hair shone and there was no need to apply powdered rouge as my face was glowing. By the second week in July I was heaving my swollen body up the hilly streets and wishing the baby would arrive. The contractions began in the evening but several hours later I had an agonizing pain in my right side. The doctor thought that the placenta had erupted but the baby was born, slipping out into a world of scurrying midwives and cries for boiling water and bandages. I heard them say "it's a girl". There was no sound at the foot of my bed. The doctor put down the stethoscope and turned away. There was no heartbeat. The baby was dead.

They took her away. I wasn't allowed to hold her. Joseph was told about the legal requirements: he had to register the baby's birth and death. All I had to show for nine months of pregnancy was two certificates; confirmation of a loss of expected happiness. I no longer had the one thing in life that mattered.

My body made no sense of what had happened. In the next few days I couldn't fasten my frock. It stretched tight across my bust. With each passing hour the hardness became worse. I threw the frock on to the bed and climbed into the bath. A tear slid down and mingled with the white flow swirling in the water.

Our daughter never had a name. Joseph and I passed each other in the apartment. I prepared meals, brushed my hair, went to bed. He spent more time at the office, waking early and leaving before I was dressed.

His mother came to visit from Gibraltar. She'd been hoping to care for a grandchild—now she sat knitting in an armchair. I didn't ask what she was making, assuming she had left behind a pile of unused matinée jackets. The needles clicked, breaking the silence in the room. Joseph would have liked his father's company but Dan had made a fuss about running the business on his own, so Samuel had stayed behind. After two weeks we were alone again.

Barely a month after that Dan telegraphed to say their father was ill. Joseph was preparing to travel to Gibraltar when a second message came to say that Samuel had died. He was sixty eight; he had deserved a longer life. He was a good man who treated his sons with dignity and respected their differences. The number of people pouring into the house in Gibraltar was a testimony to his standing in the community. While Joseph and Dan sat together on the low stools at the shiva they were spared the burden of communicating as people shuffled past, mumbling condolences, speaking of their father's courtesy and upright business dealings.

After the week we returned to Lisbon, to an apartment filled with the smell of grief. I remembered how Joseph had comforted me after my own father's death. Now I pretended to be asleep when he came to bed. We were unable to console each other, nervous that a word or remark would bring on tears. For Joseph the sudden loss of his father was like a second stone that he carried round his neck.

The only thing that helped was the sunshine. When I opened the heavy door to the street, the light flooded the hallway. Outside the sky was relentlessly blue. The flowers in the pots were a savage red. I walked and walked, feeling the warmth seeping into my body, pouring into the veins. When my feet could take me no further, I went home. Our apartment had been like an island—far away from the world. Now Joseph tried to persuade me to have company, to invite my neighbours to come up for a cup of coffee, a brioche.

The question of another pregnancy was never discussed, but it happened two years later. We were both filled with a hope, tinged with fear, desperate to replace the necessary sadness that had seeped into our lives. Joseph would rush home twice or three times a day to see how I was. I avoided meeting other pregnant women, waiting for the question: "Is this your first baby?" There was no cause for concern during those months. It was the moment after the birth that we were both dreading.

Rachel was born on 12th August 1895—a perfect, breathing 7 lb baby, with dark hair and Joseph's deep blue eyes. After a few days she still had no name. There wasn't much discussion as it was usual to call a child after a grandparent. The question was merely about the order: the dead or living one first. In the end we named her after my mother and Joseph was happy that the birth certificate said 'Rachel Regina Levy'. But she was never called by either of those names. Joseph would hold her up and whisper *bonitinha* in her ear. That was only one of the names he used. He was always the first to lift the baby out of her crib. (It was a Moses basket, lined with pale pink organdie and broderie anglaise, but he didn't notice how pretty it was.) He would lean over and pick her up calling her his treasure—*tesouro*. Sometimes he'd whisper *rainha*—Queen. But most often he would hold her high above his head and say *bonitinha*—sweetheart, so Boni was the name that everyone called her.

To escape the intense heat of the summer months we went away to a house in Sintra just outside the city. It had belonged to Joseph's father and when he was alive he was happy for us to stay there. We took the train from the new railway station at Rossio Square—a masterpiece of a building with two vast doors in the shape of horseshoes, with *dentelée* stonework and glass. Sintra was on a hill and just opposite the station was the house. It had stone pillars in the front, shuttered windows and a courtyard behind crenellated walls. The gardens in the street were full of orange trees and a wild profusion of lilies and shrubs with harsh yellowy blooms. Ours was the only one with purple bougainvillea.

Perhaps we expected to inherit the property in Sintra. Dan would eventually take possession of the parental home in Gibraltar and another property that his father owned, so it seemed natural that the house in Portugal would go to Joseph. But it was not to be. It appeared that Samuel had left no will; no document to ensure that both his sons would have an equal inheritance. The question of ownership was never discussed. We simply enjoyed the use of the house in those languid summer days.

chapter 32

Sardinhas Assadas

Wipe the fish but do not remove the heads.
Season the sardines with olive oil, salt and
pepper. Lay them on the charcoal grill and
cook for some minutes on either side. Pour
over more olive oil and serve with a hand-
ful of parsley. Vinho verde is the best wine
to drink with griddled fish.

From Dina's notebook, 1897

LISBON 1897—DINA

We often talked about fish in bed. Joseph was telling
me that he needed to go to France to purchase some aged
sardines.

"What do you mean? How can you tell how old a fish
is?"

"You ask its mother."

"I don't think sardines have birthdays."

I remember this conversation because that was the
first time we talked about Joseph travelling for his work.
He was planning to go to Marseilles and arrange a ship-

ment. He told me that the French keep their fish for at least a year to improve the flavour. There's quite a skill in turning the cans so the oil permeates the sardines and makes them taste richer.

The next evening we were sitting together after dinner. I was making a frock for Boni's second birthday. To make a smocked dress you need different tones of silk. I'd bought four shades of pink to do the bodice. But there were so many interruptions I forgot which line I was sewing. The problem was the monster. Boni claimed it was sitting in her room and one of us had to keep taking her back to bed and reassure her that it had gone away.

Joseph finished winding the clock and went to check that Boni was finally asleep. That night as we lay in bed I thought how we had changed. Joseph still made jokes but we no longer played games and teased each other. We were even discussing the business: how he was hiring two more clerks and was planning to rent a property near Poco do Bispo.

"What happened to working 'just enough'? You're always at the office now."

"That's not fair. I've been working long days for years now, since the ... since we ... " His voice tailed off.

"And what about this new property?" I asked. "You're not planning for us to live there, are you?"

"Who said anything about moving? It's a poor neighbourhood, so it's not expensive. It's a warehouse."

"Talking about moving, perhaps we should be thinking about getting a larger apartment," I said.

"But why? We don't need more space."

"We will do. I'm ... "

Before I could finish the sentence Joseph sat up and gave me a long, slow kiss.

"I've always wanted another room."

"Joseph, be serious."

"I am. I was beginning to think that the rooms in this apartment are a bit lonely and could do with some company."

"You're being ridiculous."

For a moment neither of us spoke, then I told him what was worrying me:

"How does anyone manage with two children? Boni takes up all my time. How will I deal with a baby as well?"

"I'll be here to help you and when I'm not, we can find someone else."

"What do you mean. 'when you're not'? Where will you be?"

"I was telling you before. I have to do some travelling, but I'll be home before the baby's born."

I ran my fingers over the linen sheet, tracing the initials J & D which were embroidered at the edge. Joseph leaned over and took my hand:

"Dan has taken over the Gibraltar side of the business but he wants me to do the selling. So it means a trip once a year."

He pointed his finger and made a triangular shape.

"It's like this: I buy the ordinary sardines here in Lisbon, go to Gibraltar for the olive oil and from there I go to London to arrange the sales. You know I was talking about the French sardines? Perhaps I'll forget about them this time."

When Joseph left on his first trip I went to look at a house in Rua do Salitre. It was faced entirely with cool blue tiles, but the incline would have been impossible. I couldn't imagine pushing the perambulator up the hill. We were sent details of several other houses and eventually found one which was perfect. It was in Rua Alexandre Hercolano, a broad avenue in the modern style. The stone building had double doors in heavy mahogany. There were four storeys with wrought-iron balconies and airy rooms inside. The whole of the second floor was available. The house was within walking distance of the synagogue at one end and a hospital at the other. Fortunately there was a pastry shop on the corner, painted pink and green to match the cherry blossoms.

Moving house seemed to take weeks. There were packing cases in every room and I didn't have the energy to find places for the linen and glassware. My days began with a feeling of nausea that lasted until noon. Preparing food for Boni made me feel worse but I soon learned to save small portions from our previous night's dinner so I wouldn't need to cook. By the afternoon I felt better and as soon as Boni woke up from her nap we would go down to the pastry shop and buy a *yemma* tartlet.

Our son Isaac was born in 1898. Everyone made a fuss of the new baby. Clothes and gifts came pouring into the apartment. The neighbours arrived at the door and squealed "where's this bebé, *querido*, darling … ." Boni was less pleased. When she thought no-one was looking she poked the baby and planted heavy kisses on his cheek, almost squashing him with her weight.

Joseph handled the children much better than I did.

He knew instinctively how to distract Boni when I was feeding the baby. Afterwards, he would pick them both up together, one in each arm. When I was alone with them, the feeding seemed to take hours. The slower Isaac sucked, and the more he wriggled, the more Boni teased and pulled at my skirts. She always wanted to go outside; she knew we couldn't pass the pastry shop without buying her favourite—a soft almond ball with a pistachio nut in the centre.

We decided to have a governess. An English girl called Jo responded to our newspaper advertisement. She was just eighteen and came from a village in Dorset. I watched her play with Boni and help to get Isaac dressed. She had a natural instinct for child care. Though I didn't want to be with the children every minute of the day, I was disturbed at the thought of Jo taking care of them. I think, looking back, I was too preoccupied with my own emotions to notice that Boni was feeling unsettled. Her brother had arrived on the scene, a new contender for what she saw as a limited amount of love from her parents. As Isaac grew, Boni seemed to slip into the role of a responsible older sister, but Jo would have none of it, claiming that she was 'a bossy little madam'.

I would have been happy with a girl and a boy, but it was Joseph who wanted a bigger family. It may have been that we were both turning forty and he felt that our youth was passing. I didn't argue because I thought a pregnancy at my age seemed an unlikely possibility. I was wrong.

It was nearly five years since I'd felt that lurching in my throat. I recognised the familiar signs of nausea. The pregnancy followed the familiar pattern: three months of exhaustion followed by a ten-week period of glowing hair and renewed energy. In the final months I was relieved to have Jo looking after the children while I rested in bed. Mercifully it was winter so there was no excessive heat to deal with. In the last week I felt as if I was carrying a baby elephant inside me.

Jo offered to take the children out for the day. I heaved myself out of a chair and started to look for their shoes. She was packing a picnic and called to me from the kitchen that she was going to take them to a place called Mafra where there was a palace.

The contractions began minutes after they had left. By the time the midwife arrived I was already in the second stage of labour. It passed so quickly that I remember little except that moment after the birth: waiting to hear the first cry; to hold the baby in my arms, to feel it breathing. By the time Jo came back with the children, I was sitting up with fresh sheets on the bed and flowers on the satinwood dressing table. Joseph and I were cradling our new baby and having a discussion about names:

"You like the name Hannah?" he asked. "I don't. Why does it have to be a biblical name?"

"Why not? Hannah was persistent, rather like me," I said, hoping to change his mind.

Joseph responded with surprising force:

"She certainly waited a long time for a child. But after all those prayers, when she eventually had a son, she gave him away."

"What a ridiculous way of judging her decision. She didn't 'give him away'. You make it sound like she had no feelings. It was the opposite."

I was quite carried away defending Hannah's character and was about to explain how strong she was, when Boni burst in the door.

"Mama. The palace ... it was built by a king and it has 4,000 doors and windows."

"And he built another palace for the Queen and they hardly ever went there," interrupted Isaac.

"Do you want to see your new baby sister?" I asked. Jo led them to the crib and then took them into the kitchen for their supper.

"We could leave out the 'h's," I said to Joseph, half seriously. He'd forgotten what we were talking about.

"The name. Hannah. We could make it Anna."

It was wrong to have favourites but Anna was the most beautiful of all the children, with dark hair and a soft complexion that made people stop in the street when they saw her. Boni would screw up her eyes and scowl. We should have taken more notice of her. It took her a year or two to settle down, to accept her role as the responsible older sister.

Joseph was so besotted with his youngest child that he hated being away, even for a few days. He was about to leave on one of his yearly journeys to Gibraltar when Anna toddled into the room and climbed on to his knee. She was just beginning to put words together:

"Papa coming back."

"Careful, you're spilling my tea," said Joseph, wiping his trousers.

I lifted the camel teapot to pour out another cup:

"How long will you be gone? Are you going straight on to London?"

"I'm late, I have to start packing," he replied, taking a couple of pastries. He popped one in his mouth and held the other one in his hand. Then he called from the bedroom:

"I forgot to tell you, I have some new contacts in Brazil and I'm having a meeting with Joao Silva when I get back."

I knew he didn't want to go. He needed to sell a lot of barrels of olive oil to pay the rent on our apartment. I went to help him fold his clothes. He began to talk about his plans to take bacalhau to London.

"The English won't like the smell of salted cod," I said, turning up my nose at the thought of the rock-hard slabs of dried fish. "You'd do better with figs and raisins, I should think."

The suitcase was nearly full. On the top were some embossed metal sheets.

"Look at our new advertisements," he said, picking one of them up. There was a picture of a jockey holding up a tin of sardines with the words '*Derby sardines in finest olive oil sold here*'.

"You'll need different ones for the North of England," I said. "They only like sardines in tomato sauce up there." I clicked the locks on his case. "Go on, you're going to be late." As he was closing the door, he called:

"Why don't you go to Cascais for a few days?"

Jo helped me pack a trunk and we took the train along the coast to the fishing port. I sat with Anna on my knee while Boni and Isaac were jumping up and down with excitement. The fishermen had brought in the catch for the day and we found a stall set up with small tables and chairs. We ordered griddled sardines and watched as they cooked the fish over white charcoal. When it was ready they handed us wooden platters to hold and slid three sardines on to each one. The children complained about the bones but Jo and I finished off the crispy blackened bits on their plates, squeezing some lemon on to the succulent fish. It made me think of Joseph. We often laughed because his business was mainly sardines—but not the fresh ones that were cooked over hot coals.

"Your father had the right idea," he'd say "the tinned ones are for buying and selling, not eating."

Isaac was pulling at Jo's skirt. "Can we go to the Roca?" he asked. "Will the waves be high?"

Isaac and Boni loved the Roca do Inferno, where the sea hammered into the rock, creating a spectacular spray. The two of them went off hand in hand with Jo. Anna stayed behind with me. She was scared of the booming noise. We played on the smooth sand till the sun started to go down.

We stayed in Cascais for three days and were just arriving back at Rua Hercolano when I noticed a crowd of people standing by our doorway.

"There's a telegram for you," said one of the neighbours, handing me the envelope.

I opened it slowly and read each word several times. It dropped from my hand and I collapsed on the floor.

chapter 33

*Visitors, in paying condoling visits, should
be dressed in black, either silk or plain-
coloured apparel. Sympathy with the af-
fliction of the family is thus expressed, and
these attentions are, in such cases, pleasing and soothing.*

The Book of Household Management, by Isabella Beeton, 1861

LISBON 1905—DINA

There were three words on the telegram: *Joseph sudden
death*. I thought about the waves at the Roca—hurtling
with massive force and leaving the stone standing with
nothing but a trickle of foamy bubbles sliding down into
the sea. I was like that rock, alone with the miseries of life
washing over me.

Memories of that first week are blurred. I was exhausted from incessant crying. I almost believed that if enough
tears drained from my body, there would be nothing left
and I would die too. Solomon came immediately and then
some days later Dan arrived from Gibraltar. I imagine he
was torn between leaving his mother and coming to tell
me how Joseph had died. It was only the second time he'd

been in our house. The previous visit had been uncomfortable; he'd behaved like he did at my first meeting with him, constantly making jibes at his brother and the way he ran the business. Now he was sitting opposite me at the table. He took my hand, looking around as if someone else could deliver the news of what had happened.

"We were having dinner. Joseph had just sat down."

I waited for him to continue.

"He clutched his left arm and began to fall. The chair tipped backwards and he was on the ground. We tried to revive him but he was dead. It was a heart attack."

I found it hard to speak. Dan began again:

"Did he ever..? Was he ill?"

"Of course he wasn't. Would I have let him go if he'd been ill?"

I shouldn't have been so abrupt. The truth was that he did get out of breath sometimes, walking up the hills. But we both did. The tears were pricking behind my eyes. Dan had brought back the suitcase Joseph had taken to Gibraltar. I picked it up and walked into the bedroom. I opened the cupboard and started to hang up his jacket, then lifted it out again and pushed my arms deep into the sleeves, burying my face in the silk lining. I put my hand in the pocket. There was half a crushed pastry. Why did I keep feeding him pastries? He was getting too large. I should have taken more care of him.

Letters and telegrams were pouring in. Neighbours came to the door with steaming pots, covered in linen cloths. Boni and Isaac were taken to play with friends. Jo took care of Anna from the moment she woke up. The apartment was empty. A man called Joao Silva came to the door. He mentioned something about a shipment of sardines. I told him Mr. Levy wasn't there.

At night I lay in bed listening to the clock ticking. And then it stopped and for a few days I didn't even know the time. Joseph was the one who wound the clock. I had a dream. Joseph was holding out his arm to me, asking me to dance, and I was talking about the price of olive oil and he took me down to the beach and the sea had turned to olive oil and it was lapping over the sand … . I woke with my hair damp, sticking to the pillow. The next morning I went out and walked to the Black Horse statue. When I came home I realized I had no key. Joseph was the one who always took the keys. How could he leave me? He knew I couldn't manage without him.

Jo opened the door for me and went back to giving the children breakfast. Boni was arguing with Isaac over who should have the green cup. She pulled it out of his hand and the milk went all over the floor. I couldn't move to go and mop it up. My legs felt heavy, as if the soles of my feet were stuck to the ground.

Solomon was there, in the background, all the time. He looked thinner than I remembered and there were fewer strands of hair covering the bald patch on the crown of his head. He listened as I went over and over the last few days. When I blamed the travelling he tried to reassure me. Joseph was young, barely forty-five. How could the journey have been too much for him? No-one could have predicted that a healthy man of his age would drop dead with no warning.

In my mind I thought about our last few hours together. Why did our conversation have to be about sardines? I can't remember when I last told him "I love you". I didn't say it when he passed the milk at breakfast or when he'd finished brushing his teeth at night. All I said when he walked out of the door was "You're going to be late." I began to think of every insignificant exchange we'd ever had. My thoughts were a tangle of regret and blame.

I went to the desk and picked up some letters. The inkwell was empty. I didn't know where Joseph kept the ink. He even sharpened the pencils for me and put one by a notebook in the kitchen so we could write down what was needed from the tradesmen. Solomon told me I didn't need to deal with the correspondence straight away. We were reading one of the letters when Dan came in carrying a box with folders and ledgers. He'd been out the whole day at the office, trying to sort out any urgent matters. He told me not to worry about the business. There was little more to say: I couldn't wait for him to go. It may have been my imagination but I had the impression he was assessing the contents of our apartment: the furniture bought at auction, and the few fine rugs we'd acquired for the cool winter months.

At that time I wasn't concerned about money. I assumed that for the time being Dan would take control of the day-to-day running of the business and we would continue to live on the proceeds. Solomon might have mentioned finding a manager to keep the Lisbon office running. So when he suggested that I should return to London with the children, I agreed. Perhaps he expected an argument. The question of where we lived no longer mattered.

Our apartment was rented so there was no property to

sell. Solomon arranged the removal of our furniture, and he took over the task of supervising the packing. I moved from room to room while boxes and suitcases were being filled. In our bedroom was a large packing case, marked '*not for London*'. I didn't need to ask what was in it.

Solomon put some money in an envelope and handed it to Jo. I could see he was getting ready to leave. The steamship tickets were on the table. He picked up the jacket of his suit and held out a folded handkerchief. I took it from him and he put his arm round my shoulders.

"I'll see you in London," he said and then he was gone.

The children never stopped talking. Isaac told me about a trip to the Castle:

"Jo took us up on the tram, through all those curly streets in Alfama and when we got there we played in the hollow trees. When we came down, Jo wanted to go into that place and it was horrid, all dark and scary."

Boni interrupted "It's the Cathedral, silly," and to show she knew more than him she added "they call it the Sé."

I heard what they were saying but I wasn't taking it in. Boni carried on:

"Then we went to Belem to get some pastries. There's pictures on the wall in tiles—there's ships and flowers and birds, and we played hide and seek running through the rooms and under the arches. Then we played a game by the big 'man picture'—you know, the one of the man in fancy clothes made out of tiles too. I told Isaac he had seventeen buttons on his coat but he could only count nine because he hadn't counted the ones on his sleeves."

"Boni, go and eat your dinner," I murmured. "Jo, please take them in the other room."

How could I not see that Boni and Isaac were suffering too? I assumed that it was best for their lives to continue as if their father had gone away on a short trip. I never sat down with them to explain the finality of what had happened. My eyes were closing. The sleep that eluded me at night was forcing my eyelids to close, dragging me down with fatigue. I looked at Jo and thought how she'd changed. From a shy girl in her teens, she was now twenty-five, unruffled and diplomatic, but slightly gauche in the company of adults. Her fair hair was tied back in a bun. She had the palest eyelashes and long fingers with neatly manicured nails. I could hear her cajoling Boni into eating a few mouthfuls of the meat stew she had made.

"Won't" said Boni. It's got onions in it. I hate onions."

I would have given in, for the sake of peace. When I went into the kitchen Boni's plate was clean. Isaac was complaining about his spectacles. A few months earlier he'd suffered from a severe bout of influenza. When he eventually recovered from the high fever—which I must say had caused me serious concern—his eyesight had been affected. The doctor told me that he'd need to wear spectacles and that he should take care never to get his feet wet. Jo didn't understand how I worried about him. If he caught a cold, it might make his eyesight worse. He complained that the wire frames were digging into the back of his ears. Jo told Isaac to take the spectacles off and then he said he couldn't see what was on his plate. I would have been more sympathetic but Jo simply told him a story while he prodded his fork into the potatoes. He speared the last one and pushed it round the gravy while she muttered something to me; she was always telling me he should be more robust.

Anna started to cry.

"Want Papa."

What could I say? If I couldn't explain to her sister, who was eight years older, how could I tell a two-year-old that her father was never coming back? I didn't know how to manage the children—I couldn't deal with one on my own, let alone three.

"Where are you Joseph? Come and help me."

When everyone was in bed I looked for the bunch of keys to lock the front door. It wasn't on the sideboard. It must have been in one of Joseph's pockets. The rail in the bedroom cupboard was empty. I couldn't even lock the door now.

"Damn it Joseph. Where are the keys?"

Jo took charge of the removals. She went from room to room, labelling crates, picking up toys, even putting the steamship tickets into my hand. The coach arrived, we closed the door of the apartment, turned left and left again into Rua do Salitre. We passed the house I'd wanted to live in. The plasterwork was crumbling above the blue tiles and the paintwork on the sills was peeling. Behind the window was a cat with ginger eyes.

On the sea voyage back to England Anna followed Jo everywhere. I was relieved but at the same time I felt uneasy. In the Bay of Biscay the waves pummelled the ship and the heaving passengers moved queasily between their bunks and the decks, hoping that a move from the horizontal to the vertical would calm their stomachs. A woman remarked at how lucky I was to have a governess who could look after all three children. I never minded when Joseph took charge. It was different with Jo. She was so calm and persuasive. I watched and wondered why they behaved better with her. She couldn't love them like I did, yet they clearly adored her.

We docked at Plymouth on Thursday at 7 a.m. and arrived at Tilbury on Friday morning. I was surprised to see Jonah, not Solomon, there to meet the ship. He was standing on the quay, puffing away at his pipe. The unpredictable brother I remembered had turned up on time. His suit was well-cut and he had a fine watch and chain in his waistcoat. Business—or the card games—must have been going well.

He took us to stay with him in London for the first few weeks. Then he arranged for us to move into a mansion block called Kings' Gardens, in a winding road that I believe had once been a river. It was a long way from the square we'd lived in when I was a child. We drove through one of the two entrances with lamps on either side. I helped the children climb the first flight of stairs. At each landing we stopped to catch our breath and eventually trudged up the last few stairs to the third floor. The door to number twelve was open.

There were two reception rooms and three bedrooms, with nothing except a dull brown carpet on the floor. I stared out of the window, waiting for the removals van. Jo sat on the floor with Anna between her legs and began a word game with Boni and Isaac. The furniture arrived and Jo directed the men to leave the packing cases in different rooms. I didn't know where to begin; she had labelled each one and got the children carrying toys and crockery while she stacked the shelves and piled up the empty crates. By the evening everyone was exhausted, ready to fall into bed. Isaac had a small room of his own, Boni shared a bedroom with Jo and Anna curled up in the bed next to me. I woke several times in the night to make sure my precious little one was still breathing.

chapter 34

PISTACHIO CAKE

Take one pound of pistachios, scald them and crush them adding a little white of egg. Mix with them half a pound of crushed sugar, some grated lemon peel, the yolks of ten eggs and then the whites beaten up to a froth. When the whole is well mixed pour it into a buttered mould, leave it at a slow fire for an hour, then turn the cake out of the mould.

From Dina's notebook, 1890

LONDON 1906—DINA

I had settled into a pattern of existing, seeing the older children off to school, waiting anxiously till they came back. The months passed. In Lisbon, after we lost our baby, I was always going out. The bright sky and the sun had seeped into my skin like a healing ointment. Now I stepped out on to the pavements and held up my hand to see if the drizzle was about to turn to heavy rain. The endless grey days turned into a winter of sleet and wind.

When the spring came two trees blossomed on the grass outside.

I took Anna with me when I went to buy provisions. I lifted her on to the counter to watch while the grocer tipped a pile of tea on to a sheet of paper and folded in the sides to make a neat package. He cut the cheese with a wire and handed her a piece to taste. The pound of cheddar was too big. With the hot weather coming, it wouldn't keep for long, even in the cool of the larder.

The kitchen in Kings' Gardens was poorly equipped. After we'd unpacked most of the crates I didn't have the energy to sort through items I thought I'd never use. The fish kettle, the mincing machine and the stockpot—they were at the bottom of a cupboard in one of the bedrooms. I bought a new pestle and mortar but what I really wanted was one of the new gas cookers. It was out of the question.

At the beginning of every month I received an allowance from Solomon and Jonah. Dan had also sent me some money; four or five bankers' drafts at irregular intervals, but I hadn't heard from him for a while, so I was relying entirely on my brothers. We were managing on far less than we had been used to. By the time I had paid for some scrag of mutton and a boiling fowl for *Shabbat* there was precious little left to buy new kitchen utensils. I didn't even have a decent set of weights for cake making.

I had little idea of time passing. Was it six months or a year since Joseph had died? In the weeks before the anniversary I began to feel ill. It wasn't a fever, like influenza; it was an ache in every joint of my body. My cheeks were covered in pimples and my hair had lost its sheen. The face that looked back at me in the mirror was not the one I recognized.

Jonah suggested that I might want to travel to Gibraltar to visit Joseph's grave. He offered to come with me but I had no wish to go, to stand next to Dan in front of a tombstone and read the words '*Joseph Levy—born 1860 died 1905*.' I sensed that Jonah was relieved. What I didn't know at the time was that he'd had some unpleasant dealings with my brother-in-law.

On the day of the anniversary I picked up a book my mother had given me.

The pages were edged in gold and the endpapers were a swirl of Florentine red. It contained Prayers and Meditations For Every Situation and Occasion of Life. In the second part was the Widow's Prayer.

Underneath the prayer book was a notebook that I hadn't opened for a year. On each page was a recipe, starting with my notes for making *yemma*. The next entry was Pistachio Cake. The last time I served it Joseph had eaten three slices and joked that he'd turn into a monkey if he ate any more nuts.

I had a sudden urge to make that cake and spent most of the day walking, looking for a grocer that stocked the green nuts. By four o'clock I'd almost given up hope when someone directed me to a small shop where I found sacks of almonds, brazil nuts and pistachios. Since I had no scales I asked the grocer to weigh me out a pound of nuts and half a pound of crushed sugar. When I got home Jo was reading stories to the children. I went into the kitchen and began beating the egg yolks. After fifteen minutes my hand was aching but it took even longer to whisk the whites to a froth. By the time the cake was in the oven, I was exhausted. I sat down on a chair in the kitchen and whispered:

> *'This cake is for you Joseph. But we won't tell anyone.'*

About a month after the anniversary I went to answer the doorbell and was surprised to see both my brothers standing there.

"Dina, my dear, we need to talk to you."

"What about?" I asked anxiously.

"Money, and other things," began Jonah, pushing down the tobacco in his pipe.

"Well,—what is it?"

Jonah made himself comfortable and waited till Solomon had also settled in an armchair.

"You know Joseph didn't leave a will. We thought it would have been a simple matter to divide the business into two—half for you and half for Dan, but ... "

"Is there a problem?"

"No, well, yes—the fact is that Samuel didn't leave a will either ... "

"I know. But what's this got to do with me?"

"Listen Dina. Strictly speaking half the business never belonged to Joseph as his father died intestate, so ... we're in a difficult position."

"But what about the properties? It's only right that Dan should have the one in Gibraltar and we should have the one in Sintra."

Solomon gave a nervous cough and smoothed the thinning strands of hair:

"Samuel probably meant to leave everything jointly,

but as it is, you have no entitlement to anything."

"Wait a minute, Joseph worked in the business. He did the travelling. How is it possible that he was entitled to nothing?"

"Dan says he has all the responsibility now: buying the goods, finding the agents etc."

I knew where this was leading. At one time I'd hoped to receive a lump sum from Dan but it was clear he had other ideas. Solomon pulled out some sheets of paper and pointed to his calculations. He explained that my rent on the Kings' Gardens apartment could be paid with the income from what Papa had left me. He then mumbled something like:

"Dan rather assumes that we are taking care of you."

It was humiliating for me to depend on my brothers but I had no choice. I tried to be gracious and told them I appreciated what they were doing.

"We don't want you to be grateful," said Solomon. "We want you to ... "

I knew what he was about to say. I interrupted before he could launch into comments about my state of mind.

"You want me to what? Pretend that it never happened ... that life is the same as it was?"

"No, but you're always in black, no-one comes to the house."

"What do you expect me to do, follow the latest fashions? There's no reason to wear anything but black. It reflects how I feel."

"Well, you could do something. You could invite us for tea. When was the last time you made a cake? "

Jonah gave Solomon a look as if to say "that's enough

for now".

They didn't know about the cake I'd made for Joseph. I'd hidden it in a cupboard in my bedroom and when I last looked, there was a green mould all over it. What was I thinking of? They were right: I should start baking again for the family. I decided to try to make those creamy pastries we used to buy from Belem. I found Mamma's copy of 'What to Eat and How to Cook It' but Monsieur Blot had obviously never been to Lisbon. It was Jo who helped me to work out the main part of the recipe. She must have been speaking to her mother about me because a few days later a parcel arrived containing a book with a little note attached:

> *"Dear Mrs. Levy*
>
> *I thought you would like this. Isabella Beeton had a sad life. She lost a boy from scarlet fever and died herself at the age of 28. I understand from Jo that you want to know about pastry— turn to page 633 and you'll find a recipe for Puff Paste for tarts. There are plenty of colour plates too, though you should ignore the first one on bacon and ham. You don't need to know the difference between collar and forelock! You may be amused by her remarks about early rising and cleanliness which I am sure do not apply to you. Nor does her advice on dealing with servants: She had a large house in Hatch End full of staff.*
>
> *Do come with Jo to visit us in Dorset sometime, yours ever "*

I opened the book and read on page 39 *'a dirty kitchen*

is a disgrace to all concerned.' I had little interest in food, but turned to the page on pastry and began rolling and folding the dough, interleaving it with layers of chilled butter. It was strangely soothing. Then I made the custard, but it was too thin and it seeped out of the tarts leaving a burnt mess in the tin. I felt so dejected but I started again from the beginning and by the time the children came home the smell of vanilla wafting out of the oven had cheered me up. While I waited for the tarts to set I turned to a page on folding serviettes. There were seven diagrams for making a shape called the Bishop.

The following Friday evening I invited my brothers for dinner. When Solomon came in he handed me a bunch of daffodils. I was so nervous I almost dropped them. When I went into the kitchen I burned my hand taking the meat out of the oven. Jonah carved and we began to talk about the Festival meals we'd had when I was a child. It seemed to me that all of them were to commemorate something sad and the pattern was the same: first you told the story, then you could eat. At *Chanucah* we lit the brass oil lamp and sang songs—then we had fried pastries—sweet rice croquettes, I think. At *Passover* I remember how my mother worked for weeks turning the house upside down. It seemed such a huge effort. And I would have preferred to do without the long *Seder service* and just get to the bit where we ate the soup with matzah balls.

About five years after my tragedy—it happened to be *Purim*—Jonah made a surprise announcement. We were playing cards, gambling with mother-of-pearl counters in the shape of fish. I wished it had been real money because

345

my pile was the largest. In the weeks before, I had been thinking a lot about my finances and had been saving the shillings to buy the ground almonds for the sweets. Well, Jonah was eating one of them—a date stuffed with marzipan—when he told us he was going on a trip. He was planning to go to India, taking a ship from Marseilles to Sicily and from there to Egypt, through the Suez Canal and on to Bombay. My finger was tracing the shape of a triangle on the table. Whenever I thought of travel I could only think of three points: the trip that Joseph was planning when he died.

Isaac was excited at the thought of his uncle travelling so far. He was probably imagining what presents he'd bring back. Jonah promised to send the children post-cards. The first one arrived on 4th November 1910. It was from Southampton and had three lines:

> *"Uncanny sight of baggage being taken ashore just before steamer started. A Mr. Wiggins had fallen dead in the saloon and his body quietly taken off in an ambulance."*

Boni collected the cards and put them in order. Sometimes there were two in a day and then there would be a gap of a week. The next one was from Sintra:

> *"Dance in the hotel. Women nearly all washed out looking, or catlike."*

"What does he mean 'catlike'?" asked Boni. "It doesn't sound like a compliment to me."

The ship docked at Port Said and the postcard arrived a week later:

> *"Dirty town but natives picturesque—only the poorest are repulsive."*

346

We imagined Jonah besieged by beggars, pulling at his fine silk scarf and scrabbling in the dust for the coins he tossed from his pocket.

Sometimes the cards referred to his dinner companions. He even recorded the menus and the temperature in the cabin. He seemed to be particularly interested in men and their clothes and the postcard from Bombay read:

> *"Hindus in white with bare legs, long, brown, thin, dirty, shapeless, uninteresting legs, but coloured turbans in shades of apricot, green and blue."*

I didn't show this card to the children. They might have wondered why their uncle was so interested in the men's legs. I would have liked more description of the saris worn by the women, or the flower petals that were strewn in patterns on the ground outside the hotels.

Jonah was away for two months, leaving a rather sulky Solomon to carry on the business. Boni made a surprising comment for a fifteen-year-old. "All that travelling? It's useful, really. Look at the postcards: *meeting new contacts; possible agents*."

I could only think about meeting our debts. While Jonah was abroad Solomon made sure we were managing on the allowance they had agreed. It was all right for my brother to go swanning off to foreign parts. but we had to watch the pennies, When I made frocks for the girls, I couldn't afford the best taffeta. Jonah had fine notepaper and smoked Abdulla cigarettes. Goodness knows what luxuries Dan had in Lisbon.

I was always concerned that our outgoings were too

high. A year or so after Jonah's trip, I saw the chance to economize. Jo told me she was leaving to get married and I must admit that my first thought was one of relief. But I was nervous about breaking the news to Anna. I tried to tell her that a girl of nine didn't need a governess. She interrupted and shouted that she needed Jo and couldn't bear it if she left. Her temper tantrum lasted for half an hour. Of course I had mixed feelings about Jo leaving; on the one hand it would save money. But Anna had become so fond of her that I was concerned. I didn't have the patience to invent games and I would miss the help in the house.

The solution seemed to be to find a houseparlourmaid. I interviewed two sisters. The older one wanted ten shillings a week. That seemed rather a lot. The younger one, Beatrice, was prepared to come to us for 7s. 6d. She washed and ironed, and even helped clear up after my baking, but the first time I saw her laughing with Anna, I put down the rolling pin and went into the bedroom, closing the door behind me.

chapter 35

ASPARAGUS ROLLS

*1 tin asparagus (white or green), thin slices
of white and brown bread, butter*

*Drain the asparagus well. Cut the crusts
off the bread and flatten each slice with a
rolling pin. Butter generously and place a
spear of asparagus at one end. Roll up the
bread, enclosing the asparagus, and place
on a plate with the seam side down. Keep
covered with a damp cloth until you are
ready to serve them.*

From Anna's notebook, 1970

LONDON 1970—ANNA

Sadness—like happiness—can be transitory or semi-permanent. In Anna's life there had been moments that she never forgot: the day that Jo left, the row with her mother over going to Palestine, the shock of hearing that Isaac had died. There was nothing to be done to change any of these events. But the day-to-day struggle with Nathan was different. With each passing month a new problem arose. Anna believed that she was the only one who could help him: the doctors only signed repeat prescriptions and saw no cause to visit.

When Nathan stopped eating there was clearly a new development. He would push away his plate and claim that he wasn't hungry. The district nurse came to give him a bath, and it was then that he explained the real problem. It wasn't a matter of simple constipation; it was more serious as the muscles of the bowel were unable to perform the necessary movement. Before the stroke he rarely gave a thought to the way his body functioned. Now he was like an asthmatic, obsessed with a simple matter that others took for granted—the process of breathing in and out. Nathan's mind was dominated by a similar introspection—the daily intake and expulsion of food.

After the nurse had gone Anna would struggle to get him dressed. It seemed—in spite of his decreasing weight and the bones that protruded from the sagging skin—that Nathan was getting heavier. He was unable to manoevre himself into position, leaving her to heave both his legs on to the bed. Whereas before he'd tried to pull on his clothes with his good hand, now he waited for her to struggle with pyjama trousers and sleeves and sat there with a look of resignation on his face. His expression concealed what he was thinking. As the functions of his body were progressively failing, he remembered a passage in Genesis, where Pharaoh asked Jacob how old he was. Jacob replied: "A hundred and thirty years; few and evil have been the days of the years of my life." For Nathan the last few years had certainly seemed evil.

In the early days he had tried writing with his left hand, and at Nina's suggestion had even tried to tap out a few words on a typewriter. Now he faced each day with a bleak depression, rejecting any suggestions of an article to read, showing little interest in the flicker of the television news.

In bed at night Anna turned over, pulled up the covers and made an effort not to look at the clock. If she started worrying, the thoughts would come piling in, turning blackest around midnight. By two o'clock she would be feeling utterly desolate, yet by the time the daylight broke through a gap in the curtains the picture began to look less bleak.

It was the bridge games that brought some brightness into Anna's life. Her teacher, Elena Marouk, had once owned a hotel in Egypt. She came to England in 1956, with the other Jews who were expelled after the Suez crisis. With no assets apart from a solitaire diamond, she had to find a source of income, and she established herself as a bridge teacher. But the fees were waived for Anna and the two friends she'd enlisted for the weekly game. Mr. Gardner and Mrs. Edwards were fast learners and soon picked up the basic ideas of bidding, but it was Anna who had a natural feel for the cards and a sharp memory which served her well in playing the hands. As they all improved Mrs. Marouk stepped back from her role as teacher and came to look forward to their evening games.

Midway through the session, Anna fed them handsomely. The cards were laid aside, and a cloth was put on the table. In the early weeks it was a full meal, but as her friends could see the strain of looking after Nathan, they insisted they should come after supper. Anna agreed reluctantly but her idea of a snack meant sandwiches and fruit cake, meringues or éclairs. Mr. Gardner was usually impatient to continue the bridge, but Mrs. Edwards believed that if your hostess offered you food, and especially such delicious food, it would be a sin to leave anything uneaten when the plates were finally cleared away. Anna could never resolve her feelings about these two friends. Mr. Gardner's haste to finish eating and get back to the bridge was faintly insulting. She wanted to ask him if he'd prefer a cream cake, if the meringues were perhaps a little too soft? But Mrs. Edwards's enthusiasm was definitely annoying. Had the woman not eaten dinner before she came? Was she intending to demolish everything, including the whole of the fruit cake that Anna had hoped would provide something sweet for Nathan to eat before he went to bed? Anna herself ate none of it as she was always watching her weight. While they piled their plates she allowed herself two crackers but when she was clearing up at eleven o'clock she slipped a couple of éclairs into her mouth as she put the milk back in the fridge and dried the last of the dishes.

For a bridge player, it's tantalizing to play just once a week. It's like being allowed to eat only once a day. Worse, a bridge game is often followed by regrets and a kind of intellectual indigestion. After the friends had gone home, and Nathan had been finally put to bed, Anna lay awake going over the hands of the evening's play. Why had she made that Three No Trump bid when she had no stop in Spades? It was so humiliating to watch the opponents take the first five tricks. And letting Mr. Gardner make that game contract in Four Hearts was completely unnecessary. She only had to play her trump when she was in with the Ace of clubs: he wouldn't have been able to ruff his losing Diamond on the table. Why hadn't she drawn trumps in that hand where she failed to make an easy Five Clubs contract? Mrs. Edwards had been so scathing about it, but it wasn't as if her own play was faultless. When she forgot that the last Heart on the table was a winner and went down in that slam hand, Anna wanted to point it out. But she had kept quiet.

In a drawer beside her bed was a leaflet with an alphabetical list of the problems of stroke patients:

Anxiety
Concentration (lack of)
Continence (pelvic floor exercises)
Depression (in patient and carer)
Energy (loss of)
Swallowing (difficulty leading to dehydration)

Their doctor had recently set aside time to sit with Anna and discuss Nathan's psychological problems.

"He may become less sociable."

"That's hardly possible," laughed Anna. "He never wanted to go out in the first place."

"But you may find that he forgets people's names," said the doctor. "He may lose interest in normal activities."

There was no point telling him that Nathan used to muddle people's names on purpose. As for 'normal activities', it wasn't a case of losing interest. Nathan lost his ability to concentrate, so his pleasure in reading had gone. What worried her most was his anxiety and feeling of hopelessness. She could cope with the physical problems; the fatigue that came over him early in the day and the difficulty in swallowing. She would coax him to drink small quantities all day and then deal with endless changing of sheets.

It was harder to deal with the mood changes that made him cry for no apparent reason. He had trouble dividing his attention—listening to the radio and responding if she asked him a question. Anna noticed with dismay that his existing personality traits were becoming exaggerated. Where before he'd been ponderous, now he took even more time to make a decision or tell a story. And while Nathan was struggling with his own despair, she was dealing with a constant tiredness and back strain from the lifting.

She was preparing sandwiches for her friends when Nathan called to her in the kitchen. He wanted a piece of cheese. It was not much to ask, but was the one thing he fancied that he couldn't have: it was incompatible with the medication he was taking. Although he knew he wasn't allowed the tiniest bit of camembert or cheddar and noticed that Anna never ate cheese and biscuits in front of him, he still thought it worth mentioning, just in case. She promised to bring him something else in a few minutes. She went back to the kitchen and cut the crusts off the white bread, spread each slice with butter and rolled it round a spear of white asparagus. Nathan smiled as he looked at the asparagus rolls and picked one of them up with his left hand. The first mouthful led to a fit of coughing so Anna took the plate away and tried to distract him by talking about Nina. When he'd recovered he wiped his mouth with a handkerchief and mumbled something:

"To tell you the truth, I feel guilty."

"What on earth about?"

"Stopping her marrying the Moroccan. Now she seems to have lost her chance."

"But she's only thirty one. She'll meet someone else. And whoever he is, he'll be a lot better for her than Samir."

"If she'd married him I might have had a dozen grandchildren by now. They could have helped to push my wheelchair."

Anna was irritated that Nathan made no reference to Nina doing anything for him. He took it for granted that his daughter wasn't required to help in any way and that it was enough for her to send letters and cards once a week. She even referred to doing some voluntary work in an old people's home in New York. Anna couldn't help thinking that with what she was earning she could easily afford the flight back and she could do some volunteering here at home in London.

Anna cleared away the plates, settled Nathan back in his chair and went to deal with the laundry—the third change of bedding in two days. In the hall was an unopened parcel from America. When Anna had finished changing the sheets she pulled off the brown paper and took out a box emblazoned with the words: Bergdorf Goodman, Fifth Avenue. Inside was a voluminous silk square with a printed note from Nina. Anna lifted out the scarf and put it round her neck, the cool silk a contrast to the vibrant hot colours. This was a scarf to wear with a tailored coat, a crocodile handbag and leather gloves. Anna squeezed it tighter round her neck until her throat began to hurt and then pulled it off and flung it back on top of the box. What Nina had spent would have paid for hours of nursing care; not something to be mentioned in the thank-you note she would write later.

For the rest of the day Anna was under a cloud of gloom, with Nathan's misery reflecting her own feelings of futility. There was no-one to complain to and no point in speaking to the doctor about his deteriorating condition. By the time she climbed into bed she was exhausted, not from the usual physical exertion of each day, but from the pent-up anger caused by Nina's gift. Unable to fall asleep Anna began to dig through the layers of discontent about their present situation. She started to worry about money and whether they could afford more than the once-a-week nursing help.

This led to the thoughts that were always simmering, waiting to be turned up to a full-blown boil: her mother's constant money worries and the row with Isaac over their refusal to come up with yet another loan.

Dina had never told her exactly how she'd been cheated out of her inheritance. She never spoke about Dan or how he'd stopped sending them any money. It was clear that Samuel had left no will so Joseph was not entitled to half the business or properties. But how could Dan have been so mean, failing to provide even a small allowance for his brother's widow? As a bachelor he had lived a comfortable life, with properties in Gibraltar and Lisbon and a flourishing business that provided him with diamond tie pins and hand-tailored suits. He'd died at the age of sixty five—probably the result of years of too much port and brandy. Whatever money he left certainly never found its way to London. If he had given her mother even a small part of his wealth, their lives would have been different. Her persistent mourning might have been lifted by the prospect of travel. If she had gone on a trip like Jonah, experiencing the wonder of the Taj Mahal and the pyramids at Cairo, she would have had a more positive outlook. Who knows, she might even have met someone on the steamship, a romance over a candlelit dinner, a loving stepfather for Anna, a man who would have taken them to live in a house in the country ...

And what if they'd agreed to Isaac's requests? He would still be living in London and Joel might have gone off to university with Nina. She might have mixed with a different crowd and perhaps married a lawyer or an accountant, someone who could have provided her with a house in Hampstead or Holland Park, with parquet floors and Persian rugs, and window boxes full of geraniums. After an hour mulling over such thoughts, Anna had almost persuaded herself that it was Isaac's fault that Nina had never married and had gone away to live in New York.

When Nathan awoke at eight Anna was in a deep sleep. She had finally dozed off in the early hours of the morning and was dreamily thinking again of the Five Clubs contract. Actually, it wasn't as easy as Mrs. Edwards said it was. If she had drawn all the trumps she wouldn't have been able to get back to dummy to make her Diamond tricks. She must remember to tell Mrs. Edwards that next Monday.

chapter 36

ARTICHOKE SOUP WITH CROUTONS

half a lemon, 1½ lbs Jerusalem artichokes*, few knobs of dripping for frying, an onion, pint and a half chicken stock (made from the carcass), 3 thick slices of white bread (crusts removed)

Peel the artichokes. Put them in a bowl of water with the squeezed lemon (stops them discolouring). Chop the onion and fry it in the dripping. Drain the artichokes, cut them up small and add them to the pan. Cook quickly, without browning, and pour in the chicken stock. Simmer for about forty minutes and then press the soup through a sieve to make a smooth purée.

Cut the bread into small cubes, fry in a little dripping until they brown. Serve with the soup.

*Jerusalem artichokes don't come from the Holy Land. The word comes from 'girasole', Italian for sunflower, as their flowers look similar and turn to the sun.

From Dina's notebook, 1940

Artichoke plants grow to eight feet tall and have yellow flowers. A friend of Boni's has an allotment and has been growing root vegetables. She brought some home the other day and I made a soup out of the knobbly little tubers. I don't know about 'Dig For Victory': I'm more concerned about our neighbours digging up their railings. We've all been told that wrought iron will be taken away and used in the production of munitions, but when I last looked they'd removed their gate and it was stacked up in their back garden. I expect they're planning to keep it till the war is over.

The bombing is getting worse. The German air force has unleashed a wave of fierce attacks, aimed at the docks, I presume. Those poor people living in the East End. Boni told me that three hundred bombs fell in an hour and a half, killing hundreds of civilians. I don't always tune in to the news; I find it depressing to hear about families whose lives have been torn apart. It reminds me of my own sadness.

In some moments I feel that I have always lived on the periphery of life. The good things always seemed to be happening to someone else. My father was a successful entrepreneur. He managed to overcome problems which were five times as great as my own loss. And my brothers? Solomon was a contented man, enjoying a close connection with the synagogue and getting satisfaction from the business. Jonah simply enjoyed the prosperity it brought. He was a bit like Joseph, always thinking of ways to escape from the office. It's strange that both my brothers were bachelors. I find it hard to understand how someone would want to live alone, from choice. In Jonah's case it may have been a different matter. Perhaps his interests lay elsewhere. The postcards he sent from his trip were full of references to young boys and the clothes worn by the men. He seemed to enjoy being mysterious. When he came back from India he had a regular appointment every Tuesday. When Anna asked him about it, he changed the subject. Some weeks later the enigma was solved: it transpired that Jonah had been sitting for a portrait and had for some reason wanted to conceal his visits to the artist's studio. I'm not sure why he was so cagey about it; we didn't much like the finished painting anyway.

Dan was a bachelor too, but the money that passed through his hands certainly found its way to female companions. Joseph used to tell me that his brother had an eye for the ladies and boasted that there was no point owning a book when you could simply choose one from a library and exchange it for another one the following week. He saw no virtue in commitment and was scathing about people who had no style or panache. After we settled down to family life in Lisbon we came into that category.

Yet it wasn't always so. The detachment I felt as a child as I watched my parents entertaining in the grand house in Finsbury Square grew into a determination to create a different life of my own. I was the youngest child in a household with a melancholic mother and a father who was repressing great sadness. I became inquisitive and adventurous and resolved not to be like them. Was it any wonder that my decision to marry Joseph and live abroad was taken within days of our meeting at the ball? Our first years in Lisbon were filled with excitement and adventure.

We had twenty two years together. I find it hard to believe now that it was so long. But that time was as perfect as I could have imagined. Of course there were trials to overcome but Joseph was so cheerful and loving that those years seem bathed in a golden glow; the colour of the sunshine in Lisbon, the *yemma* pastries, the flowers at Sintra. Dan wouldn't have understood this. For him life had to be forever changing, an endless search for new company or acquisitions. In a strange way it made him uncomfortable when our settled life came to an end. He was still able to pursue his conquests but I was a reminder of a stain in the family; a black widow to be kept out of sight, out of mind.

I blame myself for never coming to terms with my loss. It affected the whole family. It clouded my judgment. It was a mistake to give in to Boni and allow her to become so domineering. I must have been blind not to see that her early teenage tantrums were aimed at me, because she had no father. I just watched as she made poor Anna's life a misery, putting her in her place and tyrannizing the dinner table with her fads and dislikes. Once, she took Anna's best dress and cut it into pieces and left them under my pillow. When I asked her what had possessed her to do it, she said:

"I thought if I did something really bad, Papa would come back to tell me off."

How strange it is that they get on so well now, with

Boni never hinting that she might be jealous of Anna's success or her marriage. And as for the baby, Boni must have knitted Nina a dozen matinée jackets. She's only stopped because she can't get the wool any more and thinks it wouldn't make sense to unpick one of her old jumpers.

When I see the way Anna cares for Nina, I wonder if I could have been a better mother. But the truth is I only ever saw myself as a wife. Everyone assumed I was sad during those childless years, but though Joseph yearned for a family, I was content. My life revolved around him; we did everything together. Of course I was happy when the babies arrived, but I knew nothing about child rearing and left it to others; Joseph was the one who knew exactly how to handle them; Jo drew out their best features. I watched from the side, with a growing resentment. The jealousy was uncontrollable. When Jo took charge of the children on the steamship I was grateful, but filled with anger. When Anna developed an attachment to Beatrice, I was tempted to find a replacement. But she wasn't just a parlourmaid; she had such a sweet nature and came down in the mornings with a smile that seemed to lift us all out of our gloom. Would it have been different if I'd been younger? If we'd started a family as soon as we moved to Lisbon? Who knows whether it would have been harder for them to lose a father when they were in their teens, rather than as children. When Joseph died I was unable to be strong and objective and felt the burden of my widowhood compounded by the dependence of my young family.

The thought has passed through my mind that we

would have been happier away from London. If we'd gone back to Lisbon there would have been days watching the sea whisking into a foam round the rocks at Cascais, walking through the cool green air in the hills of Sintra.

Over the years I began to think about Dan and his part in the whole affair of the properties and the will. He sent me small sums of money but he never considered sharing what should have been a joint inheritance. Samuel had no quarrel with Joseph; he would have intended to leave an equal sum to his two sons. For a man of his age not to leave a will making provision for his wife and children—that was unheard of in the Gibraltar community. Perhaps ... perhaps it was not as it seemed.

It was in Dan's interest for his father to have died intestate. Without a piece of paper to prove otherwise, Dan inherited the business when Joseph died. He took over the property, the warehouse with the stock, the contacts. Why didn't I see it before? I accepted that my brothers would provide for us and never considered that Dan might have had a motive for claiming his father had left no will.

What would have happened if I'd installed myself in the house at Sintra instead of staying in the apartment in West Hampstead? If I'd settled the three children in school in Portugal, Dan would surely have found it impossible to turn us out. And while he was in Gibraltar I could have gone to the office in Lisbon and searched through whatever papers remained. I might even have found a copy of Samuel's will.

It is said that wealth never made anyone happy but the lack of it can certainly contribute to misery. If I hadn't always been watching the pennies we might have had a better life. I could have gone on journeys with the children. Perhaps one day we might have visited the Holy Land together. A degree of independence would have saved me from the resentment I felt towards Jonah and Dan, with their elegant clothes and their love of gambling or wine.

It's too late to rewrite the past. Just because Isaac had been ill as a child and had developed bad eyesight, I gave in to him, pandering to his demands. And what did that lead to? Giving him money I could ill afford. And Anna—I see now that I should never have been so possessive, refusing to allow her any freedom. But there is something I can do to make amends to my two daughters. I shall make sure to leave a will, making my intentions clear to all of them. What little I have left will be divided equally between Anna and Boni. If this seems harsh Isaac should remember that he has already received his share. His constant appeals over the last few years have left me weary. As far as I know the money has all gone down the drain.

I shall also leave £5 to Beatrice. After all, she was a good parlourmaid. She was very young when she first came to live with us, probably happy to escape from a poor home. She seemed to appreciate fine things and took such care of the smocked dresses I made. Anna used to perch herself on a little stool in the kitchen and chatter away with her while she pressed the sheets and bolster cases. I didn't know what they were giggling about, but it irritated me. I expected to see that Beatrice had scorched a piece of linen, but no, everything was neatly folded and piled up in the airing cupboard. Beatrice married a postman and then had a son. She couldn't have any more children and she adored him with the kind of passion that is reserved for an only child. As a young man he was very good looking; blond hair with a wave in the front. He decided to go and live in Australia. I remember her bringing in letters from him. She never saw him again. I should have learnt something from Beatrice: she lost her only son, yet she was always smiling. She's gone to work for Anna now, doing a bit of ironing twice a week.

Now we have no help in the house. Boni takes care of everything. She tut tuts at little things but never says a word about the way her life has turned out. She never complains at having no husband—unlike me, who can't forget for a single minute. I worry that I have become a burden. The doctor tells me I have a heart condition but apart from some difficulty in walking, I don't feel as if I were nearly eighty. Isaac suggested I should use a wheelchair. I'd rather not go out at all. It's so undignified to be pushed along in a chair. People might see me and realize how dependent I am on my daughter. And though Nina and Joel are only babies I don't want them to see me in a wheelchair. That's how they'll remember me—an old woman, unable to walk.

My grandchildren have brought me such joy—far beyond any feelings I had for my own children at that age. I was frightened to allow myself that boundless love that I felt for our first baby. After she died, it was as if all the tenderness had evaporated and I was left with nothing but anxiety. What began as concern turned into possessiveness. I've never spoken to anyone about this. But it may have been obvious—to Jo, to Beatrice.

What's the purpose in mulling over the past? I should concentrate on getting stronger so that when the war is over I can invite the children to come for a proper tea. If I'd been younger I'd be planning a visit to Bertram Mills Circus. I suppose Olympia is closed down now the war is on. I wonder what they've done with all the animals? The bear that rode a motorbike, and the elephants that could stand up on their back legs? I heard that their trainer slept on a camp bed in the tent with them.

I have a memory of my grandfather Reuven taking me out and bringing me presents when I was small. Most children can expect to have four grandparents but of course I only had one. But my father more than made up for that as he bought me frocks from Paris and the finest of dolls. I couldn't have wished for more.

What possessions can I pass on to my children? My father gave me the camel teapot and a letter with the words 'Forget the sorrow and use it with joy'. I think he was wrong: one should remember the sorrow since happiness is transitory and sadness lies deep inside our souls.

I have every faith that I shall soon be reunited with my beloved. Yet the moment of death is a chilling thought. What if I become unconscious, presumed dead? There have been many cases of people being buried alive, unable to communicate from the depths of the ground. I should investigate what measures can be taken to avert this possibility.

chapter 37

For delicate persons of all ages, the
following preparation has been found
most singularly useful:

*Take six fresh eggs, six lemons, half a
pound of castor sugar and half a pint of
white rum. Put the eggs in their shells inside a jar, without injuring the shells, peel
the lemons and after removing their pith,
squeeze the fresh juice over the eggs, then
lay above them the rind and the pulp. Cover
the jar lightly and put it in a cool place for
seven days, not forgetting to shake it well
on each day. At the end of that time strain
through muslin, when it will be found that
the lemon juice has dissolved the eggshells.
Add the sugar and the rum, then bottle
and cork it lightly. A wineglassful taken
each morning before breakfast is the full
dose, but it may be desirable at first to give
only half this quantity.*

Meals Medicinal, by Dr W T Fernie, 1905

Nathan's mind was troubled with dreams. He had been in bed for ten days, too weak to get into the wheelchair. The district nurse was coming in three times a day, to deal with the catheter and to help where Anna was unable to do the lifting. He had little to say to either of them. One night he dreamed that he couldn't speak any more and someone came and closed his eyes and put a sheet over his head. Then they took him off the bed and laid him on the floor with his feet facing the door. Anna was sitting in a chair and stayed there all night.

When he woke up he recalled every detail, but his voice was weak and it would have taken too much effort to relate the whole dream. Instead he talked about the things he missed:

"I remember ... what it was like ... having a bath." The words came out as if he were struggling, breathless, up a steep hill.

Anna waited.

"... with the water gushing out. I could turn off ... turn off the taps ... with my toes."

She smiled. For months he'd said so little. She waited for him to continue:

"I've gone on too long."

"Don't talk like that," said Anna, stroking his hand.

The unspoken thought—which couldn't be denied—was that he'd been a burden. He'd tried to limit the number of times he called, but the frustration of his paralysis led to a depression that infused the house like cigar smoke lingering in the morning air. Anna was trying to think of something positive to say. Nathan looked at her, his watery eyes fixed on her face. In that moment she realized that he understood her occasional bursts of short temper, the huffing at changing sheets, the less-than-instant response to the ringing of the bell. Summoning another effort of breath, he began:

"You know what I'd like?"

"What?" she whispered.

"I'd like ... a piece of cheese ... and I'd like to be able to hold a book. And turn the pages and read it to the end. Then I'd walk to the library to get another one."

Nathan closed his eyes. When she thought he was asleep Anna left the room and squeezed the door till the latch clicked. For weeks he'd said so little and in the last few minutes he'd said everything: he was miserable about his condition and since it couldn't be altered, he didn't want to carry on. For nine years she had watched him struggle. It seemed, looking back, as if it had all been a slow stream of decline, sometimes meandering through a patch of calm, but for ever trickling downwards. When the stroke was diagnosed they both knew that Nathan would never recover; that he'd never regain control of his own life. Neither of them admitted it, but the realization struck them both in that first week. It took another four hundred weeks for the machinery of his body to reach the same conclusion.

Anna was in the bathroom getting ready for bed when Nathan gasped and opened his mouth to call. She was brushing her teeth but it wasn't the swirling of the toothpaste water that stopped her hearing his voice. She didn't hear because there was no sound. There was no-one there when he breathed out for the last time; when his damaged brain sent a final message to his heart and his thoughts faded. When Anna came back he was lying still on the bed, with his mouth open.

A doctor came and signed the death certificate. He agreed to Anna's strange request to help move Nathan on to the floor, with his feet facing the door. They covered his face and body with a sheet. Anna sat in the chair and glanced at the two empty beds before she turned off the lights. She dozed and woke, constantly startled by the lack of breathing in the bed beside her.

In her whole life she had never spent a single night alone, never gone to sleep without leaning over to give someone a kiss. As a child she'd shared a bedroom with her mother and fallen asleep to the sound of sobbing every night. There had always been two single beds. When she moved away and married Nathan he persuaded her to have the iron bedsteads from his parents' house in Clapton. By the time they could afford new beds, in high walnut frames, they'd got used to being tucked in, side by side, never having experienced the expansive freedom of a king-size sheet thrown across legs and arms that entwined during the night.

The second hand on the clock chugged round, surely taking ninety seconds to complete each minute. Anna unwittingly completed Nathan's last dream, sitting curled up in the chair, not leaving till the undertaker's men arrived. She was woken by the doorbell and she hovered outside the bedroom waiting for what seemed like twenty minutes; like that period at the dentist when he says: 'just keep your mouth open a bit longer' and the drilling goes on and on. The two men finally came out of the room, carrying a long black bag between them. The weight of it seemed so slight. Anna watched as they passed her and without a word left the house. She closed the front door and collapsed in an armchair, her body heaving with sobs, crying the tears she'd held back for so long.

Nina was already on her way back from New York, unaware that her father was dead. She ate her airline meal, flicked through magazines and let a stream of guilty thoughts wash over her. Why hadn't she gone home more often? How could she leave her mother struggling to cope, alone? She should have been there, instead of the district nurse, so Anna could have gone out for more than a few snatched hours in a week. Most of all she regretted the postcards: the weekly note scribbled on the back of a view of the Chrysler Building or Central Park. Even when she wrote a letter it was brief with no discussion of books she had read or her work with the agency. She could have written about items in the news and asked what her father thought of Harold Wilson becoming Prime Minister or Richard Nixon ordering the Christmas bombing of North Vietnam.

Boni met her at the airport and Nina knew immediately that she'd arrived too late. Her first thought was: what was expected of her? She'd imagined this moment a dozen times in the last few years and pictured herself choosing a black blouse and leaving off the make-up. The scene included opening letters of condolence and telling her friends that her father had been brave. But the relationship with her parents was heavily weighted towards her mother. Nathan had been fifty when Nina was born, so by the time she was five he was hardly able to join in pass-the-parcel and choosing hair ribbons. She had no memory of talking with him about hating the junior school or the embarrassment of being a Jewish child from North London in a class of girls whose parents played tennis on the elegant lawns of the Hurlingham Club. Meal times were an opportunity for him to talk about books, the ones that he'd read, not the Balzac or the Dante on her exam syllabus. Yet it was in that year, when Nina was seventeen, that she came to know her father. It began with a pile of letters, written from Italy or Switzerland, revealing the real man: eager to amuse with his practical jokes, constantly thinking of his daughter back home and sending her advice on how to deal with money, or with men.

On their way to the house she asked her aunt how her mother was coping. The answer came as no surprise: if there were things to be done, Anna would do them. She wouldn't let her feelings get in the way. She wasn't the kind of woman who would collapse in tears in front of the neighbours. She'd be able to deal with death certificates and funeral arrangements. For someone who had learned to change a fuse or remove a spider from the bathtub, the burial was a simple matter. It had to take place immediately and there were no decisions to be made. The coffin had to be of a standard wood with no brass handles; there was no music to choose, no flowers to organise. Like all Jewish funerals the ones at the Spanish and Portuguese

374

cemetery were identical—the same for the poorest member of the community or a high-flying banker. Even the headstones were laid flat, so there was no scope for grandeur or embellishment.

What Nina didn't expect was the silence. Her mother was exhausted; too tired to speak. While the burial service was taking place Nina talked and waited for Anna to agree with her:

"I don't see why we can't go to the cemetery. It's all happening without us. I hate that. Why couldn't we go?"

"That's how it is."

"It's all about the men, isn't it? They need ten men to be there, but when it comes to public prayers, women don't count. There's not one man who cares about Dad like we do, let alone ten."

Anna sighed.

"You're being harsh. Perhaps they think it's too emotional for a woman to stand by the grave. I can imagine it, that thudding of the earth on the wood."

They were silent. Boni was busy in the kitchen preparing the meal for the mourners. Nina told her aunt not to bother with hard boiled eggs for her. She found it hard enough to eat them at a normal meal, let alone one where you were struggling to swallow anything at all. She came back and looked at her mother. Anna had a prayer book open on her lap. Nina didn't know if she was getting comfort from the words or whether it was a choice between that and the morning papers lying untouched on the table.

"Mum" she began. "You know I'm sorry, don't you?"

"Sorry about what?"

"That I didn't do more. That I didn't come back more often. That I was buttering bread in the old age home in Brooklyn instead of bringing my father a cup of tea."

Nina's face was stained. She wiped her eyes with the back of her hand.

"Did I ever say anything?" asked Anna.

"No, that's just the point. You didn't. But you probably thought it."

The week of the *shiva* passed. For most of the time the house was quiet; the silence broken by the arrival of a few bridge friends or the odd neighbour. The talk revolved round Nathan and his antics; which since his death had changed from being a source of embarrassment to one of amusement. He didn't make fun of people; it was affectionate observation. Anna remembered an incident when Joel and Nina were about four. An encyclopedia salesman had come to the door and was explaining to Anna the benefits of purchasing his product in monthly instalments. "It would be a good investment for your children" he'd said, looking at the two cousins playing. Anna agreed that she believed in teaching them to read early and was considering signing a payment form when the salesman began to tell her something:

"It's so good to meet an educated woman," he said. "I've just had a conversation with a man, sitting on the bench up the road. I don't think he's a tramp, but he looked pretty scruffy. He told me he didn't know how to read or write."

Anna was studying the conditions at the bottom of the form when the front door opened and Nathan walked in. He took off his old overcoat and put the battered hat on a chair. The salesman looked aghast, picked up his papers and began to move towards the door. Nathan closed it behind him and smiled.

Nina offered to change her air ticket and stay longer. Anna dismissed the suggestion, perhaps a little too swiftly, claiming she had to get used to living alone. She even joked that life would be easier as she wouldn't have to make endless cups of tea for the district nurse. On the way back from the airport Anna looked at her watch, wondering if she should hurry back. There was no-one at home; no one waiting for her to make a meal. And then she remembered: someone was coming to take away the wheelchair. She had to be back in forty minutes.

chapter 38

Madeleinas

2 eggs, 3 oz vanilla sugar, 3 oz self raising flour, 3 oz cooled, melted butter

Whisk the eggs and the sugar till pale yellow and add the flour. Pour in the butter and mix till smooth. Bake in greased tins in a moderate oven for five to ten minutes.

From Dina's notebook, 1912

LISBON 1974—ANNA

Nina phoned from New York every day, calculating only the time change, not the cost. At first Anna found the frequent contact difficult as she was used to the more detached weekly conversations they'd had on Sundays. These had always begun with Nina asking after her father and Anna editing what she said, to avoid giving details of her day-to-day problems. She'd never known where to start. Do you talk about the washing machine that stopped working with two sets of sheets soaking inside the drum? Do you tell your daughter you can't fit into your winter skirts, in spite of a constant diet that cuts out the cakes that everyone else can eat without putting on weight? Perhaps the conversation could turn to the new decimal currency and how hard it is to sift through a purse with no half-crowns and florins? Nina too found it difficult. She asked how her mother was managing and interrupted the reply to tell her about the Peggy Lee concert in Central Park. In the end the conversations were brief, always ending with one of them saying: 'must go', though neither of them had the urgency of a child needing a potty or a postman needing a signature for a parcel delivery.

Now that they had begun to speak every day, the talk was somehow easier; each one spilling out details of day to day life, picking up where they'd broken off the previous morning. Anna didn't find it hard to remember that Nina was waiting for a cheque, and had it come yet? Nina got a full description of the two things dominating her mother's life: her bridge games and her diet.

A month after Nathan's death the bridge evenings began again, with Anna starting the preparation in the middle of the Monday afternoon. It took time to roll and fold the puff pastry for custard tarts; to pass the tea cakes through the cinnamon sugar syrup and to arrange a plate of sandwiches, cut into hearts and spades, each one decorated with a sliced olive or a sprinkle of paprika. It was some time before it occurred to her that she could spend the evening in someone else's house and for a change they could be the ones to provide the food.

What did Anna expect? She hoped they would take as much trouble as she had done, yet in their homes there were no sandwiches with the crusts removed and no home-made cake. Instead there was a bought apple pie or a box of chocolates that had started to go white at the edges. It shouldn't have mattered. But it would have been nice if one of them had provided a few plain crackers to go with the cup of tea without milk.

The diet made Nina sad. At seventy-one her mother was still struggling with her weight; vain enough to want to look good in a silk dress; careful never to choose horizontal stripes or skirts that showed her heavy legs. Nina argued that it couldn't matter if her mother treated herself to the occasional pastry, but secretly she didn't believe Anna's claim that she had heavy bones and hardly ate a thing. It was more likely that she was eating buttered melba toast and spooning *yemma* on to matzah with her morning tea.

In an effort to compensate for neglecting her parents, Nina took too much interest. She wanted to know her mother's timetable and planned the phone calls around the bridge games and the exact time of a visit to the hair-dresser. What she didn't know was that Anna was waking up to a new life; one that didn't involve anyone else. She could eat her breakfast in bed, read all the Sunday news-papers with no interruptions; ignore the doorbell. Her greatest pleasure was to run a bath in the evening and lie back undisturbed, with the scent of almond oil floating in the air and a glass of chilled wine by her side. One thing was certain—she wasn't going to wear black for the rest of her life, like her mother.

The stories that Nina had heard about Dina were a mystery. As a young woman her grandmother had been spirited and daring. Yet when she was left a widow with almost no means of support, she became dependent on her brothers, lacking the fight to pursue what was rightly hers. Nina wondered if there was a chance of discovering what happened in 1905, when her grandfather died and his brother claimed all the business for himself. The office in the centre of Lisbon had long been closed but she made enquiries and learned that the warehouse where they stored the olive oil had been taken over by a man called Filipe Primeiro. If there was anything to find out, it would be there.

Nina planned to take her mother to Lisbon for a week's holiday. While she booked flights she calculated the journeys she should have made to London. By way of compensation she chose a hotel with class, one that advertised 'quiet elegance overlooking the river'. The trip was arranged for the beginning of September. Anna received the news with apprehension. It was years since she'd been to an airport and she didn't relish talking to people in the queue for the check-in. She'd like to find the house in Rua Herculano where her mother had lived but she'd be required to make conversation with the caretaker of the building. It wasn't a language problem—she was calm about knowing no Portuguese—it was that she'd lost the habit of speaking. After years of being confined to the house she'd forgotten the art of small talk. Living with Nathan for nearly forty years involved a different kind of communication. She would complete his unfinished crossword clues, know without asking what he thought about an item in the newspaper. She could tell by a lift of the eyebrows or a curl of the lips, if he was about to tell a joke. Words were redundant. After Nathan died and there was no-one to talk to, the bridge games were ideal, demanding only minimal communication between the hands.

Anna had little enthusiasm for sharing her thoughts with strangers and was already imagining the next hurdle: signing a hotel register as a single person, Mrs. Anna Grant. For the first time in years she remembered when she had changed her name from Mrs. Grunthal. Nathan had taken her to the Trocadero for their first wedding anniversary: February 4th 1938. They'd had a discussion about his crumpled suit and in the end he'd put on a new one. While they were waiting for the wine he began to look uncomfortable.

"What would you think of changing our name?" he asked.

"What's wrong with Grunthal? Except that it's German and some people can't pronounce it?"

"That's the problem—I don't want to have a German name if we are going to war with Hitler."

"We should just have the English version," said Anna. "But Greenvalley's a bit of a mouthful."

Nathan began to tell her about a man in Cambridge who did a brilliant name change. His name was Stoutzker. He wanted to sound less Jewish and more aristocratic, so he simply deleted one letter and replaced it with a dash. He removed the 'z' and changed his name to Stout-ker, but the master stroke was the pronunciation: calling himself Stout Carr completed the rebranding. Anna was amused and they spent the rest of the meal thinking of English versions of Grunthal. Eventually they came up with a name that didn't have to be spelt out: Grant.

The first time Anna used her new name was on a shopping expedition. She and Freda were both pregnant and they planned to go to the West End to look at baby clothes. They met in the layette department of Marshall and Snelgrove. Freda was in a fog of indecision and chose one shawl. Anna ordered everything, ticking off the items she needed and happily signed the bill 'Anna Grant'.

Nina's intention was to whisk her mother off for a silky week of luxury at The Ritz Hotel in Lisbon. She booked a room with a terrace overlooking the park. They ordered breakfast and an immaculate waiter set up a table with a starched cloth and set out coffee and rolls. There was also a plate of small scented cakes. Anna knew her daughter would tell her to forget her diet so she took one and bit into the soft, crumbly muffin. It tasted like one that she remembered from her mother's recipe book. Under the cakes was a card:

> *Madeleinas from the convent of Santa Maria, Lisboa.*

Over breakfast they planned their day. Nina would spend the morning with Filipe Primeiro and Anna might go for a short walk. They would meet back at the hotel and then find a quiet café for lunch.

Filipe's office was in an industrial area near the river. Nina took a taxi to Poco do Bispo and found the building called Edifício Levy. She climbed several flights of stairs and walked into a reception area devoted to a display of items from Joseph Levy's office. Filipe showed her the old leather desk, a safe and five or six ledgers that were the size of a paving stone. He was happy for Nina to look through the accounts, but he also directed her to a small room which was filled with boxes of books and documents. He told her she was welcome to take whatever she wanted: he had simply brought everything from the office and had no further use for it.

She began with a ledger dated January 1901. On the opening page were the words *Diario, pertenente a D & J Levy, Praca do Municipio 20, Lisboa.* Inside were the details of olive oil and sardine sales, written in flowing copperplate. There were the names of the banks—Kleinwort, Bank of South America, then the customers and finally the sums involved, in millions of reis. Nina moved into the unused room and began to sort through boxes filled with dusty letters and papers. She'd been there for nearly two hours when Filipe came in and asked if she'd like a coffee. He wondered if she'd found anything of interest. So far she'd come across some Hebrew books and an account book dated 1887. Some of the documents were copies, but inside a folder was the original conveyance of a house in Gibraltar from January 1804. An hour later Nina had made a small pile of what she wanted to take. She was about to leave when she turned to one last box that she hadn't opened.

Back at the hotel Anna had returned from her walk. She was asking the concierge to recommend somewhere for lunch when Nina came into the foyer. They took the tram to Alfama and walked down from the top of the hill looking for the cafe with trees and tables shaded by bleached umbrellas. For some reason Nina seemed restless and preferred to walk rather than go straight to lunch. Anna was already tired and didn't relish another half hour stepping on cobble stones. As they came down the hill they looked at the houses with their wrought-iron balconies and honey-pale walls. Anna wanted to remark on the terracotta roof tiles but could only think how much her feet were hurting. At each turn in the zigzag road, she hoped to find the cafe. Looking down over the rooftops she caught a glimpse of the sky and sea—a sapphire blue that almost made up for the pinching leather and blistering skin.

When they sat down to lunch Nina was preoccupied and didn't seem to hear when the waiter asked what kind of sherry they would like. She began to talk about the converted warehouse and Filipe's collection of old Levy documents. Anna wanted to tell Nina about her morning; how she'd been intrigued that the hotel would buy cakes from the nuns. On a whim, she had gone in search of the convent of Santa Maria. Inside she discovered that to buy some of their home-made confections, you needed to conduct the transaction without speaking. The nuns were members of a silent order. One of them invited Anna into the back where there was a dark wood cupboard. Inside was a turntable and on each shelf was a different pastry. Written underneath was a price. Anna chose two of each type. She paid the nuns and went away with a neatly packaged box.

She began to tell Nina what she'd heard from another

customer.

"It's all to do with the monks, you know."

"What is?" asked Nina, her mind clearly not on the subject of cakes.

"The monasteries used egg whites to clarify wine and probably gave the surplus egg yolks to the convents. What's much more interesting is that the recipes are secret. They say that they are passed on by the Mother Superior, on her deathbed, wrapped in the beads of her rosary."

"So how come the Levy family knew about them? None of them were nuns, as far as I know."

Nina thought that would end the conversation. She wanted to tell Anna what she'd found. She described the dusty store room at the back of the office and even suggested that they should try to bring one of the massive ledgers home. They had nearly finished their lunch when she reached for her bag. Anna insisted that she was paying, but her daughter was searching for something else—not a wallet. She opened the clasp and pulled out a long envelope. Inside was a document, written on parchment. It was a copy of Samuel Levy's will.

Anna shook her head:

"But he didn't leave a will. That's why Dan wouldn't share the business with Mother."

Nina moved the cutlery and spread out the sheets.

"In the Supreme Court of Gibraltar ... PROBATE ... in the goods of Samuel Abraham Levy deceased. 4th day of February 1904."

The will was written in English and Spanish and read:

"This is the last Will of me Samuel Abraham

387

Levy of Gibraltar and Lisbon, Merchant. I give and bequeath to my clerk Anthony Ferro the sum of two hundred dollars for the good services he has rendered ... to my sons Daniel Levy and Joseph Levy the sum of five hundred dollars to be distributed by them amongst such Hebrew Charities in Gibraltar as they may in their discretion think proper. I give to my son Daniel all the furniture, linen, glass, china, plate, books and other articles of household use which may be in my house situate in Turnbulls Lane in Gibraltar and to my son Joseph Levy all the furniture, linen, glass, china, plate, books and other articles of household use which may be in my house situate in Sintra. I also recommend my said sons Daniel and Joseph Levy to continue the business both in Gibraltar and Lisbon as co-partners, following as heretofore the same system of rectitude and honesty which has always characterised both the said houses of business in Gibraltar and Lisbon. I give, devise and bequeath all the rest and residue of my real and personal estate unto my said two sons Daniel Levy and Joseph Levy, to be divided between them in equal shares. In witness whereof I the said Samuel Abraham Levy have to this my last will set my hand this nine day of February one thousand eight hundred and ninety four.

chapter 39

Fijuelas

> 2 eggs, 1 tbsp orange flower water, 1 tbsp oil (and more for frying), 3 tbsp cold water, 9 oz plain flour

for the syrup:

> 8 oz granulated sugar, 10 fl oz water, 1 inch cinnamon stick or a vanilla pod

> *Beat the eggs with the oil, orange water and enough flour and water to make a pliable dough. Knead it well and roll it out very thinly. Cut it into strips about 8" long and 2" wide. Prick the strips with a fork. Have ready a pan half full of hot oil and taking one end of each strip, carefully lower it in. As it touches the oil, turn the bottom of the strip round with a long-handled fork, coiling it round in the hot oil to fry each part of it. Remove the fork and leave it to fry for a couple of minutes while you lower in the next strip. When they are golden brown, drain well and arrange in a bowl. For the syrup, bring the sugar and water slowly to the boil, flavouring with a cinnamon stick*

or a split vanilla pod. Leave to cool slightly
and strain the syrup over the fijuelas.

From Anna's notebook, 1970

LONDON 1974—ANNA

Nina heaved the massive ledger on to the table in Anna's kitchen. Layers of newspaper wrapping were all over the floor.

"Why did you bring that thing home?" asked Anna. "I thought you didn't want it."

"We just had to have it. It's all about the Levy business, when it was thriving, four years before your father died. We should try to work out the value of some of the transactions. What would a million reis be worth now?"

Anna didn't reply. Nina thought she was exhausted from the argument with the airline staff about carrying the ledger as hand luggage. But it was the discovery of the will that had left Anna shaken and subdued. Finding that Samuel had left his property and money equally between Dan and Joseph had shocked them both.

There was only one explanation: Dan must have known about it and suppressed the will so that he would inherit everything. If Dina had suspected, she remained silent, never hinting to her children that her financial situation was anything but a misfortune.

Anna, always prone to petty resentments, now had a reason to feel justifiable anger. Knowing what Dan had done would have intensified her mother's dislike of him and she might have used all the energy she expended on being miserable into fighting for her part of the inheritance. If they'd had the house in Sintra and enough money to live comfortably their lives would have been different. Above all it would have affected their relationship with Solomon and Jonah. Instead of a feeling of obligation, tinged with envy, they could have had an affinity, a closeness based on shared experiences. Anna never forgot the postcards that Jonah sent from his trip—each one received and read aloud with great excitement, and more than a hint of jealousy.

Nina was unpacking more documents: notepaper from the Levy business, a Current Price List dated 1890, and a schedule of the deeds of a house in Gibraltar dated 1788.

"Listen to this: '*part of the said estate situate in the back lane under the Moorish Castle, originally bounded towards the East by the Rock, towards the West by the said back lane, towards the North by the house of John Macasland and towards the South by the house of John Guthrie and the ground left to the Poor by the Widow King, having been parcelled into three lots.*' Do you think that was the property in Turnbulls Lane that Dan inherited from his father?"

"It might have been. I suppose you want to go there now," said Anna.

"No, there's nothing to be gained by it. Dan has been dead for nearly fifty years. We're hardly likely to be able to trace any of his money now."

Nina had little interest in the money. Discovering the will was a prize in itself. Her family history was like a jig-saw puzzle; tantalizing snippets of information surrounded by blanks. At the heart of the story was her great-grandfather David and how he'd survived the earthquake. She didn't tell her mother then, but she was planning to take her on another journey.

There were four days before Nina's return to New York. Anna hoped she'd spend some time looking through boxes of books. Nathan had collected sets of leather-bound classics and she'd finally decided to clear the bookcases and replace them with glass shelves to display a Chinese chess set in carved ivory. Nina promised to take the books to a dealer and on her way to the car, Anna pointed to a painting that she also wanted to sell.

"It's the one of Jonah. What a puffed up opinion he had of himself. Who would think of having your own portrait painted? It's not as if he had any children to leave it to."

Nina was amused at the strength of her mother's feelings. Anna had no reason to dislike Jonah but she'd inherited from Dina a sneering tone whenever his name was mentioned. Disapproval can pass through a family faster than an infection, turning a spot of antipathy into a full-blown rash, out of all proportion to the original cause. Nina loaded the books into the boot of the car and since the painting was too large, she lifted it on to the floor of the back seats, where it stayed for a few days.

The books went for a surprisingly low price. Dealers claimed there was no market for sets of Thackeray or Dickens in perfect condition. The painting proved even harder to sell. With a friend Lynn, Nina went in and out of small galleries, and each one offered less than ten pounds. As they lugged the portrait back to the car, Lynn said she thought Uncle Jonah's face showed character.

"If you like him so much, you can have him," said Nina, on an impulse.

"I couldn't possibly. He's your great uncle. I don't know why you're trying to get rid of him." Lynn looked at the painting: "He's got a calm expression."

"That decides it. You can keep him." They both ended up laughing as Nina drove to Lynn's house with the painting. When she got back to Cricklewood she called to Anna that she'd had a successful morning.

"Didn't get much for the books, but I sold the painting for £50."

"That's wonderful. I'm glad I don't have to look at him any more."

Nina pulled some notes out of her wallet and handed them to her mother. Lynn was glad to have the picture, Anna was delighted at the thought that it had raised some money. Nina thought it a small price to pay for making two people happy.

There was one more item that she hadn't sold. Sifting through her father's books she'd pulled out a copy of The Life of Lord Birkenhead (F.E. Smith). It brought back memories of meal times when Nathan had repeated stories of the great man and his exploits in court. At the time she never wanted to hear the initials F.E. again, but Nina imagined herself, sitting at her table in New York, reading the book and hearing her father's voice.

Anna interrupted her thoughts and handed her a parcel. The handle was made from several strands of string.

"Don't open it now. I've packed it up for you to take back. It's the camel teapot and the matching jug and sugar bowl."

Nina protested that she wasn't ready to start accumulating the family heirlooms, but Anna insisted, telling her there was only one condition.

"I know, I've got to keep them polished."

"No," said Anna "just make sure they're insured."

Nina admitted that she had no enthusiasm for cleaning silver but she did love the teapot. While she was packing Anna offered to make her a final treat: a batch of *fijuelas*. Nina couldn't resist a smile. Who else but her mother would be considering rolling out pastry into wafer-thin strips and frying it into coils half an hour before her daughter was due to leave for the airport?

As a child she'd thought *fijuelas* were made of fish and refused to eat them. When she was persuaded to try one, she found out they were sweet pastries, covered in a rich vanilla syrup. Nina adored them, but told her mother not to bother as she was leaving soon. Anna was thinking about the last time she'd made them. It was quite an effort rolling out the papery strips of pastry, curling each one with a long-handled fork as it touched the boiling oil. Mrs. Edwards had been impressed. She'd started with two, and then—would you believe this—she'd eaten another two, spooning over more of the thick sugary syrup. Anna watched and spread a couple of crackers with a smear of cream cheese. When they'd gone she cleared away the empty plates, lifted the largest of the remaining coils into a bowl, covered it with the syrup and ate it slowly. But the pleasure was already spoilt. It was all right for Mrs. Edwards, who was as thin as Wallis Simpson, but Anna would step on the scales the next day and find that she'd put on two pounds.

Nina returned to a damp, empty apartment. It was too early for central heating when the old-fashioned radiators turned the building into an equatorial fug. She left the chilly bedroom, put on a jacket and walked through the park, kicking at a carpet of russet and gold leaves. Going home to London was always unsettling. Thoughts about the family reinforced the nagging feeling that she was alone, without a husband or lover. Her mother was tactful enough never to ask questions.

After Samir Nina had learned to be detached. She would meet a man and feel the beginning of an attraction between them. The relationship would progress and while they were still at the discovery stage, the meetings would be filled with excitement. When there was a hint of commitment, Nina would step back, explaining at length that she couldn't live with anyone, that she needed her own space, that she couldn't cook for herself, let alone a partner, that she had to wake up in her own bed—and it wasn't big enough for two. Her friends were perplexed: Nina had a stream of admirers and as soon as one of them showed a serious interest, she would back away. What they didn't know was that she was searching for someone who didn't exist: a suitable marriage partner who was intelligent, well-educated and solvent. Most important of all, he had to have black eyes that made her heart melt.

Unlike her mother, Nina didn't dwell on the past. She went back to the apartment and found a bag large enough to hold the silver tea set. Then she searched the Yellow Pages for Silversmiths. She took the three pieces to a specialist called Newman on W 43rd Street and Madison Avenue. He told her the valuation would take him a couple of days. Nina went on to the agency where she picked up two new commissions—work that would last her a month.

When she returned to Mr. Newman, he went to the back of the shop and brought out a box with her name on it. He lifted the teapot on to the counter.

"Interesting, Miss Grant. An unusual piece."

He picked up the two smaller items.

"Both of these are English and they are nineteenth century."

"How can you tell?" asked Nina.

He reached for a book about English silver and turned to the section on hallmarks.

"Look, you see, the first mark is a guarantee of assay, or a test that the silver is 92% pure; the second is a two-letter symbol identifying the maker and the third is a letter of the alphabet denoting the year."

He pointed to a page in his reference book:

"The jug and the sugar bowl were made by a firm called Savoury, in Cornhill, London, and the date was 1856. If the set were complete, you'd be looking at a value of several thousand dollars."

"What about the camel teapot?" asked Nina.

Mr. Newman examined it, turned it upside down and

ran his finger over a small dent in the side.

"As you see, this has no hallmark. The style of the teapot is North African. I'd say it came from Tunisia or Morocco. But the ivory handle ... "

He stopped and turned the teapot over, examining the beaten work around the lid and the base.

"The piece is certainly old. The ivory handle may have been added to match the jug and the sugar bowl. But the teapot on its own—you could probably find a similar one in the souk in Marrakesh. If I were making an offer I'd start at $50 and be prepared to go up to $100."

Nina paid Mr. Newman for the valuation and left with the silver tea set. It didn't tie up with what she knew of the story. Her mother had told her that the camel teapot had come from the earthquake in Safed. She never mentioned the other two pieces. Nina knew from the dates that the silversmith was wrong in putting a greater value on them, but had no way of proving it. His final words had been:

"I'd value the milk jug and sugar bowl at $1800. I would forget about insuring the teapot."

chapter 40

"It is the most odiferous and pestiferous place it has ever been my fate to sleep in. One seems transported into the ghetto of some Roumanian or Russian town, where the Ashkenazim wear the high hats, greasy gabardines and ear-curls of the Jews of Europe. The few Eastern disagreeables (Sephardi or Spanish Jews) wear Oriental costumes."

From the journal of Laurence Oliphant
A trip to the North-East of Lake Tiberias, 1885

SAFED 1976—ANNA

When Nina was unpacking the documents from the Levy office a plan started to form in her mind. In the year following their trip to Lisbon she became increasingly obsessed with finding the origin of the camel teapot and unravelling the mystery of her great-grandfather's life. She was determined to take her mother on one more journey—to Safed in Northern Israel.

The flight to Tel-Aviv landed after midnight. The next morning they travelled by car up the Mediterranean coast to Haifa. Nina had no wish to linger. The car smelled of air freshener—a synthetic sweetness aimed at disguising the smoke from the pile of cigarette ends in the ash tray. Dangling in front of the windscreen was a photograph of a young girl and a child's drawing of a car, with the prayer for travellers stuck on with oozing glue. The driver asked if they'd like to see the Bahai shrine which dominated the city. They replied together:

"Yes we would," said Anna. "Not now," said Nina, keen to continue the journey to Safed.

As if to avoid any further discussion, the driver turned the car away from the harbour area and began the ascent through the central commercial district. The road continued for five or ten minutes up a continuous incline towards the upper part of the town. Anna was wondering how anyone could carry shopping up such hills. The engine slowed as the golden dome of the shrine came into view.

"You want to visit?"

They declined politely, Anna thinking wistfully of the formal terraces and manicured hedges she'd read about, knowing it would be impossible for her to mount the hundreds of steps leading to the fountains. The amateur guide continued to talk:

"Italian marble, pink granite pillars, Persian gardens."

"Thank you, but we really must get on."

Nina watched the driver's shoulders stiffen as he turned the car and followed the sign to Acre. She was hoping he wouldn't launch into the chequered history of the city. For his part, he decided to keep silent about how the town projected into the sea and was surrounded on three sides by water. He began to drive at speed, hurtling past Karmiel through forests of olive and cypress trees set in yellow scrubland bordered by wild rosemary. Nina saw that her mother's eyes were closing and nudged her gently, pointing towards the mountains and the pale city perched in the hills. The approach to Safed went past an old cemetery and up through cobbled streets, designed more for donkeys than motor vehicles.

They booked into a small hotel in the heart of the artists' colony. It was built on ruins and the existing stone arches may have been part of the original structure. A wall of glass windows overlooked the sombre mount Meron. In their room Nina began to unpack a pile of books. Anna had brought just one: Madame Bovary by Gustave Flaubert. The heat was oppressive and she was wiping her forehead, unwilling to admit to feeling tired already. If she hadn't been so hot and uncomfortable she would have smiled, remembering the letter that her mother had written to Jo, more than fifty years before. She recalled the exact words Dina had used, objecting to her staying in the Holy Land: 'My daughter is ill-prepared for life in a hot, sandy city'.

Among the books that Nina had brought was an up-to-date guide to the town and a journal written by a traveller from a different era: a man called Oliphant who had spent years exploring the Middle East. She read his comments about Safed and decided not to repeat them to her mother. Instead she picked up another volume, about the history of the synagogue at Lauderdale Road.

"Look, it mentions Solomon Levy, your uncle, who was one of the founding members."

"If you're looking for David's father, that's the wrong Solomon Levy."

"Mum. don't interrupt. I know that. But there's a reference to the one we want. Here it is:

> *"His grandfather, Solomon Levy, had gone as a young man from Gibraltar to Safed, the centre of Jewish mysticism, and was killed together with his wife and four of his five children in the earthquake in 1837."*

"We know that," said Anna.

"But you didn't listen. It says 'four of his five children'. Is this a mistake? I thought David only had one brother and two sisters: Abraham, Miriam and Rebecca. Could there have been another child?"

Nina was perplexed. She knew so little about her great-grandfather but she'd seen the letter he had written to Dina. There were two things that made her curious. What did he mean when he said: '*on that fateful day I made the wrong decisions. I have lived with a feeling of guilt for all these years*'? And what was he referring to when he wrote: '*there were other things I didn't take. I should have done*'? Why would he have felt such guilt at taking the camel teapot and leaving a pile of drawings?

"Could it be that he left something much more important?"

Anna knew what her daughter was thinking. David had picked up the teapot, the only item of value. But as for the possibility that there was another child—no, it couldn't be. The writer of the book must have been mistaken.

402

It was late afternoon and Nina wanted to see something of the town before nightfall. The air was surprisingly still and cool, unlike the heaving heat of Tel-Aviv or the golden warmth from the stone buildings of Jerusalem. She left her mother in the room, happy to be reading in a chair with a view of the cobbled streets below, instead of feeling the pinch of the stones under her feet.

Nina began to walk through the alleys and vaulted passages. She looked at the arched windows and wondered why so many of the doors and walls were painted blue. She'd heard that there was a museum that contained the earliest book, printed on the first Hebrew printing press. But it was sure to be closed. She'd have to go another day. She saw a group of people queuing at what looked like a hole in the wall. Inside was a brick oven and an array of salads. She bought some food and walked back to the hotel. Anna was asleep in the chair. Nina sat on the bed and unwrapped one of the packages. She took a bite of the still-warm pita bread and the crunchy falafel balls. The salad fell out on to the wax paper. She dipped a hot pepper into the hummous and scooped up the chopped vegetables with her fingers. Anna's falafel was getting cold.

The next morning Nina set off to search the records in the town museum. She offered to take her mother but Anna could imagine all the stairs and preferred to stay in the hotel, reading her book. She was engrossed in the story of Emma Bovary, a married woman searching for happiness with various lovers. It was written in the 1850s and within months of publication the author found himself on trial, accused of a 'glorification of adultery'. The court case did him no harm. The publicity after he was acquitted led to the sale of fifteen thousand copies of the novel. The main character, Emma, lived in a village and dreamed of Parisian society. Did it ever occur to Anna as she read the book, that there were similarities between the heroine and her own grandmother Rachel? Both of them lived in a world of grand balls and in their private life, both were unhappy. There had been so much talk about understanding David's personality that the family had overlooked what was happening in Rachel's apparently settled and uncomplicated life. Like Emma, she concealed a deep melancholy. The cause of their misery may, or may not, have been similar, but one thing was sure: an acceptance of unhappiness can be passed from one generation to the next.

While Nina was out Anna had a leisurely breakfast, hoping none of the residents would try to strike up a conversation. The very thought of talking to strangers made her nervous. She had no wish to share her thoughts with someone she would never meet again.

The museum was in a sixteenth century building, which had been partially destroyed. Nina crossed the courtyard and passed the two vaulted halls with an exhibition of recent history. She went upstairs and through a passageway to some low rooms which had been the cellars of the house on the top floor. Another flight of stairs led to what used to be a schoolyard. Did that mean that the houses were built on top of each other?

The story of Safed is told through exhibitions of paintings, documents and utensils, depicting life in the city. Nina began to understand how the houses were constructed: the town spread from the foot of the hill upwards, beginning in the fifteenth century, when people fleeing the Inquisition built the first narrow street. Alleyways on the roofs of these houses became the floor of the house above. Separate steps led to a door at each level, which explained how the basement of one house was in fact the roof of the one below.

With the help of a translator, she read some letters referring to the earthquake. A Rabbi Naaman wrote of the moment that *'two thousand souls were trapped in a single moment and rose to heaven.'* His account described how the entire city and the walls were reduced to a pile of stones. The survivors sat in tents outside the city and there was not a single house without several dead. The Rabbi believed it was *'because of our many sins.'*

There was also an eye-witness account from a Christian resident of the town. A man called Denus told his story to a Dutch geographer:

> *'I was accustomed to going out to my fields early in the morning and I did this on the first of January 1837. Suddenly the ground shuddered with a terrible blow. The earth rose and fell. The abyss made a noise and a low thunder threatened the soul. The earth was torn apart. The blood froze in the arteries from fright. The heights of Safed shed its houses the way that the fig tree sheds its leaves in the autumn."*

Denus returned to his house. His wife and children were buried under the ruins.

The translator offered to take Nina on a tour of the synagogues. He led her first towards the Abuhav synagogue. As they walked together, Nina was calculating how much to pay him. Thinking that it would be dark when they got inside, she checked the money in her purse. To her surprise the light flooded in through small windows around the base of a sky blue dome. Set in a circle above the glass were childlike paintings of musical instruments, crowns and trees. In a corner a group was listening to an explanation in Hebrew. Nina picked up a few words: '*twelve tribes, fruits of the garden of Eden.*' Her guide was pointing to the bright blue steps and railings around the reading desk and said:

"The blue, it's to ward off the evil eye."

Nina remembered the ultramarine splashes she'd seen on woodwork, pipes and even the tops of plant pots. The guide was telling her about an earlier earthquake in 1759 and a plague that left only seven families alive. As they stepped outside into the sunlight she saw across the street a bright blue mural. Above the carefully drawn lines was a crumbling wall, revealing layers of plaster and paint, each one a paler tone of blue. After each disaster, a fresh coat of blue paint, in the enduring hope of protection.

It took more than an hour—and two more synagogue visits—to locate the place where David's father had perished. The rebuilt synagogue was called the Ari, named after Rabbi Isaac Luria, the best known of all the Jewish mystics. There were several explanations for the name, but Nina was only concerned to see what was left of the building. The guide, looking forward to a generous tip, took her inside and pointing to highly decorated panels around the ark, began his speech about the great man:

"He was born in Jerusalem in 1534 and only lived in

406

Safed for a few years. He used to trade in pepper and grain, but he became famous for acts of levitation and prophecy."

Nina was cynical, thinking *"he was a businessman doing magic in his spare time"*, but immediately felt guilty as the guide continued:

"He died of the plague at the age of thirty-eight, but the people in Safed believed that he was still there, with them. Some years ago a group of religious Jews claimed they had seen him dancing to greet the Sabbath."

The man lowered his voice and continued:

"Other people too, have seen him. There's a rumour in the town that he came back two years ago. You remember the dreadful massacre in Ma'alot?"

Nina did remember. In 1974 twenty-two schoolchildren from Safed went on a hiking trip to the nearby village of Ma'alot. They were sleeping in the schoolhouse there when terrorists broke in. The gunmen murdered nineteen children. Nina wondered what this atrocity had to do with mysticism. The guide told her that the bodies of the children were brought back to their home town for burial. He then pulled out an account of the funeral:

> *'High up from the military cemetery, above the civilian one, came the figure of a white robed man. It passed through the iron bars of the fence and skipped down amongst the brambles and rocks, wearing strange woven shoes. The shoes left no tracks as the figure began to dance. It hovered by the freshly turned earth of the small graves and called the names of each of the children. One asked him if they were going to Jerusalem. 'In that direction' was the reply. A long*

407

*line of children was then seen to wind its way
up, over the hills and roofs of the town to be lost
in the glow of the setting sun.'*

Nina wandered back to the hotel through the stone
streets. She'd parted with the guide, leaving him a generous tip—more than she'd first considered—but she was
relieved to be on her own again. Anna was keen to hear
what she'd found out, but she seemed just as eager to find
a restaurant for lunch. After all, one thing was sure, here
in Safed the food was kosher and there'd be no surprising
pieces of bacon in any of the dishes she ordered.

In the afternoon they discussed the chances of finding any records. It seemed unlikely that the graveyard,
built on a hill near the old city, would contain the remains
of those who perished in the earthquake. Most of the
people who died would have been buried underneath
piles of rubble; the bodies found in the streets taken to
a mass grave. But there must have been lists: names of
those who were buried on that day before the sun set.
Anna believed they would find something at the synagogue. Nina, disappointed that there was so little about
the earthquake in the museum, agreed. They began to
walk to the Ari, past old limestone buildings and newly
built archways with curling vines and modern gas lamps.
Nina hurried, thinking she knew the way, but her mother
was trailing behind, each step sending a shiver of pain
through her knee. After a while Anna found a bench and
said she'd wait there. Nina carried on, irritated, and be-

ginning to wonder why she'd brought her mother all the way to Israel when she was unable to walk more than a hundred yards. Anna too was thinking it was ironic that for fifty years she'd nursed a wish to travel and now that she'd made the journey she was unable to walk through the cobbled streets.

She waited while her daughter went in search of the lists. The walls of the Ari were lined with glass covered shelves, containing crumbling leather volumes of Talmud. An elderly man was sitting by the entrance and seemed surprised that a woman was taking an interest in old Hebrew books. Nina explained what she was looking for and the man led her to the other side of the ark, to a cupboard, locked with a padlock and key.

Inside were three shelves, two of which were empty and covered in dust. The third was stacked with folders, bulging with sheets of yellowing paper. Nina opened the first one which contained plans for the rebuilding of the synagogue in 1847. A second folder had a list of names of those who died in the typhus epidemic of the first World War. At the back of this folder were some loose sheets. The date 1837 was written at the top of each one.

The records of those who died were catalogued alphabetically. There were ten families with the name Levy. Nina ran her finger over the entries on the page: Ezra (from Tangier), Moses and his brother Gideon (from Fez, Morocco) and finally came to Solomon (from Gibraltar).

The entry read:

Solomon Levy, died January 1837.

It included details of his wife Paloma and the ages of his children:

*Abraham 16, David 14, Miriam 12, Rebecca 6
and Joshua 1.*

Underneath was a further note:

*"Solomon's body was found with that of his son
Abraham at the ruins of the Ari. His wife and
daughters died in the street near their house.
It is believed that the boy David survived. The
body of the baby was never recovered."*

So the reference in the book was right—David was
one of five; four children had died. Yet he only ever
mentioned one brother and two sisters. Nina replaced
the sheets, closed the cupboard and thanked the man at
the entrance. She made her way slowly back to the bench
where she'd left Anna sitting. It was getting dark and she
hoped her mother would have the strength to walk back
to the hotel.

Anna pulled herself up and calculated that the walk
should take about seven minutes. To take her mind off
the ache in her knee and the jabbing pain as each foot
crunched on the cobbles, she counted the number of
houses with blue doors. She was sure that the colour was
to remind the residents of the sky and heaven.

Back in their room, Nina explained what she had
found. Anna was hoping she had discovered a shop selling silverware like the camel teapot. When she learned
about the baby, she couldn't believe it was true.

"Let's try to piece together what may have happened.
What did mother tell me? Yes, David stayed at home
while his father went to the synagogue with Abraham."

"Perhaps ... " interrupted Nina "perhaps he had been
looking after the youngest child, Joshua, while his mother

410

and sisters went out? That's the only explanation. When he talked about his tremendous guilt that he had left behind the images of his family, he was trying to say that he'd left behind his baby brother."

'That's not possible," said Anna. "He would have told someone, surely."

"Not if he felt guilty. If he'd been rescued and gone back to the house ... and then, he picked up the teapot, knowing that his baby brother was buried in the rubble. Mum, try and remember. why did he stay in the house when the rest of the family all went out?"

"He'd had a quarrel with his sister and she had hidden one of his shoes."

"But his mother wouldn't have gone out with the girls, leaving a baby alone ... "

"That's it," said Anna. "The baby must have been in the house. Otherwise he would have been with his mother. The reason David never mentioned him was that he blamed himself and consciously or subconsciously blocked out all memories of his brother's existence, even the thought of his name."

"So he hid it all those years and never told anyone. How could he tell his aunt Deborah, who thought he was brave? How could he tell Rachel, the wife who tried to help him deal with the nightmares?"

Nina fell silent, wondering what difference it would have made if his sons and daughter had known the truth. An Act of God was responsible for the death of six members of David's family. yet throughout his life he carried the guilt that he had survived and was unable to save Joshua. Perhaps he even convinced himself that he never had a baby brother. Yet if he'd confided in Rachel, she would have understood. How could he know that the misery caused by his silence would be passed on to their daughter Dina, when a tragedy in her life dug deep into a seam of dormant unhappiness.

An object—like the silver teapot—can be handed from one generation to another. We have no control over the genes that we pass on, but we have the power to nurture an inclination towards sadness or happiness. For the first time Nina understood that Anna had broken the chain of grief that she had inherited. Faced with the discovery of the will, Anna never considered pursuing a legal claim to her mother's rightful inheritance. When dealing with Nathan's long, protracted illness she refused to be drawn into a world of depression.

The journeys to Lisbon and Safed were far from the pleasures that Anna had imagined in her youth. And yet she continued to travel. Despite the aching feet and knee, and the struggles to avoid talkative strangers, she notched up a dozen stamps in her passport. It was Nina who provided the motivation. She finally married—an American professor, a man of humour and insight, a man who looked nothing like Samir. Over the next twenty years Anna made many trips to New York. She knitted shawls for her grandchildren and taught them to play Bezique, and when they visited her in London, she offered them chocolate éclairs served on elegant china.

What do we know of the past? We know the tales that our parents choose to tell us. It's not that they intentionally hide the facts; the brain blots out painful scenes, pushing them in to the background, out of reach. Memories deceive us: in our mind an event may seem real—but how much of it is embellished with the telling, diminished by shame or embarrassment, or even overheard in conversation and accepted as true?

Was David to blame for what he did—for the train of events set in motion by his blurring of the truth? He carried the burden all his life and kept himself apart from anyone seeking to understand his past. When challenged, he revealed a tarnished story of survival. Who are we to judge? In a lifetime of memories we all choose our own truth, obliterating events and emotions that disturb us. Yet there are moments that always float to the surface, indelible and unforgettable.

THE END

Acknowledgements

One benefit of writing a cookbook is the constant output of food. Writing a novel is different. There is a stream of questions to be answered and at the end of the day, often no food at all. I have been sustained from the earliest idea to the final editing by the boundless help that Michael has given me. Is there any other husband (or computer consultant) who will drop everything to advise on the details of bridge, the finer meanings of words and anything to do with a laptop?

The concept for The Camel Trail came long after my parents had died. Now it is too late to ask Tess and Rudolph Blackburn what really happened, but they told me enough to make me want to know more. My interpretation of their lives springs from a deep love for them.

I am grateful to my sons for preventing the first draft of this book from being published. Daniel and Adam made corrections and comments on both style and content; Tim gave me constructive and valuable criticism—especially with regard to writing. David helped to widen the range of my reading. My American daughters-in-law have all been supportive—Claudia and Karen encouraged me from afar, and Emily provided much appreciated editorial advice. Kate Whiteman, Barbara Arden-White and Monika Sears all read the manuscript and suggested improvements to dialogue and characterisation. The collections and newspapers of the British Library have been a source of much detail, as was the website victorianlondon.org, compiled by Lee Jackson (no relation). When the internet failed, I found immediate answers in the wisdom of Marguerite Patten. Thanks also to Yvonne Mocatta in London and Haim Sidor in Safed who gave me information willingly and to all those who don't even know that they have contributed. The Camel Trail is based on a set of true events but fiction grows from facts learned through conversation and shared experiences. I hope my friends will forgive my interpretation of such moments and I give them all permission to use anything I have told them in their own books.

Permissions

Extracts from the following books have been included by permission of The British Library:

The Art of Conversation, 1840 (8409.a.46.)
Robson's Housekeeper's Account Book (P.P.2505.f.)
Lady's Guide to the Ordering of Her Household, 1861 (7943.e.32.)
What to Eat and How to Cook It by Pierre Blot, 1866 (7955.aaa.21.)
Cassell's Household Guide, 1869 (7943.f.22.)
The Family Handbook, 1838 (RB.23.a.28000.)
Cookery for Every Household by Florence B. Jack 1931 (D-07942.k.38.)
The Dinner Question by Tabitha Tickletooth 1860 (7953.b.15.)
*The Art of French Cooking,*1965 published by Paul Hamlyn (7951.g.8.)
The Book of Household Management, by Isabella Beeton 1861 (7953.d.28.)
Meals Medicinal by Dr W.T. Fernie, 1905 (B.203.e.19DSC)
A Trip to the North East of Lake Tiberias by Laurence Oliphant, 1885 (2356.b.12.)

Other books by Judy Jackson

Cookery
The Home Book of Jewish Cookery
Microwave Vegetable Cooking
A Feast in Fifteen Stories
The Passover Menu Planner
The Essential Jewish Cookbook

Biography
Tess Blackburn

Lightning Source UK Ltd.
Milton Keynes UK
UKOW03f0856290414

230775UK00001B/3/P

9 780951 722022